THE RIVER IN WINTER

THE RIVER IN WINTER

A novel by
MATT DEAN

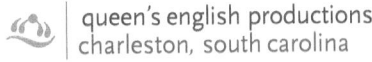
queen's english productions
charleston, south carolina

ISBN-10: 0-9825552-0-2
ISBN-13: 978-0-9825552-0-0

Book design by Matt Dean

To order additional copies, please contact us:

Queen's English Productions
Number 276
1643B Savannah Highway
Charleston, South Carolina 29407

http://qepro.com

TO TODD

Mein unsterblicher Geliebter

Who is now reading this?

May-be one is now reading this who knows some wrong-doing of
    my past life,
Or may-be a stranger is reading this who has secretly loved me,
Or may-be one who meets all my grand assumptions and egotisms
    with derision,
Or may-be one who is puzzled at me.

As if I were not puzzled at myself!
Or as if I never deride myself! (O conscience struck! O self-
    convicted!)
Or as if I do not secretly love strangers! (O tenderly, a long time,
    and never avow it;)
Or as if I did not see, perfectly well, interior in myself, the stuff
    of wrong-doing,
Or as if it could cease transpiring from me until it must cease.

Walt Whitman
Calamus #16
Leaves of Grass (1860)

PART ONE

1   PORT FORWARD, STARBOARD BACK

On the river the air was sharp and cold, smelling of mud and peat. The current drew me southward, downstream. The oars pulled easily. Brown water swirled away from the blades and, whispering, fell in on itself. Ahead of me, pennants of mist waved skyward; behind me, above my small wake, they scattered toward the riverbanks.

A pocked buttress of concrete—the Lake Street Bridge—stretched high above me. Traffic between Minneapolis and Saint Paul—light traffic, this early on a Sunday—whirred and thumped across the bridge.

I lifted and dipped the oars, port forward, starboard back, guiding my new shell in a quarter turn. Pulling harder now, I rowed diagonally across the current. A few yards from the river's eastern shore, I spun another quarter turn and settled into the rigorous upstream cadence.

The effort of rowing upstream warmed me; my sweatshirt—and under it my unisuit—clung to my back. Feeling muscular, loose, strong, I pulled the oars harder, rowing at full pressure.

As I drew even with the square of sand where the entrance to the beach—Bare Ass Beach, as I knew it—met the water, I slacked off. At the foot of the asphalt switchback to the street, two boys in ragged black denim sat side by side on a picnic table. One passed a cigarette to the other. Both glowered at me, as if I'd caught them at something illicit. One of them pulled the last drag off the butt and flicked it toward the water. It spun toward me in an angry arc.

◆   ◆   ◆

Toward the end, during the gloomy months when nothing had pleased him, Tom had taken up smoking. He'd hidden cigarettes and lighters everywhere. Cigarette packs in the closet, one in each mate of a pair of fraying, grass-stained running shoes. Lighters in jacket pockets, at the back of the sock drawer, behind a row of books—why so many lighters? He'd come home every night with the stink of smoke in his hair and on his clothes. A carton of Marlboro Reds had appeared in the freezer. Again, just as it had on the day I'd found the carton, my gut seethed. My cheeks burned.

Fixing on a patch of brown water ahead, I pulled hard and regained my rhythm. Shafts of sunlight slanted now through the nude-limbed trees on the riverbank. I passed the section of beach where, in the few warm weeks of summer, men sunbathed and cruised among reddening sumacs. Decades of footprints cut the upward-sloping strand into countless switchbacks and risers.

Tom and I had come here almost every weekend in summer, had driven the other men crazy with our aloofness, our conspicuous togetherness. Now I would be free to come alone—as if I wanted to be free. I could try my luck unencumbered—as if I wanted to be unencumbered. But Tom's and my customary place among the sumacs would be one of the numberless commonplace things that would remind me of him and make my heart swell and thrum in my chest.

Just south of the Franklin Avenue Bridge, a complicated stair of wood and steel rose to the street. I passed the stair, passed through the icy shadow of the bridge. Against cliffs of crumbling rock, an asphalt path walked on fat stilts above the surface of the river. A skeletal birch marked the path's sharp inward turning. Beyond, in a little inlet, the boathouse, a homely A-frame of dark wood and multiform shingles, huddled beneath a pair of ailing ash trees.

Shallow waves lapped and silvered the low T-shaped dock. With a flick of the port oar, I nosed the shell toward the longest stretch of planking, the post of the T. Where the dock met the shore, a man in a sheepskin coat stood with his brown-booted feet planted far apart, his arms folded across his chest.

Except for the denim-clad boys, I hadn't seen anyone all morning. Seeing the man—all the lean length of him—standing there, where I had not expected to see anyone, startled me so much that I nearly tipped the little boat.

The man strode out onto the decking. His boots thumped; the planks sang and squealed. He did not seem to mind the water darkening the round toes of his boots.

Careful now, I drew alongside, pulled to, nudged the port side of the rigger onto the dock. Snatching off his glove, the man stretched out a raw-knuckled paw, his left. I took it. It was warm and damp, the grip strong. He lifted me off the shell and snagged my feet out of the shoes. In his scarred boots he stood inches taller than I was in my sock feet.

"John," he said. "John Peterson. My friends call me Spike." He yanked away the other glove. Tucking both gloves under his arm, he enclosed my one hand in both of his. A rough spot on the heel of his right hand chafed the matching place on my hand. It set me on edge, like a crackle of static electricity. "You must be Mike?"

Michael Walton, he must mean, one of the Saint Paul coxswains. I knew him a little—Michael, never Mike—from rowing club meetings where he and his eight rallied like a drove of fraternity boys in matching US Rowing jackets. I never saw them on the water; they rowed before dawn, because the river is never so calm after sunrise as it is before.

I shook my head. "Afraid not," I said. "I'm Jonah." Spike didn't reply. To fill the silence, I said, "My name is Jonah." I added, "Jonah Murray," as if my last name explained why my first name was not Michael. At any moment my mouth might disengage from my brain altogether, and I would repeat last night's weather report.

Frowning, he said, "Not Mike?"

"Michael Walton?"

He shrugged. "Mike something."

"You were meeting him *here*? Today?" It was—plainly, manifestly, unequivocally—too late in the season to be on the water. I had a reason, if not an excuse. My boat had taken longer than I'd expected to build, and then I'd run short of cash and it had taken much longer than I'd expected to pay for it. This was the first chance I'd had to row in it. If Michael Walton had intended to row today, then—. Then—plainly, manifestly, unequivocally— Michael Walton must be out of his mind.

Spike nodded. "He was supposed to be here."

"I guess you've been stood up."

"Were you supposed to meet him as well?" he said.

"No, just getting out on the river. Trying out the boat. Why were you meeting him here, of all places?"

I had a sense of the boat bobbing in the water, drifting. I glanced down at our hands, my right hand still folded in both of his. Dipping as much as I could to my left knee, I hooked the toes of my right foot in the boat's rigging.

Color bloomed slowly in the hollows of his cheeks. He released my hand. "I'm not sure Mike would want me to tell you about that."

His eyes were fierce, a glittering Wedgwood blue. Ridiculously, supernaturally blue. I couldn't look into them for long. I looked instead at his mouth, at the square tuft of black whiskers below his lower lip.

He ruffled that knot, that upside-down mustache below his lip. He squinted into the distance beyond my shoulder. I was not Michael Walton. The hugger-muggery of their meeting had not rocked my world. I must have dropped off his radar.

I dropped literally as well: my foot, wet and cramping, was just losing its grip on the oarlock. Squatting at the edge of the deck, I reached for it, caught it just in time. As I pulled it to, ready to lift it by the gunwales, I felt Spike beside me, his long body hunched parallel to mine. He fumbled for a grip on the crescent moon of the rigging. Abandoning that, he reached around it for the foot stretchers. For a second, I thought he might slip his hand into one of the shoes.

He said, "How the hell do you lift this thing?"

"I can get it. It only weighs about thirty-five pounds." When I lifted the shell from the water, the effort pulled from me a humiliating, constipated grunt. "Besides, this is the only safe way to hold it." I wanted to keep talking, to show how effortless it was to hold and carry the boat, but the tightness of my voice belied me.

My socks were sopping and muddy. I hustled the shell along the length of the dock and up a hill of hard-packed earth. Under the steep eaves of the boathouse, I tipped the shell into the cradle of a drying sling.

The western clouds had slouched closer. They hemmed in the left bank, drove clammy wind before them. My body ached from cold. I had to get my socks off, along with my sweat-soaked uni and sweatshirt. The sweatshirt clung to me, chilled me, and I could wait no longer to peel it away. I laid it flat over the shell's upturned hull.

My cap had somehow gotten knocked to the ground. I fetched it and laid it, too, on top of the shell, until I pictured my hair—damp, wild, and as bright as flame. Every redheaded boy has heard himself called "red" and "carrot top" and "orange crush"—every redheaded boy who has ever been in the company of other boys, at least. In seventh grade health class, during a lecture on sports nutrition, Mr. Burns had patted my carrot-orange hair. Look for this color, he'd told us, if you're trying to get beta carotene in your diet. Good for the eyesight. Cures acne. Fights the flu. Carrots, cantaloupe, sweet potatoes, he'd said. Look for this shade of orange. For years after that, my nickname had been Beta Carotene, until Mr. Burns himself had taken to calling me Beta. Sometimes even my mother still called me Beta.

I pulled the wool cap down tight again.

When I moved toward the door to the boathouse, Spike was already there. Inside, we stood looking at each other in the narrow space between the racked boats. He unbuttoned his jacket. Underneath, he wore a shirt of blue and green plaid flannel. The top three buttons were open, showing the white of his undershirt.

I craved the warmth of dry clothes, but he stood between me and my duffel bag. "I don't really know Michael that well," I said.

"I'll see him tonight." A smile warmed his face. His front teeth were crooked, one overlapping the other. "There's a beer bash at the Gay Nineties. In the Men's Room? The back bar?"

"I know it. I've been there."

"How long have you been rowing, Jonah Murray?" His voice, low in pitch, contained a promise of thunder. He lifted my cap from my head, dropped it to the floor. His eyes dipped. "How long to get thighs like those?"

"Since high school." I blinked. "Rowing since high school. Six years. No. Seven. Yes, seven years."

"And is rowing the only thing that brings you to the river, Jonah Murray?"

Between us lay a space not quite as long as his booted foot. The warmth of his body crossed the gap first, followed by one ham-pink hand. He laid his thumb in the hollow at the base of my throat. The tips of his fingers were hot and rough on the back of my neck.

"Not always," I said, or meant to say, or would have said, if my throat had not suddenly filled with cotton. I felt my mouth noiselessly working, and then Spike's left hand joined his right around my throat. His thumbs and fingers met, intertwined. He kissed me.

I plunged my frigid hands into the humid gap between Spike's jacket and his body. Beneath layers of cloth—flannel, waffle-weave cotton, jersey—I felt the workings of muscle and bone.

"Red hair," he said, his mouth close to mine. He stroked the back of my head, where my hair was cut almost skin-tight. "I have a weakness for red hair."

Strange, that a compliment can seem cruel. I drew away, but Spike pulled me closer. He kissed the cool place on my neck where his warm hand had just been. His lips and unshaven cheeks were dry and rough. My fingers, warming swiftly, touched the planes and margins of his shoulder blades. My eyes lolled shut.

His right hand was still around my neck. Driving his tongue against mine, with the fingers of his other hand digging deeply into the muscle of my buttocks, he pulled me against him.

But as suddenly as he had drawn me in, he released me. I stood before him, blinking and bereft. Now parted from him, I felt so cold and so naked that my gray unisuit with its racy vermilion stripes might never have existed. He touched the fabric at my shoulder. With an effortless clutching motion of his fingers, he could have torn the uni from my body. A sense of his power over me crackled like lightning.

"I like what I see, Jonah Murray," he whispered. "I like it very much."

"I like you, too," I said, or thought I said. The moment stretched. "You're a really handsome man."

The corners of his mouth turned upward. He drew my body against him. "I want you in a bed." He kissed me again. "Come with me to my hotel."

I told him I would go anywhere he chose.

• • •

Bulbous clouds hung low, as if a burden dragged them toward earth. The river, lean and silver, carried crumpled reflections of the sky southward toward the bridge. Spike stood at the edge of the dock, balancing on his heels, watching the water pass underneath the toes of his boots.

Only when my own footfalls rattled on the planks did he look up. "You look even better in real clothes," he said.

I had changed into jeans and a T-shirt, and a thick sweater that made me feel itchy and hot. Lifting my duffel bag from my shoulder, he slung it over his own.

Until we reached the top of the wood-and-steel stairs, we walked in silence. "Where's your car? You must have a car," he said. "Do you want to follow me or ride together?"

"Why not come to my place? We'll be more comfortable there than in a hotel. It's not all that far. I can drive." All these words emerged in a rush.

He smiled, nodded.

I'd parked half a block away. Side by side, we walked along the curving sidewalk. Across the street, amid a thicket of Bush-Quayle signs—a dozen or more lined up along the curb like a fence, dozens more scattered across the sparse and sloping lawn all the way up to the house, a white saltbox with black shutters—a gray-haired man stooped over a silver-headed cane, watching us. He appeared to have no other purpose in mind. Cars passed, and he crossed toward us.

Doors unlocked, opened, we sank into the houndstooth seats of my tan Chevette. Our weight shook the car on its ancient springs. Spike tossed my duffel bag lightly into the back seat. Somehow, in the same motion, he let his hand come to rest on my thigh.

The old man, the gray-hair from across the street, appeared suddenly behind Spike. Mouth open, hair streaming, he knocked the head of his cane against the window. Spike lurched in his seat, but when he saw the old man—a mere caricature of violence—he laughed and waved me on. "Guess we wore out our welcome," he said.

In some of the neighboring lawns there were Clinton-Gore signs. I saw no other Bush-Quayle signs, but it was difficult to believe that, after the little gray-haired man had taken his share of signs, there were any left for the rest of the seven-county metropolitan area. "I wonder what the neighbors think of him," Spike said with a laugh. His hand still rested on my thigh.

◆   ◆   ◆

As I turned onto my street, I rehearsed concessions and vindications. The house wasn't much to look at, one story of often-patched stucco, no off-street parking. Yet it stood on a roomy corner lot, the rent was reasonable, and my landlords loved me like family. But I said nothing. As I drew the Chevette even with the front walk, Spike tumbled from the car and stood in the yard. Arms akimbo, he scrutinized the house as if calculating the windows' exact deviation from the golden mean.

"It's home," I said, walking backwards toward the front porch. "A house of my own. A brick residence, adjoining royal palace."

He cocked his head. "Royal palace?" he said. "Brick?" he said. "It looks like stucco to me."

"Sorry. I was listening to *The King and I* earlier. Et cetera, et cetera, et cetera."

If he had any idea what I meant, he hid it well.

Inside, I hung his jacket and my sweater in the closet. With a wave of my hand, I conducted a grand tour: a square, low-ceilinged living room with walls the color of warm sand, a curtained window set in a shallow bay, a dark green sofa, an easy chair upholstered in beige tweed worn smooth, in places, from use. No pictures or mirrors or posters on the walls, no plants in the window.

The other rooms were the same: square, warm, beige, dull, full of used and useful things.

I invited Spike to sit in the easy chair. Under the table next to it lay a brown vinyl case containing Tom's cassette collection, one of the many things he'd left behind. Sometimes I stood in the middle of the floor and stared at the cassette case, or sat in the chair petting its hinges, helpless until the phone rang or a record ended or something shook me out of my stupefaction. The reminders that he'd lived with me—the clothes bunched on his side of the closet, the cheesy 'eighties porn stacked up on the bedroom floor, the un-opened packs of Marlboros in the freezer, the cassettes—somehow, these pained me more, even, than his absence.

"Can I get you something?" I said to Spike. "I don't have any beer or any-thing, but I think I might have some iced tea." Very old iced tea, I remem-bered, probably as ripe as cheese by now. "Or Diet Coke. I always have Diet Coke around."

Still standing in the entryway, Spike stepped out of his boots. "Water'll do." Bracing himself against the closet door, he tugged at his gray wool socks, straightening the red toes and heels.

When I returned from the kitchen, he was bent over, squinting at the ste-reo. He punched a couple of buttons, and Karen Holmes leapt mid-syllable into "This Is Love." "—Ate of confusion that makes you see everything plain," she sang.

He took the glass of water from me. Ice cubes cracked and rattled. He didn't drink. "Who's singing?" he said.

"Karen Holmes. A jazz singer—vocalist. One of my favorites." Last night I'd been listening to all of her albums in reverse chronological order, recording them afresh onto cassette. The LP's still stood on the floor, leaning against the subwoofer.

He touched the volume control, edging it up.

"My mother took me to see her in New York," I told him. "A couple of years ago. It was a college graduation present, that trip. It was an amazing night."

An awkward moment passed. How could we get back the chill-driven intimacy of the boathouse?

"It was at the Algonquin," I said. "We"—that is to say, Tom and I. Having dragged the whole bulk of him into the room on the back of that tiny pronoun, I didn't know how to get him back out again. Spike scratched a bit of smut from the knurls around the circumference of the volume control. "I actually got to meet her, because her son, who was her accompanist for a long time, Patrick—. Patrick Holmes, her son, came to my college to give a lecture."

Spike's attention seemed to be wandering. He turned to the bookshelves, picked up a book, put it down again, brushed his fingers along the rows of record albums in their motley jackets. Admittedly, the story, just begun, was already convoluted. I waved away the rest of it.

He said, "Can I pick something else?"

"Go ahead. I'll be right back."

I went to the bathroom and softly closed the door. I primped: rolled up my sleeves, washed my sweat-roughened hair with hand soap and tepid water from the tap, gargled with Listerine, smoothed the folds of my shirt, hiked up my jeans.

I peered into the living room. Spike sat in the easy chair, reading the back of an album sleeve. A dozen others lay in his lap. Mindful of creaking floorboards, I crept to the bedroom, where I stripped the blankets and sheets and remade the bed with starchy new linens. On the way back, I shut the door to the music room, the spare room where I kept towers of music textbooks from college, scores and sketches, and sprawling heaps of staff paper.

By then Spike had put everything back. He stood sipping his water, staring at the spines of my books. Baudelaire and Verlaine in red boards, Whitman in green, Crane in ten-cent paper covers—they stood in sagging ranks. Karen Holmes sang "Easy to Love."

"You have a lot of poetry here."

"I collect it for writing songs—art songs, et cetera, et cetera—." He rolled his eyes. "I'm a composer," I said. But that was too much to claim; my voice faltered. I cleared my throat. "I *wanted* to be a composer. I studied composition in college."

His finger had fallen on Cummings—a scruffy *Tulips and Chimneys* I'd unearthed in a used bookstore. He tipped it forward and slipped it off the shelf. He weighed it in his hands. Over and over he turned it, studying the frayed edges and corners with no apparent intention of opening it.

"A songwriter first, then a composer."

He looked at me sidelong. "What are you, then," he said, "if not a songwriter or a composer?"

"I work for the state legislature. A legislative commission. We're supposed to create a policy that encourages tolerance and eliminates harassment in the workplace."

"So you're the political correctness police."

"That's what everyone says." Sitting on the sofa, I untied my sneakers, slipped them off my feet. "There is something I've been working on since college. A longer sort of composition."

It was called *The River*. "The Mississippi," I told him. "At first it was going to be a tone poem—like *Metamorphoses* or *Má vlast*. That's Smetana. *Má vlast* was Smetana. That is to say, Smetana wrote *Má vlast*. It depicts various—various scenes from Bohemia. Not to be confused with *La Bohéme* or anything." Spike raised an eyebrow. I felt feverish. "He was deaf—Smetana was—like Beethoven."

"Him I've heard of."

"That got out of hand, though," I said.

"Which? Smetana or Beethoven?

"My thing."

He grinned. "Your thing is out of hand?" His tongue darted across his crooked front teeth.

"My tone poem. *The River*. I thought maybe a symphony, like Beethoven's Ninth. You know, where there's a chorus in the last movement?" I sang a couple of bars of the "Ode to Joy."

Spike observed me with an avuncular grin. "Fucking redheads," he said. He tossed the book into the easy chair.

As if he were my Fred and I his Ginger, he held out his hand; when I took it, he drew me toward him. Nuzzling his bare neck, I pulled his shirt free of his jeans. I tucked my hand between his skin and his belt. His arms were iron bands around me. Our lips touched.

Releasing me, he said in a whisper, "Bedroom?"

Taking his hand—I was Fred, now—I led him down the hall. I switched on the small, dim light by the bed. When I turned, I saw that he'd spotted the television and the stacks of videotapes. Looking up, he smiled to show that he knew what they contained. Squatting, he pawed through the tapes. The plastic cases clattered and clacked. He chose one and wagged it in the air. I could see that the label was simple black lettering on white, but I couldn't read the title. With a prankish smile, he slipped the tape into the VCR's toothless mouth.

He was a genius with buttons. He punched just two, and tawdry disco music filled the room. On the screen, two men in leather soul-kissed.

"This'll do, won't it? Music-wise?" he said, still grinning.

◆　◆　◆

I laid him on the clean sheets. I freed him of flannel and denim. I palmed and stroked his shaggy thighs, smoothed and raked the prodigal black hairs like the nap of a lavish carpet. I pulled off his sweat-damp socks and T-shirt and underwear. His white boxer shorts were old and much-laundered, translucent as vellum. Down the steep insteps of his high-arched feet, fat veins meandered—like the channels and distributaries of a river delta—toward his blunt toes.

I touched him, exploring planes, mesas, canyons, the whole winter-white landscape of him. Against his cool, pale skin, my hands were hot, my freckles as dark as cinnamon.

He tugged the hem of my undershirt, pulled it up over my torso and head, tossed it aside. Again, as in the boathouse, he wrapped his hands around my neck. He drew me toward him, drew my mouth to his.

In one swift motion, he rolled us so that I lay under him. Straddling my thighs, he fumbled with the buttons of my jeans. He stood, yanked at the frayed cuffs. Even before I heard the soft tumble of fabric landing on the floor, his weight again covered me. He licked my chest, nuzzled my armpits. I tasted my own sweat in the air. His hands trapped my hands behind my back. As he settled his weight, my spine cracked against the bones of our wrists and knuckles.

Blood sang in my ears. Spike moved against me. His hands were on my shoulders. He turned my body beneath him—laid me on my belly—and smoothed the cool of his chest across the heat of my back.

Spike said, "I love fucking rowers from behind. Your backs are bulked up like all fuck." He said into my ear, "Condoms?"

There were no condoms. My body went limp. "I don't have any," I told him. I spoke into the sheets. "Tom and I—. My boyfriend—." I hugged a pillow to my chest. "We didn't use them."

Spike rocked back on his haunches. "Not to worry," he said. "I was a Boy

Scout. Always prepared." He dropped to the floor and pawed through our mingled clothing.

"What are you looking for?"

"My wallet." It had slipped under the bed.

"You were a Boy Scout?"

"Not exactly. Had my share of them, though."

With one hand he swung his wallet open; with the other he fished out a square of bright yellow cellophane. A vending machine novelty, it looked like—glow-in-the-dark, or a tickler, "ridged for her pleasure." Holding a corner of the packet between his teeth, he tore the cellophane. As he unrolled the condom, he twirled his finger in the air, motioning for me to lie on my belly. Again he straddled my thighs.

"Damn," he said.

I lifted, turned. Through a diagonal gash across the rubber's tip, I saw the dark pink of the flesh inside. Peeking from the ruined latex, his cock looked more bare than if it had been actually bare. Spike ripped off the condom, tossed it away.

"I can run to the drugstore," I said. "It's just a block." More than a block. A block, and then an acre or two of parking lot. How long would it take to walk that far? How long would I have to leave him alone in my house?

"No need," he said. "You prefer it raw, so do I."

I stared at him. "That wasn't—. I didn't—."

"I'm clean," he said.

I said, "So am I," but that wasn't what he wanted to know. He stroked the small of my back, his thick finger trailing downward. With the other hand he stroked the nape of my neck.

"You want it or not? I think you need it pretty bad."

My breath caught in my throat. I closed my eyes. I said, "I do."

♦   ♦   ♦

We moved in counterpoint. On the TV screen, I saw through blurred eyes a title card, white on black, "John and Pete." Then, an apartment or townhouse somewhere—it could be anywhere—hopelessly dated, never exactly fashionable. Two men on a grimy tweed couch. No, one on the couch, the other kneeling on the floor.

Spike forced my head back and at the same time hunched forward, so that we could kiss. His crooked front tooth snagged my lip.

He broke the kiss, saying, "Ah. Here it is. Me and Pete."

I may not yet have been in that place beyond language where two people can go, but this utterance meant nothing to me. My addled brain simply couldn't parse the sentences.

Spike was looking at the video. I looked with him, and then it all came into focus. The kneeling man had Spike's white skin, the same black-furred thighs. And then his face filled the screen; a younger and thinner face, clean-shaven, but unmistakably Spike's.

Present-day Spike, in-the-flesh Spike, nuzzled my neck. His whiskers tickled me behind the ear. I bucked against him, crazy to make him stop. He misunderstood, or perhaps my thrashing piqued his desire. In either case, he hunkered down, redoubled his efforts.

The perfect counterpoint resumed. I buried my face in the sheets, yowling like a dog.

2   CLEAN

I woke in an itchy tangle of sheets and a panic of having been robbed. The fitted sheet had peeled away from two corners of the mattress, and in my brief and fitful sleep I'd wrapped it around me. My cocoon was mine alone; Spike had gone.

But he hadn't gone far. I found him in the living room. Naked, he lay rod-straight across the length—and then some—of the fat sofa, his tousled head lolling on the cushion of one overstuffed arm, his crossed ankles propped on the other. The original cast recording of *Oklahoma!* played softly on the stereo—"I Cain't Say No." One of my high school yearbooks lay face down on his belly. As I knelt quietly beside the sofa, his eyes snapped open. He took my hand in his, kissed the palm.

He sat up. Smiling, he patted a spot next to him. I sat.

"Who's Beta?" he asked.

"Beta?"

He opened the yearbook, pointed at the loopy writing on the endpapers. "'Beta. Good knowing you. Mark.'" He moved his finger down the page to something written sideways along the bottom right corner. "'Beta. Best of luck at Bemidji State. Friends always, Bruce,'" he read. He looked at me. "You went to Bemidji?"

I shook my head. "It was my second choice, but I got accepted there first. I ended up going to Woodland College." I could see by his blank expression that he'd never heard of it; almost no one ever had. "A little private school in Partridge Lake."

He nodded and read more: "'BC. Keep singing! Love, Lori.'"

"That would be me. Beta Carotene, Beta, BC—all me. Stupid nicknames I picked up in junior high. It's a long story. Kind of ugly."

He was smiling. "You tell me yours, I'll tell you mine."

"I'm sure it was all in good fun," I said. I wanted to hide in the sofa cushions.

"Can I call you Beta? It's kind of cute."

I shrugged. "I guess if I'm Beta, you're Alpha."

He frowned. He said, "I'm not sure I understand what you see in this music."

"This was the first cast recording of any musical, made back in nineteen-forty-three. More recent versions sound a bit less dated."

I stopped the record. Lifting it from the turntable I put it back in its sleeve. I stepped to the bookcase. Third shelf, halfway over, between *Oh, Kay!* and the nineteen-fifty-five *Oklahoma!* film soundtrack, a narrow gap marked the spot where the cast album belonged.

"I'm not in a Rodgers and Hammerstein kind of mood," I said, walking my fingers back along the row. *Oh, Brother! Of Thee I Sing. Nine. My Fair Lady. Music Man. Mack and Mabel.*

Spike came up behind me, wrapped his arms around my belly. "It all seems a little too clean and wholesome to me." He bit my earlobe.

I wandered farther afield: *Bitter Sweet, Crazy for You, Here's Love, Pipe Dream.* It was useless. Dozens of overtures and interludes and intermezzi, hundreds of ballads and soliloquies and choruses, and nothing capable of chasing out the words swimming like tiger sharks in my head. *Clean*, and the word it brought with it, *dirty*. "I'm clean," he'd said, with the implication that he might not be, that—as someone who had, for example, had unprotected sex for money—he might be dirty.

I turned to face him. "How many have you done?"

"How many what?"

"Videos, movies. Porn movies. How many?"

He stepped away. "A dozen, maybe. It was eleven years ago. I was twenty-two years old."

Eleven years ago. Nineteen-eighty-one. I would have been thirteen. While I'd been dreading showers in gym class, dodging jocks and bullies out of equal portions of fear and lust, had he spent his days flying from one porn set to another, his nights skulking from the Mineshaft to the Slot?

I spotted *The Very Thought of You* among the group of Holmes albums on the floor. I floated the record onto the spindle. I handed him the sleeve.

"I guess you weren't entirely impressed with Karen earlier, but this is my favorite of them all. It's a tribute to Billie Holiday."

Spike squinted at the album cover, with its photo of the singer looking for all the world like a Texas oil billionaire's shopping-addicted spouse. "Christ. Bad hair day." He handed back the album cover. "I told you," he said. "I'm clean."

I said, "Clean." I didn't know what else to say. "Okay. Me, too."

"Let's hear the record, Beta."

I turned to look at the stereo. I had put the record on, but hadn't yet started it. I set the needle down on the first note of "I'm a Fool to Want You."

◆ ◆ ◆

I dropped Spike at his car. Afterward, the day was dry and aimless.

Over and over I watched the "John and Pete" segment of that old video of Tom's, until the tape began to track oddly from all the rewinding.

I ate a late lunch or early supper of canned soup, sitting naked in front of the television and drinking Diet Coke straight from a two-liter bottle. I fast-forwarded through some videos I'd rented—*The Music Man, Funny Lady, Hello Dolly*. The grinding away of frivolous plots and clever dialogue made me anxious and impatient.

At last I grew weary of moping. It was barely six o'clock, not too early for a Sunday beer bust. I changed the bedding again. I dumped my salt-smelling clothes into the laundry hamper. I showered and shaved.

On half of a crumpled old grocery store receipt, crosswise over the prices of lettuce and bread and sliced deli meat, Spike had written his name and phone number. He'd stuffed my phone number, scrawled on the other half of the receipt, into his back pocket.

While I brushed my teeth, I stared at the round digits and rakish dashes of his phone number. The three eights were stacked circles, headless snowmen.

Naked and still sticky from the steamy damp of the bathroom, I scrounged in cabinets and drawers for notebooks and scrap paper, and copied the number carefully, over and over, and stashed the copies in ten different places, insurance against misplacing the fragment of receipt. I slipped the original into my wallet.

I dressed in my tightest white T-shirt, my oldest and most faded jeans, and my surplus-store Army boots.

I called Christa. She picked up on the second ring. I heard water running.

"Are you up for some dancing? I hear there's a beer bust at the Nineties tonight."

"It's buttons," she said.

"Buttons?"

"Something I'm trying to get started. It's sewn up, like a button, or done up, like a button. It's a done deal."

"Why not say pinch pleats, or tab collars?"

The water stopped. Something clattered—something plastic, it sounded like. She sighed and cursed. "Who drives?"

"I'll drive," I said in a hurry. Her driving frightened me. "I'll come by and pick you up."

"Give me thirty minutes."

♦　♦　♦

Ninety-six minutes later, Christa dropped into the passenger's seat of my car. A cloud of billowing fabric settled around her. Meticulously untidy short blond hair, leather jacket, thick-soled shoes, and floral-print chiffon: if ever Agnetha Fältskog set out to audition for a role in *Grease*, this was how she would dress. Lips the color of a bruise parted in a smile. Christa kissed my cheek.

"I have *never* been so in the mood to dance," she said. "I didn't even know it till you called."

As I navigated the maze of carport-lined driveways surrounding Christa's apartment complex, she wiped lipstick from my cheek. "I got some on you." Twisting the rearview mirror toward her, she blew elaborate Marilyn Monroe kisses at her reflection. "Do I need to redo?"

I slapped her hand away from the mirror and righted it. I said, "There was this guy, this morning. At the boathouse."

We sat, now, at the place where the driveway emptied onto Cleveland Avenue. A half a block to the left, cars clogged the strange spot where Cleveland forked onto Saint Paul. I signaled a left turn. Christa poked my leg. "Go. Go."

There were cars coming from the right. I pointed to them. "How can I go?"

"Go right. It'll be faster." I didn't see how, but I obeyed. "So? A guy at the boathouse?"

It took only a few blocks, until Mississippi River Boulevard, to tell her about Spike, and his mysterious appointment with Michael Walton.

"Walton?" she said. "Is that his last name?" She pointed right; I turned.

"He never did explain why they were supposed to meet."

"Isn't it obvious? He's a male prostitute."

My face turned hot and itchy. "Michael Walton? A prostitute?" I dodged a blow to my shoulder.

"Dimwit."

I paused at a four-way stop. On our left, a city park entrance curved down and away toward the river. On our right, houses stood in the deepening autumn night, their curtained windows glowing creamy yellow. "Should I be turning somewhere along in here?"

"Why on earth would you do that? Stay here all the way till Franklin."

Her route took us along the river road, past the Jewish Community Center, past the University of Saint Thomas, past houses turreted like castles, past apartment buildings and bridges and a train trestle, past Prospect Park. Past Bare Ass Beach. As I rounded a curve, the Chevette's headlights swept over a pair of boys in black. Long after we'd passed them, I realized they were the two who had been smoking at the beach that morning.

At Franklin I stopped for a red light. Ahead of us lay the University of Minnesota campus, mostly obscured by the trembling branches of trees. For some reason, the brick buildings were never as clear from the ground as they were from the river.

"Left, left, left," Christa said.

I turned left.

Franklin to Riverside. Riverside to Cedar to Washington. Washington to Hennepin.

"See?" Christa said. "Easy."

•   •   •

People thronged The Gay Nineties' central bar, the old west saloon. Above our heads, above the mirrors and the bordello-red walls, were smoke-darkened murals that might have been unchanged for decades. Beneath our feet, gum and trash flocked the carpet.

I followed Christa to the coat check, where we paid a dollar each for leather-sitting. We sped by a pair of men in chaps and leather jackets. I felt or imagined that their eyes followed me as we passed, and my heart fluttered.

But before I could make eye contact, Christa and I were in the black cave of the Dance Annex.

Music thundered and thumped. On the big screen behind the dance floor, Janet Jackson canoodled with buff men in sepia clothing. Except for two bartenders and one white-whiskered old man on a black leather couch, the place was empty of people.

"I can't dance here," I said. "Not until some more people show up."

Christa rolled her eyes. "Don't be an infant. Let's get a drink."

The bartenders stood talking at the other end of the bar, near the narrow hallway to the restrooms. Both men wore jeans and boots, but one wore a crisp white banded-collar shirt, and the other had strapped his brutish torso into a leather-and-chrome harness. Looking vaguely put upon, the white shirt met us halfway down the length of the bar. Christa ordered a Corona for herself and a Diet Coke for me.

Over the bar a black-lit banner gleamed. In foot-high letters of Day-Glo orange it read, "Thank God It's The 70's." Smaller letters below that: "Disco Lives All Night Long."

Christa handed me Coke-moistened ice in a slender glass. In unison we sipped, turned, leaned back against the bar.

The DJ booth filled with the dim glow of orange and green lights. As Janet Jackson faded out, the Village People faded in. "YMCA."

Christa set down her drink. "You *have* to dance to this, or I'll start to suspect you're really straight."

I let her drag me to the dance floor. Spotlights faded, replaced by flashing colors. I hopped around for a minute, like a boxer loosening up in the ring. By the first chorus, I was ready for the hand motions. Christa and I did them together, facing each other. She added fillips and filigrees to every movement, and I mimicked her.

By the end of the song, we were no longer alone on the floor. "Brick House" came next. Christa was just warming up. The chiffon seemed to inspire all manner of pirouette and glissade. Once, she took my hand and somehow managed to dip herself against my arm.

When the DJ put on "Dancing Queen," no one fit the role as well as Christa. Agnetha herself would have run for the ladies' room, tears streaming down her cheeks. The crowd hung back at the edge of the dance floor, watching Christa.

For the right song—and none came closer than "Dancing Queen"—I could

stand having the floor to ourselves, but not with all of Minneapolis watching. I slipped into the crowd. By now traffic had formed a circuit from one
entrance to the other; people clogged the narrow corridor behind the Dance
Annex. I inched my way through.

There were restrooms, and a line at each door. Beyond the men's room lay
the Men's Room—the back bar, the "leather" bar. Men crowded the space,
but in no semblance of the organized event Spike had promised. No posters
announced a party. No volunteers sold raffle tickets at the door. No patrons
queued for twenty-five-cent keg beer. Men lined up against every vertical
surface, drinking, posing, staring.

A voice behind me: "Jonas?"

It was Michael Walton, of all people. For some reason he carried two
beers, a Rolling Rock in his right hand, a Heineken in his left. With neither his eight nor his US Rowing jacket, he seemed shorter. He was, in fact,
close to my height. At the last rowing club meeting he'd worn his hair in a
high-and-tight. He'd looked like a Marine, like a honed-steel warrior on a
recruitment poster. Now his dark hair fell in unruly cascades from a central
part almost to his shoulders.

"Jonah," I said. Someone squeezed past me, and to make room I moved a
step closer to Michael.

"Right. I hear we have a mutual friend," he said. He took a long pull from
the Heineken.

"Which friend is that?"

As someone slithered past me, a hand or arm brushed my lower back. I
tumbled through a kind of time warp. All at once the loneliness and hyste-
ria of the last months vanished, and I knew it was Tom, returning from the
men's room, slipping his arm around my waist in that intimate, slightly pos-
sessive way he had when we were among other gay men. But no, it couldn't
be Tom. It was no one I knew. In fact, by the time I turned, half-smiling,
there was no one at all.

I felt as if I'd crashed through a series of alternate dimensions, as a silent
film comedian might crash through all the floors of a shabby building. I felt
bruised and exhausted. Barely a second had passed.

Michael Walton was still chugging Heineken. He said, "Spike. He couldn't
stop talking about you."

"Is he here?"

Michael looked around, and I watched the muscles in his thick neck move under his skin. "Holy fuck. Did you see the guy with the chaps?"

"When did you see him?"

He pointed the neck of the Rolling Rock bottle toward the bar. "He's right there."

"Spike, I mean. When did you see Spike?"

"Oh. Spike." He laughed. "About two, I guess."

"I thought there was supposed to be a beer bust here tonight."

Michael was still watching the guy in chaps. "That's funny, so did Spike. It's next week. Next Sunday."

"Will he be back for it?"

He sipped the Rolling Rock. "Hell if I know."

"He came looking for you at the boathouse this morning. Spike, not the guy in the chaps."

At last Michael's eyes fixed on mine. "He mentioned that. Said he helped you dry your boat." He smiled. An enigmatic kind of smile. "Spike, not the guy in the chaps."

"Is he still in town?"

"He got a call. Had to go back to Duluth. We could only talk for a few minutes. He might be back next week. He owns a bar up there. He's doing a series of fundraisers for us. The Gay Games and all that. Local dudes go to the Games, blah, blah, blah. Support your Minnesotan brothers, blah, blah, blah."

This was the very first I'd heard about Michael's team rowing in the Gay Games. Maybe Christa knew something about it. I nodded placidly, as if I might not be the most inconsequential rower in the Twin Cities.

"Of course," he said, sipping his beer, "now he can pull people in with a bunch of bullshit about our courage in the face of adversity." A shirtless, absurdly muscular man—his triceps were so overbuilt that his arms curved out to either side of his torso like parentheses—winked at Michael and gave a tiny nod. Michael's head bobbed and swiveled, watching the bodybuilder strut away.

"Adversity?"

The shirtless man dissolved into the crowd, and Michael's attention returned to the guy in the chaps. After a moment, though, his face dropped, and he turned to look at me. Leaning toward me, squinting, he scrutinized my face, as though all the signs of my flawed character were written there for him to see, if only he looked closely enough.

"You don't know."

"Don't know what?"

"About the boathouse."

"What about it?"

"It burned down."

"Burned down? No. No, I was there this morning. I met Spike there this morning. I put my new shell in there this morning."

"It happened this afternoon," he said. "Some old guy across the street saw the smoke and called the fire department. About two o'clock, I guess. By the time I heard, Spike was already on his way back to Duluth, so, I guess, about four o'clock?"

The very idea seemed preposterous, scandalous. The boathouse had no electricity—no faulty wiring to spark a blaze, no creaky space heater that might have been left on. Spike didn't smoke. I didn't smoke. Few of the rowers smoked, and I doubted that any of them would have tossed a smoldering butt into the corner of the boathouse among the racked shells.

"Well, who—? What—?"

Rolling the mouth of his beer bottle across his lower lip, Michael shrugged. "Don't know anything more than that yet. Guess it must be arson."

"I just put my new shell in there this morning," I told him.

"You said." He drained the Heineken and tossed it into a trash can behind me.

"You're bizarrely calm about this. Won't this affect your training for the Games, at the very least?"

He shook his head. "Everything's insured. The boathouse and everything in it. The river'll be freezing up any day now. And we've got a year and a half to go anyway."

"I just put my new shell in there this morning. I saved all year. I stopped buying records."

"Records? *Vinyl* records?" He put his hand on my shoulder. "You need to rejoin us here in the 'nineties, buddy." He smiled and winked.

I'd rarely given Michael Walton a moment's thought without the word "jerk" bobbing up from my subconscious like a cork, but it was undeniable that when he smiled, he was as beautiful as the sky. Watching him suck Rolling Rock from its emerald green bottle, watching his meaty neck muscles churn as he swallowed, I felt giddy. His hair glistened blue-black in the neon light. Tom, Spike, Michael Walton—all black-haired, all so beautiful that the sight of them could make my heart knock like a mistuned engine—could it be that I had a weakness for black hair?

He said, "It'll be fine. Your boat's covered under the insurance. I just renewed it, too. Sent in the check a couple of weeks ago. Just get me a copy of the paperwork at the next meeting. To prove the replacement value."

He must be rowing club treasurer. Was there anything about the rowing club that I *did* know?

"Sure," I said. "I—. I guess I'll see if I can find—."

Just then the shirtless bodybuilder appeared at the bar, leaning over an empty stool to give his order to the bartender. Michael's whole attention appeared to rest worshipfully somewhere between the bodybuilder's trapezii and latissimi dorsi.

"Catch you later," I said, backing away.

◆ ◆ ◆

Christa had attached herself to a pack of lesbians. Four of them stood in a circle around her. She snapped and pranced, shaking her breasts at them, oblivious to their breaking hearts. Someone swept up behind her, a guy so young-looking in his cardinal-red letterman jacket that he must surely have used a fake ID to get into the bar. He put his hands on her waist. Without so much as a flinch, she leaned back against him.

On and on they danced. They swayed together, smooth as milk. Their feet didn't seem to touch the floor. They were so good together, and so blind to everyone around them, that the lesbians eventually decamped.

When they came to quench themselves at the bar, Christa made brief introductions. His name was Tory. "Like the conservatives in England, not like Aaron Spelling's daughter," he told me.

"Aaron Spelling's daughter?"

He looked puzzled, as though I had spoken Swahili. He said, very slowly, "Tori Spelling. From *Nine-Oh-Two-One-Oh?*"

"No one ever sings," Christa said. "Jonah wouldn't be interested."

Tory smiled at me as one might smile at a small child before mussing his hair. "You're seriously missing out," he said.

I touched Christa's elbow. At last she looked at me, and even took half a step closer. "Listen," I said, "I just talked to Michael Walton."

"So was I right? Was he a male prostitute?" She grinned at Tory in a way that bespoke fascinating intrigues which must remain concealed.

"The boathouse burned down."

"Oh, sweetie! Your new shell!" She stroked my forearm. "It's insured, though, right?"

I nodded. "I was thinking I should go down there and see if anything's left."

"That's crazy. We'll go down tomorrow." She turned to Tory. "Jonah just bought a new rowing shell and the boathouse burned down."

Tory displayed a puzzled, pitying smile. "Sorry to hear about it, man. You're insured, right?"

· · ·

Somehow, when they returned to the dance floor, I ended up holding his damned letterman jacket.

While Michael Jackson sang "You Can Cry on My Shoulder," and Christa laid her head on Tory's shoulder, I seethed with envy for his deltoids. I ruminated on the fact that he appeared much older up close than he had at a distance. He must be at least thirty-five, and didn't that make the damned letterman jacket unutterably sad?

When they returned to the bar, briefly, for more Corona, I said to Christa, "Well, this was a real nice clambake, but—."

She looked at me, dabbing the damp hair at her temples with a little square bar napkin. "And I am telling you I'm not going."

I felt my eyes narrow. She must have been saving that for a while. I said, "Just you wait, 'Enry 'Iggins."

Tory took Christa's elbow. He said, "While we still have the chance, let's face the music and dance."

She frowned. "You're both scary as hell."

After sullen and suffering hours, during which I tried to recall all the lines of "I Could Have Danced All Night" in the right order, the DJ announced last call. There were boos and catcalls—even some hissing—from the few patrons who remained, but my joy was Brobdingnagian. While the other dancers started shuffling toward the doors, Christa and Tory made the most of the last song. They turned and glided, inventing moves that belonged in a soft-core revival of *Funny Face*. At last Christa turned to face him, and as the chorus repeated and faded, they kissed under the spinning lights. The song was "Heart of Glass."

· · ·

As I descended the stairs, I could smell the river, an icy, clean smell. Snow swirled among the trees. Where the path turned away from the river, the birch tree stood orphaned on the riverward side. Its bark shone like bronze in the pink glow of distant streetlights.

I stopped. In the wind and snow I hugged myself. The leather of my jacket creaked. The boathouse would be there, I told myself. Some mistake had been made. Michael Walton had fallen for an adolescent prank. Or perhaps he'd perpetrated the prank, and I had fallen for it.

But then, just beyond the birch, I smelled stale charcoal.

Where the boathouse had been—all around it, down to the dock, and into the trees on every side—there was a tract of black earth and, in the center of that, a heap of charred timbers. Nothing resembling the weathered A-framed building I'd loved, with the mismatched shingles that had given it the crazy aspect of a fairy-tale cottage. And of course, nothing resembling the boats that had been inside it.

A squall kicked up. The snow wrapped around me like a living thing, or a rout of ghosts.

3 ARCHAEOLOGY

Naked in the pink glare of streetlights, I stumbled down Nicollet Mall. A man emerged from a darkened doorway. As he strolled away from me, shadows gathered to him. I beseeched him to turn back, to speak to me.

People lined the pavement. I felt them there, felt them waiting and watching, as if for a parade, but I could not bear to turn my head and look at them. I thought I heard them whispering—some in horror, it seemed, and some in amusement.

At last, the man turned. Shadows concealed his face. He spoke with the voice of my alarm clock. I woke.

The churlish boiler had drenched the air; the bedroom was as sweltry as a rain forest. My sweat dampened the bed where I lay. In my sleep I'd tossed the sheets and blankets to the floor. I shook off the dream and rolled over to silence the alarm. It had been warbling for fourteen minutes. The fat red numbers glimmered in the half-light: twelve after eight.

I walked stiff-legged to the bathroom. I blotted my face with a hand towel. I sat to pee, slumping against the cool tile.

I squeezed toothpaste onto my toothbrush. I squinted at the mirror. Dark orange whiskers crowded my upper lip and the tip of my chin; I looked as if I'd begun to rust overnight. Reflexively I gripped the toothpaste tube, and a white ribbon of the paste splattered to the floor.

As I squatted to wipe up the mess with a towel, I saw that a bit of white paper had fallen to the floor, who knew how long ago, and had somehow partially worked its way under the vanity. I picked it up, turned it over. It was a business card bearing the name of my dentist, George Bell, DDS, in raised type. A smiling cartoon tooth held a toothbrush. The thick blue ink of the toothbrush handle and the tooth's rickety legs shone and rippled like old window glass. In a shaky slanted cursive, Dr. Bell's hygienist, Miss Morton, had written, "Monday, November 2, 1992, 9:00 am."

"Holy shit," I said.

•   •   •

The snow had vanished. Glistening puddles were all that remained. The dank air carried a whiff of woodsmoke. Ordinarily it was the cozy perfume of winter hibernation, a pleasant reminder of my youth, of the snow days I'd spent listening to *Cabaret* and *South Pacific* with liner notes spread across my lap and my bare feet propped on the hearth, but now it reminded me of my lost boat, of the acid smell of the charred boathouse.

I'd parked the Chevette at the end of the front walk. As I slipped the key into the ignition, I looked up. A neighborhood rogue had written on the windshield in angular strokes of flaky white soap—a belated Halloween prank. The delinquent had formed the letters backward, so that they would be legible from inside the car, but he—it seemed natural to assume the prankster was male—had strung them together from his left to his right, so that they spelled "GAF."

Laughing, I turned the key. One thing in the engine pecked softly at another. After that, silence. "Shit," I said. I rested my head on the steering wheel. "Shit." Somewhere behind me—a couple of blocks away, I guessed, somewhere on University Avenue—a siren keened and faded. I turned the key once more. Nothing.

I would have to walk, and hope for a bus.

•   •   •

A teenager stood at the corner of University and Simpson, in front of the Spin Cycle Coin Laundry. Tucked under his arm he carried a stack of bright yellow leaflets. He wore a gigantic black parka and, under that, a tight white T-shirt short enough to reveal a little tuft of hair below his navel. As I approached, he offered me a leaflet and a gap-toothed grin.

"Love is all around, bro," he said. His voice was throaty, laryngitic.

The leaflet advertised an Election Day prayer vigil at a church in Golden Valley.

Protect Freedom
Preserve The Family
Save America
Pray For President Bush And Vice President Quayle

In the middle of the page there was a big block of text. It began:

Join us for an evening of praise, worship and prayer for the future of our Great Nation. The Liberal Media is falling all over itself to declare Bill Clinton the next President of These Great United States of America, but according to *our* sources, he is nothing but a Liar, a Cheat, and a Whoremonger.

Tiny type at the bottom read:

Vote for Perot if you must, but if you love God, you *must not* vote for Slick Willy Clinton!

Below that, in even tinier type:

Copyright 1992, Sam Stinson Ministries, LLC.

I heard yelling, a man's voice, deep and sharp like the woof of a big angry dog. A woman's anguished bawl answered him. On the other side of University, in the Rainbow Foods parking lot, a tall, bone-skinny black man strode away from a short, plump white woman. He was bare-chested. He wore bleach-stained sweatpants and slippers, or perhaps sandals. She was barefoot. Her pink peignoir flapped in the wind; grime blackened the hem.

The woman extended her hands and raised her voice in an apotheosis of desolate pleading. I could hear her wailing, but the noise of passing traffic obscured her words. The man turned. He shambled backward a few steps. He stopped, then moved around her, crabwise in widening circles, as if she were an explosive device set to detonate at any moment.

Stopping some yards away from her, he said something that struck her—doubled her over—like a kick to the gut. He turned on his heel and, with a snap of his wrist, disappeared behind a row of cars.

The woman, too, turned, but staggered toward the street, away from the man. Just watching the heavy tread of her bare, grubby feet made the bones of my own feet and ankles ache. She flung herself to the ground, onto a muddy strip of lawn alongside the Perkins. She clawed at the grass, dug her fingers into the earth, scratched at it like some kind of wounded animal digging its own grave. Her mouth opened—in a silent scream, I thought, until, belatedly, I heard her howling, her ululant sobbing.

And then she seemed suddenly to calm herself. She sat on her haunches and regarded the ragged gash she had made in the ground. She began again to scoop away the sod, but in a more methodical way, squaring off the sides of the hole she'd made.

As I stood and watched the woman dig meticulously in the mud like an archaeologist searching for a few mire-caked shards of her pride, a bus rolled to a stop along the curb in front of me. Hydraulics hissed as the bus knelt; by luck or skill the driver had stopped the bus so that the lowest step was even with the curb, with a gap of just a couple of inches. I waited while a stooped, gray-haired man with a three-footed cane doddered off the bus.

A cluster of passing cars stirred the air, and the sharp black stink of the bus's exhaust struck me like a slap. My eyes watered. The smell of diesel exhaust had pervaded my dream. Or rather, there had been a smell, and diesel exhaust had been part of it—diesel exhaust mixed with tar, sweat, rotting fruit, and something else I couldn't name. The stench welled up in the back of my throat. My stomach lurched.

I still held the prayer vigil leaflet in my hand. As I crumpled it into a knot that fit in the palm of my hand, I glanced back toward the boy who'd handed it to me. I supposed the heavy-lidded head shake he gave me was intended to convey pity, but it succeeded only in making him look a little stoned.

•   •   •

The bus windows were misty, and the bus was so crowded that I had to stand in the middle of the aisle, clutching the overhead railing. I couldn't see very clearly where we were, but as we approached what seemed like our fortieth stop, I thought I spotted the Arby's at Fairview and University. I pulled the cord, and the bus eased to a halt in front of the Griggs-Midway building.

Dr. Bell's office lay on the other side of Fairview in the Midview Center, an old strip mall that had been converted into professional offices. Dr. William Andersen, MD. Ralph Estes, DO. George Bell, DDS. Venetian blinds masked the last window in the row. At eye level, the name of Eliot Moon, MA, formed an arch, a half moon. "Family And Individual Counseling" inched across underneath, like a kind of horizon over which the moon rose.

Eliot Moon's door opened, and a man emerged. Thickset, of no great height, a small bear of a man in baggy jeans, rumpled flannel, and shiny Doc

Marten boots. He wore an unruly blond goatee. His head was shaved and shining. Our eyes met. He smiled and nodded by way of greeting or farewell. He ambled away, hands in pockets, whistling.

I opened Dr. Bell's door. It moved stiffly, with a shivering creak. Empty of people, the waiting room was barely large enough for the furniture it contained, though it contained only a round glass coffee table and two leather-and-chrome sling chairs. The walls were cinderblock, a shade of pale green that reminded me of hospitals and breath mints.

Dr. Bell himself sat at the reception desk. He looked up and smiled through the sliding window. Since my last checkup he'd grown a mustache. His hair seemed thicker, with a little more gray in it. He was everything I was not. Tall where I was short, dark where I was pale, bulky where I was lean. Every six months or so, I fell in love at first sight.

"I didn't expect to see *you* sitting there," I said.

"We're short-handed," he said. "Jonquil should be here any minute." He handed me a clipboard. "Just check that everything's current, if you please."

The door groaned. A tall young woman with calamitous posture and ruinous fashion sense clattered into the waiting room. Her calf-length jacket—or was it, God forbid, a dress?—had apparently been adapted from someone's grandmother's prize quilt, cut into pieces and dyed black. She wore her platinum hair in an odd hybrid of a bob and a high-and-tight. In the front, two curving locks—one tinted blue, the other green—framed her face and pointed like arrows to her cleft chin.

"Speak of the devil," Dr. Bell said, "and she shall appear. How was breakfast?"

In two steps Jonquil reached the counter, where she set down the remnants of her breakfast—a crumpled white paper bag and a Styrofoam cup.

"I *devoured* it on the way back," she said. She turned to me. "I'm *totally* compulsive abozut hash browns. Fried potatoes in any form, really. As you can see." She planted a hand on each hip, as if to demonstrate her girth, when in point of fact she was at her broadest point not much wider than a sheet of notebook paper. "I'll be back in a sec," she said, and disappeared through a narrow door.

I handed the clipboard to Dr. Bell. I surveyed the furniture arrangement. The room was so cramped that I didn't dare sit. Surely I would stub a toe or bark a shin in the attempt. There wasn't room enough for a coat rack; it hardly seemed there could be room for a person. I slipped off my jacket and laid it on the back of one of the chairs.

"Sorry to say, no magazines," Dr. Bell said. "We don't have any delivered now. All that paper makes the earth weep." He rolled his eyes.

I stepped to the counter and peeked into Jonquil's Styrofoam cup. It was half-filled with black coffee. "On the other hand, I heard that Styrofoam makes the earth giggle."

Dr. Bell smiled. "Come on back," he said.

Beyond the little door lay a warren of tiny rooms—two exam rooms on the left, a restroom and a filing closet on the right. Dr. Bell pointed me into the first exam room.

"I'll be right with you."

The exam room was miniscule, roughly square. Here, instead of green, the walls were yellow, perhaps a shade too close to the color of mustard. On a poster pinned to the acoustic ceiling, a kitten hung by its claws from a tree branch. A caption read, "Hang In There!"

I settled into the exam chair. The vinyl was smooth from many years of use, cool to the touch. Again, the sickening smell of my dream filled my nose. I leaned over the porcelain cuspidor. Water trickled into its honey-comb drain. The freshness of the water and the clean scent of astringent cleared my head.

I lay back in the chair. Dr. Bell stood just inside the door, a file folder tucked under his arm. Staring absently at the ceiling, he tugged at the cuffs of his smock. I wondered how long he'd been watching me lean over the cuspidor. Perhaps for so long that—as a passenger of a crowded bus might hide behind a newspaper, on the off chance that the people surrounding him might at any moment begin raving or hallucinating or quoting Bible verses—Dr. Bell had invented a way of occupying himself, of ignoring my eccentric behavior.

But then he said, "I had to remind Jonquil to do some billing, otherwise she'd spend the whole morning fixing her makeup."

So he'd been distracted with personnel issues. Perhaps he hadn't even noticed me leaning over the cuspidor. He sat on a stool, rolled it toward the exam chair.

"Black lipstick and eye shadow," he said, shaking his head. "*Black.* I just don't get it."

"These kids today," I said.

He opened the folder. "No X-rays today. Great." He spread out the open folder on the cabinet. "Shorthanded, as I said. You're stuck with me for your cleaning."

"What happened to Miss Morton?"

"Retired," he said. "She was overdue, I think."

From a drawer in the cabinet Dr. Bell took a bib, fastened it around my neck with alligator clamps, and smoothed it down across my chest. I touched the bib, imagining that the warmth of his hand remained in the thick tissue.

"How's your mother?" he asked me.

He half-stood to position the dental light. Sitting, he flicked the switch, and the reflector filled with an amber glow.

"My mother is ... my mother."

He arranged his tools on the instrument tray. Mirror, hand excavator, explorer—he laid them side by side, exactly parallel to the sides of the tray. In his thick fingers the tools looked slender, delicate, precise.

"Actually," I said, "I haven't talked to her in a while."

"When you do talk to her, tell her I miss her show. It was the best thing on the radio."

"I'll tell her. She'll probably send you a balloon bouquet."

"All right," he said. "Let's have a look."

I turned my face toward him, but locked my eyes on the kitten poster. The dry warmth and the girth of his bare fingers as they eased my mouth open had always suggested a deep intimacy between us. A fantasy, of course, part of a puerile crush, perhaps, but I delighted in it. I felt my breath coming a little rougher.

But he wasn't ready yet. "What did she think of that mess with Howard Stern?" he asked.

"Howard Stern?"

"The FCC just hit him with a big fine. The biggest ever, I heard."

I looked at him. His eyes were hazel. For a moment I stared into them, lost among the pale striae and flecks of green. "I hadn't heard about that. I'm sure she has opinion to spare on the subject, though."

He laughed, shook his head. "I'm sure she does."

Mirror in one hand, explorer in the other, he leaned in. I opened my mouth. I stared at the poster on the ceiling, fixing on the kitten's pink nose. Dr. Bell's warm hand brushed my chin. He tucked the mirror between my teeth and my lower lip.

"Oh, bother," he said, and withdrew. "I will never get used to this."

I had no idea what he meant. I lifted my head. He had rolled away on the stool. He rummaged in the storage cabinet and pulled from it an unopened box of latex gloves.

"I usually leave them out on the counter, so I don't forget," he said. "But then, when I run out—." He plucked two gloves from the box. "You're not allergic to latex, right?"

The gloves appeared to be a couple of sizes too small for his hands. He spent considerable effort and time wriggling his thick fingers and thumbs into the latex. Once his left hand was covered, it was even more difficult to slip a glove onto his right. The ring finger of the second glove split at the tip, and he had to start over. He grinned at me—bashfully, I thought.

At last both hands were gloved. "By the way," he said. He tugged and snapped the latex down toward his wrists. "What's going on with Tom? He missed an appointment last month." He wiggled his fingers. They moved stiffly, like corseted ladies trying to bow. "Jonquil *swears* she called a 'million times'"—he made quotes in the air with two fingers of each hand, and the latex creaked—"but you two don't have an answering machine, so—."

Again I stared up at the poster. Suddenly, it irked me—the triteness of it, the cuteness, the soft focus, the absurdly unnatural cobalt blue of the kitten's eyes. The smell from my dream rose once more in my throat. I must have eaten something foul, but what? Surely I would remember eating something that smelled like tar and diesel exhaust.

I managed to say, "He—," and then no words would come. Only that damned stench, and the tang of latex and antiseptic on my tongue.

I covered my face with my hands; tears soaked my fingers. All at once, I was leaning sideways out of the exam chair, hugging the cuspidor, sobbing. My body heaved and shook. Choking noises ripped my throat.

Around me, whole worlds seemed to spin and churn, lost in murk. I saw only the blur of chrome at the bottom of the cuspidor. Dimly, I heard casters squeaking, doors banging, water running—not the trickle in the cuspidor, but a faucet gushing, wide open.

Then Jonquil was there, beside the chair. The patchwork thing had been a coat after all, I saw; she now wore a blue smock with a mini-skirt underneath. She placed a damp cloth on my forehead. I was leaning back, my head on the headrest. When had that happened?

"It's only a cleaning," she said. Her voice was so kind, so solicitous, that I broke out in fresh sobs. She smoothed the bib over my chest. She stroked my arm, held it so that I couldn't lean over into the cuspidor again. "It's okay," she said. "Whatever it is, it'll be okay."

I meant to protest, to say, "It won't, it won't, it won't," but the words came out in a slur of random vowels.

Jonquil moved away. I heard whispering at the door. "He's saying something about a boat," she said.

"A boat?"

The boat? Had I mentioned the boat?

Suddenly I went numb. I lay still. Jonquil wore the expression of a mother sitting vigil beside her child's deathbed. I closed my eyes.

The door opened with a protracted squeal. Dr. Bell whispered, "He's here."

I opened my eyes. A man sat in the stool. I noticed his hands first of all. He held them on his knees, plucking at his the creases of his khaki trousers. His fingers were long and slender. Whorls of flesh puckered at the knuckles, as if they were made of knotted rope. The pads of his thumbs were fat, though— or broad, rather, slightly flattened. A crescent of grime darkened one thumbnail. His face seemed to be formed of ill-fitted pieces—high cheekbones, thin lips, eyes set too far apart, eyebrows so pale they seemed not to exist. Crooked bangs covered his forehead. He smiled. "I'm Eliot," he said.

Eliot Moon, MA, Family and Individual Counselor. Now I was mortified. Like the batty maiden aunt in an old film, I had become completely unhinged in public, compelling the management to cry out for any doctor who might be in the house. By now, in some psych ward somewhere in the Twin Cities, a bed surely had my name on it.

"They tell me there's something about a boat," he said. "I doubt there's much I haven't heard, but that's a new one." Again, he smiled.

I pulled the bib off and scrubbed my face with it. I wasn't sure I could trust myself to talk, but I sat up and with a few deep breaths primed myself for the effort. "I'm sorry. I think I should just go." My voice was thick, sluggish.

I stood. Eliot put his hand on my forearm. "If you need someone to talk to, I have some time."

Jonquil appeared behind him. "Did the boat sink?" she said.

With an urgent whisper I couldn't quite understand, Dr. Bell pulled her away from the door. His hand and arm reached into the exam room, like a hook dragging a vaudeville juggler from the stage.

Eliot spun in the stool and, standing, closed the door. The stool squeaked.

The door squawked. I discovered that I was gritting my teeth. I sat in the exam chair.

"Maybe some privacy wouldn't be a bad thing right now," he said. He sat on the stool, his fingers gripping the seat between his splayed legs.

"I appreciate your offer of help," I said, "but I'm really so embarrassed about all this that I think I should just sneak out of here and—and find a new dentist, I guess."

"Would you like me to create a diversion?"

In spite of myself, I smiled. "Why don't *you* start sobbing like a little girl, and I'll make a break for it."

"What's this about a boat, then?"

"There's no boat." I paused, rubbed the whiskers on my chin. They were coarse; it almost hurt to touch them, like stroking finely ground glass.

"I didn't think it was really about a boat." He seemed relieved.

"Well, there *was* a boat, but I never—." I was about to say that I'd never told Jonquil or Dr. Bell about the boat, that they wouldn't know about the boat, but really, did I even know myself what I'd said and hadn't said?

"Okay. Tell me about the boat." He shrugged, as if to suggest that the idea of the boat made him slightly weary, but he was resigned to it.

I said, "Do you have issues with boats? Did you get jilted on a cruise, or were you made to watch *The Love Boat* as a child?"

He squinted as if focusing on something at a great distance, or as if enduring some dull pain. His forehead bunched up in the middle, making his wide-set eyes seem closer together. "Tell me about the boat."

I told him. The shell, brand new, senselessly destroyed. The ruined boathouse. The smell of ash. Somehow in the telling I ended up recounting my dream. Suddenly it occurred to me that the figure melting into the shadows on Nicollet Mall had been the arsonist.

But no. Surely the man in my dream had been Tom. Again the tears came. Eliot drew closer. I could smell his cologne, or maybe it was his shampoo— something spicy, a whiff of cloves or patchouli. I thought he might literally offer me a shoulder to cry on, but he made no move to touch me.

"It must have been Tom," I said.

"Tom?"

"In the dream."

There was a tap on the door, so soft that I didn't hear it. Only when Eliot held up a finger to signal that I should wait, only when he spun on the stool to open the door, did I know that there had been a knock.

A whisper, Jonquil's voice: "I'm sorry." She hung back out of sight.

I blotted my face with the bib. Again, I stood. "I can't believe this happened," I said. "I won't take up any more of your—."

Jonquil leaned into the room. "No, no, really, don't be—. I mean, it's—. It's just—. You've been in here quite a while. The next two patients are here, and we need—."

God, how long had I been wailing and sobbing? Twenty minutes? Thirty? Forty?

Eliot touched my arm. "Let's go to my office." His eyes were brown—so commonplace a color, so unremarkable that I might never have bothered to notice them. But now he gave me a look so filled with tenderness and empathy that I found myself staring into them—staring at the tiny, pale gray rings that marked the boundaries between irises and pupils. "I have a gap between patients. I have a couple of hours free on Monday mornings, so I have some time, if you want to talk," he said.

I remembered the bearish man I'd seen leaving Eliot's office, and found myself picturing the fellow's Doc Marten boots, the yellow stitching around the soles. I stared thoughtlessly at the floor, as if the boots might appear there.

Eliot touched my elbow. He said, "I think it would do you good to have someone to talk to."

As I passed Jonquil in the narrow hallway, she leaned in to whisper, "Did the boat sink?"

God, she was tall. Even stooped over as she was—an adolescent habit to compensate for her Amazonian height, I'd be willing to bet—I had to lift my head to look at her face. She had a smear of kohl below her right eye.

I shook my head. "It was destroyed in a fire."

She stepped back. Her mouth snapped shut, as if she'd been struck dumb. I touched my forehead, thinking to hide behind my hand, thinking my face must be a puffy, reddened mess. But then she put her hand on my forearm. "Oh, my God, that's awful. Was it insured?"

• • •

Dr. Bell's office looked like exactly what it was—an old storefront in a strip mall, uneasily converted to a dental office—but Eliot's office was something much finer. Halogen lamps washed the sesame-colored walls in clear, diamond-bright light. His desk was honey oak, possibly an antique, immaculately polished, the size of Liechtenstein. White bookcases filled one wall. Books lined half of the shelves, arranged by height and color. Texts concerning the treatment of mental illness wouldn't have surprised me. *DSM-III* wouldn't have surprised me. That every book was about baseball—that surprised me. Memorabilia crowded the remaining shelves: baseballs in acrylic cubes, an autographed bat in an ebony cradle, programs and tickets, baseball cards gilt-framed like sacred icons.

Eliot waved me toward an armchair upholstered in mahogany leather. He sat in its mate. "You were telling me about someone named Tom," he said. "You thought it was Tom in your dream. Who's Tom?"

I stared at the baseball bat in its cradle. The pale wood shimmered in the halogen light.

"Your lover," Eliot said. It wasn't a question. Maybe Dr. Bell had said something.

"For five years," I said. "We met in college."

"And something happened."

Thoughts tumbled, rose, crumbled, collapsed. It was a simple enough thing to say: *Tom died. Alcohol poisoning. A stupid accident.*

But no. First there was the dry gray morning I spent searching for him.

No. Before that. The baseball game. He'd gone to a Twins game with his friends, the drinking buddies that had become his entire social circle. I hadn't been invited. I hadn't *wanted* to be invited, but even so, I'd stewed about it all night.

In the early dawn I'd rolled over in bed and had found that Tom was not there. He was not in the house. His car was not parked out front, or on the side, or on any nearby street. I drove around in the Chevette, searching for his car. It was not in the Rainbow Foods parking lot. It was not in the Montgomery Ward parking lot. It was not in the Target parking lot.

Each time I widened the circle, I doubled back to the house to see if he'd come home. There was no sign of him. The Chevette's fuel gauge listed toward empty, but I couldn't bear the thought of stopping the car. If I walked into the house, and he wasn't there, then I would know for certain that something was terribly wrong. As long as I kept driving, then he must be driving too, somewhere between Minneapolis and Saint Paul, on his way home to our bed.

"He died," I said. At last, there it was, the simple declarative sentence that had eluded me all morning.

"I'm sorry for your loss," Eliot said.

I looked at him. His brown eyes gleamed, not exactly brimming with tears, but certainly showing deep, true sympathy.

"You're the first person to say that," I told him. "Somehow, everyone seems to know what happened, but no one mentions it. I feel like I'm not allowed to talk about it."

"You can talk about it now, if you want."

Eliot's office was overheated. My skin felt itchy and dry. It occurred to me that I'd left my jacket in Dr. Bell's office. The prospect of going back for it made me feel heavy, enervated. I felt as if I hadn't slept in a month. Maybe I hadn't.

Eliot touched my knee. For some reason, the black curve of dirt under his thumbnail troubled me.

"What happened?"

"That's one of the hardest things. He was my lover, my best friend, but I don't really know what happened. Not for sure."

"Tell me what you *do* know."

I said, "He and his friends—these fucking club friends he was hanging out with all the time—they went to a baseball game, a Twins game."

"When was this?"

"September seventh."

He nodded. "The Twins beat the Mariners, four to two."

I looked at him, blinking. If there was an appropriate reply, I couldn't think of it.

"I'm a Mariners fan. My hometown. Seattle. I was at that game."

I leaned forward. "You were there? Where? Maybe you saw them. I'm pretty sure they were sucking down beer for seven innings, making a lot of ruckus."

"I don't think I noticed them. Sorry."

I sank back. "They must have gone somewhere else after that. I don't know what they did or where they went, but you can't drink enough near-beer to overdose. You just can't."

"And you're sure it was alcohol poisoning?"

"That's what the nurse told me at the hospital."

"So you were called to the hospital?"

"No one called me," I told Eliot. "I didn't know what happened till the morning, when I saw he wasn't back." I described how I'd gone looking, how

I'd driven in spirals around the Cities, looking for his car, or for some sign of him.

First, I'd stopped at Fairview. I'd slowed for the left turn into the parking lot, stopped at the gate. I'd looked up at the hospital—the big rectangular block of red brick, the tidy grid of little black windows. Taking a ticket meant rolling down the car window; I couldn't do that. I didn't know why, but I couldn't do it.

I went around the block. I followed Riverside to Cedar. I drove around downtown. I drove by Hennepin County Medical Center. An ambulance and a taxi sat nose to nose in the curved emergency room driveway. Behind the taxi there was a blue minivan, a Lumina. Tom's parents drove a Lumina.

I drove to the parking ramp across the street. I rolled down the window this time, took the ticket. I parked. I trudged down the concrete stairs to the street. I crossed against the light.

Even before I got into the waiting room, even before I saw Tom's parents talking to the ER doctor, a man in mouthwash-blue scrubs, I knew that Tom was there. Somewhere in the curtain-walled spaces behind the registration desk, he was there.

•   •   •

"His parents never thought to call." No, that was too charitable. "They refused to call." They actively shunned me when I stumbled into the emergency room, blinking and bewildered as if I'd emerged from a cave into full sunlight. When they saw me, they turned their backs, stared at the vertical blinds, studied the leaves of a potted palm, looked at the aquarium between the waiting room and the corridor, watched a lionfish swim through a forest of plaster coral—anything to give the appearance that they had not seen me at all.

Fucking vipers, I thought. And then I said it aloud. I spat the words, feeling heat blossom in my cheeks. My ears burned like lanterns. "Motherfucking vipers," I said.

Eliot nodded gravely. For a moment I half-expected some words of reproach, an admonishment to clean up my potty mouth. But no, of course that was ridiculous; he said, "But someone finally talked to you?"

"There was a nurse." A tiny black woman, no higher than my shoulder, with a buzzed scalp and one gold hoop earring. She would have looked like a diminutive African pirate, if pirates wore mauve scrubs. "She figured out who I was, and even though she shouldn't have, she pulled me aside. She said a cab driver brought him in. A group of teenagers, it seemed like to him, poured Tom into the back of the cab, and halfway to Saint Paul he passed out and the driver couldn't wake him. That was all she could tell me."

"It must have been very difficult, sharing your life with him, but then having everyone act as if none of that existed."

My head sagged back against the chair. I lacked the strength even to nod.

Eliot said, "This was two months ago, and you haven't been able to talk to anyone about it in all that time? It's no wonder you had a breakdown this morning. The wonder is that it didn't happen sooner."

"Maybe you're right."

"You have a right to grieve, Jonah. This is a big loss. You can't let anyone take that away from you because they're uncomfortable talking about it."

"Or maybe no one knows, and they're all wondering why I suddenly stopped mentioning him."

"I'm sure at least some of your friends know. And what about your parents?"

"My mother knows. But I don't get to talk to her that much. The time difference—she lives in San Francisco—plus she sleeps in the day and works all night."

And Christa knew, of course. The game had been on a Monday night. Most of Tuesday I'd spent at HCMC in fruitless longing and profound invisibility. I had called Christa that night, had told her all of it—all that I knew—and we'd cried together over the phone. On Wednesday I went back to work, and her doe-eyed "How are you doing?" seemed to require something breezy—"Holding up," and then—in answer to the stern, quizzical expression she adopted, rather self-consciously, I thought—"Better today." Neither of us had mentioned Tom since.

"I'm not even really sure he died at all. Maybe he recovered in the hospital and just never came back." Maybe he'd gone to Thailand, as he'd been planning to do. Or maybe he'd gone hitchhiking in Europe. Or maybe he was living with his parents in Roseville, bagging groceries at Cub Foods.

"That sounds like wishful thinking," Eliot said. "The way things happened, you never got to say good-bye. It's all open-ended. Ordinarily there's a funeral, there's a burial. You see with your own eyes that the person is gone. You didn't get any of that."

"No closure," I said.

Eliot's face puckered, as if he'd sucked a lemon. He was silent a moment, as if considering something, but he said only, "Yes."

Perhaps I'd overstepped, using a therapy word before he could utter it himself. Or perhaps he disapproved of it, considered it pop-psych jargon.

He said, "You and Tom weren't married. It wasn't possible for you to marry, but for whatever it's worth, he chose to live with you, possibly to spend his life with you, and even if his parents aren't obligated to accept that or approve of it, they could at least recognize it."

I wasn't so sure that Tom and I had been headed toward a life together. So many fights, so many frigid silences, so many evenings apart: I knew it would all have come flying apart sooner or later. Before I could give voice to any of this, Eliot went on.

"I think before you can move on, before you can even grieve properly, you need to say good-bye, or at least establish for certain that he's—that he's gone."

"There was no funeral, no obituary."

Leaning back in his chair, he crossed his legs, ankle over knee. The cuff of one trouser leg rode up, showing his slumped beige sock, a couple of inches of shin, and a few long, wiry black hairs. *In olden days a glimpse of stocking*, I thought.

"He must be buried somewhere. I think you need to confront his parents."

My chest tightened. Before that Tuesday in the hospital, I'd met Tom's parents only once, years ago, when Tom and I had just begun dating. We hadn't even slept together yet. As far as his parents knew, we were friends, and both straight. Even so, the way they'd looked at me, I might have been some kind of predator or parasite infecting their son, corrupting his very blood and marrow.

"I didn't think therapists gave advice," I said to Eliot.

He laughed. "I'm not a therapist, first of all. I'm a counselor. And, secondly, I think of myself as a kind of coach, more so than a traditional counselor. And lastly, I'm afraid I've got another client coming in about fifteen minutes, so I was thinking it might not be a bad idea to cut to the chase, so to speak."

I nearly leapt out of my chair. "I'm so sorry. I can't even begin to say how sorry I am for derailing your day like this."

Eliot rose as well, so that we stood a few inches apart, between the two leather chairs. In the prickly weather of the office, he was an island of greater heat. I thought of Spike, the heat of our bodies in the chill of the boathouse, thought of the way he'd wrapped his hands around my throat. It had felt threatening, but oddly intimate. He had dared me—had *forced* me, really—to trust him even before I knew him, and I had.

I stared at the braided veins and muscles of Eliot's hands, imagined them grasping my neck in the same way. I longed to kiss him, to fold myself into his arms.

As if he could read my thoughts, Eliot stepped back. He motioned toward my chair. "I'm the one who should apologize. I wasn't trying to rush you out of here. I shouldn't have mentioned the time."

Neither of us moved.

"Jonah," he said. "Please. Ten more minutes."

I sat. He perched on the edge of the chair, leaning forward with his elbows on his knees. He said, "I hope it's been helpful to talk out some of things you've had to keep bottled up, but I feel there's a lot more ground to cover. I hope you'll come back and talk some more."

Of course, he was right. There was more, much more. We were archaeologists just beginning a big dig, still surveying the site, with all the shattered pottery and rusted weapons yet buried in the ancient loam. I knew now what had driven that woman—the barefoot woman in the pink peignoir—to scratch at the muddy turf alongside the Perkins. Clawing at the earth would be so much simpler than what Eliot and I had just been through, and what lay ahead.

"If you're hesitating because of cost—."

I started to shake my head, but stopped. "I—. It's true, I can't really afford a lot of—."

He waved the subject away as if waving away a gnat. "There are programs I can look into. Assistance programs. Leave that with me."

"I suppose the more important thing is—. That is to say, I—. I guess I never thought I'd be crazy enough to need therapy." Once uttered, this immediately seemed ill-advised, an ignorant and insulting thing to say to a therapist—or a counselor or coach or whatever he called himself.

But Eliot laughed. "By rights I should give you a lecture about the word 'crazy,' but I'll spare you. So you'll come back later this week? Next time will be just an hour, I promise."

We arranged a meeting for Wednesday afternoon. He walked me to the door, and as he opened it, he handed me a business card. He pointed at the phone number. "If you need to talk before Wednesday, call me," he said.

◆ ◆ ◆

Clouds had gathered. Streetlights glowed pink in the grim, half-hearted light of noon. Out on the street, snowflakes eddied in the beams of passing headlights. The wind blew, stiff and icy. I had no choice: I had to fetch my jacket from Dr. Bell's office.

Every door in the building squeaked; there was no way to sneak in. Jonquil sat at the receptionist desk. She looked up when I entered. She gave a tenderhearted smile. "How are you?"

"Embarrassed," I said. My jacket lay across the back of the chair, where I'd left it. I picked it up.

"Don't be. We all have our days."

I put on my jacket. I pretended to be utterly absorbed in the process of zipping it. "Well. Good-bye, Jonquil."

"Take care of yourself," she said, and stared at me intently, as if by telekinesis or sheer force of will she could make me treat myself kindly and with love.

4 ONSLAUGHT

When I got home, the phone was ringing. Martin, my boss. "Christa tells me you're ill. Why do you want to be sick, Jonah?"

Martin believed in neither accident nor coincidence. Incident and destiny alike, he believed, were ordained by conscious or subconscious intention.

"I don't know," I said. "I guess I'm just weak."

He cleared his throat. Not the answer he'd expected. "How long—? Will you be back—? When—?"

"I'm teasing, Martin. It was just a dentist's appointment."

"Ah. The importance of good dental hygiene can scarcely be overrated."

"Agreed."

"However, I'm calling because there's this meeting with Thorstensen, and—."

Of course. The meeting with Thorstensen. Two appointments in one day, completely forgotten. Somewhere on my desk at work lay a Day Runner, but it wasn't much help if I never looked at it. I took the portable phone into the bedroom, where the alarm clock's red numbers shimmered in the half-light: twelve-thirty-two. Easy enough to get to the office by one o'clock, if not for the death of my car. Damn, I'd have to take the bus again. How long would *that* take?

"I'm sorry, Martin. I'll be there as soon as I can."

"Good enough," he said. "We'll start without you." He hung up as he always did, after a tense pause and a clearing of the throat.

Halfway to my car I had my keys in my hand, although barely forty seconds before, on the phone with Martin, I'd been chafing at the prospect of riding the bus twice in one day. I stopped, twirled the key ring on my finger. Apparently, conscious or subconscious intention had dictated that my brain go smooth as a pebble, that my memory wipe itself clean on a minute-by-minute basis. I put the keys in my pocket, then pulled them out again. What the hell, why not give it another try?

The salt spray of passing cars had splotched and spotted the Chevette on the street side. As I walked around it from the back, keys jangling, I again saw the GAF on the windshield, and I noticed something new—someone had tucked a sheet of paper under the left-hand windshield wiper. A Sam Stinson leaflet, pink instead of yellow, but otherwise exactly like the one the gap-toothed teenager had handed me earlier. Melting snowflakes had pocked and puckered the surface of the paper. On the back someone had written in a rounded hand, "Homosexuality is an abomination before the Lord."

The leaflet lay in tiny flecks in the mud-choked gutter by the time I sat at the Chevette's wheel. I slid the key home, turned it. My foot was heavy on the accelerator—I fully expected this to be an exercise in futile optimism, after all—and the engine roared to life. Startled, I pulled my hands and feet away. The engine dropped its voice.

So it wasn't the battery. The starter? The distributor cap? The dual overhead cam, perhaps? What was a dual overhead cam, and did I have one, and why was I pretending, even to myself, that I knew the first thing about cars?

I sprayed the windshield with washer fluid and let the wipers scrape away the soapy GAF. The word smeared and dissolved into sudsy white streaks.

I switched on the radio. It was tuned to Minnesota Public Radio. A string quartet I dimly recognized, one of Beethoven's late quartets, perhaps. *Serioso?* Certainly it sounded quite serious. Or perhaps it was the sixteenth quartet.

Traffic on University Avenue moved sluggishly. I passed the familiar landmarks: the Target at Hamline, an abandoned furniture store and the Frank's Nursery on either side of Lexington, the second-hand store with six rooms' worth of furniture on the sidewalk, the Vietnamese restaurants and groceries of Frogtown.

Yes, it was Beethoven's sixteenth quartet. The finale. I recognized it, now, from a report I'd written in Form and Analysis in my junior year. No, that wasn't right. I'd chosen it, enamored with its German subtitle—*Der*

Schwer ... something. Translated, it meant "The Difficult Decision," or more exactly and more meaningfully, I'd thought, "The Hard-Won Decision." I'd imagined Beethoven on his deathbed, parchment staff paper strewn across the coverlet, expressing acceptance of his imminent mortality in the language he knew best. I'd soon rejected the piece, though, finding that its many eccentric key changes boded poorly for an easy A.

A halting, then flowing, series of imitative sequences gave way to pulsing chords high on the violins. Beneath these the viola and cello sang mournfully, then venomously: *"Muss es sein? Muss es sein?"* I remembered seeing the figure in the score, remembered reading its final interval as a tritone, an augmented fourth or diminished fifth, an awkward interval, in Bach's day considered a sign of the devil in music. But then I'd played parts of the score on a piano. The "tritone" was, after all, a garden-variety major third. Only Beethoven could, with a single accidental, transform the simple, euphonious interval at the core of all Western music into something bitter and sullen.

In front of the Wendy's restaurant at Dale, two cars had collided. A bottleneck had formed around the accident. Traffic crept around it. I cursed and pumped the brake and glanced at the dashboard clock every six seconds.

The violins sawed away in double-stopped chords. The cello and viola answered, booming like bullfrogs. And then a sudden *cantabile* passage gave way to dance, which gave way to stridency, followed again by *cantabile. Cantabile*—singable or singingly. Indeed, I found myself singing along. *Fugato* flowed effortlessly, water over rock.

One of the cars, a tugboat in champagne and gold, sat with its nose in the street, its hind wheels in the Wendy's parking lot. The driver had tried to turn into the nearest lane of traffic, but instead had struck and crumpled the second car, a white Cabriolet.

A white Cabriolet. Christa drove a white Cabriolet.

"Es muss sein!" the second violin said, the three-note motif simple, exultant, reassuringly diatonic. *"Es muss sein!"* the first violin answered, an octave above. *It must be.*

I bullied my way between a matched set of Nissan Pathfinders into the right turn lane. Fudging the red light, I turned onto Dale and swerved without signaling into the parking lot. A knot of people stood gesturing and shouting—a pair of Latino men in gray coveralls, a black couple flanked by two bored-looking teenaged girls. Christa was not among them. The teenagers stared wretchedly toward the Wendy's, as if a bowl of chili were all they desired in the world. The adults turned and looked at me. I shrugged, smiled, and backed away.

And now the going was easy. I sped through the empty parking lot of the Unidale Mall and onto University through the far entrance. The street was nearly clear of traffic now.

The quartet played, *arco* against *pizzicato*, each instrument dancing lightly, high in its register. And then, just when it seemed a whole new section had begun, the entire movement ended in three booming chords—second-inversion tonic, dominant, tonic—simple, uncomplicated, expected, deeply traditional, as if Beethoven hadn't just dragged the listener through four remote keys.

A hushed female voice confirmed what I had guessed. "That was Beethoven's sixteenth and last string quartet, Opus one-thirty-five," she said. "In Beethoven's own hand, we find the words '*Muss es sein?*' 'Must it be?' Under the faster main theme, Beethoven wrote, '*Es muss sein.*' 'It must be.' Since the composer was suffering in ill health at the time, legend has grown up around these words, but apparently in truth it all stemmed from a dispute over money with his housekeeper. Interesting trivia for your next cocktail party."

I stared at the radio, blinking. Dispute over money? With his housekeeper?

The announcer promised another quartet, Dvořák's "American." But first the news. More newspapers had endorsed Clinton than Bush; not since nineteen sixty-four had a majority—or even a plurality—of newspapers endorsed the Democratic candidate. A former client of Dave Durenberger had claimed that, decades ago, he'd raped her. More than three centuries after the fact, and after a dozen years of study, the Pope had at last conceded that Galileo was right. I switched off the radio.

At Rice Street, I turned right, then left into the State Office Building parking lot. The granite parking structure rose in two levels. The leggy skeletons of last summer's nasturtiums fainted at its foot.

My assigned spot was in the farthest corner of the ramp's ground level. Martin rarely drove to work, but today his rattletrap Volkswagen bus stood in his space, angled to accommodate the right rear fender of Christa's white Cabriolet. Here it was, intact, if crookedly parked.

• • •

People thronged the first floor lobby of the State Office Building, stamping the black marble with muddy boot prints. They carried signs. Their voices tangled and thrummed. Compared to the average class of protestor, they seemed quite placid. One of the signs read—what else?—"Love Is All Around." Another was angled away from me and was difficult to read, but it seemed to say "A Vote For Slick Willy Is A Vote For Satan."

The elevator could not come fast enough. I punched the button forty times before the cantankerous elevator on the northernmost end of the bank rumbled up from the ground floor.

When I opened the door to the office, I found Christa sitting at her desk. She sat with her hands flat on the desktop in front of her, staring ahead as though she'd been doing nothing at all except watching the door. I feared a catatonic state.

"Are you all right?" I said. Something occurred to me: "We haven't been abolished or something, have we?"

Rousing herself from her trance, she waved away the suggestion. "Nothing like that. I've just been waiting for you." She lowered her voice to a portentous whisper. "And so has Martin."

I threw up my hands. "I know, I know. He called."

On a legal pad set before her, she'd scrawled a short list:

Eat a Bowl of Tea
My Dinner with Andre
Surviving Desire

"That's an interesting to-do list," I said.

She sighed. "I was just trying to think of movies where nothing happens."

"I'd have thought you'd rather have your toenails painted pink than see *My Dinner with Andre*."

"It's true, I like a movie with a few good explosions, or at least a car chase. But Tory likes movies where nothing happens." She wrinkled her nose. "And subtitles."

And perhaps movies where middle-aged men wear letterman jackets, I thought. I bit my tongue.

A false wall separated our cubicles. I rounded it. I hung my jacket over the back of my chair. From my desk I grabbed a pen and my Day Runner; I promised myself I'd never again let it out of my hands. I peeked into Martin's office. He wasn't there. "He's up there already?"

"You bet."

"Where's Thorstensen's office again?"

I heard pages rustling. When I returned from my cubicle, she was consulting the big calendar on her desk. "Two-sixty-three," she said. "If it's any consolation, Martin's been torturing me, too. He wants to cut our budget by reducing every number to the tune of—get this—one nickel. *Literally.* I have to figure out how many paper clips we get for five cents. Can a person die from pure annoyance?"

I let my shoulders slump. "If don't come back, that'll be your answer."

In the elevator lobby, I stopped for a long drink from the water fountain. The tunnel to the Capitol curved away out of sight. From its ceramic and stone depths issued the reverberant voice of a crowd. The Sam Stinson folk, no doubt. *Love Is All Around,* I thought.

◆   ◆   ◆

Each floor of the State Office Building had a color theme. The second floor was blue. I followed a strip of navy carpet past robin's-egg walls to Thorstensen's corner office. A fortress of navel-high cubicles—the workspaces of pages, legislative aides, and lackeys, all empty now, all the surfaces clear—surrounded the Minority Leader's office. Thorstensen's door was closed. Muriel, his administrative assistant, was away from her desk. A mug of tea steamed on a tiny hot plate.

In an alcove behind Muriel's cubicle I waited beside brass-framed windows. Patches of sun mottled the wet streets. In the distance, past the Department of Transportation and the Kelly Inn, the cathedral stood on its hill, wrapped half in cloud. To its left, downtown Saint Paul filled the hollow between Summit Avenue and the river. Red and black towers huddled together like parents gathering in their children.

"Jonah?" It was Martin. He stood at Thorstensen's open door. He wore a Twins sweatshirt, faded blue jeans smeared with greenish dirt, and his battered canvas bicycling shoes. "What are you doing?"

I shook myself awake. "No one was here. I didn't think—."

"You could have knocked." He lowered his voice. "You *should* have knocked."

I followed him into the office. How strange that Thorstensen's desk, though surely smaller than Eliot's, seemed so outlandishly out of scale by comparison. Jokes about the size of this slab of dark-stained cherry—bigger than either the Speaker's or the Majority Leader's, so big that it scarcely left room for the Minority Leader himself—were rife throughout the Capitol

Complex. Thorstensen sat in a chair of dark blue suede so tall that it eclipsed all but the topmost foot of the office's only window. Martin and I sat facing him in matching vinyl chairs as narrow as airline seats.

Thorstensen leaned back in his chair, coaxing a complaint from its springs. Smoothing his puckered red vest over his round belly, he said, "Martin has been telling me that you've been out of sorts the past couple of days."

I looked at Martin. He'd had his hair cut to a yarmulke of white bristles. Long yellowish-white whiskers formed a crescent-shaped beard. Steadfastly he kept his eyes on the Minority Leader.

I cleared my throat. For Martin's benefit, I said, "I guess I'm just weak."

Now Martin was looking at me. But I watched Thorstensen. He wheeled back his chair. Elfin eyebrows climbed the craggy cliff of his forehead. He said nothing.

"I thought we were here to talk about the forums," I said. I looked back and forth between them. "Is that not the case?"

Martin said to Thorstensen, "We've planned a series of discussions with staff—we're calling them forums—designed to gather facts about the kinds of harassment—."

Thorstensen held up his left hand. With his right, he rummaged in a desk drawer. He plopped a book, a thick hardcover in a bright red dust jacket, onto his desk. It slid toward us. *Onslaught: How Political Correctness Erodes Our Culture and Belittles Our Values,* by Sam Stinson.

My face burned. If I heard, read, or saw that name one more time to-day—.

"Everything I need to say on the subject is contained in this book," Thorstensen said. "I will not stand by while excellence takes a back seat to some liberal idea of *diversity.*" He spat the word as if it impugned the virtue of someone's mother.

"Representative Thorstensen," I said, "were you aware that in a survey conducted in nineteen-ninety, a mere six percent of university faculty identified themselves as holding leftist—."

Martin touched my arm. "I think what Jonah is trying to say is that that is not our goal. We have been charged with the task of creating a policy that deals with forms of harassment—."

Thorstensen held up his hand again. "I've read the law, Martin. I know what your charter is. And I can read between the lines. I am not going to idly sit by while you draft a policy that prohibits my staff from complimenting one another on their clothing, for fear that someone who has an inferior fashion sense—who's not even in the room, mind you—would be offended if they *were* present—."

I said, "That's *so* beyond the realm of what we can possibly accomplish—."

"I think what Jonah is trying to say is—."

"Martin, I *know* what I'm trying to say. You don't have to—."

Thorstenson shook his head. He pushed the book toward us. "Read the book and you'll know where I stand. I can't forbid my staff from participating in your *forms,* but you should know I'm not kindly disposed to what you're doing."

The meeting was over. I half-expected Thorstesen to spin in his chair in a dismissive gesture, but there was no room for the chair to spin.

•   •   •

In the elevator, I said to Martin, "*Forms?*"

He was holding the Stinson book, ruffling its pages. "I suppose we'd better find out where he stands, so to speak." He closed the book and handed it to me.

"You're joking."

He shook his head. "I doubt there are Cliff's Notes. Best get cracking."

I flipped to the end of the book. Six hundred, forty-nine pages, not counting the index. The elevator doors slid open. Engrossed in the book, I blindly followed Martin. On a hunch, I checked the index for "excellence." Page thirteen, in the preface.

"Listen to this," I said, and read from page thirteen:

> This is a movement so bent upon erasing the natural order of things that they want to make it a crime for us to compliment one another on our clothing. Their wrong-headed idea is that they are protecting someone, some theoretical person with an inferior fashion sense (someone who's not even in the room, mind you), who *might* be offended if they were present.

"Almost exactly the words Thorstensen used," I said. "Did you notice? 'Mind you.' Didn't he even say the 'mind you'?"

I looked up. I was alone in the ground floor elevator lobby. Martin had vanished. The tunnels to the Capitol and to the Department of Transportation were empty, still as a church. Reading, I wandered toward the Capitol.

"*Es muss sein! Es muss sein,*" I sang. The ceramic brick walls sang back.

5 **POPULAR INDICATORS**

On Tuesday morning I drove to work through flurries of fat snowflakes. Snow swirled across University Avenue. The Chevette felt inclined to fishtail, a little unruly, like a skittish pony on a rocky, unfamiliar trail.

KSJN was playing Mendelssohn's Italian Symphony, the first movement. It was a little too early in the day for such ebullience, too wintry for such sunny, shimmering music. I switched off the radio.

At every intersection—or at least every traffic light—some stalwart stood holding a Clinton-Gore sign. Most of the signs were tabloid-sized, but some were as big as sails. Passing motorists honked and waved.

I blinked, rubbed sleep from my eyes. Oh, yes. Election Day. After the previous day's Stinson saturation, the Clinton-Gore signs were a relief, a balm.

What would the little gray-haired man who lived across from the beach be doing now? Marching up and down among his yard signs, shouting, "Bush-Quayle, Bush-Quayle"? Plucking placards from the earth, shaking them menacingly at passing motorists? Perhaps simply standing at the edge of his lawn, leaning on his cane, glowering at passersby, daring them to vote incorrectly?

On second thought, I switched the radio back on. The violins played the jubilant main theme against an accompaniment in the cellos and violas that sounded like a diminution of the melody. So radiant, so celebratory, so recklessly exuberant. All the strings took up the diminution, and the horns broke in with the theme. I found myself humming along, tapping my fingers on the steering wheel.

After the music, election news. The announcer, the same woman who'd told the tale of Beethoven's housekeeper, said, "In a presidential race that has grown more and more heated, and with pollsters predicting a close election, the faithful among both parties are looking backward in order to predict the future. Over the years, would-be prognosticators have made use of a number of popular indicators that have been surprisingly—one might say inexplicably—accurate in predicting election results. Bill Harmon has more."

Bill Harmon's voice was reedy, phlegmy, unpleasantly like an oboe played in its lowest range. He said, "Thank you, Susan. There are indeed several popular indicators which may seem random and which are certainly not statistically valid, but which nevertheless have an excellent track record. For example, since nineteen-fifty-two, no candidate has taken the White House without winning his party's New Hampshire primary."

Susan said, "And as we know, Bill Clinton came in second place in New Hampshire."

"That's right, Susan. His second-place finish was strong enough to reinvigorate his beleaguered campaign, but this traditional rule of thumb bodes ill for his chances in today's election." Bill Harmon sounded as if he badly needed to clear his throat. "Some of the other popular indicators people are looking at seem considerably more tenuous. For example, in eight of eleven past elections, whenever the American League has won the World Series, it's coincided with a Republican win in the election. And the Toronto Blue Jays, this year's World Series champs, are in the American League."

"Another bad sign for Clinton."

"That's right, Susan, but that's not the most unusual of these popular indicators. The most unusual, certainly, would be the quality of the year's Bordeaux harvest. A bad year usually bodes well for the Republicans."

"And this was a bad year?"

"A very bad year. Meaning it's possibly a bad year for Mr. Clinton."

Bill and Susan droned on. According to the dashboard clock, it was eight-thirty-three. For once, I wasn't running late. My polling place was just a few blocks away, on Albert. I had long passed Albert; I would have to double back. Just before Lexington Parkway I edged into the left turn lane. At Lexington I waited for the light. A pair of Clinton volunteers stood on the opposite corner, in front of the Kentucky Fried Chicken, smiling and waving. As I made my left turn, I honked and waved back.

• • •

Christa sat at her desk, *Onslaught* open before her.

"Are you volunteering to read that instead of me?" I asked her.

She slammed the book shut and drove it across her desk with the butt of her stapler, as though it had at just that moment become the most revolting thing on earth, too filthy to touch with bare fingers. "It's all yours," she said. "I'll tell you, though, having read about six paragraphs, I think I might actually vote."

"Please do," I said. "I just stopped on the way, and I was one of about seven people."

From Martin's office came a crash, a metallic clatter, the rustle of paper. Martin swore loudly.

To Christa I said, quite softly, "Not a good morning, I take it?"

She shrugged and pushed the book a couple of inches farther away from her. "Take that, please."

• • •

The previous afternoon I'd read about a hundred pages of Stinson's book—that is to say, about as much of it as I could stand.

The book's first few chapters described a case study of political correctness run amok, an initiative undertaken by the Minnesota State Legislature to make statutory language gender-neutral. Stinson vilified the "time-wasting pinheads" who had conceived the idea. He bestowed his sympathies upon the "loyal servants of the public good" who had been forced to spend their valuable hours working on the project. He ridiculed the countless statutory passages that, "in the cause of correctness," had been rendered gawky or inelegant. His contempt for "awkward constructions" and "passive voice" filled nearly ten pages.

Sitting now at my desk, I picked up where I had left off. The next chapter was an orgy of invective; in it, Stinson enumerated the many gender-neutral word choices he found egregious. "Firemen" had been replaced by "firefighters," although at the time of the initiative there had been no female "firefighters" anywhere in the state of Minnesota. "Fishermen" had been replaced by "anglers," although as anyone knew, "angling" referred only to fishing with rod and reel, and not all who fish do so with rod and reel. As for the rejected alternative, "fishers," Stinson spent a page and a half expounding a theory that the Biblical echo—"fishers of men"—made the word anathema to liberals. "Flagmen" had been replaced by "flaggers." For Stinson, this was the worst example; "flaggers," he wrote, "is an ugly, made-up and patently ridiculous word."

He wrote:

> Any child knows, men and women are biologically and emotionally different creatures; vastly different. It is not without reason that firemen have always been and should be *firemen*, that fishermen have always been and should be *fishermen*, and flagmen have always been and should be *flagmen*.

> Saith the Lord (Corinthians I, 14:34-35), women "are commanded to be under obedience as also saith the law. And if they will learn any thing, let them ask their husbands at home. . . ."

> Our language is being watered down, thinned out. One has the sense that these champions of "correctness," "neutrality" and "diversity" want to strip everything of its meaning, to make everything contain any meaning that any potential reader is "comfortable" with. Look at the newspaper of record for any large city. You will find any number of classified advertisements for "waitstaff" and "servers." "Servers"? Is a subpoena to be delivered to the table with your tiramisu? What's next? "Persons prepared for or engaged in armed struggle" instead of "soldiers"?

By noon I'd read seventy-five pages, but I'd had to reread—and reread and reread—so many paragraphs to get their sense that I felt as if I'd read several hundred pages.

Without a word or a glance in my direction, Martin strode by, out of the office. He wore a distracted, pinched look that—I knew from long experience—meant things weren't going well with his colon. I stood and stretched and peered over the cubicle wall. Christa's chair was empty, angled toward the wall. She'd slipped out without my noticing.

In the hush of the office, without the distraction of Stinson's execrable prose, I found that I still heard the Beethoven string quartet in my mind's ear. "*Es muss sein! Es muss sein!*" Could it really have been about a dispute with his housekeeper?

One of my favorite places in all the world was a small room on the third floor of the Saint Paul Public Library—the Art and Music Room, a high, narrow space, overheated in winter, with a catwalk of creaking wood and thousands of musical scores filling its tall shelves. I knew I could find a copy of Beethoven's string quartets there, and surely the library's nonfiction section would contain something that described the history behind them.

The walk to the library could seem toilsome even on a pleasant day—and today was certainly *not* a pleasant day—but it usually took only half an hour round trip. Parking always seemed more complicated, somehow. I slipped into my jacket and dashed out the door before Christa or Martin could reappear to distract me.

♦ ♦ ♦

After the walk and the cold air and the climb up the wide marble stairs, the Art and Music Room seemed even more overheated than usual. I was alone with the tall wind-rattled windows and the many scores. As I climbed the narrow steps up to the groaning catwalk, I felt as if I were mounting the forecastle of a ship. I found the Beethoven string quartets, complete in three slim paperbound volumes. Along their purple spines they were tattered and frayed.

Downstairs, in the card catalog, I found a book titled *Beethoven: The Seventeen Quartets*, by someone named Terrence McNamara. *Seventeen* quartets? A librarian fetched the book from the stacks. It was a chunky book in ordinary reddish cloth covers, shabby around the edges. On the way downstairs, I glanced at the preface. Within a couple of paragraphs McNamara explained that he counted the Great Fugue as a seventeenth quartet; it was, he wrote, "ahead of its time in every particular, not least of which is a singularly modern sensibility as to structure. It is no less than a full quartet in a single movement."

I paged through the table of contents. The sixteenth quartet had a chapter to itself. I turned to it and skimmed the first few paragraphs, which described Beethoven's health and finances. The opening of the chapter didn't answer my question, but it certainly seemed to be leading up to it.

At the circulation desk a librarian handled the volumes of quartets as if they were precious icons. "You've been up to Art and Music," he said. I nodded. "Someone was telling me that the librarian who designed that room was in the Navy in World War Two. He added the catwalk because it reminded him of being aboard a ship."

"Interesting," I said. I brushed my hair back from my forehead. Clearly, the world's librarians and Public Radio personalities were conspiring to fill my brain with cocktail party trivia. "Did you know," I said, "that Beethoven's last quartet was inspired by a dispute with his housekeeper?"

• • •

The clocked ticked slowly that afternoon. I worked my way diligently through Stinson's book, but the quartets and McNamara's book sat at my elbow, tempting me.

When I could no longer resist McNamara's mute seduction, I turned again to the first page of chapter fourteen.

> In 1826, at the chaotic end of a chaotic life, Beethoven found himself in the midst of pandemonium. His health was poor. His accounts were in extravagant disarray. His relations with his brothers, always argumentative, were ever more fraught.

Fraught. What a good word. I resolved to use it more.

> The appearance of his room and of his person were peculiar and untidy. Friends and acquaintances eschewed public contact with him. The reader has no doubt heard that Beethoven was supposed to have caused a cattle stampede?

Cattle stampede? More cocktail party trivia. So McNamara was part of the conspiracy.

Again as before, Martin debouched from his office, looking grim. Chastened, repentant, I closed McNamara's book, slid it aside, and returned to my assigned reading.

At last, some forty-two hours after I'd first stepped into the office, it seemed, I heard Christa shuffling papers and slamming her desk drawers. I waited for the rustle of her vinyl typewriter cover. Five o'clock at last. I marked my place in *Onslaught* and packed up to leave. I leaned into Martin's office to say good night. He looked up from a book, peered at me over pince-nez, and grunted.

Christa and I walked out together.

"Any plans?" I asked her, and immediately regretted it. Her plans, if she had them, would surely include Tory.

"Dinner and a movie where nothing happens," she said, and gave an appreciable sigh.

Ancient machinery trundled in the elevator shafts. Above the brass elevator doors, numbers glowed: *4, 3, 6, 5.*

"Let's walk up," I said. "It's only one floor, for pity's sake."

As we climbed, she said, "I hate to jinx it, but things seem to be going well. With Tory, I mean."

With my forefinger I tapped the dark cherry paneling in the stairwell. "Better knock on that before you say anything else."

"Taste in movies aside," she said.

"And jackets."

"Beg pardon?"

"Never mind."

◆   ◆   ◆

At the library I'd neglected to pick up a recording of the Beethoven quartets, but Cheapo Records might have one. I took a circuitous route home—up the hill to the cathedral, right on Summit, past the James J. Hill House and the opulent homes of robber barons, past the governor's mansion and Hamline University, past Craftsman bungalows and enormous Victorian painted ladies set back from the tree-lined boulevard, and at last to Snelling. The streets were wet and slick. Snow had begun to collect in the gutters. The going was slow.

In Cheapo's Classical section, I found several recordings of the string quartets on CD, and a two-cassette compilation of the early quartets, but nothing on vinyl. The clerk, a tall woman who, in spite of her dark brown hair, reminded me of Jonquil, led me to the used section, where at length she found a boxed set of LP's: The Guarneri Quartet, *The Complete String Quartets and the Grosse Fuge*. On the box cover, wavy rays of orange and red issued forth from a bust of Beethoven in silhouette. I would have bought it at almost any price, but it cost only thirty dollars; I couldn't pass it up.

When I got home, I dropped the books and my jacket inside the door. Tearing the quartets from their acetate envelope, I rushed to the stereo. I flipped through the records until I saw number sixteen. I eased the platter onto the turntable. I set the needle at the beginning of the second and final track. Instead of the cello moaning the familiar motto, all four instruments played in octaves. A brief, mysterious, emphatic theme ended in a strangely ominous trill. A pause. And then, still in octaves, a couple of snippets of something that sounded like incidental music for an old melodrama, the kind of music that might accompany a black-cloaked villain as he snuck from tree to tree, stalking the pinafore-clad heroine. Another pause. And then, again, something completely different—a slow theme of ravishing beauty and pathos in the first violin, answered by weeping chords in the other instruments. What *was* this?

I paged through the liner notes until I found the track listing. Of course. I'd put on *side* sixteen, not the sixteenth *quartet*. Side sixteen, track two, was the *Grosse Fuge*. The Great Fugue. The liner notes referred to the work's "spartanic, gaunt power" and called it "one of the most difficult pieces in the entire literature."

The instruments hammered away at an obsessive dotted rhythm, a march for goblins or witches. The countersubject seemed to be the first theme— the mysterious organ-like unison—but played on the odd beats, with rests in between. I sank to the floor, scanning through the index of McNamara's book. The longest passage relating to the Great Fugue began on page two hundred.

The piece had originally been the finale of the fourteenth quartet, Opus 130. Beethoven's contemporaries had found it difficult, remote, abrasive. I understood completely. If someone had announced this as a Stravinsky piece written in *nineteen*-twenty-six, rather than as a Beethoven piece written in *eighteen*-twenty-six, I wouldn't have blinked an eye. At the urging of Matthias Artaria, Beethoven's publisher, the composer had split off the Great Fugue into a stand-alone piece; his last completed work had been a new finale for Opus 130.

The goblin march ended abruptly. A new, softer theme began. Arpeggios eased upward. A whole new fugue, in a new, remote key. No, not a fugue; the viola and cello played a pulsing, homophonic accompaniment underneath the new theme. Surely Bach had begun spinning in his grave even before Beethoven's ink had dried.

•   •   •

In college, I'd been crazy to write a fugue. Counterpoint in general had exerted a strong pull on my imagination, but no other species of it had captivated me quite like the fugue. Even so, fugue had eluded me. I'd written a dozen canons or more for my senior composition symposium with Dr. Benton. All had looked so good on the page, and all had sounded like garbage when played. The first two I had titled "Fugue in A minor" and "Fugue for Piano, Four Hands," but in reviewing each piece Dr. Benton had said sourly, "Good work, but not a fugue."

Somewhere in the spare bedroom where I kept my sketches and my staff paper and my old theory textbooks, somewhere in a notebook or in a manila envelope, I still had those old canons I'd hoped to turn into fugues by sheer force of will.

I set aside McNamara's book and cranked the volume on the stereo. In the workroom I sat cross-legged on the floor and sorted through my sketches and notes. Months had passed since I'd looked at *The River*. I'd barely thought about the piece since that nightmarish night in September when Tom had disappeared from my life.

Now, I tried to impose some kind of order on the scattered pages. I created a stack for each section. The prelude was a chaotic contrapuntal work—*not* a fugue, Dr. Benton surely would have said—in which the themes seemed to spin out without end, into more and more remote keys, with no clear path to a resolution. The four choral sections were full of parallel fifths and un-resolved tritones. I tapped each stack against my knee to straighten it. I laid the stacks in parallel lines along the wall.

There was a box, a square cardboard box that had grown wonky from rid-ing in the back of my car and from being shoved around in the workroom. In the box I'd stored all the scraps of poetry I'd collected and had begun to set to music. I'd started with a few stanzas of Hart Crane, from "The River" sec-tion of *The Bridge*. Gradually I'd begun to accumulate anything to do with the Mississippi, and then anything to do with any big river. I dug through the box and found a tumult of prose and poetry—wavy and smudged photocopies, tidy hand-printed transcriptions on ragged sheets of staff paper, half-legible scribbles on Post-It Notes.

I found the three-subject spiral notebook I'd bought for my last semester in college, the disastrous semester in which I'd cut almost half my classes. Each section of the notebook contained a few pages of notes, a few pages of Tom-related doodling, and then dozens of blank pages.

On page after page of college-ruled paper I'd written our names in my ju-venile scrawl. Jonah Thomas Murray and Gregory Thomas Hill. Hearts en-closed pairs of Thomases. Circles and arrows linked them. Tom and I had made much of the fact that we had the same middle name. It had seemed like some kind of sign.

I stripped away the used pages, crumpled them, tossed them aside. Dip-ping into the box, I dredged up a handful of poetry scraps and began to copy them neatly into the notebook.

6 THE C MINOR MOOD

A little after seven o'clock, Christa called. "It took *forever* to vote, so we decided to skip the movie, but Tory knows this great Thai place he wants me to try. Tag along?"

She was talking very fast. My brain felt sluggish, addled. After a time, I said, "I was planning to stick around here. I was just going to—."

"What on *earth* is that music in the background?"

The Guarneri Quartet coaxed flash and pomp out of the Great Fugue. Near the end, a series of chunky chords ushered in a brief passage, seemingly a parody of old courtly dances. "It's Beethoven. I was—."

"It'll do you good to get out of the house. We won't be late. You can put shelf paper in your kitchen cabinets tomorrow."

"*Shelf* paper? I wasn't putting—."

"You *know* you want pad thai."

Now that she'd mentioned food, I realized that I hadn't eaten all day. I was famished. Except for a few Healthy Choice dinners buried in the hoarfrost of my freezer, the cupboard was bare.

"Lobster clasps," I said.

She paused. "It's *buttons*, you dick."

◆ ◆ ◆

Just as I emerged from the house, Christa's white Cabriolet slid sideways into the front curb, coming to rest so that it blocked the snow-clogged street. Bluish smoke poured from the tailpipe and bruised the snow beneath. The bass line of an old Prince song rippled the plastic window in back, a mallet hitting a drum skin. When I reached the car, the rusted-out passenger door swung open. It rattled to the crazy beat of the mistuned engine.

Tory sat in the passenger's seat, damned letterman jacket and all. "Hello again," he said, clambering out of the car. He fumbled with a lever near the floor, flinched when the seat snapped forward. "I'll sit in the back. I can stretch my legs across." He went in feet first, trying to step all the way across the back seat in one ungainly movement.

Christa jabbed a button on the dash, silencing Prince's oscine falsetto. "Get in, get in," she said. "I made a reservation, and I don't want to be late."

It was colder inside the car than on the street. My leather jacket crackled as though it might shatter. As the car fishtailed away from the curb, I looked out my window just in time for a last glimpse of my house, lights still burning within, Beethoven stilled, books and papers spread across the floors. What in the hell was I doing out in the cold and snow, in search of pad thai? The Cabriolet slid around a corner, and a neighbor's unkempt arborvitae obscured my view of the house.

Behind me Tory was still arranging his long limbs. He held the back of my seat for leverage, and jerked it every time he moved.

Christa's earrings were Calderesque shapes in primary colors, dangling on spidery black curves of metal. I fingered a red blob hanging from her right ear. "Are these new?"

"Had them forever. Never wear them." Without stopping, signaling, or looking for oncoming traffic, she turned right onto University Avenue. Tory balanced himself by pushing against my seat.

Christa shoved her pink wool cap up and back, so that it sat on the crown of her head. With lavender-painted nails she pricked up the hair above her forehead.

"You actually voted?"

She folded down the lapel of her jacket to reveal a sticker above her left breast: "I Voted!"

Signaling for the first time that I could remember, Christa turned left onto Snelling. She barreled through the next red light, tailgating a salt truck. She swung the car onto the I-94 on-ramp. The highway was wet but, happily, clear of snow. Christa stomped on the accelerator and crossed to the far left lane. My right foot pumped an imaginary brake pedal.

The Mississippi River overpass was slick. To compensate, Christa lifted her foot off the accelerator for half a second.

"We both voted," Tory said.

"I fear we canceled each other out, however," Christa said, looking at me.

I glanced at Tory. He was staring at the Minneapolis skyline, his face awash in pink mercury light.

"If only I'd known," I said, "I could have lent him that Stinson book."

Tory leaned forward, between the seats. He said, "Christa was telling me about that. I don't care about all that shit. I just know Clinton's itching to raise taxes. For me it's all about the money. The right-wingers can talk all they want about family values. The social stuff is what it is. People who want to fuck are going to fuck."

"If Bush wins I'll send you a post card from the concentration camp," I said.

Tory snorted. "Never happen, man. Actually, I'd imagine for guys like you it'd be more fun when things are tightened up."

"Tightened up?" If he was prescribing Kegel exercises, it was one hell of a non sequitur.

"Sex is more fun on the sly, when it's a little sleazy."

Christa giggled. She'd never giggled before, that I could remember, but this was manifestly a giggle. She looked at Tory, then at me. He sank into the back seat. To me, Christa said in a stage whisper, "I'll tell you later."

I wanted a change of subject, very badly. "Do you ever get a word stuck in your head?" I said. "Just some random word?"

"What's the word?" Tory asked.

"Diflucan," I said. "On and on and on. Diflucan, Diflucan, Diflucan."

Christa said, "Edible underwear."

Tory's turn to giggle, now.

"You have edible underwear stuck in your head?" I said.

"That's what I was laughing about," she told me. "We were buying some yesterday and ended up—you know—putting them on before we even got out of the store."

"Both of you? Are the sizes pretty true, then, in the edible panties game? What about spoilage? Do you have to keep them refrigerated, and if so is it part of the thrill to put them on cold?"

An MTC bus sped by us on the right, and Christa edged our speed upward, keeping resolutely in its blind spot. "Weigh 'nough," she said.

Clouds obscured the top of the IDS building. Soon, the bus obscured the rest of it, and the whole of the skyline besides. A second later it peeled away from us and exited onto Eleventh.

"'Weigh 'nough'?" Tory said. He enunciated the two syllables charily, as a spelling bee contestant might sound out some phonetic trap of a word. "What does that mean?"

"What about mold, or yeast? Couldn't you get a nasty infection of some kind?"

"Well," Tory said, "that's why there's Diflucan."

I had to award him points for timing and aptness of thought. Over my shoulder, I smiled at him. He nodded and winked. I subtracted points for winking.

"Weigh 'nough," Christa said to me. For Tory's benefit she added, "Rowers' talk for 'stop.'"

I obeyed her command, at least until she could navigate the snarled Hennepin Avenue exit. Lanes crossed and merged willy-nilly, and Christa—already distracted by her own cuticles—didn't need further interference from me. She stopped for the light at Lowry Hill.

Tory leaned forward between the seats. "Why not just say 'stop'?"

"Centuries of tradition? Who knows?" I said. "'Let it run' means the same thing—'stop'—though it always sounded to me like something that would mean the opposite."

Music rumbled from the car next to us. I opened my window a quarter of an inch to hear it. "Super Trouper." Two middle-aged men with earrings and graying goatees sang along. They bobbed their heads and did Motown hand motions. I felt the car shake, and turned to see Tory following along with the hand jive. A look passed between Tory and the two men, and they all waved at each other as the light changed and we sped away from them.

Christa stopped, her fingers pattering on the steering wheel, while she waited for our lane to merge around a parked car.

"Or sometimes it's a jingle."

"What?" she asked, squinting at me.

"Stuck in my head. Sometimes I get a commercial jingle stuck in my head."

Tory chanted, "Brush your breath, brush your breath, brush your breath . . ."

"What?" Christa said again. She cleared the parked car and lurched into the outside lane. The Cabriolet slid sideways. The rear tire on my side scraped the curb.

"Have you driven a Ford," I sang, "lately?"

♦   ♦   ♦

Larn Thong was the kind of restaurant where the servers wear starched white jackets, and the walls are bathed in the golden light of wall sconces, and the tabletops are spotless beveled glass. And yet the incongruities, the tiny failings of the place, were what I noticed—the kitschy paper lanterns, the dust on the ivory carvings, the bent forks and insubstantial knives, the flimsy water glasses, each bearing a palimpsest of scratches and nicks where it had jostled its peers during thousands of trips through the dishwasher.

Reservations, as it happened, had been unnecessary. The restaurant was nearly empty. A waiter, a tall, cadaverous man, an Asian Ichabod Crane, showed us to a table near the window. He passed around menus in inch-thick red vinyl binders. In college I'd read academic journals less arcane and elaborate than Larn Thong's menus.

Somehow I ended up sitting across from Tory. He was looking at me, a little too knowingly, I thought, as if he knew—or thought he knew—everything about my political views, my sex life, my taste in music. As if he knew, even, that I hated that damned letterman jacket. I couldn't meet his eyes. I stared off at a portrait in oils of the king of Thailand; it hung in a carved gilt frame, the centerpiece of a tiny shrine near the kitchen.

When the waiter came with water, I ordered a Singha. Christa raised an eyebrow.

"I thought you weren't drinking any more after—."

After Tom, she meant. She shot Tory a sideways look. A rather *fraught* look, to use McNamara's word. It seemed as if she intended to show me that Tory didn't know what she meant, while also trying to convey to Tory that he did know what she meant, and while also warning him not to let on how much he knew.

"One beer won't kill me."

Christa looked at me now, her eyes filled with warning and worry.

I cleared my throat. "Pardon my unfortunate choice of words." I opened my menu. "So. Tory. What's good here?"

For a time we barely spoke, except to place our orders. Christa said something to Tory about Martin driving her crazy. Tory claimed that, if we compared bosses, his would prove infinitely more difficult than Martin. We fell silent, fiddling with our silverware. I gulped my beer.

At last the food came. While a server assistant set a tray on a folding rack, the waiter stood by, his back held very straight, his chin tipped toward the ceiling, a white cloth draped over his arm. The waiter served the food, announcing each entree as if it were a guest at an embassy ball. Pad thai. Red curry duck. Pad see ew. Masaman curry with beef. He withdrew with a little bow, and the server assistant spirited away the tray and the rack. We passed around plates of noodles and bowls of rice.

"I went to the library today," I said. "When you called, I was reading a book about Beethoven's string quartets. I heard his last quartet on the radio yesterday, and—."

"*Der schwer gefasste Entschluss,*" Tory said.

I looked at him. "Opus one-thirty-five. F major. But I was actually reading about the Great Fugue."

"*Ja,*" Tory said. "*Der grosse Fuge.*"

"What the hell are you two talking about?" Christa said.

Tory said, "If you like the F major, you should definitely check out the C-sharp minor. It's possibly Beethoven's greatest work—even if you count the symphonies. And even though it's in C-sharp minor, it's got the C minor mood in spades. The sixteenth is lightweight by comparison. Which recording, by the way?"

"Guarneri Quartet," I said.

He rubbed his chin. "'Sixty-nine or 'seventy or something, wasn't it?"

"Guano Quartet? Minor sharp mood?" Christa said. "What the—?"

Tory looked at me. I looked down at the pile of noodles and scallions on my plate.

"Beethoven held the key of C minor in a special kind of esteem," he said. "It was a very spiritual, very meaningful, key for him. The Fifth Symphony is in C minor. The Fifth is my favorite. What about you, Jonah?"

For some reason, I'd always thought the Fifth Symphony was in C-sharp minor. I didn't dare say so. "I like the Seventh, or maybe the Ninth." He wrinkled his nose. "Were you a music major?" I asked him. I couldn't help glancing at his damned letterman jacket, draped over the back of his chair. The letter itself—an R—Richfield? Robbinsdale?—was blocky, squared off, an athletic letter, surely. My own letter, earned at the expense of four years of Mrs. Martin's tantrums in chorus, was a cursive C.

"Just an enthusiast." He shrugged, cutting his pad see ew into bite-sized pieces. "The Fifth is so familiar—'A Fifth of Beethoven,' 'Hooked on Classics,' all that. I used to think it was a little embarrassing that I loved it the best. But it's a damned good piece of music." As he ate, he hummed a fragment of the scherzo theme.

When the waiter passed by again, I ordered another beer.

◆ ◆ ◆

The waiter brought the check on a little silver tray. Tory scooped it toward him. "I've got this," he said.

Christa stretched and purred like a contented kitten, not even making a show of resisting his offer. I raised my hand to protest, but Tory waved me off with one hand while reaching for his wallet with the other.

I finished my beer, my fourth, and glanced at my watch. It was a little after nine-thirty. I wanted badly to get away from Tory, and yet because of the beer I felt loose and reckless, and I didn't want to go home to Beethoven and the hard-won decision, or the C minor mood, or the hopped-up dotted-rhythm turmoil of the Great Fugue.

"Anyone feel like a cocktail?" I said. Perhaps, over cocktails, I could make use of some of my cocktail party trivia.

Christa, still stretching, dropped her arms and stared at me. "What is going on with you?" She said it quietly, in the way of a mother chiding a misbehaving child in a crowded place.

I said, "I'm *fine*. I just feel like going out and having a little fun."

Tory tidied a stack of twenty-dollar bills and dropped it onto the silver tray. "I think a little drinkie is a fantastic idea," he said. He leaned over and kissed Christa on the cheek. "I'll drive, if you'd also like a little drinkie-pooh."

Drinkie-pooh?

She smiled and kissed him on the lips. "To tell the truth, I could simply *murder* something fruity. Maybe something with a tiny paper umbrella in it?"

Tory drove us to a seedy sports bar—a place called Winners—at Lake and Bryant. The building looked as if it had long been neglected. The exterior paint had peeled and blistered. The tin soffit above the front door and the brushed-steel frames around the windows were all crooked and crinkled.

As he held the door open for me, Tory told me that he lived nearby, that this was "his" bar. That seemed about right, given the felt pennants and—yes, of course—the letterman jackets that decorated the walls. The ceilings loomed in smoky darkness above us, yards or perhaps miles away. The floors were tiled in fussy little white octagons, so old-fashioned they were retro—or would have seemed so, if not for the decades of grime in all those tiny grout lines. The booths, tables, and bar were heavy old wood, much darkened by the innumerable drunken hands that had grasped them over the years.

There were three television sets above the bar. Hockey, football, and the election. Behind Dan Rather, a map of the United States showed New England, the Midwest, and most of the South in red. The mid-Atlantic states and a column of plains states were blue. The Western states were white.

Rather's lips moved, but the set was muted. A jukebox played some sort of 'seventies country rock. Not the Eagles. The Band? Lynyrd Skynyrd? I hardly knew.

While Christa went to find a table, Tory and I stood at the bar. "Which is Clinton and which is Bush?" I asked him.

"Red is Clinton, since he's a big Commie." He laughed. "What'll you have? They have some decent beers, but the wine list isn't so hot. Mostly stuff from Napa." He grimaced.

"Well," I said, "the wine of my country is beer."

"Beer is the wine of my country, I think you mean. I'm going to recommend against a mixed drink, for sure."

I shrugged. "Better stick with beer."

"Guinness okay? They have it on draft here, nice and cold."

Wasn't it supposed to be served warm? I nodded. "Sure. Guinness."

Tory ordered a Guinness for each of us. For Christa he ordered a frothy concoction in a brown plastic glass shaped like a coconut. A wedge of pineapple and a pink paper umbrella adorned the edge of the glass.

Christa had found a booth in the back, in the pool room. A young man in a tank top and jeans leaned over the table, lining up a shot. Older men in camouflage trousers and hunting pacs sat on stools along the wall, watching—with significant envy, it seemed. Off to one side, two old phone booths, little closets with folding doors of wood and frosted glass, flanked a pair of doors marked "Linebackers" and "Cheerleaders."

Christa accepted her drink with a little squeal of delight. She tucked the umbrella behind her ear and appreciatively sucked the pineapple.

"It looks like Clinton is winning," Tory said. He slid into the booth beside Christa. She scooted closer, and he put his arm around her. "Many, many red states. The whole country is going Commie." He laughed again at his own sour joke.

I hunched against the wall and stretched my legs across the bench. One of the hunters, standing near the left-hand phone booth, stared at me. He had dark hair—it was difficult to tell in this light whether it was black or dark brown—and Spike's little tuft of whiskers below his lower lip. For a moment I thought he *was* Spike, but this fellow was thickset, a little jowly—not Spike.

It was the beer, perhaps. Or maybe the hunter's unexpected passing resemblance. Possibly I just craved an excuse to be away from Tory, even for a few moments. In any case, I was suddenly eager to hear Spike's voice. The receipt with his phone number was still in my wallet. Inside each phone booth, a light glowed, dim and yellow; surely that meant they were in working order.

I excused myself and crossed to the phone booth on the right-hand side. My legs felt a little unsteady. I bumped an empty stool, and it clattered against a wall. The hunter watched me. I pretended not to notice.

In my wallet I found Spike's number and my calling card. After a couple of rings I heard a series of short beeps, followed by a longer one. What did I want to say, exactly? I hung up, rehearsed, dialed again.

"This is Jonah—Jonah Murray." I swallowed hard. "Beta. I was just—just thinking of you." Another long beep cut me off.

As I returned to my seat across from Christa and Tory, I said, "Strange. His answering machine had no outgoing message."

"Whose answering machine?" Christa said.

"Spike's. Spike—that guy I met the other day?"

"No outgoing message?" Tory said.

I sipped my Guinness. It was intense, bitter, not altogether pleasant. "Just a few short beeps, then a long one. And then it cut me off after about five seconds."

Christa leaned over the table to smack my shoulder. "It's a pager, you dope." She took a bite of her pineapple. "I *told* you he was a male prostitute."

"What time is it?" I said.

"You're wearing a watch," Christa said. She tapped the crystal of my chrome Seiko. "What the fuck?"

"I'm afraid you're a lightweight, Jonah," Tory said.

I rubbed the face of my watch against my shirt, wiping away Christa's fingerprint. It was ten-twenty-five—seven-twenty-five in San Francisco. My mother would be at home, getting ready to go out for dinner before her show. No, it was Election Night. She'd already be on the air. The station aired a special team coverage show on Election Night.

"I'll be right back," I said. I took a gulp of Guinness. A burly, robust kind of beer. Spike in beer form. It was growing on me.

I returned to the phone booth. The hunter who'd been watching me had disappeared. I knew the toll-free number by heart. I dialed. Petra, Barbara's producer, answered.

"It's Jonah," I said. "Is my mother—?"

"Jonah!" she cried. "So good to hear your voice. When are you coming to see us?" After decades of living and working with native English speakers, she had smoothed her German accent almost to nothing, except for an over-compensating elongation of W's and a tendency to swallow R's.

"Soon, soon. Are you on the air?"

"We're on a break. The network feed is live now. Let me put you through to Barbara." When Petra said my mother's name, it sounded like "*Bah*-blah."

A few seconds later, Barbara's show voice: "You're up late on a school night."

"Can I ask you a stupid question?"

"Don't be silly. You've never asked a stupid question in your whole life."

"Sweet of you to say, but—."

After a moment's pause, she said, "Let me put you on hold a second so we can do this—you know, this thing."

Faintly I heard the Mozart aria she used for her opening theme and as a bumper before and after commercials. One of the Queen of the Night's coloratura pieces from *Die Zauberflöte*. It faded after a few bars, and then through a caul of static I heard Barbara's biggest voice: "It's Election Day, San Francisco. Polls are still open for a few more minutes. Get out there and let your voice be heard. The voice you're hearing now is the voice of Barbara Murray, the Queen of the Night, continuing our very special Election Night team coverage. But first we have to do just a little business."

After a single note of some commercial jingle, the line cleared and Barbara came back. "Now what were we saying?"

"Are the red states Republican or Democrat?"

"Usually Democrat, but it varies by network. You know it's already being called for Clinton, don't you? It's not official yet, but he's already *very* close. And looking at the exit polls, it's pretty clear what's going to happen."

It was silly, crazy, unexpected: I began to cry. Strange, happy-sad tears. I couldn't quite speak.

"Jonah?"

"That's really, really—. That's good news."

"We all certainly think so out here." I could hear the smile in her voice.

A series of clicks came across the line, and then Petra again. "Your mother wants to know if you've been drinking."

I choked back a sob. "A little. Just a couple of beers." My face grew hot. "Shit. Was I on the air just now?"

"No. I'm sorry. I didn't know you wanted to be."

"I didn't. I just wanted to hear her voice."

"I hear music behind you. Are you at home?"

"At a bar with some friends. This election was kind of a—. It was—." What was it? *"Der schwerer gefasster Entschluss? Yes?"*

"Perhaps you should go home now. Get some rest."

"Maybe you're right."

• ◆ •

The neighborhood wit had struck again. Leading up the front walk, a hop-scotch grid drawn crudely in pale blue chalk bore, instead of whatever customary markings, a ladder of squared-off letters and numbers in yellow and orange and pink:

2

4 6

8 he's

1

queer

we ♡

2 hate

Christa and I stood side by side at the grid's baseline.

"I don't need this right now," I said. "I can't even *think* of hopscotch until I sober up."

Tory had been waiting at the car. He stepped up behind us. "Does this happen often?" he asked me.

I shook my head. "This is the second or third thing. Neighborhood kids, I guess. Can you help me?"

Together, we three kicked wads of snow onto the chalk outline and rubbed it into obscurity. Every move caused my stomach to churn anew. I felt light-headed and dizzy. I sat on the stoop, supporting myself on the way down with both hands, like a pregnant woman. As Christa blurred the last cross of the last T, with a snow-footed cha-cha-cha, she let go a peal of laughter that, for all its depth and timbre, was the laugh of a wholly pleased little girl.

7 POLITE CONDUCT

I lay in bed, exhausted and wakeful.

As a small child, sleepless on the eve of a new school year, I'd gone to Barbara, had lain beside her in her bed, had listened politely as she'd suggested counting sheep.

"Why sheep?" I'd asked her. "Why not cows or chickens?"

"Sheep have the force of tradition."

I'd crinkled my nose at her. "Speak English," I'd said.

"Well, why *not* sheep?"

"I've never even seen a sheep in real life," I'd said. "I've seen a cow. I've seen chickens."

"Count cows, then. Count chickens." In a dippy nursery-rhyme voice, she'd said, "Moo, moo, cluck, cluck." Smiling, then laughing, she'd poked my belly after each syllable.

Now, picturing chickens and cows, I counted backward from one thousand, but my restless thoughts—a jumble of Beethoven and McNamara, Tory and Christa, Spike and Tom, and above all, Clinton and Bush—crippled, then halted, the series of diminishing numbers. I couldn't stop thinking about the famous photograph of Truman holding a newspaper, the headline in enormous type reading, "Dewey Defeats Truman."

By trying to force myself awake, I thought, I might be able to trick myself into sleeping. I kept my eyes open and stared at the light fixture in the center of the ceiling. The glass shade glimmered in the pink light of streetlamps coming through a chink in the curtains. The bed seemed to rock from side to side, a raft afloat in a gentle surf.

At last I arranged pillows against the headboard and sat up. In the dark I groped for the television remote, aimed, brushed the power button with my thumb. The TV crackled to life. Cold blue light twitched around me, tinting the walls in trembling sheets and tendrils. Standing before the columns of some government building—the state capitol in Little Rock? the governor's mansion?—Clinton addressed a crowd of people shivering in the glare of bright lights. The television's volume was set low; the roaring crowd buzzed like faint static.

I fat-fingered some buttons on the remote. I raised the volume, but also managed to engage the VCR. A synthesizer and drum machine chirped and twittered. Spike's young, clean-shaven face, upturned, filled the screen. For a moment he wore the anguished expression of a man in the throes of either passion or torment, and then his face relaxed into smiling bliss. The camera panned abruptly and shakily away, stopping on a potted palm. Fade out.

I rewound to the title card, "John and Pete," and then there he was again. Spike, amid a flutter of grayish electronic snow. Spike, naked but for a pair of striped tube socks. Spike, improbably young, badly lit, enthusiastically erect. He virtually devoured his partner; I imagined he'd lusted after the fellow for some time, that the camera had captured the enactment of a cherished fantasy. By contrast, the other man was barely more avid than a damp tree stump.

◆　◆　◆

Porn had always been Tom's thing, never mine. Soon after my twenty-first birthday, I'd worked up the nerve to enter the Main Street Video in Partridge Lake, and then to rent an adult video, *Powertool*, with two Jeffs—Stryker and Converse. I'd had no idea that the camera would record the act of sex in such graphic detail, that lights and lenses would venture so close to a cock splitting an ass—and what a cock it was, and what an ass!

At first I felt an impossibly erotic voyeuristic rush. Soon, though, the video's flaws ruined the thrill. The music was too chattery and cheesy to suit me, too synthetic, as if it had been pulled, all of a piece, from a jar or can. The lighting was bad, either too dim or too bright. The acting—well, the men recited lines, but it could hardly be called "acting." The plot, sketchy as it was, eventually came to seem illogical, unsettling, odd. To enjoy a pornographic video, I would have to—and yet could not—overlook its many defects.

For Tom, the gimcrackery was a virtue, not a detriment. Once, as we lay in bed watching plucked and overbuilt men fucking robotically on a shabby mauve couch, I began to complain about the tawdry music, the generic 'eighties décor, the lackluster sexual chemistry, the rote prattle of dirty talk.

Tom shushed me. He said, rather grandly, "These things are artistically as well as sexually transgressive. Porn is a degenerate art form."

Ugliness, like beauty, was in the eye of beholder, he said. Degeneracy could be a badge of honor, under certain circumstances. I thought of Stravinsky and Chagall running afoul of the Nazis.

I started to say, "The enemy of my enemy is my friend," but Tom cut me off.

"It's an act of rebellion, making one of these things," he said. Wagging his erection at me, he smiled, looked at me sidelong. "Besides. Admit it. You like that big dick, don'tcha?"

♦ ♦ ♦

The more I thought about it, the more astonishing it seemed that for months, perhaps for years, one of the many videos sitting in a stack in my bedroom contained the image of a man I was destined to meet. One video of the many—or more?

I rewound to the beginning of the video, to the credits. The title, *Streets of Los Angeles,* filled the screen, rugged red letters on a field of flinty gray. The title spun away into space, the gray dissolved to flickering black. A list of names scrolled up the screen in a smallish and plain white font. John Peterson was not among the names. Of course not. He would have used a pseudonym. I remembered Spike saying, or implying, that he was John—the other guy was Pete. There were two Johns, John Bambrick and John Clancy.

I switched on the light. Tucked away, deep in the stack of videotapes, I found an old catalog. It listed hundreds of titles, each with a strange grayscale image of its box cover. John Clancy appeared in only one title, *Streets of Los Angeles.* Six others featured John Bambrick; I found half of those in Tom's collection. I took the three tapes into the living room, where the air was cooler, the television larger. I watched them all, fast-forwarding until I saw the black hair, the uncanny blue eyes of John Bambrick, also known as John Peterson, also known as Spike. Often, in close-up, his expression was almost foolish in the rawness of sexual need. I noticed, I could not help noticing, that in all his scenes, he was the bottom.

♦ ♦ ♦

Even as Eliot and I sank into his leather armchairs, he said, "Have you had a chance to think about what I suggested on Monday?"

I rubbed my hands together to warm them. That morning, in a narcoleptic stupor, I'd forgotten my gloves. "I think you'll have to be more specific."

"Confronting Tom's parents."

I shook my head. "I don't see it happening. I barely even met them, and it's just not the kind of thing I'd ever do."

"It's up to you." He raised his hands, his fingers spread, as if surrendering. "Have you been having an easier time of it since we talked?"

"Up and down."

"How so? In what way?"

"I haven't been sleeping well."

"This is a new problem?"

I shook my head. "Not so new. Since—. Since Tom—."

He nodded. "Understandable."

"Comprehensible," I said. "Not a bit reprehensible."

He squinted at me. "I beg your pardon?"

"From *Chicago*. It's nothing. Never mind." I cupped my hands together, blew warm air against my fingers and palms. "Last night I ended up going out for a few drinks with some friends. Well, a friend and her new—. Her new whatever-he-is."

Eliot studied his fingernails. Today, they were all clean. "It sounds like there's a story behind that."

"Not an interesting one. Eventually, after a couple of beers, I even tried to call Spike, and I found out he gave me his pager number, which freaked me out. And then—."

"Spike? Who's Spike? Your friend's new whatever-he-is?"

After a mostly sleepless night, my brain was hopelessly fogged. Many long moments passed before I fully understood how Eliot had gotten from Spike to Tory. He might as well have mistaken Bush for Clinton. I said, "Spike is a guy I met a few days ago. Kind of a—. We—. It turns out—." I sighed. I tucked my hands under my knees. "It's a long story."

"You had sex with him."

I laughed. "I guess when you put it like that, it's a short story, after all. There isn't much more to tell than that."

He raised his hands again, the gesture of surrender. "What else has been going on?"

I'd spent the entire day struggling through *Onslaught*. Stinson's diatribe concerning gender neutrality in statutes had been uncomfortable enough to read, but what followed was far more difficult. "There's this *thing* I have to read for work," I told Eliot. "This book by Sam Stinson. Today what I read was all about the Saint Paul human rights ordinance, adding sexual orientation to it."

The middle third of the book comprised a venomous Philippic, a splenetic rant against the city of Saint Paul—mainly the City Council, but also its benighted citizenry. In the 'seventies the good people of the city had sensibly beaten back a cancerously dumb attempt to codify amorality into law. But then, over the course of barely ten years, the forces of evil had changed the city for the worse. Saint Paul had embraced the idiot cause of our time, "diversity"—in my mind's ear I could hear Stinson *spit* the word, as if it were the foulest kind of curse—and had consented to permanent debasement in the form of a human rights ordinance guaranteeing the right to be sinful.

As I remembered Stinson's words streaming across the page, blurring before my eyes, a cold hand squeezed my stomach. To Eliot I explained some of this, the few hints and highlights that I could stand to utter aloud.

"I would never read this book if I didn't have to," I said.

"You don't agree with him, I take it."

I stared at him. His face was the very image of clinical detachment. "Like anything else, political correctness can be taken to an extreme, to the point where it isn't safe to speak the truth. But that's not the intention of it, as far as I can see."

"And what is the intention of it?"

"Being kind to each other. Saying something kind when you could otherwise say something hurtful. The Golden Rule. That's all it is, as far as I'm concerned. The Golden Rule. Polite conduct."

Eliot cocked his head, as if listening for muffled voices in an adjacent room. "But you say yourself, it's been taken to an extreme."

"It *can* be. Some people *have*, obviously. But Stinson doesn't even see the good intentions behind it. And his opposition is more extreme than what he's opposing."

"Do you—?" He cleared his throat, shifted his weight in his chair. "Do you have issues with Stinson personally?"

"Every time I see Sam Stinson's name, or that damned slogan he stole from Mary Tyler Moore, or his people, I feel anxious. Out of sorts. Cranky. It doesn't have to be Sam Stinson. It could be Billy Graham, or Jimmy Swaggart, or Bill McCartney. Or Anders Thorstensen."

"Why do you think that is?"

"Because I'm gay." He flinched, as though my answer startled him. "Did you think it would take more thought?"

"I expected you to say something different."

"What?"

"We may still get there. Tell me what you mean."

"There are—what?—dozens of denominations?"

"A couple thousand," he said.

"A couple *thousand?*" For a moment I stared blindly at the shelves behind Eliot's desk, at the souvenir bat in its black cradle.

"Yes? What about the denominations?"

I shook off my stupor. "They can't agree on how often to have communion or even what communion *means,* but when it comes to hating *me,* none of them can wait to pinch a penny—that is to say, *pitch* a penny in the hat."

"You think they hate you, personally?"

Blood rushed in my ears. Was he making fun of me? "As a group, *most* Christian types—*like* Sam Stinson, *like* Billy Graham, *like* Jimmy Swaggart, *like* Anders Thorstensen—hate gay people, as a group." My throat felt clotted, spasmodic. I coughed and swallowed. "Without bothering to know any of the *people* they're so busy hating." My voice had risen in volume and pitch. I paused, took a breath. "As individuals, most of these people's followers would likely hate me if they knew me to be gay."

"How does that make you feel?" He smiled—effortfully, I thought, as if following a stage direction in a script. "Sorry for the counselor question."

"It makes me angry." With the palm of my hand I raked back my hair. It moved in stiff waves between my fingers. I needed a haircut. "It scares me."

"Why?"

"Why? Why *not?* I don't want people to *hate* me."

"But what does it matter if Sam Stinson hates people like you? What would it matter if Sam Stinson hated you personally?"

"I don't understand the question. How could it not matter? Hatred is a bad thing, isn't it?"

"Have you never hated anyone?"

Like bile, the name of Anders Thorstensen boiled to the top of my throat. I said, "Of course."

"Did you have good reason?"

"Of course."

"Think of one person for whom you've felt hatred. One person you knew and talked to and hated." He waited a moment, reading my face. With his eyes on me, I felt how the corners of my mouth were pulled down, how my teeth were clenched. "You already have someone in mind." I nodded. "Now tell me this. What did your hatred do to that person? How did he—? He?" I nodded again. "How did he react to your hatred?"

"If he even knows about it," I told Eliot, "if he even recognizes it, I doubt he cares much about it."

Letting his head fall back, Eliot ran his hand up the length of his neck. A little fringe of black hairs he had missed in shaving circled his Adam's apple. Gazing at a point on the ceiling, he said, "Why do you suppose he cares so little?"

"Why should he? What am I to him?"

Glinting, pupils narrowed to pinpoints, his eyes met mine. "What is Sam Stinson to you?"

I had nothing to say to that. I looked away.

"What is Billy Graham to you? Jimmy Swaggart? Anders Thorstensen?"

My eyes found his again. "Anders Thorstensen very likely has the power and means to put me out of a job."

"And the rest? What reason is there to give them that much power over your life?"

With my mouth already open to protest, I remembered crumpling the gap-toothed kid's leaflet. And taking the time to make confetti of the second leaflet, the one I'd found on my car. And skulking away from the Stinson people in the State Office Building. I felt again the mixture of thumping rage and quavering fear I'd felt in each case. I breathed deeply, pressed my hands together, calmed myself. To Eliot I said, "I guess a little more equanimity would be good."

"You said something earlier. Something about communion. Where did that come from? Is your family religious?"

"Not at all."

"Not at *all*? Never?"

"A long, long time ago, when I was a little kid."

"Tell me about that."

"I don't remember, really."

But that wasn't strictly true. I remembered sunlight streaming through an open window. An airy white room with braided rugs on a linoleum floor. An ancient, enormous upright piano nearly filling one narrow wall. A younger Barbara sitting on the claw-footed piano bench, a book perched on her arm, open to a sunny drawing of giraffes and antelopes parading up the broad gangway of Noah's ark.

"Tell me anything you can think of. One thing leads to another, as they say."

I told him. One thing indeed led to another: "Jesus Loves Me." "Go Tell It on the Mountain"—how I'd loved shouting "Go Tell It on the Mountain" with the other kids in Sunday School. A jar, a clear glass jar, shaped like an apple and filled with M&M's that I'd won in Vacation Bible School. How I'd won it, I couldn't quite remember. Memorizing the most Bible verses? Perfect attendance? Random luck?

"How old were you when you stopped going?"

My father wore a leisure suit to church every Sunday; it would have been the late 'seventies. I said, "I must have been—what?—eight or nine?"

"Why did you stop?"

"My mother left my father and took me with."

"Why?"

I closed my eyes. "I don't know." But again, I wasn't telling the whole truth. Barbara and I had never talked about it, and so I didn't *know* why she had left, but I could guess.

"You were very young," Eliot was saying. "At that age, and at that time, parents tended to hide their emotions from their children." I kept my eyes closed. He spoke quietly, rounding the edges of his voice. "What about your father? Is he still in your life? Jonah?"

I looked at him. He wore a powder-blue Oxford shirt, open at the neck. Staring at the pale triangle of skin at the base of his throat, I felt salt prick the corners of my eyes. "I haven't seen him since we left."

"Can you remember anything about him?"

The rainbow of leisure suits. Sky blue, mint green, chocolate brown, mustard yellow. I couldn't picture him without a Bible tucked into the crook of his elbow. At church he'd always carried around another book, a little paperback with a photograph of a smiling baby on the cover. I couldn't remember the book's title, but I remembered the name "Stinson" in large white letters along the book's creased spine. Any mention of the book, or of Stinson, had been enough to set my father fulminating against lax discipline, against the pestilential surfeit of unruly children he saw all around him.

I shook my head.

"Nothing at all?" Cupping his left hand over his right kneecap, Eliot rolled up his sleeve until the rectangular cuff nestled in the crook of his arm. "Let's back up." He started on the other sleeve. "Have you had any exposure to religion, or to spirituality, or to—well, to *God*—since you were a small child in Sunday school?"

With two narrow fingers he canted the face of his watch toward him. He wore it with the face against the delicate vein-tangled bones on the inside of his wrist. My eyes followed the curves and slim bulges of his forearm muscles.

"Are we over?"

He shook his head. "We have about twenty minutes. Tell me about your relationship with God."

A laugh escaped me. "It won't take the whole twenty minutes. I don't have one."

Eliot tilted his head, tugged his ear. "Do you consider yourself an atheist, then? An agnostic?"

"I've just never thought about it. I never cared enough about it to choose a label for myself."

"You laughed a second ago. Why?"

"As I understand it, you talk to God by praying, but evidence for his ever talking back is—. Well, let's say it's anecdotal and subjective. It sounds like God may be just a little bit passive-aggressive."

"Have you considered that the trouble you have in your human relationships are caused by not having a relationship with God?"

I had nothing to say to that. Where my heart had been, I felt a small, jagged shard of stone. What had been a smile tightened into a grimace.

"Jonah?"

"I've never considered that."

"Does it sound reasonable?"

"Is our time up yet? I might need to leave a little early. I just remembered—." I paused, trying to think of an excuse, any remotely plausible previous engagement. Laundry? Grocery shopping? Dinner plans?

Again he checked his watch. "It's only been a minute, Jonah. Why is this such a touchy subject?"

"I don't know."

"Tell me what you're feeling." He leaned forward and placed his hand on my wrist. "It can't hurt to tell me what you're feeling, and it might help."

He'd made his voice into velvet. Peace lived in the heart of that voice, and in the warmth of his palm through my sleeve. "It scares me," I said. "If—. Even if I want any of it, and I have to take all of it, it scares me."

"I don't understand." He scooted his chair a few inches closer to mine. He moved his hand from my wrist to my hand. Our fingers intertwined. "Make me understand."

Blood pulsed in my ears. Was it fear, now, or Eliot's hand in mine? Again as on Monday, I thought of Spike's hands, encircling my neck as if I were territory he wished to claim. "If I want God, but he only comes as a package with Sam Stinson, then it scares me. If I have to become a hateful, self-righteous bigot, then it scares me."

An inch closer. "What makes you think that's the way it works?"

"*Onslaught: How Political Correctness Erodes Our Culture and Belittles Our Values*, by Sam Stinson."

With his free hand he waved Stinson away into air. "That's not how it works, Jonah, and if you let go of the fear, you'll see for yourself."

Freeing my hand, backing away my chair, nearly knocking it over, I stood. "I'd better go."

He stood, too. "Do you want to make another appointment?"

"Let me call you. I have to check my schedule."

He nodded. His face was grim. I could tell that he knew what I meant. He knew that I had no intention of calling him or seeing him again.

I turned toward the door, then turned back. "What do I owe you?"

He frowned. He looked at his desk, scanned the neatly arranged accessories, the pencil cup, the blotter, the empty file tray. He picked up his stapler, snapped it open and shut. "I looked into some programs, like I said. It's—. You know, don't worry about it. I'll need some more information, but there's no rush. I think I have your number. I'll call you." He looked at me. "Take care of yourself, Jonah."

I felt him watch me as I crossed the room, as I yanked open the door with a clatter of mini-blind slats and a squeal of hinges in need of grease. Outside I jogged through icy, needling rain to my car. Turned the key, tugged open the door. Slumped into the driver's seat. Ignition.

Nothing. Nothing. Nothing.

I'd parked at the far end of the parking lot, in the row facing University

Avenue. An eastbound MTC bus passed. Yes. The buses.

I locked the car door as I climbed out. Slammed it behind me. Heedless of traffic, I jogged across the street. The bus shelter on the far corner had been stripped of its schedules, leaving a messy collage of ripped paper and jagged graffiti scratched in the plastic. To the west I saw nothing but cars. To the east, one block away, the bus that had just passed sat taking on passengers. Just as I started toward it, it pulled away from the curb. Even by doubling my walking pace I couldn't catch it.

I ran.

8   LOVE AND DISCIPLINE

By the time I reached the next corner, the bus had traveled blocks. I ran until my shins and my lungs ached. The rain burned my cheeks and forehead. Phantom teeth gnawed at me. At Snelling, I stopped, doubled over, caught my breath. Panting, I limped across the street, toward home. I crossed against the light. Car horns sounded around me; I ignored them.

From more than a block away, I could see white—no, yellow—rectangles of paper plastered to the house. Three of them on the front door at cock-eyed angles. Two more on the front window. More, I thought, on the steps. I quickened my pace.

Sam Stinson bumper stickers. *Love Is All Around.* They started at the sidewalk, stuck directly, if tenuously, to its rough wet surface. Dozens of them formed a ladder—another kind of hopscotch grid—to the house. I stepped over and around them. On the stoop, seven of them overlapped each other in a wagon-wheel pattern. The three on the door, I saw now, formed an arrow pointing toward the mail slot.

Fumbling for my keys, I looked around me. There was no one. No one on the street, no sign of anyone stirring in any of my neighbors' houses. My keys clattered to the ground. Moving quickly but shaking hard, I at last unlocked the door and fell through it. I slammed it behind me. Locked it.

The outside mail slot fed a copper-lined compartment built into the stucco. A matching trapdoor on the inside gave access. I opened it. A sheet of yellow paper fell out. A duplicate of the one I'd found on my car: "Protect Freedom" and "Save America" and "Love Is All Around" on one side; "Homosexuality Is An Abomination" on the other. Nothing more.

I called Luther, my landlord, at work. While I waited for him to pick up, I realized that I still held the leaflet. "The Liberal Media," it read, "may already have sent Clinton to the White House, but according to *our* sources, he's going straight to Hell."

Luther answered. In a clumsy rush, I started to tell him what had happened.

"Tenant," he said. "Tenant. Tenant. Whoa. Hush. Slow down. I can't make heads or tails of what you're telling me. Breathe. That's it. Now. Start again."

I felt feverish. The story comprised one sentence, maybe two. Had I really made such a muddle of it? I started over. While I described the prank, I went to each window in the house and looked for bumper stickers. Each save the bathroom window wore at least one.

"Bumper stickers?"

"Everywhere." Cradling the phone against my shoulder, I slid the bedroom window up its warped and rusty track. "On the porch, the door, the windows."

"Sam Stinson bumper stickers?"

If I kept the window mostly closed, I could stick my hand out the space at the bottom and reach the bumper sticker. With my thumbnail I picked at one corner of it. "Don't you just feel how love is all around?" I said. The sticker wouldn't budge. "Should I call the police?"

"You could, but I don't think it'll do much good. It's a funny kind of vandalism. There hasn't been any damage, not really. Nothing a razor blade won't fix. And there was no breaking and entering."

To close the window, I brought my weight to bear on its lower frame. It rattled home. I locked it. "That's your lawyerly opinion?"

"That's my landlordly opinion. Speaking of landlordly stuff, have you heard from Tom's parents?"

I felt my jaw working, heard the hinge snap like a cracked knuckle. "Why would they—?"

"They called me to ask for his half of the security deposit. They implied they were hassling you for it."

"I doubt they'd ever contact me." And if I sent them a check, I doubted they would cash it. "Are they—? Are they even entitled to it?"

"As long as you still live there, it's up to me to decide," he said. "I can be nice." He cleared his throat. "Or not."

"I'm not leaving any time soon."

"Good. Good. I don't like to lose good tenants. Not the ones who give me presents at Christmas. By the way, the wife and I have been wanting a bread machine."

"Good to know."

"I'll come over tonight and take care of the bumper stickers. Have dough-nuts and coffee."

"It's okay. I'll take care of it."

"Are you sure?"

"It's buttons," I said.

"*Buttons?* What the hell?"

• • •

Next, I called my mother. "This is Barbara Murray," she said. "We won Or-egon and lost Colorado." Her voice was thick.

"What? Oregon?" I looked at my watch: six-twenty-two. Only four-twenty-two in San Francisco. "I'm sorry. I woke you."

"Jonah? It's okay. I'd be up in another—another eight minutes anyway. What's wrong?"

"There was this book," I said.

Through a noisy yawn, she said, "Book?"

The radiator gurgled. My face still felt febrile from running through the winter air, but my fingers ached with the cold. "A book that Dad carried around a lot. It had a baby on the cover. A pink-skinned smiling baby in pink blankets."

After a time, she said, "You remember that?" Her voice was clear now, bright and hard.

"I remember he hit me with his belt. With the buckle." During our first night together, Tom had found a few crisscross scars in the small of my back. I'd told him I'd fallen off my bike.

For nearly a minute, she said nothing. "Why are you thinking about this?"

"I'm seeing a counselor. It came up today in our session. What did I do to deserve the belt?"

"A counselor?" She paused. "Do you know that that's why I left your father? That one time? That was all it took."

"What did I do?"

She cleared her throat. "It was nothing." Her voice was shaky and too loud, as if she were trying to sound more assured than she felt. "You asked him if 'fuck' was a bad word. I think one of your playground friends tried to convince you that it was, but you didn't believe it. It sounded like an innocent word to you. Duck, truck, muck, luck, fuck. Fuck, fuck, goose," she said, and gave a humorless laugh. "He set out to show you just how bad he thought it was."

"Did he hit you too?"

She said nothing.

"What was that book?"

"It was a book he taught in the adult Sunday School. I can't remember the name of it." I heard, on her end, the squawk of bed springs. "*Love and Discipline. Discipline and Love.* Something like that. It was a small book, a couple hundred pages at most. It was a kind of meditation on 'spare the rod and spoil the child,' interspersed with some sort of weird exposé of Dr. Spock's personal life and political ambitions. He ran for president, you know."

"Stinson?"

"No, sweetie. Spock. Spock ran for president. Excuse me one second." With a muffled honk she blew her nose.

"Are you all right?" I said. "I don't blame you for any of this. You know that?"

She said nothing.

"I'm sorry to wake you up with this," I said. "I'll call you on Thanksgiving?"

"In the evening, after everyone's gone." Every year, she invited forty of her closest friends for a potluck. Usually she provided a turkey roughly the size of a Volkswagen Beetle. "Or any time you want. I'll be here."

Barely a second after I pressed the button to end the call, I pressed the button to redial. "Me again," I said.

"What did I—? Did I—?"

"No, I hit redial. I was thinking—."

"Mm?" she said.

"What if I came out for Thanksgiving instead of Christmas?"

"That'd be lovely." I could hear that she was smiling. "Just lovely."

"Can you—?"

"Of course, darling, I'll call my travel agent tomorrow."

"Call me with the details?"

"The second I know, I'll call you," she said. She rang off with a squeal of joy.

• • •

I looked everywhere, but couldn't find my gloves. Maybe I'd left them at work. Bundled up in mittens, sweater, and parka, armed with the ice scraper from my glove compartment, I peeled the bumper stickers from the windows, from the front door, from the walk. The rain had stopped, more or less, but the temperature had fallen a few degrees. All the darkened windows of the neighborhood seemed to conceal watching eyes. I looked over my shoulder so often that I felt like a dog chasing its tail. My lungs smarted as I filled them with the frigid air. It felt good, in a way.

When the windows were as clean as I could make them, I walked across University to the auto center at Montgomery Ward. All of the tow trucks were out on calls, but the service manager promised me the next run. I sat in one of the orange-upholstered armless chairs in the narrow hallway that passed for a waiting room. A tempest of torn magazines covered a low, square table. I shuffled through the pile and found an old issue of *People*, its pages folded open to an article declaring Patrick Swayze the sexiest man alive. I picked it up. Underneath lay a book of children's Bible stories. It had long ago shed its cover, and a crazy crosshatch of crayon marks covered it from its naked end papers to its stitching. I dropped the *People* and opened the book.

Pictures—impossibly colorful drawings, their subjects happy enough for the Sunday comics, missing only thought balloons and symbolia—filled every other page. I started to read about Noah's ark, but the second and third pages of the story were missing. Only scraps of torn paper remained to show where they had been. The story of Jonah and the whale came a few pages later. I checked; the story was entire. I began to read.

Perhaps it was a stretch to equate Jonah's flight to my own. But after all, hadn't we both chosen one form of mass transit or another? And hadn't we both lost our rides? And of course, we'd both run from the same thing.

The service manager reappeared with a broad-shouldered Latino man—the tow truck operator—at his heels. A few inches shorter than I, he wore greasy coveralls, heavy black boots, and a threadbare twill jacket. His silky black hair was swept back, held in place with gel or pomade. When the service manager introduced us—the driver's name was Jaime—we shook hands. His warm, callous palm stayed in mine a second too long. His easy grin was a whisker too broad.

"Ready?" he said. "Let's go."

I followed him outside. The seat of his coveralls fit his trim ass neatly. Looking over his shoulder, he waved toward his truck—it sat across three spots along University Avenue. Catching my eyes on him, he smiled again.

Nodding, I said, "Nice." No lie: as tall as some houses, its red doors and chrome brightwork sparkled uncannily in the dim and watery November twilight. It sat idling, its engine surprisingly quiet. White plumes of exhaust billowed upward into the cold air. "Is it yours or Ward's?"

By now we had reached the truck. Stepping up to unlock the door on the passenger's side, he said, "Mine and Norwest's." He lighted on the ground and held a hand out to help me up. For a second, as I climbed aboard, his hand filled the small of my back. The bucket seat welcomed me coolly. I sank into it. The spotless interior smelled of leather and new carpet.

The driver's-side door opened with a hefty clunk. In a single smooth leap Jaime settled into the driver's seat, a clipboard in hand, a grin crinkling his face. "University and Fairview?" he said, scribbling on the clipboard.

"In the Midview Center lot."

"Won't start, huh?"

"It's an intermittent problem," I said, and wondered if "intermittent" might be too pretentious a word. "I don't think it's the battery."

He was still writing. "Maybe the starter." Sliding the clipboard into a slot on the console between us, he shifted the truck into gear. "Ready?" he said.

"For anything."

We traveled wordlessly west on University. He poked along in the right lane. It seemed, even, that he slowed on approach to green lights, as if willing them to turn red. I watched his hands move over the wheel; they stayed always in motion, gripping the wheel, letting go, gripping again. His brown fingers moved in rococo flourishes.

Soon we reached Fairview Avenue. As we sat at the red light, Jaime dropped his right hand to his knee. He lifted the hand again and dropped it in his lap. He cupped, squeezed. I looked up. How long had he been watching me watch him? He smiled. I blushed.

The light changed. Using both hands, he steered into the Midview lot's narrow entrance. I pointed to my car. The lanes between cars were narrow; luckily, I'd parked in a space perpendicular to a lane, so that my car had nothing but open space behind it. After a three-point turn Jaime backed the truck into place.

"You can stay here if you want. Just give me the keys?"

I did. He rattled them, smiled, and hopped out of the truck. Over the quiet chuckle of the idling engine I heard chains rattle, and my car door swing closed, and steel scrape blacktop. I watched the mirror on my side, watched Jaime move and work in the cold. His breath rose in a white mist.

Off to my right, Eliot's front window, now dark, chided me for my earlier flight. What had I been so afraid of? If I stopped for a minute and thought about it, wasn't the idea of God comforting? If I stopped working so hard to drive it—that is to say, *him*—that is to say, *God*—away, didn't I feel something like peace?

The truck's winch kicked in with a deep whir. Soon Jaime would be back, and the smiles and the coy gestures would resume. If he wanted me, I knew he would have me. But afterward, wouldn't I yearn for him pointlessly, half-afraid to call him? Wouldn't I listen, terrified, to his answering machine, and then hang up without a word?

Eliot's door swung open, and there was Eliot. Leather jacket, leather satchel slung over his shoulder, a bright red knit cap tugged down over his ears. I heaved my door open and jumped down from the cab.

Eliot seemed surprised to see me. He looked around him, as if this might be some kind of prank, as if nearby bushes concealed Allen Funt and a cadre of videographers. "Jonah. Are you all right?" he said. "I'm sorry if I made you uncomfortable."

"It wasn't you, really. It was the subject matter."

"Not a bit reprehensible," he said, smiling.

I pressed on. "I was a little taken aback," I said. "I guess I kind of thought that therapy—."

He wagged a gloved finger at me. "I'm not a therapist," he said.

"Counseling, then. I didn't think that—." I looked up at the impenetrable sky, the clouds shell pink in the mercury lights.

"In my experience, when people are grieving, unhappy, adrift, they cling to all sorts of physical things—shopping, alcohol, drugs, sex—when really what they're missing is something spiritual."

I took this in. It seemed completely apt. "I think I'm ready—or, at least, I think I *was* ready to start talking to God again. I remember saying my prayers as a kid, and I remember how safe and peaceful it made me feel. I think it could make me feel that way again."

"But?"

"But when I got home today some vandal had plastered my house with Sam Stinson bumper stickers."

He tilted sideways, readjusting the satchel's strap on his shoulder. "And?"

"And it made me angry and scared all over again."

For a long moment, he looked at me, his face still and calm. "Whatever your father did to you, and under whatever pretext, it had nothing to do with God."

Tears welled at the corners of my eyes. Without forethought, on pure instinct or reflex, I fell into his arms. The shoulder of his jacket was frigid against my wet cheek. Softly he stroked my back.

"It's okay," he whispered, his lips nearly touching my ear. "It'll all be okay."

We stood for a long time. Icy rain began to fall, but his body heat warmed me. At last I drew away, sopped tears away with my mittens.

"What should I do next?" I said. "What's the next step?"

"Talk to God. Just like you remember."

"Can we get together next week? I'd like to talk some more."

"A couple of years back I started a support group for gay men. We meet on Thursdays at my house. Would you like to join us tomorrow night?"

"I'm not sure."

"I'm booked into next week. If you come tomorrow, you won't have to wait. I promise you all of these men are struggling with the same issues you are."

I heard a car door slam and remembered Jaime, the tow truck, my car. I turned to look behind me, and saw Jaime standing in the parking lot, tugging on his gloves.

"All right," I said to Eliot. "I'll call you for directions?"

Eliot set a gloved hand on my shoulder. He grinned. "Do that. And I'll see you tomorrow."

As I crossed the parking lot toward him, Jaime said, "All set?"

Again, he helped me into the passenger's set. Again, his hand lingered in the small of my back.

To maneuver through the tightly packed lot and then through its needle's-eye exit required both hands and cost him a deep frown. But as soon as my car's back bumper cleared the curb, Jaime's face split into its crinkled grin. His hand dropped again to his lap. First with two gloved fingers, and then with the palm of his hand, he rubbed the leg of his coveralls. A longish bulge appeared.

My mouth went dry. I wanted that. Whatever its shape, size, color, or proclivities, I wanted it. But it seemed an unwholesome temptation. If Jonah swallowed Jaime, the whale would swallow Jonah.

I kept watch out my window. Once, when some pine trees along the street darkened my view, I saw Jaime's hand, still stroking his thigh, reflected in the glass. It seemed impolite, somehow, to ignore him after having shown such interest. I glanced over, watched him for a few seconds, smiled, and turned away again. By the time we got back to Ward's, both his bulge and his smile had vanished.

Leaving Jaime to set free my car, I went inside to talk with the service manager. No one could look at the Chevette before morning. At some point during the following day, I would receive a call.

When I left for home, I noticed that Jaime and his monster truck had disappeared.

At ten o'clock Martin had a meeting with the Speaker. I waited until then to call Eliot. While I wrote down and read back his directions to an address in the intricate maze of Prospect Park, Christa bustled about in her cubicle, slamming drawers, bumping her chair into walls, ripping paper, rattling her trash can.

I said goodbye to Eliot, and before I could fit the handset into its cradle, Christa stood beside me. She dropped a fat gray cloth-covered book onto my blotter. A thick sheaf of notebook paper, folded lengthwise, marked a spot near the front of the book. I turned the book over, looked at the worn imprint on the spine. Thomas Mann. *Doktor Faustus.* Below that, in smaller type, *Die Entstehung des Doktor Faustus.*

"What's this?"

"*Doktor Faustus.*" She spoke the words with extreme care, as if she'd rehearsed their pronunciation.

"I can see that." I set the book down, thumbed a spot on the edge of the front cover where the cloth had frayed and split. "Why are you giving it to me?"

She tugged at a corner of the notebook paper. She pulled the stack of pages free of the book and dangled them in front of me. "Tory asked me to give it to you. There's something about Beethoven. He translated it."

"Translated it? *Tory* translated this?"

"In case you don't read German. I told him he was being completely ridiculous. Doesn't *everyone* fucking read German?"

I opened the book, flipped pages. It was in German, all right. "Let me make sure I understand. *Tory* translated a section of this book. From *German*."

Christa flung the pages of Tory's translation into the air. Turning abruptly, she fled the office. I closed the book and watched the sheets of notebook paper flutter down around me.

What the hell had just happened?

I followed her. She sprinted down the hall. Her black skirt flitted around her legs like a colony of bats. By the time I reached the elevator lobby, she'd vanished. I went to the stairwell and listened for her footsteps on the stone treads. All was quiet, but then I heard a soft creak behind me, and turned to find the ladies' room door swinging closed.

I waited for her. At last she emerged, pallid and shaky. She clasped her hands over her stomach. "I'm sick," she said. "Food poisoning or the stomach flu, I think."

"Isch. Have you been to the doctor?"

She rolled her eyes. As we turned back toward the office, she lurched sideways. To steady her, I took her elbow. She yanked her arm away.

"Back off, Mom," she said. "If you kiss my forehead to check for a fever, I swear to fucking God I'll knock your block off."

"You're not a very good patient, are you?"

When I returned to my desk, I gathered the papers—dozens of them— Christa had scattered. Tory's penmanship was impeccable—whatever his faults, I had to give him that—but page numbers would have been nice. As I stacked the pages, I scanned for mention of Beethoven.

> Actually in his middle period Beethoven was more subjective— or we might say "personal"—than at the last. At that time [middle period] he was heedless of the conventions, formulas, and ornamentation of which music is of course full, instead allowing personal expression to consume [overwhelm?] them, to melt away into the subjective dynamic.

What?

> Of what did he speak? Now, the man was capable of devoting a whole hour to the question: "Why did Beethoven write no third movement for the Piano Sonata, Op. 111?"—an item worthy for discussion, no doubt. But one imagines the advertisement

fastened to the Community Center, or advertised in the Kaiser-saschener *Railway Journal* [made-up newspaper], and asks one-self if such a thing can arouse any measure of common curiosity.

Of what did *who* speak? Beethoven? No, surely Beethoven wouldn't adver-tise and deliver a lecture about his own piano sonata. *Worthy for discussion?*

After all, Beethoven—so we'd heard—had an acknowledged reputation for being unable to write a fugue, and now we asked ourselves to what extent this bitter defamation in reality applied. Plainly he had tried to refute this claim. Several times he had in his earlier piano music inserted [inlaid] fugues in three voices— in the Hammerklavier as well as in the one in A-flat.

"Christa?" I said. "Is Tory going to expect me to discuss this with him at some point?"

In reply she fed a pencil into her electric sharpener for something like four minutes.

• • •

I parked in front of Eliot's house. A concrete stair climbed an unkempt low slope of red grasses, pine bark mulch, and dead leaves. At the top of the stair, at the back of a narrow rectangle of lawn, a homely two-story cottage sat, white and square, among short, bare-limbed trees. Black earth circled the base of each tree and paralleled a short, crumbling brick walk to a small rectangular porch of ramshackle concrete, about four inches high, unshel-tered, off-center from the front door.

The sky was an overturned bowl of dirty cloud. Eliot's windows glowed, the curtains clad in golden light. From inside I heard the happy din of voices. I rapped the iron knocker and waited for answer. I stood back from the door and tried to read the faded lettering on the rush welcome mat. Not "Wel-come," certainly—not enough letters. "Moon"? No, too many letters.

When the door opened I first saw a pair of tasseled loafers, polished al-most to the sheen of patent leather. I didn't think it possible that Eliot could own a pair of glossy tasseled loafers. Indeed, it was not Eliot, but a thewy, sandy-haired, bearded man in khakis and a rayon shirt of forest green. He smiled. Lines crinkled around his pale gray-green eyes. Blond whiskers on either side of his mouth folded and bristled.

"I'm Charlie," he said. "Charlie Kent." He shook my hand. His grip was sure and warm. He turned my hand so that it was underneath his. I lost myself for a moment in the whorls of brown hair on the back of his hand. He tugged me gently toward him, into the entryway.

"Jonah Murray," I said.

He helped me out of my jacket and hung it on a hook by the door. With a wink and a lavish gesture he swept me into the fire-warmed space beyond. The living room, far larger than I had expected, seemed to extend the full length of the house; there were curtained windows on three sides. The carpet was plush, beige, spotless; I wondered if I should have taken off my shoes. Only five men—far fewer than I'd expected—crowded the sofa and matching chairs near the stone fireplace.

A double-hung door, barely three feet from my elbow, swung abruptly toward me. Eliot emerged, carrying a lacquer serving tray on which he'd arranged silver bowls of potato chips and nuts. As he walked, he stared at the bowls as if daring them to spill their contents.

To avoid a collision, I stepped back. "Eliot," I said, more sharply than I'd intended, so that his name sounded like a warning or reproach rather than a greeting.

Eliot turned and looked at me. "Jonah," he said, a little breathless. "Glad you could make it. Did you have any trouble?" He set the tray on the coffee table.

"Car's still in the shop," I said. "I called a cab."

He smiled absently, as if he hadn't quite bothered to hear my answer. To Charlie he said, "Can you make introductions? I'm still working on the refreshments." By then he was already pushing open the kitchen door.

Drawing closer, Charlie grasped my elbow and aimed me toward the sofa. He whispered in my ear, "Be not afraid." His breath smelled sweetly of mulled cider. "They're noisy but harmless."

Fred was the oldest of the group. His hair was a ring of white bristles around a shiny pink tonsure. Creases showed the path of his easy grin. He handed me slim fingers the color of unbleached cotton. I hoped I was supposed to shake his hand rather than kiss the enormous signet ring on his pinky finger. "Welcome to our happy little group," he said. His voice rattled like a sack full of gravel.

I fought an impulse to reply in French. I said, "Pleased to meet you."

On Fred's right sat Jeremy. His perfect skin had the color and gloss of bittersweet chocolate. High, sharp cheekbones and short dreadlocks reminded me of Erma, Luther's wife, but his narrow chest and toothpick limbs precluded further comparison. He opened his small angular mouth in a small angular smile. "How do you do?" he said.

"How—." I was about to say, "How kind of you to let me come," but I stopped myself. "How do you do?"

Rob and Tigger shared an armchair, Rob on the arm, Tigger crowded into the opposite corner of the seat. Rob stood and gripped my hand strongly in both of his. He wore a brown plaid shirt with pearl snaps. Years of ironing his store-brand jeans had drawn a white crease from the cuff of each leg nearly to the fly. He'd shined his round-toed cowboy boots until they gleamed like polished ebony. Somehow, by applying any number of pomades, mousses, or gels, he'd managed to do the same thing to his hair. He said, "So glad you could join us."

"We're always looking for new meat." That was Tigger. Now that I looked at him, I realized I'd seen him before—just days ago, in fact, coming out of Eliot's office as I'd gone into Dr. Bell's. I glanced down and saw the shiny Doc Marten boots he'd been wearing on Monday morning.

As his broad warm hand engulfed mine, I asked him, "Why are you called Tigger?"

"I picked it up as a kid. I was always bouncing around."

"On his tail," Jeremy said.

Tigger blushed. Even his hand, still holding mine, flushed red. Everyone screamed with laughter.

That is to say, everyone except Mason. Moving with great care, as if approaching a dotty and irascible monarch or a cornered and possibly rabid animal, Charlie escorted me to the chair where Mason sat. He hugged his knees, slouching as if he longed to disappear into the carapace of his pilled and faded beige cardigan.

"Pleased to meet you," I said.

Mason nodded. He muttered something that might have been "likewise," or just a pair of random syllables. I had a suspicion that, if cajoled and prompted and bribed with *Star Wars* action figures, he could be persuaded to quote entire chapters of *The Hitchhiker's Guide to the Galaxy* verbatim.

After all of the introductions, there was nothing else to say. Charlie and I stood side by side in front of the fire. The others stared into their empty laps or empty hands. Rob snapped and unsnapped the cuff of his left shirtsleeve. Jeremy leaned into Fred's shoulder and whispered something. Fred nodded and coughed. Silence.

Directly across the room from the fireplace, a tarnished mirror hung above a marble-topped console table. The mirror's gilt frame was a baroque topography of acanthus and anthemion. The table's base was an elaborate concoction of iron scrollwork and bronze filigree. I couldn't quite make these pieces square with the simple furnishings of Eliot's office, with the orderly arrangement of books and souvenirs on his plain white shelves.

Within this single large room, in fact, the furnishings seemed to represent an unpropitious marriage of two styles. A pair of simple ladder-backed oak chairs flanked the console table. The sofa and armchairs—overstuffed and upholstered in blue and gold stripes—looked utilitarian above all, comfortable and possibly durable, but hardly the pinnacle of the decorative arts. Yet the round tables on either end of the sofa were florid meditations on the rocaille style.

When I looked again into the mirror, I saw that Charlie had been watching me. I turned to him. His face rucked up into a grin, the jubilant, ungovernable smile of a lottery winner. I wanted to reach up and touch the deep furry dimple on his left cheek.

The others—all but Mason—chatted and chortled, but I had lost the thread. They might have been enacting a pantomime. It was as if I could hear only my own slow pulse. It was as if my breathing and Charlie's had fallen into the same rhythm, as if our bodies—though not even touching—had become intertwined, interdependent. I hated to speak if by speaking I would spoil such a perfect moment.

Charlie glanced toward the kitchen door, then at his watch, then again toward the kitchen door. "I wonder what could be taking him so long," he said. "I'll just check."

With that, the perfect moment was over—indeed, it had never been. Surely this was the casual stewardship of a partner, not a client. *I'll just check.* Keeping things on track, managing the schedule. I'd been dreaming. All this time Charlie had just been the polite host.

After he'd gone, I looked about me, feeling foolish and bereft. Again I saw my reflection in the clouded glass of the old mirror. My face burned red.

Now I understood. The mirror and end tables were Charlie's. The sofa and chairs were Eliot's. The room looked as if it had been cobbled together from two disparate styles, because it had been. Of course. Two households had become one.

I feigned interest in a Terry Redlin print—Eliot's, surely, not Charlie's—hanging in a corner. I moved toward it as if to examine it in detail, as if admiring the expert depiction of pond and trees and drifting snow. When I turned away from the print, Tigger motioned with a kind of reverse nod for me to come over. Rob had moved to the hearth and sat on its ledge of flagstone, his back to the fire. I settled on the arm of Tigger's chair.

"Doing okay?" Tigger said.

"I'm wishing I'd gotten more sleep last night, I'll say that."

"Were you doing something fun, I hope?"

"Listening to Beethoven."

Jeremy screamed. Startled, I looked over. He had both hands over his mouth, and his eyes were saucers. But then he collapsed against Fred, slapped the older man's wrist to chide him for some outrageous thing he'd said.

Tigger said, "Beethoven?"

"String quartets. The Great Fugue."

He crinkled his nose. "You could have been doing more sinful things than that, I suppose."

"Somehow, I prevailed against temptation."

"Right on, brother."

It was all getting a little too Baptist for my taste. I said, "Do things usually take this long to get going?"

Tigger shrugged, shook his head.

Rob reached over to tap my elbow. He said, "We were just talking about our plans for Thanksgiving." I looked around. Fred and Jeremy whispered together like schoolgirls. Mason stared into space, fiddling with the mother-of-pearl buttons of his cardigan. Tigger had been talking to me. Whom did Rob mean by we? He said, "I'm thinking of having a little gathering at my place. Kind of an orphans' Thanksgiving. What about you? Are you going anywhere?"

"San Francisco. My mother lives there."

Rob said, "San Francisco." He stretched the syllables until they sounded almost as separate words. "Very nice. Are you from there?"

I'd been born in Ohio, in Youngstown, and that's where we'd lived until my father had gotten a job in Charleston, South Carolina. We'd stayed in Charleston for a few years, until Barbara packed us up and moved us to Minnesota—of all places. Whenever I said I'd lived in Ohio, though, people heard it as Iowa, and whenever I mentioned South Carolina, I always had to follow up with a five-minute geography lesson, explaining the relative locations of Charlotte and Charleston and—for whatever reason—Myrtle Beach. The whole thing was always more trouble than it was worth. I decided to tell the simplified version. "I grew up here. Barbara moved to California a few years ago for a job."

"Barbara?" Tigger said. "You call your mother by her first name?"

"She insists," I said.

"Sounds like your mom's pretty cool," Tigger said. "Mine won't even speak to me."

"Barbara's pretty cool as mothers go."

"What do you have planned while you're there?" Rob said.

"I go every year, so there isn't much in the way of sightseeing that I haven't already done."

Fred said, "Are there any good churches there?" He and Jeremy had been silent for a while, I realized, listening in. "Around the holidays you can usually get in on some pleasant church gatherings."

Where did *that* come from? "I—. I don't really know. I never paid attention."

Mason said something. I looked at him. He said, "Good for you." He spoke softly. Everyone fell silent. "About listening to Beethoven, I mean."

"Beethoven?"

"Listening to the Beethoven quartets, you said. Good for you. Young people today—." I found myself cocking my head, turning one ear toward him. "I work in a library. Young people today, they—. All they seem to be interested in is pop culture."

Speaking in a room full of people appeared to cost Mason some effort, an effort I doubted he would make in order to utter an insult, and yet I felt vaguely insulted. Had he assumed, until I mentioned Beethoven, that I was one of those "young people" who bothered librarians with requests for *TV Guide* and tell-all memoirs? Hadn't Beethoven been part of pop culture, when he was arranging concerts and courting the favor of patrons and a paying public?

I feared that if I replied rashly, Mason might never speak again. While I weighed alternatives and tried to sustain a polite smile, Charlie returned, his loose sleeves rolled halfway up his forearms, his hair pointing in a dozen new directions. He wiped his hands on his khakis.

"You're all suddenly quiet," he said.

Jeremy said, "Mason farted, and we were trying to be polite about it."

Jeremy giggled. Mason blanched. Eyes wide, he looked up at Charlie and shook his head. "I swear I did no such thing."

"I know, Mason, I know." He sat on the arm of Mason's chair. It was a kind gesture, I thought, a vote of confidence. "There was an incident in the kitchen. I guess a couple of two-liters of Coke burst in the freezer. Eliot'll be out in a few." Standing, he tugged the folds out of his trousers. "While we're waiting, I think I need to get some air."

I wanted badly to go with him, and more than that I wanted him to know how badly, and more than *that* I wanted him to know without it being obvious to everyone else. At the front door, Charlie turned and looked at me. He cocked his head back, toward the door. I stood to follow him, patting my pockets as if looking for something I might have left outside—what, I couldn't have said—but then I stopped. Let the queens think what they might.

◆   ◆   ◆

We stood shivering on the porch. A chill wind cut through the weave of my sweater. I zipped my jacket. Unrolling his sleeves, buttoning the cuffs, Charlie looked sidelong at me. "I guess this wasn't such a great idea," he said.

"Do you want to get your jacket?" He shrugged, shook his head. I said, "Let's walk."

"That'll help."

The steps to the sidewalk were narrow; Charlie waved for me to go ahead. When we met at the bottom, I paused, trying to get my bearings. Everything seemed both familiar and strange. Already I had forgotten which way the cab had brought me in.

"I always find this neighborhood incredibly bewildering."

"You get used to it."

"Barbara—my mother—and I once got lost driving around in this neighborhood. Back when I was a kid."

He turned right, strolling uphill. I followed him.

"I'll bet you were looking for the Frank Lloyd Wright house."

I nodded. "On the snowiest day of the year. She had this Volkswagen Thing, this ridiculous Army-green rattletrap with no working heat. She plowed through drifts as high as the running boards, up and down all these streets, laughing like a maniac."

"Did you ever find it?"

"The whole adventure ended with me finding a pay phone so we could call Triple A."

He laughed. "It's on Cecil, I think. Or, no, Bedford. It's a couple of blocks from here, anyway." We walked in silence to the end of the block. Charlie stopped, folded his arms. His sleeves tightened over his biceps. He said, "I feel like I should apologize for Eliot."

"Why?"

"He's so disorganized about these gatherings."

"So it would seem."

He clenched his jaw. His whiskers rippled as his cheeks tensed and slackened. "It happens every week. That's why I promised to help. But he won't let me do anything useful."

"How did you meet him?"

"An ad in *Equal Time*."

"And how long have you been with him?"

He looked to the clouds for his the answer. "It must be five years now?"

Tom and I had been together for five years. I started to say as much, but before I could, Charlie spoke again. He said, "I'm finally starting to feel things are fitting together."

"I'm glad to hear it," I said, but then I wondered, why it had taken five years for things to *begin* fitting together?

"Eliot's just so—." Squinting at the sidewalk, he stroked his cheek. "He's so perceptive. Don't you find it helps to talk things out with him? And the group helps too. I think it was a great idea he had, to start it. We all get such benefit out of it."

And now my heart grew impossibly light. Charlie was Eliot's client, after all, not his lover. A member of the group, not its polite host.

In an instant I had it all planned out. A three-bedroom Tudor house in a quiet glade of Eagan, a sprawling emerald lawn, pansies in the window boxes. Low junipers filling the air with the sloe-gin scent of their berries. A copse of birch at the back of the property. Matching Honda Civics, silver with black leather upholstery. Two tomcats, an Abyssinian named Kander and an Egyptian Mau named Ebb. I said, "Pal, if I were a salad, I know I'd be splashing my dressing."

"Were you really bad off?"

"Getting there." He took a step toward me. He wiped a tear from the inside corner of my eye. "Windy," I said.

"I'm glad I found Eliot when I did. I have a sense it's the same for you."

"Are you ready to go back? I'm freezing."

"Me too."

As we turned, I said, "Do you want to hear something funny?"

"What's that?"

"When I asked you how long you've been with Eliot, I meant it a different way. I thought you were lovers."

Charlie stopped. He stared at me for so long that I thought I must have said something unwittingly cruel. "Can you not know? Jonah, how can you not know?"

"What? Can I not know what?"

"This—. These men—. We're—. Eliot brought us together because we're all struggling with the same issue. He told you that?"

"You're all gay. He told me. That's why—."

"No, no, no, not at all. We all *used* to be gay."

We stood between a birch tree on the boulevard and a stone retaining wall. I slumped against the tree. "*Used* to be? How—?"

"That's Eliot's gift." In the yellow glow of the streetlights his eyes were strange. "His gift to us, his gift to the world. He's curing us."

"*Curing* you?"

"I thought you were just another—."

"Victim? Just another victim?" *Faggotry's the thing that has licked 'em,* I thought. *And it looks like Jonah's just another victim.*

He winced. "I know how it sounds. I probably didn't say it quite the right way. I guess I shouldn't have mentioned it at all."

After a moment's silence we walked on. At the foot of Eliot's stair, I said, "I should go. I'm not comfortable with this at all."

"Please don't. I'm sorry I said anything."

"It's okay. I just—. I have to go. It was—. It was nice to have met you."

"I'm sorry. Will you shake my hand?"

I did. His skin was as cold and smooth as granite. All the while I walked away—down the hill, toward University Avenue, I hoped—I felt his eyes on me. After about half a block, I turned back. Charlie stood, now, at Eliot's front door. He waved. I turned and never looked back.

At the next cross street, I waited for a traffic light. I looked around for a street sign.

Franklin. The cross street was Franklin. That meant I'd probably gone the wrong way, away from University. I stood, now, facing a downward slope. I remembered that, as the cab had turned off University into Prospect Park, I'd caught a glimpse of some kind of tower—a bell tower, perhaps, or a shot tower—a fat column of gray stone with a pointed roof like a witch's hat. It had stood high on a hill. I didn't see a hill or a tower anywhere in front of me.

I wanted very badly to turn. If I could see the tower behind me, then I would know how to get back to University—but I imagined the entire bastion of Christian queens standing on the sidewalk, their arms folded, their eyes narrowed, watching me, and I decided that I could not—would not— turn. I would not even look back over my shoulder.

I looked, instead, to the left and to the right. Franklin stretched away in either direction, sloping up to the left, down to the right.

One direction would lead toward the University of Minnesota campus. Most likely, I would have to walk many blocks before I could find a cab or a bus, or even a pay phone.

The other direction would lead—where? Perhaps to some cross street that would get me to University Avenue, or perhaps to a cross street that led to another cross street, and another, and another. There was every chance I'd get hopelessly lost—or, worse, end up back on Seymour, in front of Eliot's concrete stairs.

And I wasn't sure which direction was which. Left toward the campus? Right toward the campus? If Franklin sloped downward to the right, then that should mean the campus lay in that direction.

On the other hand, the streets of this neighborhood were convoluted and perplexing. I'd never understood how everything fit together. Whenever I found myself in this maze of hilly, curving streets, it always seemed either larger or smaller than I remembered. Whichever direction I chose, I might find myself in some vast park I'd never heard of or in the midst of a tract of close-set houses that I didn't recognize.

Ahead, at the bottom of Seymour, the street curved to the right and followed a tall grayish-white wall or fence. To the left of that, there was a narrow ramp of some kind, flanked by a chain link fence that glowed stark white in the lamplight.

Left or right? Left or right? I couldn't make myself decide, and I couldn't stand to think about it any longer. I still felt that eyes were on me, that Eliot and his group watched me from his windows or his front walk.

I crossed Franklin. The light may have been red or green—I scarcely noticed—and I didn't bother to look for traffic. I fixed my eyes on the bottom of the hill, and I half-ran, half-walked toward it.

Pools of yellow light dotted the buckling sidewalks. Bony tree limbs waved and darted in a stiff, chill wind. I huddled deeper into my jacket.

Seymour didn't, after all, curve to the right. It ended at a cross street. The grayish-white wall I'd seen from above stretched away in both directions. Rough panels of concrete alternated with smooth. A patchwork of paint in various shades of white marked the spots where graffiti had been covered up. I heard the thump and hum of freeway traffic.

On the left there was a small park, a patch of dead grass with a jungle gym and a picnic table, and then the concrete ramp curving upward, rising above the rough-and-smooth wall. From above, from a distance, I'd thought that the fences on either side of the ramp had been painted white, but I saw now that they were constructed of bare galvanized steel.

At the top of the ramp, I could see a structure of some kind, a series of black arches. I climbed the ramp's shallow slope and found myself on a pedestrian bridge, a narrow, deeply shadowed walkway caged in chain-link fence. Below it, I-94 ran through a channel of concrete. Beneath my feet traffic sped by in a river of light and noise. It was surprising, with all the bright lights along the freeway, how dark it was on the bridge.

Shivering, I stood in the center of the bridge, where there was a spot of pink light. On the concrete walkway someone had painted in blue:

KILL YOUR

EGO

The wind was a frozen blade. Barehanded, I clutched the fence. The cold steel numbed my fingers.

Eliot's gift to the world, Charlie had called it. *Curing us.* As if they—*we*—were all diseased.

In the eastbound left lane, a semi rumbled along, spouting black exhaust. As the truck passed under the bridge, the pavement trembled alarmingly under my feet. I walked on.

Well beyond the center of the freeway, the bridge crested above some train tracks. More blue paint. I crouched to read the graffiti.

THE

UNIVERSE

WANTS TO

PLAY

What the fuck did *that* mean?

I stood. To the left, far below me, a yellow boxcar sat on the tracks, looking as if it hadn't been used or even moved in years. On the right side of the bridge, a gap in the trees offered a view of downtown Minneapolis, of gold towers and obsidian columns encrusted with white lights.

At the far end of the bridge there was a stairway. I hurried down it. My feet and fingers ached with cold. At the first landing I paused and cupped my hands around my mouth and blew warm air into them.

On either side of me, houses stretched away, their leaf-strewn lawns filled with flagstone-ringed flower beds and patio furniture and barbeques shrouded for winter. Somewhere high above me, a plane droned. Behind me, the freeway traffic moaned, loud and low-pitched.

I looked down and saw that the stairs gave onto a sidewalk. To the right of the sidewalk, a big stucco duplex or apartment building sat mere feet from the pavement. To the left, a row of pine trees bordered a strip of lawn. Directly across the street, on the corner, a street sign read, "E River Terr."

East River Terrace. I was near the river. The river was just ahead.

I dashed down the stairs, flight after flight. My footsteps fell on more graffiti, illegible in the shadows.

I ran down the sidewalk, toward the river. The boulevard was mostly clear of trees, and I could see that, yes, after the next block, the sidewalk ended at the river road.

At the river road, I stopped and looked up and down the street, trying to get my bearings. The main entrance to the beach would be far off to the left. The stairway to the beach would be far off to the right. Heedless of traffic, I crossed and turned right along the path.

As I walked, I realized that I would have to pass the little gray-haired man's house. I stayed as far from the street as I could, walking along the line of trees at the top of the slope. I could smell the river, could feel the chill of the water. Even bare and leafless, the trees were so thick that I could see the river only in pearly-white stripes and blotches.

The little gray-haired man still had all his lawn signs out. From a long way away I spotted the field of red, white, and blue. A few signs had tumbled down—had loosed themselves or had been pulled loose by vandals. They flapped in the breeze.

Fuck. There he was. The little gray-haired man himself, on this side of the street. He was in his bathrobe, leaning on his cane, waiting while his dog shat. He called out a challenge, wanted to know what the fuck I thought I was doing.

What the fuck did he *think* I was doing? I was walking. Walking along a public path through a public park.

I ignored the barking man, ignored his barking dog. I doddered, faltered, rushed.

At last I came to the stairs. I plunged into the beach's narrow gullet. My footsteps thundered against the wood and steel in a fugal basso crescendo. At the bottom, I paused to catch my breath. In a grove of trees and bushes, off to my left, branches rattled. A twig snapped.

A figure—broad and tall as a truck, indistinct but undeniably male—emerged from the shadows. His face was a pale blur. I sensed movement near what must be his beltline. I feared he might have a knife or a gun or a club. But then he moved aside his hand to reveal what appeared, in the dark, as a white smudge. With a gloved hand he pawed himself. The white smudge burgeoned into a column. A little way off the path, I sank my knees into the dirt and took him into my mouth.

He was thick and meaty and tasted of wool and mint. I reached up to fondle his balls. He leapt back, tittering. "Cold hands," he said. For a man so large, his voice was astonishingly high in pitch. I muttered an apology, not caring if he heard or understood. I walked forward on my wet knees. I sucked.

For many minutes, I worked him with my lips and tongue. He was not quick. I felt my own erection bulge uncomfortably against the fly of my jeans, and then soften. He moaned and placed his hands on my head. I grew hard again, and then soft, and then hard.

I quickened my pace. The wet sound of my mouth on him seemed quite loud in my own ears. I feared my sucking might be heard up on the street. My tongue went numb. I gagged and choked. My jaw began to ache—his cock was very thick, and it seemed to be growing thicker—and after some time I could only suck him deeply and slowly and at as even a pace as I could manage.

After a time, though my knees ached and my jaw ached and my hands were numb, I began to wish that the man would never come, that I could go on sucking him forever.

My erection swelled, flagged, swelled again.

At last the man sputtered a warning. "I'm coming." His gloved hands brushed my ears and came to rest on my shoulders. Again I quickened my pace, and I ignored the catch in my jaw. I didn't stop. I swallowed.

He thanked me, buttoned his jeans. Whistling merrily, he mounted the stairs. I stood and wiped my mouth with the back of my hand. I veered off the path, crashed into the thicket. There were no more men—no more black silhouettes—prowling through the bare branches.

I wanted to be a mouth, an open channel, a gullet, a hole. I wanted to still my roiling thoughts, to kill my brain and its ceaseless churning. I wanted to be used, thrown away, used, thrown away, used again. I wanted to be wanted.

Now I wished I'd turned the other way on the river road. I wished I'd started at the other end of the beach. Inch by inch, step by step, yard by yard, man by man, I could have made my way toward the boathouse—no, not the boathouse, the empty place where it had stood.

For minutes or hours I waited in the thicket, wandering around in circles on its narrow paths. Time came to seem elastic, if not faintly ridiculous. I thought I heard footsteps in the brush, but it must have been a squirrel or a bird. I thought I heard footsteps on the stairs, but it must have been the wind shaking the steel frame. No one came.

Leaves rustled and crunched under my feet. I was exhausted. My legs were sore and weak.

Suddenly, I wanted to see the square patch of black earth where the boathouse had been. I returned to the paved path. I stumbled along, walking northward. I passed through a patch of black ground, the gelid shadow of the Franklin Avenue Bridge. The drone of traffic above me might have been hundreds of miles away. Somewhere above and behind was the pedestrian bridge. The cage had been open at the top. I could have climbed it. If only I'd climbed the fence, if only I'd sailed like a hawk into the open air, had fallen to the pavement, had shattered like a block of ice under the wheels of that rumbling semi.

• • •

When at last I sat on the dock, it might have been nine o'clock at night, or four in the morning.

I sat cross-legged on the frosty planks. The river slid by beneath me. Ice chinked against the dock's iron piles. My thoughts, if they could be called thoughts, were chaotic, inchoate. My beautiful lost boat. Sam Stinson. Tom. Beethoven. Eliot. Charlie. Each seemed to be an avatar of something else, of an emotion I could not quite feel, an idea I could not quite articulate.

Behind me I heard footsteps in the leaves. "Jonas?" someone said.

I turned. At first I saw only the rosy light of streetlamps, glimmering through trees. "Jonas, is that you?"

From the left, a man appeared, as broad and tall as the man I'd met along the path, so that I thought he had followed me or had found me again. I wondered how he'd learned even this approximation of my name. But I saw, then, that this was not the figure of a particularly tall man; rather, he stood a few feet above me, on a distant bank. And when he spoke again—"What are you doing here, buddy?"—I recognized his voice. Michael Walton.

He stepped onto the dock. When he squatted beside me, I saw that sweat steamed off him, that damp strands of hair clung to his forehead. He was dressed for running, in gray Asics sneakers, a long-sleeved US Rowing T-shirt, and warm-ups of whispery black nylon. His face furrowed into such a deep frown that I wondered what I must look like. I turned away and chafed my cheeks against my knees.

Michael took my chin in his hands, lifted my face toward him. "Are you okay?" He brushed something from the hollow beneath my left eye.

All at once I understood: I had been—was still—weeping. I dabbed my tears with the sleeve of my jacket. The cold, stiff leather burned my skin.

"You're not shivering," he said. "Were you shivering before? Did you stop shivering?"

Hooking his fingers under my armpits, he lifted me to my feet. He took my hands, held them up to the light. "Are your fingers numb?" he asked me. "What about your toes? How long have you been out here?" He grasped the wrist of my right hand and held it for many minutes, it seemed, while he stared at his watch. He dropped my hand, then took it up again and held it in both of his hands, gently rubbing my fingers and palms.

"Would you say something, please?" he said.

"The rain in Spain falls mainly in the plain."

"I think you might be hypothermic."

"In Hartford, Hereford, and Hampshire—." The words slurred on my tongue and lodged themselves at the back of my throat. I stopped.

"How did you get here? Where's your car?"

"In the shop," I said. "I was looking for a cab." That must sound ridiculous. Looking for a cab? Here? I had been looking for a cab much, much earlier, though, hadn't I? I couldn't quite think how to explain how I had gotten from that point to this.

He aimed me toward land, toward light. He started walking, pulling me along. "My place is a few blocks from here. You can call a cab from there, after we get you warmed up."

"You're all sweaty," I said. "*You'll* be hypo—hypo—hypodermic by the time we get there."

"Fuck that," he said, and then, "Walk faster, please."

As we crossed the scorched earth where the boathouse had been, I tripped on a charred chunk of wood. The choking smell of ash filled my nose. I fought a sneeze.

Taking my hand, Michael hauled me up the bank and onto the broad paved path where he'd no doubt been running when he'd spotted me. I glanced back. How on earth *had* he spotted me, sitting way out there on the dock? It was inky black out there, no sign of the dock at all.

Now that I thought about it, I suspected that perhaps I had for a time been bawling and shouting Tom's name. Maybe Michael had heard me.

We walked north, away from the beach. Trees arched over the path. I trudged along beside him, insensible of nearly everything but the warmth and solidity of his body against me.

A little way along we came to a stairway. Steep flights led up a steep bank. It was a tough climb. Ice, dirt, pebbles, cigarette butts, and sticks clogged the stairway's shallow concrete treads. Halfway up, a tree limb hung low over the handrail, and I hit my head. I slipped back, faltered on the gritty ice. Michael clutched my elbow, helped me up.

We emerged at last onto the campus. To our left lay a tall tower of red brick. The hospital. To the right there was a row of dormitories, also red brick.

On the street I was dimly aware of people around us. Just behind us, someone said, quite sharply, "On your left." A bicyclist, bundled up in a parka and a scarf and gloves, riding fast. He jangled a tinny bell. Michael pulled me aside, onto the boulevard, to let the bike pass. I felt drunk and stupid.

He led me through a gap between dormitory buildings, into an empty quad. Hundreds of bikes stood in sagging ranks, locked to steel racks. We passed an empty basketball court, an empty volleyball pit.

We stopped at the front door of a squat brick building. The bricks had been painted yellow and tan. Michael propped me against the door and dug a key out of his shoe. "Roos," I said, and giggled.

• • •

His apartment was a single room with a row of cupboards along one side and a closet-sized bathroom in the opposite corner. The walls were concrete block, pale green. A wall of single-paned windows, though closed, poured icy air into the room. A bare queen mattress lay on the floor in a muddle of sheets and blankets. Near the head of the bed, four stacks of milk crates and an old hollow-core door served as a desk. Everywhere there were piles of books.

Michael stripped naked. In a couple of deft moves he had me out of my jacket and sweater. It all happened so fast. I stood there like a dolt, blinking and dumb, certain that I had just witnessed some kind of magic trick.

"What?" I said. I discovered that I was staring at his penis, pink and stout in a nest of curly black hair. My heart thumped.

"You're hypothermic. More than a little. We need to get you warmed up." He fumbled with my belt buckle. "This is how it's done."

"If you want me to suck your dick, you can just ask." I thought of the man I'd sucked along the path at the beach, and my cock stiffened.

He took a step back. He looked at me. "Take your pants off," he said. "Underwear, too."

While I obeyed him, he knelt on the floor and made the bed. Flat sheet, blanket, quilt. He smoothed the covers over the mattress. Standing, he led me to the bed.

"I feel fine," I said.

"You're disoriented. Your pupils are dilated. You're lethargic. You're ataxic, which is Greek for you're a clumsy fuck. Your speech is slurred and your breathing is rapid and you aren't shivering. You're hypothermic, in other words. Get into the fucking bed, please."

He lifted the covers and I crawled underneath them. He rolled in after me. He lay facing me, pulled me toward him, wrapped his arms and legs around me. His skin was dry now, but as cool as marble. His body was dense with muscle. Against my leg his genitals were a packet of flame.

"Well," I said, "this is awkward."

"Shucks, buddy." he said. "Your effusive gratitude is making me blush. Be still, please."

His hair smelled of apples and limes. I nuzzled the briny skin of his neck. I breathed him in. His warm, dry hands stroked my arms and back. I slept.

• • •

When I woke, I was alone in Michael's bed. The air smelled of cumin. Music played softly and at some distance, so that I heard it in scraps and snatches—a male voice, intricate percussion, a riff of syncopated chords on electric piano.

I lay facing what at first appeared to be a vast sheet of duct tape. After a moment I realized that I was looking at a strange curtain of silver vinyl that Michael had drawn to stanch the hemorrhage of cold air into the room. He'd wrapped me in blankets and had placed a space heater near my feet.

I'd been dreaming. I closed my eyes, trying to sink back into sleep, back into the fading dream, if only so that I could remember it before it slipped completely away. I had been doing something—had been standing, talking, drinking—with someone who had been Tom, but also Spike, but also Charlie. There had been colored lights, streamers, loud music. I half-remembered something about a wound on my face or neck, a marking of some kind that I could not properly cover.

I turned over.

Now wearing a navy-blue sweat suit, Michael sat at his makeshift desk, reading. My jacket hung over the back of his chair. With the fingers of his left hand he absently combed and stroked his long hair. It shone as silk. I wondered if he'd showered while I slept. How long had I slept?

"How did you know all that?" I asked him. He didn't seem to hear me. Louder, I said, "About the hypothermia and all. How did you know about all that?"

Without looking up, he said, "It's just the kind of thing you pick up in med school. One sec, buddy." He read for a while longer, then set a leather bookmark crosswise on the page. He turned to face me, leaned over, felt my forehead. "Much better. How do you feel?"

"Embarrassed, but otherwise, surprisingly, as if nothing happened. You're in med school?"

"Going on my seventeenth year."

"Seventeenth—?" He rolled his eyes. "Oh. You mean it only *seems* like—."

"Right. Give me your hand." I lifted my right hand, and he checked my pulse. As he counted, he wiggled his bare toes. Sprigs of black hair darkened the knuckles.

"Your mother must be very proud," I said. "Her son the doctor."

He cut his eyes at me. "Your pulse seems fine."

"Thank you." I meant to thank him for finding me, for pulling me off the cold dock, for bringing me here and warming me. After a moment's thought, though, I feared it might seem that I meant to take unwarranted credit for my strong pulse. While I was still trying to think how to explain, he spoke again.

"I'm not going to be that kind of doctor," he said. "I'm more interested in the research side. I'm getting an MD/PhD. Immunology. Molecular virology. Beating HIV, basically."

"I think I need to use your bathroom," I said.

"It's not hard to find."

"Where are my clothes?"

"I washed them. They were soaked and filthy." He cleared his throat. "Especially the knees of your jeans."

To my relief, he returned to his reading. Although we had both been naked, although we had shared a bed and he had held me in his arms—or perhaps because of these things—I felt shy about showing myself to him.

The bathroom door sounded hollow and fit poorly in the jamb. I jiggled it, jammed my shoulder against it. Leaning over the toilet, eye to eye with a poster of Jonas Salk, I peed.

The painters had been sloppy. Where the frame of the medicine cabinet met the wall, streaks and drips of green and lavender and yellow paint over-lapped. The cabinet door was ajar. I craned my neck to see in, but the over-head light was dim, and I could see only the blue edge of a box of Q-tip swabs.

Stepping to the sink, I turned on the water. No soap. Perhaps in the medi-cine cabinet? I glanced around. There were no closets, no cupboards, no shelves, no baskets. The extra soap, if it existed, could only be in the medi-cine cabinet.

I nudged the mirrored door, and it opened a few more inches. No soap. The Q-tips. Toothpaste, the crinkled tube squeezed in the middle. Two tooth-brushes—why two?-—lying bare on a water-spotted glass shelf. Nyquil. A bag of cotton balls, squeezed into a pudgy white lump and shoved into a cor-ner. A razor. A can of shaving cream with a crust of white around its nozzle. A bottle of rubbing alcohol. Two amber bottles of prescription medications.

One bottle sat with its label facing out. Tylenol III, long expired. It had been prescribed by a DMD. The name on the bottle read, "Michael Walrath."

Walrath? Not *Walton?* Holy shit. Had I ever, in all the dozen or more times that I'd met Michael at rowing club meetings or at the Gay 90s, referred to him by the wrong name? I was sure that I had. Of course I had.

I turned off the water. I eased the cabinet door shut, leaving it open a frac-tion of an inch. The bathroom door was more difficult to open than it had been to shut. I tugged, and it came free with a raw squeak.

The room was empty. Michael had gone—to fetch my clothes?

On a two-burner cooktop near the door, a pot of rice and black beans bub-bled and simmered. Between the burners, a spoon lay in a puddle of purple muck. I leaned over the pot and whiffed the haystack scent of cumin, the bite of chili powder, the bitter woody warmth of oregano.

A boom-box sat on the counter, still softly pouring music into the room. The percussion grew more complex. The piano thrummed with deep rolling chords. The man's voice veered into a high falsetto.

It was a beautiful voice—the tone clear and round and full, the intonation perfect—but in his upper range the singer's diction was slack and muddy. I rewound the cassette a couple of times and raised the boom-box's volume, but I couldn't make out the words. When the melody returned to earth, the man seemed to be singing, "It's always warmest where you are."

Among the books and papers on Michael's desk I found a photograph in a silver frame. In the flicker of tiki torches, a sunset seascape behind them, Michael and one of his rowers leaned forward into the camera, their heads touching. What was the rower's name? John? Jake? Josh? Something with a J. He was almost preternaturally blond, his hair—even his eyebrows—nearly white. Across the bottom of the photo someone had written in silver ink:

> Though we may wander or get lost,
> I'll never feel the winter's killing frost
> It's always warmest where you are

On the desk, underneath the frame, there was a letter on flimsy, powder-blue air mail stationery. I didn't dare move the photo, didn't dare touch anything, but I could read the last few lines. "I miss you so much it hurts," I read, and, "I couldn't wait to get to Paris, and yet now I'm counting the days until I can see you again, till I can lie in bed with you," and, "I'm sitting up in my bed as I write this, wishing you were next to me."

Well. That explained the second toothbrush.

A Day Runner lay open at the edge of the desk. The pages were filled with miniscule handwriting. Classes, labs, meetings with advisors, study groups. The evening slots were mostly blank, but on Wednesday, "Pink House" was written across a four-hour block.

The textbook Michael had been reading lay open in the middle of the desk. The leather bookmark lay on the left-hand page, marking a section heading that read, "Acute HIV Syndrome." I lifted the bookmark.

> In a certain number of patients, an acute syndrome develops
> 2-4 weeks after initial HIV infection. This self-limited syndrome
> manifests through the appearance of symptoms including, but
> not limited to, rigor, lymphadenopathy, arthralgia, myalgia,
> weakness and fatigue, rashes, nausea, and diarrhea. Viremia of-
> ten accompanies a precipitate drop in $CD4^+$ T cells, followed by
> a rise to normal or near-normal levels.

Arcane, but comprehensible. Subsequent paragraphs became more and more dense with acronyms and words derived from Greek and Latin. CTL's. PBMC's. $CD8^+DR^+CD25^-$. GM-CSF. IFN-α. IFN-β. IFN-γ. Monocyctes. Follicular lymphocytes. Dendritic reticulum cells. Michael understood all this? I carefully returned the bookmark to its place.

At the top of a stack of books beside the desk lay a hardcover copy of Stephen Hawking's *Brief History of Time*. I picked it up, thumbed through. Dozens of pages had been dog-eared and annotated in the same cramped cursive as the Day Runner. On the title page of chapter eight, tiny words filled the space around the chapter title with a digressive meditation on Einstein, absolute time, and the existence of God. It seemed that Michael believed in Einstein, but not in God or absolute time. It *seemed* so, but I couldn't be certain; the handwriting was difficult to decipher, and the prose was convoluted or perhaps simply beyond my understanding. I returned the book to the stack, squaring its edges with the book beneath.

On the wall above the desk, Michael's undergraduate degree hung in an ebony frame. It was an elaborate, professional framing job—a creamy yellow matte, a bronze medal in an oval cutout, a ribbon of black, yellow, and red stretched across the bottom. According to the Gothic-lettered parchment, Michael—Michael *Walrath*—had received a Bachelor of Science from Heidelberg College and had graduated magna cum laude.

The door swung open. Michael stepped through, kicked the door closed behind him. Though he carried my sweater, jeans, and embarrassing candy-striped pink boxer shorts in a neatly folded stack, he stopped short just inside the door, as if he hadn't quite expected to see me standing in his room.

I set my hand on the back of his chair, felt the fine-grained leather of my jacket collar, and wondered if I should have somehow covered myself with it. I might have wrapped it around my waist like Donna Reed's apron, might have cinched the sleeves into a knot at the small of my back. No matter. Too late now. I moved the chair and hid behind it.

"Your last name is Walrath," I said.

"I'm aware of that."

"I always thought your name was Walton."

In the manner of a zookeeper shoving food into the cage of a ravenous, man-eating predator, he set my clothes on the desk and sidled away. He kept his eyes resolutely off to one side. "Why do you think I always call you Jonas?"

All at once my knees felt weak. I sank sideways onto the chair. I let out a long laugh, a crazy bark of a laugh, a mad song of a laugh.

When I'd met Tory, I'd thought he was sad, over the hill, a dim bulb, and yet it turned out that he knew more about Beethoven than I did, that he could quote Berlin and Hammerstein as well as or better than I could. For pity's sake, he could read, could *translate*, German.

I'd thought that Eliot meant to help me, to deepen and enrich my life, but to him I'd been just another queer in need of a cure. Through a series of lies and blandishments he'd dragged me into his bizarre missionary fantasy.

For more than a year I'd thought that Michael Walton—*Walrath*—was a self-centered frat boy, beautiful but wanton, working his way through the Twin Cities one ass at a time like some sort of sexual conquistador. I'd never have guessed that he was a medical student, an MD/PhD candidate, one half of a committed couple, a saver of lives.

"What?" Michael said. He was looking at me now, focusing—so it seemed—on the center of my bare chest.

"I just realized I'm not exactly a great judge of character."

"Could you get dressed, please?" he said.

As I reached for my boxers, I muttered an apology. "My mind was wandering," I said. "I didn't mean to—."

"It's not that I don't—. Never mind. I shouldn't—."

I picked up my jeans, shook out the folds. The denim snapped in the air like a flag whipped by strong wind. I said, "It's okay. I know that you and—." What the *fuck* was that rower's name? "That is to say—. You don't have to—."

"James," he said. "His name is James, and we're—."

"I saw the picture. Worth a thousand words, as they say." I put on my sweater.

As if hearing the boom-box for the first time, he turned toward it, cocked an ear. "This is his voice," he said. "This is his band, playing a song he wrote."

I put on my shirt. It was still warm from the dryer. James sang something about a scar. "She bore her opinion of me like a scar upon her face"? Was that it?

"Jonah," Michael said. He was looking at the knees of my jeans. Smudges of brown and green still marked the faded twill. My face grew hot. "I don't know what you were doing down at the beach. I don't know why you were out on the dock like that, wailing like some sort of wounded animal."

So I *had* been bawling out there on the dock. And he *had* heard me. I dropped my eyes. Michael's thick toes drummed against the linoleum. I had a crazy impulse to prostrate myself, to scatter my limbs across the floor, to cover his feet in kisses and tears.

"You don't have to tell me," he was saying. "I mean, don't tell me. I don't want to know. But you have to take care of yourself. Nothing is worth—." He put his hand over his mouth, as if stoppering it.

"I know."

He dropped his hand, fidgeted with the drawstring of his sweatpants. "I don't know if you do."

Suddenly I couldn't face him any longer. I had to get away. I had to get home. I put on my jacket. "How long did I sleep?" I looked around for a clock. "What time is it?"

Shrugging, he checked his watch. "Quarter after four."

"Fuck. I'm sorry. I didn't mean to—."

He put up his hands. "It's okay. I never sleep more than three or four hours a night. Never have, suspect I never will."

"But surely at this hour—."

He shook his head. "I go for my run every night, then I come back here and sleep for a few hours, then I get up and study. Except for the hypothermic redhead in my bed, this has been a pretty normal night."

I said, "I don't know how to thank you. I know I can never repay you." I still could not look at him. I stared at the photograph of Michael and James. In the photo they looked absurdly happy. Had Tom and I *ever* looked that happy, even in the beginning? "I can never—."

In a couple of steps he closed the gap between us. He took me in his arms. He said, "I wish I could fix it, whatever it is."

For a moment I stood rigid against him, too shocked to return his embrace. But then my arms closed tight around him, pulled him hard against me. I buried my face in his sweet-smelling hair.

11 THE GOBLIN MARCH

On the way home, in the back of a Yellow Cab, I dozed. The driver tapped my knee to wake me. Groggy, not quite awake, I looked down. Where he had touched me, on the left knee, my jeans bore a greenish-brown splotch, roughly circular, about four inches in circumference. Another stain, more irregular in shape but nearly as big, covered the other knee.

I looked up, and I saw that the driver, a jowly, whiskered man in his late fifties or early sixties, was staring at the spot on my left knee. I handed him a twenty-dollar bill and, before he could make change, climbed out of the cab on the curb side.

Dawn was a purplish vein of light in the eastern sky. The house was as I'd left it—no bumper stickers, no chalk on the sidewalk, no graffiti. The cab spun away on Sherburne. I stumbled up the walk.

First thing, I called Martin and left a message on his voice mail. Sick, not coming in, terribly sorry. I said something—no doubt something not entirely convincing—about food poisoning.

I stripped, dumped my clothes into the laundry basket. I showered, the longest, hottest shower of my life. I tumbled into bed.

The doorbell woke me. For many minutes I lay staring at the ceiling, dully thinking that I couldn't remember anyone ever ringing my doorbell. Jehovah's Witnesses, perhaps.

The windows were dark. I switched on the lamp. According to my alarm clock, it was just after six. I'd slept for more than twelve hours.

The doorbell rang again, a dozen or more times in the space of a few seconds. If some Jehovah's Witnesses had decided to pay me a visit, they must be unusually persistent. I put on my stained jeans and padded to the front door. John Peterson, whose friends called him Spike, stood on my front stoop in his sheepskin jacket, his brown boots, stiff new jeans, and an orange and blue plaid shirt. When he saw me, he smiled. "Beta," he said. Shedding his jacket, he pushed past me into the entryway.

I closed the door. He pinned me to it with a hand on each shoulder. With the full length of his body against mine, he kissed me. His scent—an earthy mix of something peppery and something sweet—filled my nose. Pulling away, he unbuttoned my Levi's. They fell to the floor at my feet.

"I've missed you," he said. He laughed, as if the idea of missing me could not exactly be taken seriously, but then he kissed me again, and the kiss was very serious indeed.

I set my hands on his forearms and squeezed, willing him to wrap his hands around my throat as he had before. An oblique gesture, a sidelong way of making the request, but he seemed to understand. He laid his hands on either side of my neck and gently pressed his thumbs into the hollow at the base of my neck.

Taking me by the hand, he led me to the bedroom. Bronze light from the bedside lamp made plain the path to my bed. He laid me across it. Still clothed, he lay atop me. His knee pressed my erection down between my thighs, pinioned it. Painful, yes, but no pain had ever pleased me more.

He kissed me, stroked my bare shoulders, chest, hips. Again, his hands grasped my throat. His weight trapped me.

But then he rolled us over, so that I lay astride his lean body. I undressed him. Half-crazed, I feasted on him, on his soft mouth, his broad neck, the damp knots of hair in his armpits, his stiff nipples, his belly, his pulsing cock. He moaned. In this position I could not have all of him. How maddening that I could not have all of him. I moved on: his perineum, dark and fragrant with sweat; his legs, broad and solid; his feet, long and gnarled. Crouching on the edge of the bed, looking up at him looking down at me, I took both of his big toes into my mouth at once.

"Get up here," he said, chuckling. He beckoned with two fingers. "Get your butt up here."

I dragged my body along his until our mouths met. I eased off him and nestled against his side. His hand traced the curve of my back. I wrapped my fist around his erection and stroked it gently.

"You want it?" he said.

No way existed for me to give my answer the emphasis and power it deserved. Perhaps if I could have scrawled it across the sky or used my own blood as ink, I could have come close. My answer came out in a ragged whisper.

Reaching for the bedside table, he switched off the light. Silver and green spots danced before my eyes.

He flipped me onto my belly and knelt astride my legs. He lowered himself over me. I held my breath, braced myself. He spat noisily. He entered me in one thorough, excruciating drive. I clutched a pillow to my face. Heedless of my squirming, he fucked me with thrusts long and savage. I cried into the pillow.

After a time the pain ceased. At every instant it seemed I might explode. I slipped my hand between my cock and the sheets, and the mere brush of my fingers finished me.

Panting and hollering, Spike drove hard to his own end. He collapsed against me. The rise and fall of his chest beat a crazy cadence on my back. His sweat drenched my body. He stroked my hair and nuzzled my ear.

Abruptly, apropos of nothing, he laughed.

"What?" I said.

"I guess neither one of us got our fill last weekend."

"I called you, but I didn't know you gave me your pager. I left a stupid message." I was glad that, in the dark, he couldn't see me blush.

"I called you, too. But you"—here he bit my earlobe, a little too hard—"are the last person on earth without an answering machine."

"You didn't—? That is to say, did you—? Did you drive all this way just to—."

He shook his head. The patch of whiskers below his lip brushed my shoulder. "I'm flying out tomorrow."

"*Flying?*" I said, too loud. I cleared my throat. I turned to face him. He laid his leg over my hip. "Where to?"

"Los Angeles." He grinned. "I'm resurrecting my porn career. I got a call from an old friend of mine. He's been trying to put something together, and a guy dropped out at the last minute."

All at once a dozen highlights of his earlier performances came to mind. Spike kneeling. Spike on all fours. Spike in a sling. I rolled away from him and sat on the edge of the bed. I turned on the light. "What kind of—? I mean, will you be—?"

Blinking, squinting against the light, he arranged some pillows against the headboard. He sat up against them. He stroked his sticky thigh, smoothing flat the black hairs there. "He wants someone ... aggressive. Someone *mean*, actually."

"Mean?"

There was a mischievous twinkle in his eye. He nodded. "'Mean as shit' were his exact words."

I swallowed hard. "What is it, some kind of—?" Some kind of what? I didn't exactly know what I meant to ask.

Leaning forward, he grabbed a hank of my hair and dragged me toward him. His teeth knocked against mine. He drove his tongue deep into my mouth. He let go, shoved me away from him. I nearly toppled off the bed.

"Like that," he said. A few flame-red hairs had come loose from my scalp; he sprinkled them on the floor. "Mean as shit."

My heart hammered in my chest. I saw that he was hard again, and then that I was, too. My mouth was dry. I licked my lips. "Do you want to—? That is to say, do you need to rehearse?"

◆　◆　◆

My hunger was bottomless. I fed on him, and could not get my fill. Hours earlier I'd imagined myself at Michael Walrath's feet, flattened against the floor, crawling and begging, worshipful, penitent. With Spike I got my wish, and it seemed I couldn't go low enough.

He stepped on me, trampled me, and yet I could not go low enough. He called me names, made me repeat the names he called me. He bent me over his knee, struck and heated my skin with the palms of his hands. I could not get my fill.

At some point, when we were in the living room, he cranked the stereo and set the needle on the platter. The Great Fugue, the goblin march. He laughed at me, kicked my thighs lightly with his bare toes, ridiculed my taste in music. Spike—the subject—dragged me—his countersubject, his answer—along behind him, molding me, forcing me to obey his mysterious purposes, to accommodate whatever remote and inscrutable harmonies he had in mind.

I could not fucking get enough.

By midnight, sweat dripped from our bodies. My skin felt branded and bruised. My knees and hips and jaw ached. Spike said, "I need to blow a fucking joint. Want some?"

My jeans still lay in the entryway. Spike put them on. They were a snug fit, inches too short. Without even buttoning the fly he dashed barefoot and shirtless to his car. Lying naked across the sofa, I watched him through the open door. His car was a great beast of a thing, green-gold in the weird light of the streetlamps. When he returned with a bag of weed and a stack of rolling papers, I sat up to make room for him on the sofa. He said, "This is some good shit. Blow-your-fucking-mind kind of shit."

Sitting next to me, hip to hip, he rolled a joint on the mud-stained knee of my Levi's. With dainty pinches he crumbled the buds into flakes and fragments. He rolled the paper and licked the glue with the darting tip of his tongue. As he passed me the unlit fatty and a lighter, I said, "I never—. That is to say, what do I—?"

He laughed. "Just watch what I do, and do the same."

He lit up. Sucked the smoke deep, swallowed and held it. Again he passed me the joint. I did as he had done. He exhaled sweet smoke and took another drag.

"Good shit, right?"

I nodded, but in point of fact I felt nothing. We smoked. Beethoven still played on the stereo, more softly now. It was not the Great Fugue. I thought it might be the C-sharp minor quartet. Certainly I felt the C minor mood in spades, as Tory had put it.

"What is this?" he asked me. He nodded toward the stereo. "I don't get your taste in music at all."

I shrugged. "It's Beethoven. I heard it on the radio. I got hooked somehow."

Curls of blue smoke escaped his lips. "Highbrow shit. Kind of stuffy." He kissed my ear. "You don't strike me as the stuffy type. Stuffed, maybe." He licked my neck.

When nothing remained of the joint but a smoking twist of paper, I at last felt a tingle, a buzz, a slight giddiness. I couldn't help thinking that beer would be cheaper, easier to get, and more effective.

As if he'd read my mind, Spike said, "Got any beer?"

I shook my head. "There's a bar more or less around the corner. A block and a half, two blocks. A gay bar."

He sucked the roach, glared at it as if reproving it for insufficient longevity. Pinching it delicately between thumb and forefinger, he sucked it again. "What time is it?"

The VCR clock blinked a series of zeroes. I couldn't remember the last time

I'd touched or looked at the clock in the kitchen. I went to check the alarm clock in the bedroom. When I came back, I told him, "Almost twelve-thirty."

"Let's go."

We didn't trouble to shower or even to wash our hands. We dressed in a hurry. As we walked, Spike draped his arm over my shoulder, held my body close against his. I glanced around, following with my eyes the cars that passed us. I couldn't stop thinking that his public display of affection and proprietorship would someday soon be repaid with more Stinson bumper stickers.

•   •   •

The Town House was crowded and too warm, rippling with blue neon light. A slow, sweet Mary Chapin Carpenter song played too loudly. Hugging couples filled the dance floor. In a chilly corner near the door, we found a stretch of empty wall and leaned against it.

"Get me a beer," Spike said. His tone was lordly, masterful. I didn't quite trust myself with a reply.

I wriggled through sweat-damp bodies. At the bar, I ordered two beers. With an ostentatious display of self-control, the bartender began naming all the beers on tap. I seized on the third, MGD. As the bartender filled two plastic cups, the song changed. Two men near me were kissing. Even over the din of a Brooks and Dunn two-step remix, even over the scuff and clomp of a hundred boots on the dance floor, I heard the wet smack of the men's lips and tongues.

When I returned to our place by the door, Spike had gone. Standing on tiptoe by the wall, I looked for him. Far across the dance floor, facing away, wasn't that his sheepskin jacket? Balancing the beers, keeping my eyes fixed on the sheepskin jacket, I worked my way through the crowd.

Halfway across the room, an arm blocked my path. I stopped short, spilled a little of one beer onto my own feet, barely avoided spilling the other. The arm was Spike's. A tall, bone-skinny man with red hair stood very close to him. The redhead leaned toward Spike, his head turned so that his ear was near Spike's mouth. I handed Spike his beer. He took it, but otherwise ignored me.

To the redhead he said, "We're just around the corner. A block and a half, two blocks."

We? I thought. I gulped my beer.

They turned slightly away from me, and I could hear only random words of their conversation. More than once, I thought I heard Spike say, "red on red," but I couldn't be sure.

The redhead wore jeans and pointy-toed cowboy boots and some kind of taupe mechanic's shirt with the unlikeliest of names—Jose—stitched in blue above the breast pocket. His face was smooth, shiny, unlined, as pink as sunburn. His orange hair was thin on top, swept back from his high forehead in parallel waves, cascading in damp-looking curls at the back of his head. A brambly strawberry-blond goatee surrounded his wide mouth. With a start, with a catch in my throat, I realized that, though he was undeniably one of the ugliest men I had ever seen, he was nevertheless oddly sexy.

I'd drunk barely a quarter of my beer, and Spike had not touched his, and yet suddenly it seemed we were leaving. With a hand in the small of my back, Spike guided me toward the door. I stumbled over his booted feet and spilled beer on Jose's arm.

"Oh my God," I said, "I'm so sorry."

Brushing droplets of gold from his sleeve, Jose looked at me. He said nothing. He grinned and licked his lips. With pale eyes, pinkish in the neon lights, he looked at me as if I were some kind of crackling-skinned roast, just drawn from the oven, that he could not wait to devour.

Out on the street, Spike and Jose walked a couple of steps ahead of me. At Pascal they stopped, conferred. I thought I heard Spike say something about "growlers."

I felt hazy, sluggish, as if somewhere in my brain a few random plugs had been yanked from their sockets. The traffic light changed. Belatedly I realized that Spike and Jose were crossing Pascal. I hurried after them.

On the far corner, Spike stopped so abruptly that I nearly collided with him. "Are there any brew pubs around here?" he asked me.

"Brew pubs? *Here?* Whaddya talk?"

He sighed and looked around. He turned back to me. "How much cash have you got?"

I dug out my wallet. I flipped through the bills it contained—twenty, five, five, one, one, one. "Thirty-eight dollars," I said. I opened my wallet again, squinted at the bills. I recounted. "Thirty-three dollars."

He sighed again. He held out his hand. "Let me have it."

Balling up the money in his fist, he strode down University. He and Jose laughed and knocked shoulders. At that hour, anyone who might be out on the street had some sort of debauchery or villainy in mind, surely, but even so, as people turned to watch us pass, I felt unclean. I thought I must reek of sex, pot, and beer. It was breezy out on the street—a cold wind blew, smelling of mud and car exhaust—and I hoped it was enough to hide or dissipate whatever stench clung to me. I scampered behind Spike and Jose, feeling like some kind of criminal, like a fugitive from respectability.

We passed the Spin Cycle, an abandoned warehouse, the Ragstock. We stopped. Spike disappeared into the Trend Bar, a dive I'd never had the nerve to enter. Jose stood at the curb, staring at his tiny, distorted reflection in the wavy mirrored windows of a bank across the street. I slumped against the brick façade of the Trend Bar. I felt weary and out of sorts. Whatever Spike had in mind—whatever it was, who knew what it was?—I couldn't help thinking that a few hours' sleep might be more in line with what I needed.

Spike emerged from the Trend Bar with a case of Budweiser. Jose looked sore impressed. To Jose, Spike said, "You just have to know the magic words. I told him I had a pretty little girl all lined up to go down on me, if I could just her get drunk enough."

Jose laughed.

Spike said, "Told him it was her first blow job, and she was nervous. A little shy, don't you know."

I looked at Spike, at Jose, at Spike again. So, then, this made me the pretty little girl?

Spike hefted the cardboard box, and I saw, with alarm, that he intended to hand it to me. I held out my arms just in time to catch it.

◆ ◆ ◆

As I led Jose up the front walk, Spike stopped at his car. Carrying a box of cassettes under his arm, he followed us into the house. I spun the thermostat to seventy-five degrees. Spike popped in a cassette and cranked the stereo. With one finger he slid all of the equalizer levers to the tops of their tracks. A crazy bass-heavy dance beat rattled the windows. The equalizer's LED lights shimmered in the dark.

Jose found some candles, set them around the room in bowls and mugs, lit them. In surprise I watched him; I didn't even know I *owned* candles. I couldn't imagine where or how he had found them.

Spike lit a joint. We smoked.

With the base of a Bic lighter, Jose popped the caps off three beers. He passed them around. We drank.

The music was as different from a Beethoven string quartet as music could be, and yet it was, even so, just another kind of goblin march, so dense with overlapping bass and drum lines that it sounded viscous, nearly tangible. My mind was hazy. My body moved to the music. I danced for them as they sat on the couch, side by side, watching me, hands in each other's laps. Without exactly knowing what I was doing or why I was doing it, I took off my clothes. Under my breath, so that they couldn't hear, I sang, "Oh, you're gonna see a Sheba shimmy shake."

For the first time, Jose spoke to me, only to say, "Aye, it's a wee little thing." Whether he meant all of me or only a part, and whether the thick Scottish burr of his consonants was genuine or the engine of some obscure joke at my expense, I didn't know. And why, with all of the possibilities equally likely— with, indeed, the possibility that all were true at once—why my dick began to harden, I couldn't have begun to explain.

Jose stood and joined me in the shimmy shake. His clothes dropped to the carpet around us. And then, in the middle of the floor, he and I wove our limbs together. Red on red.

Spike watched us. Candlelight flickered across his face. The cherry of his joint glowed crimson.

•   •   •

Early the next afternoon, I woke alone in the stained wreckage my bed. Spike had gone. Jose had gone.

I searched the house for a note, for evidence of theft. The Ziploc bag in which Spike had brought his pot, yes. The cereal bowl we'd used as an ashtray, filled with crumpled and twisted and black-edged hanks of rolling papers, yes. Bowls and mugs filled with ossified puddles of white wax, yes. Two dozen empty brown Budweiser bottles, yes. A piss-colored, vaguely heart-shaped stain where Jose had spilled most of a bottle of beer, yes. A stray athletic sock, alarmingly streaked with something brown, yes. The taste of both Spike and Jose in my mouth, the smell of them both on my skin, yes. Evidence of theft, thankfully, no. A note from either of them, a phone number from Jose, no. Anything showing Jose's true name—for it could hardly be Jose—no.

What had I done? What in the hell had I been thinking?

In the small hours, in the hissing heat of the overburdened radiators, it had all seemed so natural, one thing flowing from another. There had been three of us—Spike, Jose, Jonah. The possibilities had seemed endless.

In the light of day, there was only Jonah, naked, achy, cold.

12 GRIEVING SONGS

Hours stretched before me. Hours more to get through before sleep, and I could not imagine how I would make it. If I stood, I wanted to sit. If I sat, I wanted to stand. My heart shimmied in my chest. Nothing was right. Everything was wrong.

Except for the knocking radiators, the house was silent. Humidity and silence weighed on me like physical burdens. I felt my back hunching and couldn't seem to straighten myself.

I lowered the thermostat and turned on the stereo. I needed noise, music, something to calm and distract me. I couldn't face the Great Fugue. It was the soundtrack of my shame. For the rest of my days, I was sure, the goblin march would make me feel the mix of disgust and remorse I felt now.

Something else, perhaps. Karen Holmes. Julie Andrews. Something wholesome. A spoonful of sugar to help the medicine go down.

As I'd suspected, Beethoven's C-sharp minor quartet, side seventeen, lay on the turntable. I set the needle at the beginning of the first track.

Almost as soon as the music started—yet another fugue, sober and mournful—I craved silence again. I stopped the record.

I called Barbara. While the phone trilled in my ear, I leaned over and picked up the stray sock. It was not my sock. Gingerly and from the distance of a couple of inches, I sniffed it and caught the iron tang of blood. Not what I'd expected, but not exactly a relief. I let the phone ring twenty times. No answer. Of course. Barbara was asleep, possibly with the phone unplugged.

I called Luther. No answer. Just as well. What would I say to Luther? What would I say to Erma?

I called Christa, hoping that Tory wouldn't answer. Tory answered. Of course. Of course, Tory *would* answer.

I asked for Christa. He said, "She's in Hudson, visiting her mother."

"How did *that* happen?" I asked. Christa's relationship with her mother was, if nothing else, fraught. Almost since the day I'd met Christa, she'd been vowing to cut all ties. Routinely she referred to her mother as "the shrewish harpy" or "the raging bitch."

"Beats me," Tory said.

Something occurred to me. "Are you—? Tory, are you *living* there now?" He emitted a long sigh, but he didn't answer. "I didn't mean to—. You don't have to define your—."

"No, no, it's nothing like that. I still have my place, but I'm here most of the time. It smells a hell of a lot better over here." He laughed.

"Do you know when she'll be back?"

"Ages. Sometime tonight, or possibly tomorrow." He paused, cleared his throat. "Hey," he said. "You know, Christa told me you called in sick yesterday. And you don't sound so hot. Are you okay?"

"To tell the truth, not so great." I closed my eyes, squeezed them tight, braced myself. Tory might be the last person on earth I wanted to spend an afternoon with, but I couldn't face the long empty day on my own. I just couldn't. "Have you had lunch?"

"I was about to make an omelet. Come on over. It's easier to cook for two than one."

"That would be—." What? Awkward? Tense? Hellish? Ah, fuck. What did it matter? "That'd be nice. I'll be over in—." Shit. My car. What the hell was going on with my car? "Wait, sorry, my car's in the shop."

"Fuck the omelet. We can go somewhere. Keys or the Egg and I or somewhere. I'll come get you. Simpson and Sherburne, right?"

"Exactly."

"By the way, did Christa give you that translation from *Doktor Faustus?*" He pronounced the title as a native German speaker would—as Petra would— with the syllables clotted at the back of his throat.

"She did, but then she had a kind of fit, and scattered the pages everywhere, and I couldn't get them back in order. You didn't number them."

"Didn't number—?" He was silent for a moment. "Shit. That was the rough version. I wonder what I did with—." He trailed off. I heard papers rattling.

"It *did* seem a little—."

He sighed. "Awkward. I know. I was just trying to get the sense of it, and then I made a polished version I was going to give you." Again, the crinkle of paper. "I wonder what—."

"It's okay. I appreciate that you thought—."

"Yeah," he said, and then again, "Yeah. Not a big deal." He cleared his throat. "Anyway. Okay. Whatever. I'll be there as soon as I can."

• • •

Forty minutes later, he showed up in a silver Mercedes sedan and, yes, his damned letterman jacket. He also wore a rumpled madras shirt, pink and green plaid, tucked into gray sweatpants.

As I climbed into the passenger's seat, he said, "After we talked, I realized I haven't been home in a while. Okay if we go to my place? I picked up some stuff, brunch stuff."

"Sure," I said. "Whatever you want."

He drove to Snelling, to I-94, to Hennepin. The interior of the Mercedes was sumptuous, the suspension smooth as cream. We might have been riding in someone's living room. All around us, speakers twittered something orchestral, Baroque-sounding, jangling with harpsichord continuo.

"Is this the radio?" I asked him. He nodded. "Any idea what piece?"

"Sounds like the Mozart harp and flute concerto."

Mozart? I would have thought Handel or Bach. I said nothing.

At Twenty-Seventh he veered right. After a couple of blocks, just before Lake of the Isles Parkway, he again turned right, into a driveway, a square of cracked concrete barely large enough to accommodate two cars. He eased the car to a stop so that its nose barely touched the door of a miniscule garage, not much bigger than a potting shed. Or perhaps it *was* a potting shed. There was no way the Mercedes would fit through the door.

"Did you forget to measure the garage door before you picked this car?" I asked him.

Laughing, Tory shook his head. "Everyone says that. I saw it in the window, and I had to have it." He waved his hand to show that he meant the car, not the garage. "I knew I was sentencing myself to years of scraping ice off the windows, but I figured—you know—beauty is pain."

He turned the key and pulled it from the ignition. The sound of the engine not running was identical to the sound of the engine running.

Beyond and above the garage, a clapboard house—two and a half stories high, shallow of roof, broad of eave—sat at the top of a gentle slope. The windows were narrow but many. The clapboards were a greenish shade of taupe. The window frames and soffits were cream and burgundy. Cedar shakes, weathered to a silvery gray, covered the roof.

From the driveway up to the house an evergreen hedge swept in a long fluent curve. Bare mounds of mulch filled beds where, in summer, flowers must grow. On a flagstone patio a grove of potted arborvitae surrounded wrought-iron patio furniture.

This was his "place"? I'd pictured a squalid two-room apartment full of dirty socks and old issues of *Penthouse*. I had, in fact, a pictured a "place" much like my own. I wondered just how bad his "place" could possibly smell, if he preferred Christa's tiny apartment to this.

◆ ◆ ◆

It turned out that the house smelled of nothing—not of decay, not of grime, not of disuse, not of old carpet or of new, not even of cleanser or of furniture polish. Perhaps that was exactly what he'd meant. It didn't smell like a home.

In the living room, the Mission-style furniture sat in two groups. A sofa and loveseat faced a row of windows with a view of the lake. A trio of chairs and another loveseat faced a fireplace. On either side of the fireplace, two vast expanses of built-in shelves contained artful clusters of books and LP's, a turntable and cassette deck and tiny speakers, and a few framed photos. When I saw the LP's, a tiny thrill of kinship hummed in my chest.

As we passed through the living room on the way to the kitchen, Tory shifted his grocery bag from one arm to the other. He waved toward the shelves. "Put on some music if you want," he said. "Anything you like."

He had a lot of Beethoven, including the Guarneri *Complete String Quartets*. He had a lot of *everything*, really—Bach, Handel, Vivaldi, Haydn, Mozart, Schubert, Brahms, Mendelssohn, Tchaikovsky, Smetana, Debussy, Ravel, D'Indy, Delius, Stravinsky, Britten, Barber, Shostakovich. I didn't recognize all the names. Who was Witold Lutosławski? Who was Carlos Chávez? Who was Maria de Alvear?

Tory kept the popular music on the other side of the fireplace, well apart from the classical. He had a lot of Broadway, most of it from the 'twenties, 'thirties, and 'forties. On another shelf, Carole King, Janis Joplin, Bob Dylan, and then a whole row of Billy Joel albums. Did people really listen to Billy Joel? I chose an album at random. *52nd Street*. On the cover, the piano man leaned against a grimy white brick wall. He wore a ridiculous checked sport coat and a more ridiculous frizzy hairstyle. He held, of all things, a trumpet—or was it a cornet?—or a Flugelhorn? I supposed he couldn't very well have held a grand piano, out there in some blighted alleyway in midtown Manhattan.

The first song—"Big Shot," according to the track listing—began with a cacophonous series of chords on crunch guitar. Just as I reached to lift the tone arm from the record, Tory shouted from the kitchen. "Damn," he said. "Good choice. I haven't heard *this* in a while."

I sighed. Best to leave it.

I fled to the kitchen, where at least the noise would be muffled by intervening walls.

Tory was chopping a red bell pepper on a monumental butcher block. In one corner of the block lay tidy piles of diced onion and minced garlic, mounds of tiny gems. On the range, in a steep-sided cast-iron skillet, plump cubes of bacon browned in their own bubbling juices.

"I thought I'd do a frittata," he said. "Kind of like an omelet, but more forgiving."

He flicked bits of pepper off the blade of his knife. With the sharp edge he scooped the onion into his palm and chucked it into the skillet. The perfect squares of onion flesh jigged and sizzled in the bacon fat. The kitchen smelled of salt and smoke. Instantly, I was ravenous.

The cabinets were red oak, polished to a high gloss. Tory opened a cupboard to the left of the sink. He lifted a green ceramic bowl down to the countertop, and in the same motion knocked the door with the back of his hand. The door swung closed smoothly, noiselessly.

"Do you want coffee?" he asked me.

I shrugged. "Sure."

He nodded toward the coffee maker and a stout white canister with a stainless steel lid. "Do you mind making it? The filters are in that drawer underneath."

While he cracked eggs into the green bowl and whisked them to froth, I set about making coffee. When I made coffee at home—something I rarely did—I usually poured hot tap water over a spoonful of Taster's Choice granules. In Tory's kitchen, coffee was apparently a more elaborate affair.

I opened the white canister. I tipped it, stared into its open white mouth. In Tory's kitchen, coffee apparently started with whole beans. The beans slid and crawled toward the lower corner. I stared, and did not know where to begin. A spoon nestled into the beans rattled against the pottery. I flinched. I nearly dropped the canister, but caught it against my belly. Somehow, a handful of beans spilled onto the counter and onto the floor.

The whisk had fallen silent. Tory stood watching me. "Are you okay?" he said.

"I'm not okay," I said. I set the canister on the counter. "I'm as far from okay as—." I stopped.

"What's going on?"

He stood with his back to the window, his face partly in shadow. I had never noticed that his eyes were nearly black. I could not make out where the irises ended and the pupils began.

That first night at the Gay Nineties—could it be, really, less than a week ago?—I'd thought he was young and handsome, then old and sad. In the space of a minute I'd dismissed him, and I'd never bothered to look at him after that. He was not a bad-looking fellow—sturdy square jaw, symmetrical features, well-formed mouth and nose, good bones. And those eyes, gleaming like polished black onyx.

His ash-brown hair, usually neatly parted, was now in handsome disarray. A swirl of brown whiskers filled the hollow of each cheek. I realized that I hadn't shaved in days. I stroked the down on my cheek. By now I must look as if I'd glued scrapings of carrot flesh to my face.

Tears came all too easily to me these days; I fought them back. I straightened. I waved away his question. "It's nothing," I said. "A couple of late nights. I'm just tired."

But his dark eyes did not leave mine. "I know about Tom," he said. "I'm not supposed to say so, but I do. Christa told me."

"She told—?" I felt behind me for the counter. Coffee beans crunched underfoot.

He shrugged, glanced away. "You know how it is," he said. "When you're together with someone, you tell each other things."

"You're *together*?"

His face broke into a grin. He sighed. "I can pretend we are, if we're not. I—. Christa is something else, I'll say that."

"Does she—? That is to say—."

"You're changing the subject. Let me show you something." He nodded toward the living room, where a jazzy flugelhorn solo skittered above a rollicking boogie-woogie accompaniment.

Out of the kitchen, through the living room, down a carpeted hall, up a flight of red oak stairs, and then another flight, he led me. Every couple of steps he glanced back, as if I might at any moment bolt for the front door.

The entire third floor was an open space, a master suite. A majestic platform bed floated in the center, facing a row of floor-to-ceiling windows and a set of French doors that opened onto a three-sided balcony. Snow had begun to fall. Clusters of down drowned themselves in the churning green waters of the lake.

Here as below, shelves filled an entire wall. He led me to them. German novels filled one shelf—Mann, Remarque, Hesse, Grass. On the shelf below, poetry. Baudelaire and Verlaine in red cloth, Whitman in green buckram, Crane in tooled leather. I ran my hand along the spines. My fingers tingled.

"Were you an English major?" I asked him.

He shook his head. "Just an enthusiast."

On the bottom shelf at the far end of the room there was a wooden box. He sat on the floor, opened the box. From it he took a sheaf of onion-skin paper and a stack of photographs. He tossed the photos back into the box. Cradling the pages against his belly, he flipped through them. I sat beside him.

He handed me a thin stack of yellowed paper. The first page bore a title in hard-struck majuscules.

GRIEVING SONGS

BY TORSTEN SCHMITT

Torsten? "Tory is short for Torsten?" I said.

"If your name were Torsten, wouldn't you shorten it to Tory?"

"Point taken."

"My dad was going through some kind of genealogical craze when I was born. I was named after some ancestor back in Hamburg. Read."

I turned the page. Another title.

CRIMSON, ORANGE, AND GOLD

The commas had bored holes in the paper.

Beneath the title, a poem.

> We walk along the river side by side.
> The light is failing. He is failing too,

Although he has some strength yet to concede.
The autumn air is warm but growing cool.
Along the path the leaves are crimson, orange, and gold,
Like crackling fire beneath our feet.

I looked up. Tory watched me with brimming eyes.

"What is this?" I asked him.

"I wrote it after Adam died. My brother. My older brother. He was—. I worshiped him, but—." A tear streamed down his cheek. With the back of his hand he wiped it away. "Read."

I read. The poem described a walk along the river—*the* river? *my* river? the Mississippi? The narrator's companion—Adam, presumably—explained how autumn was his favorite time of year. Crisp weather, football games, dances, leaves turning crimson, orange, and gold. For the sake of appearances, to live up to expectation, it seemed, Adam had taken girls to the dances. But then, afterward, after a quick peck on the cheek and a courteous farewell, he had gone to the beach—Bare Ass Beach, obviously, though the poem didn't give it that name.

My face was hot. "Your brother was gay?" I said.

Tory nodded. "He hid it for as long as he could. He was the captain of the football team, everyone's idea of the red-blooded American male." He reached into the box, handed me a photo.

In the photo, a much younger Tory stood arm in arm with a slightly older, somewhat blonder, much handsomer version of himself—Adam. In the photo, Tory looked like a German club president, a drama club geek, a band fag. In the photo, Adam looked like a soap opera star, a matinee idol, a presidential hopeful, a prince. In the photo, I could not help noticing, Adam—not Tory—wore a red letterman jacket.

I looked at Tory. I tipped the picture toward him, tapping Adam's jacket. "That jacket you wear all the time? It's his?" He nodded. I felt like shit. I stared at the photo.

"As soon as he graduated, he was gone, off to San Francisco."

I glanced down at the poem. Words jumped out at me: *night sweats, wasting, lesions.* I swallowed hard. "I can guess the rest."

"He died in nineteen-eighty-eight. He was thirty years old."

"Tory, I'm so sorry."

"I wanted to show you this because I wanted you to know—." He kept his eyes, and his hands, in his lap. "I wanted you to know that I know about loss." Now he looked at me. "I would never be the kind of person who would say, 'I know how you feel,' but I know something about loss."

From our place on the floor, the windows were narrow rectangles of pearl-gray light. Snowflakes dashed themselves against the glass, melted, dribbled down in rivulets and meanders. A cardinal darted toward the French doors, lighted on the balcony railing. The bird darted away, a red stain on the vellum sky. I turned back to Tory.

"Lately," I said, "I've been thinking I need to reexamine all of my interpersonal connections."

"Where does that leave me?"

"Your stock is rising."

His smile was broad, toothy—heart-breaking. If he put so much stock in *my* opinion—. Well, wasn't that just *sad?*

"Were you on good terms when he died? You and Adam?"

Tory cleared his throat. "We were closer than ever. He and my parents were estranged, but we—he and I—were very close. He lived with me, here, until—. I was with him—." He blinked and sniffled. "It's all in the poems. It's probably easier if you read the poems."

The pages crinkled, slipped to the floor. I caught them and straightened the stack. "Tom and I fought a lot," I told him. "Thinking back on it now, I guess we—. We were probably together just because in college, we didn't really know any other gay people. We were both just *there.*"

I looked up. Tory bit his lip. He nodded. "I've had a few relationships like that."

"I *did* love him. Don't get me wrong. But maybe—. Maybe it was all one-sided. Or maybe we were just too different. I don't know."

Tory said, "I guess it makes the grief even harder. There are mixed feelings. It's hard to know what to feel."

"I know he wanted out, but didn't exactly know how to tell me. Maybe he—. Maybe it wasn't an accident, the alcohol poisoning."

He flinched as if I'd slapped him. "You don't really think he would have—."

"I don't know. Maybe I was so hard to live with that—."

"That's crazy, Jonah." He glared at me as if he were extremely angry with me. His eyes were fierce. "Absolutely insane."

"I guess you're right." I shifted my weight. The carpet was lush, but it hurt to sit on the floor.

All at once Tory turned away, sniffing the air. "Motherfucker," he said. "The bacon's burning."

• • •

The bacon was black. No longer gems, the cubes of onion were tiny charcoal briquettes. The char lay in a scum of stinking black grease.

Tory switched on the range fan and opened the windows in the breakfast nook. Cold, clean-smelling air flooded the kitchen.

From a cabinet under the stove Tory fetched a new skillet. He scrambled the eggs with shredded cheddar. I made coffee. It took me many long minutes to figure it out, but as the carafe slowly filled, the brew looked more or less like coffee.

At the same moment, Tory and I both noticed that the stereo had gone silent, that the record had ended. We stood facing each other, our heads cocked, listening to a faint hiss from the other room. Somewhere in the depths of the house a boiler or furnace thrummed.

"I'll go," he said. After a time, a factory whistle ushered in a lively syncopated piano riff. The riff halted briefly, and Billy Joel sang something about living in Allentown. Maybe people in Allentown listened to Billy Joel.

Tory closed the windows, and he and I sat in the breakfast nook at a round table barely larger than our stoneware plates. Tory set out a jug of cream and a bowl of sugar cubes. The creamer and sugar bowl matched the plates. Our forks matched each other. The napkins matched the tablecloth. In Tory's kitchen, apparently, everything matched.

I was more willing, now, to tell Tory the whole tale. Even so, I wasn't sure where to start. I began with Eliot's invitation to group, and got somehow sidetracked with a detailed description of Charlie's tasseled loafers.

"Chaussure," Tory said.

"Chaussure?" I pronounced the word carefully, mimicking him as closely as I could manage.

"Footwear. I always think of tasseled loafers as the chaussure of the pompous. They can hardly be called shoes. They are *chaussure*."

I squinted at him, unsure what to make of this.

"Never mind," Tory said. "Go on."

I told him about the members of the group, describing each man and the tenor of the group's conversation.

In the living room, the music had gone silent. I half-turned, thinking I would volunteer, this time, to change the record, but then there were wind chimes, a helicopter, chords on piano, climbing, climbing.

Licking a string of cheddar from his fork, Tory said, "Adam used to call them Kinsey queers."

"Kinsey queers?"

"Have you ever read the Kinsey report?" I shook my head. "I'm not sure why it was—probably something to do with the era—but when Kinsey set out to explore human sexuality, he found that gay men tended to be rather effeminate and campy. He depicted them sitting around talking in double entendre and quotes from Broadway shows."

I blushed. "I think I may have been the only one quoting show tunes, but the rest of them definitely were fond of the double entendre. The single entendre, too, for that matter."

"So you didn't feel particularly comfortable."

"It turned out not to be such a kick, but not just because of that. It turned out—the chaussure guy told me—they all think of themselves as formerly gay."

"Ah. An ex-gay ministry."

"Ex-gay?" I said.

"That's what they call it."

"Ex-gay. Ridiculous. I don't understand how you can become ex-gay, any more than you can become ex-straight."

"People like that take over the word 'Christian,' you know, and 'morality,' as though they're the only ones who can say what those words mean. Why was it again you ended up spending an evening with these formerly homosexual men?"

"Believe me, I wouldn't have seen the show if I'd read the *Playbill*."

"Deception as a means of bringing someone to reality. Excellent."

I thought about that for a moment. Something in me, some warm place in the center of my heart, refused to connect the Eliot whose hand on my shoulder had comforted me with the passive-aggressive Eliot who'd hid in the kitchen while his "ex-gay" minions plied me with off-color banter. "I think it was just a horrible misunderstanding," I said.

"That's some misunderstanding," Tory said.

I told him how it had happened, how Eliot had rescued me from Dr. Bell's office, and how he'd made me easy on a hard day. "It all has to do with Tom, I guess. I guess I was—. I was crazy with grief."

Tory sipped his coffee. He grimaced. "A little strong," he said.

"My first time. Sorry."

He lifted the white jug and spilled cream into his cup until the coffee turned pale. "Grief can make you do crazy things, especially in a case like yours. The shame of it is that this Eliot person offered you the right remedy, but with some unpleasant strings attached."

"I expected this group to be gay men who were struggling to get back some sort of spiritual life."

"I think the ex-gay stuff is all bullshit. God is for everyone. That's what the pastor of my church says more or less every Sunday. In God there is neither Jew nor gentile, neither slave nor free, neither male nor female, and if Paul were writing today he'd add, neither gay nor straight. Do you think it might do you some good to talk to him?"

As he spoke, I felt a familiar closing-in, the accustomed wish to run. I suppressed it, deflected it with a joke. "Hasn't Paul been dead for a couple thousand years?" Tory gave me a grave look. I cleared my throat. "I've never really been a church kind of person."

"Of course. I understand."

"That is to say, I haven't been to church in ages. I might get more from some one-on-one time, rather than just diving in. What denomination is it?" I said.

"Lutheran"

"Not Missouri Synod, I take it."

"Not Missouri Synod."

"What do you get out of it?" I said. "From church, I mean. When I was four, it was all Kool-Aid and cartoon pictures of Noah's Ark."

"First, there are all the social things, the friends you make, and the support structure you grow into. Everyone around you is on the same journey you are. There are people all around you trying to learn from the same mistakes, trying to navigate the same dark waters. And then, like I said, when Adam died, I got a lot of comfort from being among sympathetic people."

I had barely touched my eggs. Tory pointed at my plate. "No good?" he said.

"It's delicious. I'm not all that hungry." The sizzling onions had whetted my appetite, but then the burnt bacon had dulled it. In the air, still, there was a whiff of charred flesh.

He stacked my plate on top of his. Standing, he took them both to the sink. I had left his poems on the counter, near the coffee maker. He picked them up and, riffling the pages, brought them back with him to the table. He set the stack between us.

"Do you pray?" he asked me.

"Isn't it a kind of crutch?" I said. These were Barbara's words; I heard them in her voice. "Isn't it a way of abdicating thought and responsibility? A way of going all Scarlett O'Hara? As if to say, 'I'll think about it tomorrow—let God think about it today'?"

Tory laughed, a low long chuckle in his throat. "For me it's a kind of meditation. I came to it out of grief, sort of a cry to the heavens. I made demands, demanded answers. A 'who the fuck do you think you are?' kind of thing. Now it's a way to keep me sane. I'm a lawyer, you know."

I hadn't known. I fell silent, thinking how I might factor his profession into my increasingly complex view of him. I flipped through the pages he had set on the table. The final poem, "The River in Winter," began:

> The river, in winter, is not a river at all,
> But a white plain of glitter and glare,
> The prismatic dazzle of light and ice.

I read a few more lines. The river was a symbol of something—life, death, I couldn't quite make out what.

> Far beneath in the earth's deep flesh,
> In the flanks, in the cavities and bones,
> As some say Eve was hidden in Adam's rib,

> The spring is hidden. The promise of summer's
> green lies beneath the winter's white.

The words sang in my head, composing their own melody. It was a halting kind of tune, rising, falling, rising again.

"Have you ever thought of setting this to music?"

Tory nodded. "That was the idea," he said. "A song cycle, sort of Schubertian. Like *Winterreise* or *Die schöne Müllerin*. That's why I used the word 'songs.' I tried to add music, but I don't have any talent for it."

In college, for Dr. Benton's composition class, I'd set a group of Emily Dickinson poems as art songs. All of them I'd set as waltzes. I'd been thinking of Brahms's *Liebeslieder Walzer*. I'd never enjoyed a composition assignment more. "I'd like to take a shot at it. Is this your only copy? Can I take it with me?"

"I have copies." He waved toward the pages. "Take it."

He wrapped his hands around his coffee cup, cradled it to his chest, as if he needed to warm himself. He stared out the window into the side yard. I looked, too. The hedges and mulched flower beds were freaked with snow. A pair of squirrels romped across the grass and scampered up an oak tree.

He said, "It helps me to know that there might be—that there *is*—some being greater than myself watching me, yes, to see if I do the right thing, but also watching *over* me to help pick up the pieces when I do the wrong thing."

"Right and wrong. No two people can seem to agree about this business of right and wrong."

"Say again?" Tory said. He set his cup on the table and leaned toward me.

"You and your pastor believe that God is for everyone. Sam Stinson doesn't. Anders Thorstensen doesn't." I snorted. "I had just this conversation with Eliot."

"What did he say?"

"That the important thing—." This took some thought. My head had been all in a jumble at the time. "That the important thing was my relationship with God, what I needed it to be, not what other people said it should be."

Tory said, "I can't disagree with that. However reprehensible his ex-gay ministry might be, I can't fault him for telling you that."

"I suppose in theory it all sounds lovely. A big bearded father figure in the sky, taking care of everything. On the other hand, it's kind of ridiculous, isn't it? A big bearded father figure in the sky, taking care of everything? Ridiculous. Obviously, no one's taking care of anything, or there wouldn't be war, or famine, or genocide." I lifted my coffee cup. The coffee was strong indeed; the very smell nauseated me. I put the cup down again. "Or alcohol poisoning."

"Men make war, not God. And God gives men free will. We're all free to throw away our lives and our souls, if that's what we want to do."

In the hedges alongside the house, a cardinal bathed itself in the deepening snow. It might have been the same bird I had seen from the bedroom, but I couldn't be sure. White fluff clung to its back and wings. It shook and snapped its tiny body, casting off the snow, and in the same motion it took to the sky.

"I don't really want to debate theology," I told Tory. "I'm sure you know more about it. You know more—." I was about to say that he knew more than

I did about everything, but I could hear the bitterness creeping into my voice. I took a breath. "You know more about it than I do, I'm sure. I haven't given the subject much thought in a very long time."

Tory sipped his coffee. He stared out the window. Or, rather, he had turned his face in the direction of the window; his eyes seemed unfocused, the eyes of a blind man. "I don't know that much about theology, actually," he said. He took another sip of coffee. With a grimace he set down his cup. "Cold." He looked at me now, no longer blind. "What I think you're saying, really, is that you want some kind of proof, some evidence that God is there, listening, watching, ready to help. That's not how it works. Proof and faith are two different things. In a sense, they're opposites."

"That's convenient."

"Faith is illogical. By definition, it's illogical. It makes no sense. It's not meant to. Why should it?"

"It's not like I need a burning bush. It just seems like there's nothing. I'd feel stupid praying to nothing."

"Silence isn't the same thing as absence. Maybe if God is silent, it's because he wants us to work harder to find him." He cocked his head. The stereo had gone quiet again. "Speaking of silence, time to turn that record."

While he was gone, I flipped through the pages of his poetry. One of the poems was called "fuck."

> fuck hospitals
> fuck IV drips
> fuck the ER
> fuck ICU

I felt a knot in my throat. I read on. The poem ran on and on without punctuation, almost entirely in lower case, cursing oxygen, plastic tubing, syringes.

> fuck all of this
> fuck life fuck death
> fuck doctors and
> fuck nurses and
>
> fuck God who won't
> listen when all

I want is one
more fucking day

One more fucking day. In my mind's ear I heard the poem as a song. Or not as a song, perhaps, but rather as a kind of countertenor shriek, accompanied by crashing chords on piano and dissonant triple-stopped squeals on violin.

One more fucking day. One more fucking day.

If I set this poem to music, I would string out those last few syllables until the singer's voice wearied under the strain and the tuneless tune rankled the audience to the point of distraction. I would turn this poem into the Great Fugue—the goblin march—of art songs.

I stared at the poem's final stanza.

fuck God who won't
listen when all
I want is one
more fucking day

The typescript blurred before my eyes. Tears came at last. Tory returned from the living room. He stood over me, stroking my hair. Tears came and came. He squatted, his hand between my shoulder blades, stroking, softly stroking.

"That one gets to me, too," he said, softly. "The sheer rage. It's a kind of wall you have to climb over. The anger blocks the sorrow. After the sorrow, there's the acceptance, and eventually—. Well, it takes a long time, but eventually there's gratitude."

He stood, dragged his chair around the table. He sat. I wiped away tears. I looked at him.

"It's okay," he said. "It's okay to be angry. It's okay to be sad. It's okay to *feel.*"

Something in my heart snapped. It was a physical sensation, as if a rib had cracked. The fearsome thing, the hideous thing, I'd thought to stave off at last happened.

After the salt came the sweet. My heart grew still. I heard no small voice, I felt no unearthly presence. But in my ears there rushed a blood song; just as I grew still, I also surged. The fear was gone, the wall breached, and on the other side, calm. Was this conversion?

"Have you gone and made me Lutheran now?" I asked him. My breath rattled in my throat.

"There are worse things, my friend. There are worse things."

PART TWO

13 NOTHING

The sun sank behind a hill. Engines whining, the plane banked over the blackening bay and leveledw on approach. The landing was bumpy and swift. As the plane came to a shuddering stop at the gate, I grew jittery, restless, hectic in anticipation: Barbara was just on the other end of the Jetway.

And so it was. She stood at the front of the waiting crowd, her hands folded primly across her belly. When she saw me, she raced toward me, squealing, and wrapped herself around me. Sunglasses sat atop her frosted bob; our hug knocked them off. As I bent to retrieve them, I noticed that she wore a long, reed-slender black skirt, the hem a kind of hobble around her ankles.

"What on earth is going on with this skirt?" I said.

"Nowadays all the young ladies wear them this long."

"The young ladies? What does that have to do with you?"

"Mind your manners." She slapped my shoulder. "If this skirt were any more chic it would speak French. Did they feed you on the plane?"

"They tried to, but I was too smart for them. Have you noticed how they always store those little carts right next to the biffy? I find that kind of creepy."

"Do you have luggage?" she said.

I carried only my leather jacket and a canvas tote bag big enough for *The Seventeen Quartets* and a notebook containing blank staff paper and Tory's poems. I lifted the bag. "You didn't raise me to travel *this* light," I said.

Arm in arm we strolled away from the gate. She peered at me sidelong.

"Are you growing a beard?" she asked me. "I've never seen you with a beard."

I stroked my cheek. By now the whiskers there were long and stiff. Whether the growth amounted to a beard, I couldn't say; I couldn't remember the last time I'd looked in a mirror for more than a couple of seconds. I shrugged. "I've just been kind of lazy lately."

Lazy wasn't exactly the word for it. After my apparent catharsis at Tory's, after my initial euphoria, I'd felt mostly numb. Each night I'd slept long and dreamless hours. Each morning the alarm clock had buzzed me awake. Each day I'd gotten myself to the office. I had somehow plodded through my duties, had somehow finished *Onslaught*, had somehow put together a coherent book report for Martin. Some of the refinements—cleaning, laundry, shaving, eating—had gradually come to seem irrelevant.

"Do you disapprove?" I asked her.

Too quickly, she said, "No, no, no, not at all. Just surprised, is all. I've never seen you with so much as a stray whisker."

A knot of people had stacked up behind a pair of stooped old ladies who shambled along in the very center of the concourse. We slowed, hanging back until the crowd cleared. As we passed the old women, I noticed first that they were dressed just alike, and then that they *were* just alike. Twins.

We passed the beeping white sally ports and humming black conveyors of the security checkpoint. In the blue cavern of the ticketing level we passed a skycap, a hunched and rounded little man, his uniform all askew, the backs of his shoes folded down under his white-stockinged heels. Arms crossed, cap tilted over one eye, he leaned against the back of a motorized cart. Barbara stopped cold. She lifted her chin and set her shoulders in a way that usually meant trouble. I hung back while she strode over to the skycap. As she spoke to him, her face broke open in a grin, the toothy quintessence of breezy politeness, but the clipped syllables of the only words I could make out—"centenarians" and "hobbling" and "do your damn job"—were sharp and hectoring. Her gesture, too, a wave of the hand in the direction of the concourse, was abrupt, with an austere snap of the wrist.

On the other side of the security checkpoint, the concourse slanted downward. I had to squat slightly to see beyond the slope. The hunchback twins shuffled along the concourse, inexorable and slow, like zombies in a B movie, if zombies wore pink macramé shawls and carried rectangular rattan handbags.

Suddenly Barbara was at my elbow. She said, "I've discovered this new Vietnamese place—."

The skycap's cart whirred as he spun it in a wide arc and pointed it toward the concourse and the zombie twins.

Barbara said, "Well. It's not *new*, precisely. It's been there for twenty years, I'm told, but it's new to *me*, though ironically it's been seven blocks from my house all along."

The skycap helped the twins into the cart. Barbara grasped my elbow and pulled me toward her.

Barbara said, "It's a hole in the wall. One of those places. You know, nothing to look at, but the food is marvelous."

We rode an escalator to the crepuscular cave of baggage claim. The Northwest Airlines carousel loomed in a distant corner.

"Is it me," I said, "or does the light seem dim? I feel as if I'm in a casino."

Barbara made a show of looking around. "Perhaps the odds of your bag arriving are posted somewhere." She giggled. At just that moment, the carousel creaked to life. Metal blades rasped and scraped. A hard-sided orange suitcase rolled up a black conveyer belt and clattered onto the carousel. "Imagine that," Barbara said. "My melodious laughter charms even inanimate objects. Don't roll your eyes at me, young man. Bow before my grace and power."

"What if I just stand here quietly and wait for my luggage instead?"

◆　◆　◆

Barbara had parked her BMW convertible on the roof of the parking ramp. It sat a long way from the elevator, perpendicular to the yellow lines, taking up three spaces. Its black paint shone like the surface of a polished mirror. While Barbara folded the top down, I stowed my jacket and luggage in the narrow trunk.

After the rimy weather of Minnesota, the California air felt silken, balmy. As she drove up the 101 through South San Francisco, though, the air streamed damp and chill through the loose knit of my sweater. I huddled into it. All week I had been wearing it. The collar smelled musky.

Traffic in our direction was sluggish. Far off to my right, in a marina, dozens of boats, their masts as silver-white as winter birches, bobbed in the dark water. Across the bay, the lights of Oakland twinkled like earthbound stars, their reflections drowning in the rippling bay.

Nothing moved in the southbound lanes. On the far side of the highway, a broad basin or reservoir—some brackish-looking backwater of the bay—lay still and shining. Around it a commuter train—a long silver thread—chugged along in a cloud of black diesel smoke.

"Isn't this horrible?" Barbara said. She tapped her horn and dashed across three lanes. "It's getting to be as bad here as in Los Angeles."

"How do you live here?"

Stung, she looked at me. I thought she might cry. "How can you *not*? Everything you could want is right here. *Including* other gay people." She said, "I've been thinking, with everything that's happened, maybe it would do you good to have a change of scene. Get out there. You know, meet some new people."

I thought of Spike's dance music, the shimmy shake, the sweaty electric slide Jose and I had enacted on the living room carpet. I sank deeper into the beige leather of my seat. I plucked at the wiry hairs around my mouth. I couldn't remember if I'd packed a razor.

Above Candlestick Point, square-shouldered hills rose on either side of the highway. Beyond that, square houses in pink, lime, and pumpkin climbed sloping streets dotted with amber light.

"How's Christa?"

"She's been sick," I said. "Food poisoning, I guess. She's a freak about doctors, so she won't go and find out what it is."

Traffic came to a halt. Barbara coasted to a stop behind a panel truck, her front bumper inches from its chrome trailer hitch. "How long has she been sick?"

"A couple of weeks."

The truck edged forward. A purple minivan drifted into our lane. Patting the horn twice, Barbara swerved. The minivan's driver watched us go by. She was, unthinkably, one of the zombie twins. She watched us pass, her wrinkled face impassive, her eyes hooded. There was no sign of the other twin.

"No good deed goes unpunished," Barbara said.

"This can only mean one thing. Somewhere on this highway there is an identical purple minivan being driven by her sister."

Taillights shone red-orange all around us. Barbara braked. Crossing her arms over her chest, she said, "She's pregnant, you know."

Stately as a Spanish galleon, the purple minivan sailed rightward, into the side of a Cadillac. Immediately, all around us, horns squawked. I turned my head to watch the van recede as Barbara veered around the wreck. The zombie twin stared numbly at her steering wheel. "She's probably too old, don't you think?"

"Not *her*," Barbara said. "*Christa*. She's pregnant. No one has food poisoning for two weeks. It's morning sickness."

"*Morning* sickness," I said. I felt suddenly dull-witted, thick-tongued, club-footed. Slack-jawed, I stared at the dashboard. "What makes you say that?"

Barbara tramped the gas pedal and swerved into the now-empty middle lane. "Just a hunch, I suppose," she said.

We were closing fast on the car in front of us. I clutched the armrest until my knuckles whitened. I closed my eyes and clenched my teeth.

I must have dozed. Barbara nudged me awake in time to see the skyline come into view. Against a blackening, cloudless sky, the windows of office buildings glowed with yellow light. Fairy lights outlined the cables of the Bay Bridge.

"What is it about a skyline?" I said. "It's just concrete and steel and granite, and somewhere a power plant belching coal smoke to keep it all running. But there's something magical about a skyline at night."

Barbara stared at me, frowning.

"What?" I said.

"A power plant belching coal smoke? I don't recall you being so cynical."

I patted my belly. "I'm always cynical when I'm hungry."

◆　◆　◆

By some miracle, Barbara found a parking spot half a block from the restaurant, in front of a movie theater, the Lumiere. Rapt, she stood on the sidewalk, perusing the poster for a movie called *Tous les matins du monde*. Two men stood before a pair of trees. A gap between the trees revealed the sandy-beige facade of a manor house. The men wore elaborate period costumes; one held his arms outstretched and tipped his face to heaven, as if appealing to the gods for a role in a better movie.

The marquee's yellow light bathed Barbara's upturned face; her pale skin and frosted hair glowed. She wore the beatific smile of a haloed saint or votary in a Baroque painting.

I cleared my throat. Barbara shook herself out of her reverie. With a smile she led me down the hill to the restaurant.

Just as she'd said, it was a hole in the wall, a narrow, deep storefront. At the front, there was a galley kitchen and a long counter. At the back, a single cramped four-top table sat on a platform. A tall structure of bead board half-concealed the sunken entrance to the restroom. To the right of that, a closed door oozed steam.

"Strange," Barbara said. "I've never seen this place empty before."

We sat at the table. Barbara sat with her back to the bead board wall. She set her mammoth leather handbag on the chair next to her.

The cook, a tall curly-haired Asian woman, handed us each a single sheet of laminated paper. Barbara fitted horn-rimmed half-glasses to her face and pored over her menu, as if it were something elaborate, as if it did not comprise a handful of items—imperial rolls, five-spice chicken, grilled pork, noodles—in various combinations. Everything came with "meat sauce and rice."

I leaned across the table. "What is this meat sauce?" I whispered.

"The most delicious thing on earth. Just don't ask what's in it."

Another Asian woman, also curly-haired, appeared from the back. Smiling, she set two glasses of ice water between us. Smiling, she disappeared.

"Now I'm kind of wishing I'd tried to talk you into Thai food," I said.

The front door opened with a creak, and a man stepped into the restaurant. He wore a baggy, rumpled raincoat. He could not have been much older than thirty, but his hair was salt and pepper, mostly salt. His eyebrows were thick and black. He sidled past us. In his heavy black boots he clumped down the stairs to the restroom.

Without looking up from her menu, Barbara said, "I swear I raised you for higher purposes than you've yet put yourself to. Open your mind. It's a big world."

That sounded familiar. I rolled my eyes. "When you said Vietnamese, I was picturing hot and spicy chicken, ginger beef, spring rolls. Like at Vina. You know, that place in Highland Park—."

"I remember, I remember. Vina is bogus. This is the real deal."

I laid aside my menu. "How's the pork? I don't want chicken. It'll either be bone-dry or crawling with salmonella."

"You seem snappish of a sudden. I suppose I shouldn't have said anything about Christa." She folded her glasses and tucked them into a gold lamé case and dropped the case into her purse. "Never mind," she said. She sipped her water. "What shall we do tomorrow? The entire city is our playground. Do you have any interest in the wine country? We could drive up in the morning, have lunch in Napa, hit a few wineries. Or maybe the Santa Cruz Mountains. More wine, fewer tourists."

The gray-haired man returned from the restroom. As he passed our table he winked at me. I heard him say, in a mellifluous baritone, "I'll have the usual."

"I don't drink wine," I said to Barbara.

"That's not really the point, is it?"

"Won't you be sleeping all day?"

With a grin she poked my shoulder. "You're only here once or twice a year. Who needs sleep?"

The cook approached, a tablet clutched to her breast. She smiled but said nothing. Barbara ordered for both of us. She ordered by number, and the cook whisked away our menus.

"How's your show going, now that the election is over? Will you have anything to talk about, without Bush to kick around?"

"There's plenty to talk about," Barbara said. "I'll miss Dan Quayle, of course. I've seen some wretched vice presidents in my day—Spiro Agnew comes to mind—but Quayle is something else again." She brushed hair away from her forehead. "In any case, there's *plenty* to talk about. The anti-gay thing in Colorado, the ordination of women in the Anglican church."

Imperial rolls arrived, two of them, each cut into quarters. Their skins were shining and golden. I tried a piece. Crispy on the outside, melting and savory on the inside. Delicious. I popped another piece into my mouth.

Barbara narrowed her eyes at the imperial rolls, as if they were slightly suspect or possibly repellent. "Also, get this. It turns out the State Department investigated Bush's rivals in the election, looking for politically damaging muck to rake. Shades of Watergate, methinks, but no one's talking about it. I suppose because the election's over with . . ."

I'd devoured an entire imperial roll. I had my eye on the other. I nudged the plate toward Barbara. "Aren't you going to—?"

She plucked a segment of imperial roll from the plate and nibbled away its skin. She moaned with pleasure. "And of course, we do movies on Fridays, still. Friday movie nights are my favorite."

I turned in my chair so that I faced sideways. I glanced at the gray-haired man at the end of the counter. A plate of imperial rolls—a dozen or more of them, stacked like cordwood—sat before him. Nibbling one, he watched us with a contented smile.

"I would have thought Friday movie night would go dark in between Woody Allen releases."

She crinkled her nose. "It was a bad year for him personally, but a good year for his movies. He released two this year."

"What happened to him personally?"

She peered at me askance, as if she'd suddenly realized we'd never met, that she'd fetched the wrong person from the airport. "That thing with Soon-Yi and Mia . . ."

Soon-Yi? Who or what or where was *Soon-Yi?* I said, "Oh, that."

"I'm afraid, around the time that *Husbands and Wives* came out, Friday movie night got a little . . . gossipy."

"The last Woody Allen movie I saw was that one you dragged me to. The one with the e. e. cummings poem in it. Someone had an affair with Michael Caine, I think?"

She made a noise like a radiator blowing steam. "I so wish I liked Michael Caine more. He's not bad with a director who can keep him kind of tamped down. But when he does that shouting, baring-the-teeth thing he does . . ."

The front door squeaked again. A man and a woman in matching Burberry raincoats came in and sat at the counter. The cook was ready with menus. The woman tucked herself under the man's arm. They giggled and murmured happy sounds at each other.

"Speaking of movies," Barbara said, "there's the NEA debacle."

"NEA? Nebraska . . . Endocrinologists' . . . Archive?"

"Oh, stop. There are these gay and lesbian film festivals, three of them. The NEA has gone back and forth on funding them umpteen times. Just today, the acting director announced that these film festivals *aren't* going to get any money after *all*. Mind you—."

My attention wandered. The cook stood before the vast grill, flipping hunks of meat. Flames leapt at the sizzling flesh. On a tiny gas range at the cook's elbow, pots bubbled and steamed.

Barbara rummaged in her purse. She'd fallen silent. Guiltily I wondered how much of her political talk I'd missed.

"I know it's simply *ages* until Christmas, but I can't wait a second longer."

From the depths of her bag she pulled two boxes, each wrapped in bright red foil. One was smaller than a pack of cigarettes. The other was larger, the size of a cigar box. She set the packages on the counter and twiddled her fingers in their direction.

"Open, open," she said. "The big one first."

I tore the paper. It *was* a cigar box. It contained, in a nest of shredded newspaper, a Walkman cassette player, one of the bright yellow sports models.

The smaller package was a Karen Holmes album on cassette, *Command Performance*. On the cover, instead of a photograph, there was a caricature of Karen. Her hair, lips, and breasts were enormous, as if the caricaturist had thought he was doing Dolly Parton.

"I'm sure you have that on vinyl already," Barbara said, tapping the cassette case with a red-lacquered fingernail. "It's brand new, only out for a couple of weeks or so, but I know how you are about Karen Holmes. I just wanted you to have something to listen to right away."

I didn't actually own the album. I hadn't even known it existed. Barely a month ago I'd been listening to Karen Holmes with obsessive single-mindedness. Some nights I'd played all of her albums in chronological order, and then again in reverse chronological order. Now, somehow, I'd completely missed a new release.

I turned the cassette case and squinted at the track listing on the back. All of the songs came from previous albums. "This Is Love" and "Take It Uptown" from *This Is Love*. "Easy to Love" and "Well Did You Evah?" from *The Cole Porter Songbook*. "I'm a Fool to Want You" and "Stormy Weather" from *The Very Thought of You*. I turned the case over again and looked at the cover. There, at the bottom, beneath the caricature, miniscule black letters: "Recorded Live, March 15, 1992, Algonquin Oak Room, New York, NY."

The cook set before me half a chicken, its glistening skin the color of rust. It smelled of pepper and anise. A pool of pinkish gruel oozed into a mound of rice.

"This is the meat sauce?"

Barbara leaned back as the cook set a plate of pork chops in front of her. "I hope you like it. The Walkman, I mean. I didn't think you had one."

"I don't." I stared at the yellow case and gray buttons of the cassette player. I didn't feel certain I would be able to work it. "I didn't."

Again I glanced at the gray-haired man. Still munching his imperial rolls, still smiling, he watched me.

Barbara reached for a piece of my chicken. "Do you mind the white meat?" Giggling, she said, "Of course you don't." She took the thigh and leg.

I looked at her. Her eyes darted from me to the gray-haired man and back again. I blushed. "I was kind of thinking the pork would be good," I said.

She stabbed a pork chop and dropped it on to my plate. Meat sauce sloshed off the side of the plate and dripped onto the counter.

I picked up the Walkman. I pressed a button and it snapped open with a satisfying clunk. I slid the cassette into the tray and closed it. I pressed the play button. Nothing happened.

"Oops," Barbara said, chewing. "Forgot batteries. Sorry."

There was a squeak at the end of the counter. The gray-haired man had stood. He dropped a ten-dollar bill on the counter and, without a backward glance, left the restaurant.

Barbara sighed. "Gay romances are so brief."

Suddenly I felt unutterably weary. I returned the machine to its nest of shredded paper. I closed the box.

"You're not eating," she said. "What's going on?"

I picked at the pork chop she'd given me. A few strands of meat came free. The pork looked delicious and succulent, but my appetite had deserted me.

"I guess I filled up on imperial rolls," I said. "And it's been a long day."

Barbara set her fork across her plate. "It's probably my fault," she said. "All that political talk. You always ask about the show—you're a dear to ask—but I should know by now, all that political, religious, current-events stuff just makes you morose."

I separated grains of rice and coaxed them into a row around the rim of my plate. Onward, starchy soldiers. "Do you ever miss God?" I asked her.

"I beg your pardon?" She squinted at me, as if viewing me at a great distance.

"We were church folk when I was growing up. You must have believed in God then. You must have prayed. You must have felt that he was there, listening, ready to help if you needed him."

"I'm not in the habit of pining for all the imaginary friends I had in childhood," she said.

"Imaginary—?"

"People invented God to explain the world. No, that's not quite right. People invented gods—little-g gods. Men invented God—capital-G God. Now that science explains the world, they still hang onto him because they fear death." Her enunciation was frighteningly precise. "And although they have God and heaven to coddle them in the face of death, they're still so terrified of death that they have to shove all that crap about abortion and euthanasia down our throats, as if—."

She spoke distinctly, not loudly, but the man and woman turned and stared at her as if she had shouted a series of obscenities.

She went on. "All this nonsense about the inspired word of God. Bullshit."

At the counter the couple sat stiffly, no longer huddled together. I sensed that they were holding very still, the better to eavesdrop. "The Bible was all politics," Barbara said, "not inspiration. A bunch of men got together and decided to put in all the stuff that kept women down. Not to mention"—here she paused—"homosexuals." She let the final word drop hard, as if it settled everything.

"I'm not talking about the Bible. I don't know anything about the Bible, except that 'for God so loved the world' bit. And that's—. That's what I'm talking about. God and love and—." And what else, I wasn't exactly sure.

She sat ramrod straight, her hands in her lap. She crumpled her napkin and dropped it on her plate. "I'm not hungry any more," she said. "Let's go."

She slapped down a couple of twenty-dollar bills and stood. The cook gave her a quizzical look, reached for a Styrofoam box. Barbara shook her head. "No need for that," she half-said, half-sang. To me, she said, quite sharply, "Don't roll your eyes at me. Neither one of us is eating anyway. We might as well go someplace more private."

In a whirlwind she collected her purse and bustled out of the restaurant. I struggled into my jacket and rushed to catch up. Halfway to the door I realized I'd forgotten the cigar box.

• • •

Out on the street, over the roof of the car, I said, "I'm sorry. I guess I hit a nerve?"

She whirled her purse over her shoulder and landed it on the car's soft top. Gear spilled across the black canvas. Trident chewing gum, the gold lamé case, half a dozen emery boards, a bottle of red nail polish, a patent-leather checkbook, a petite silver lighter. A Bic pen, the end chewed flat. A pink compact coated in bronze dust.

Reaching across the car's roof, I picked up the lighter. I rolled it across my palm. It was a handsome thing, slim but weighty. Its surface was mirror-bright, though scratched in places from rattling around in her purse. At the touch of a button a tall flame flickered briefly, then died in the wind. "Why do you have—?"

"Where is all this coming from?" she asked me. She dug in her purse. "Does this have something to do with that wacky phone call a couple of weeks ago?"

She turned her purse upside down. Keys on a springy orange band tumbled out on top of the pile. She picked them up, unlocked her door. Wrapping the orange band around her wrist, she stuffed things back into her purse.

"What kind of Jesus freak 'counselor'"—she made quotes in the air with her fingers—"have you gotten yourself mixed up with?" she asked. "Sam Stinson? Don't get me started on Stinson."

"You brought him up, not me."

She opened her door and slumped in her seat. I knocked on the passenger's-side window. For a moment she didn't move, and I thought she might drive off and leave me on the sidewalk. But then she leaned over and shoved the door open.

"Thankfully he doesn't play well *here*," she was saying.

One foot in the car, one foot out, I said, "What? Stinson? What is it about Stinson?"

She looked at me. Her purse was a round leather bundle in her lap. She looked down at it, then tossed it into the back seat.

"Can we go home now?" she said. "Would that be all right?"

•   •   •

Through Nob Hill streets clogged with honking traffic, past trees and brownstones strung with white lights, Barbara drove in silence. Past Grace Cathedral, dark and plain. Past the Masonic Auditorium, white, square, shining. Past a crowd of windswept tourists waiting at Powell Street for the cable car. Past the glittering Fairmont. One more block, and we came to Barbara's building, slate blue, trimmed in mauve, corniced in white.

She turned left, down a narrow alley. Soon it opened into a rectangular courtyard bounded on one side by the back of the building, on three sides by carports. Barbara steered into a parking spot. She cut the engine, and we sat in quiet, oil-smelling dark.

She smiled at me, a sideways simulacrum of a smile. "I'm hungry again now," she said. "Isn't that perfect?"

Bag in hand, she stepped from the car and strode toward the building. Halfway there she turned back. She slipped the key into the trunk, twisted, and popped it open.

I pulled my bags and jacket from the trunk. I tucked the cigar box into the tote bag. Slinging my duffel bag over my shoulder, I followed her. She had left the back door of the building standing open. I bumped it shut with my hip.

The hallway was never as wide as I remembered it. Passing through it now, passing the mauve doors of the first-floor apartments, my bags scraped the dimpled plaster on either side of me. After a few awkward paces I came to the high-ceilinged lobby, lit by a single dim chandelier. Light coming through the etched glass of the front door cast lacy shadows at the foot of the stair. At the top of the first flight, Barbara's black skirt flitted across the landing and disappeared. I followed.

Her door was at the top of the last flight of stairs. When I reached it, it stood open. A dim light in the entry hall guided me as far as the living room. I dropped my tote bag and duffel on the living room floor, at the foot of a console table crowded with silver-framed photographs.

At the far end of the room, another short hallway led to the two bedrooms—one on each side—and to the bathroom. A light in Barbara's bedroom cast a cockeyed yellow square on the mahogany floor.

She sat on the floor with her back against the side of her bed, an open box across her skirt-straitened legs.

"How ladylike this pose," I said.

"I've been keeping this shit in the closet for years," she said. The closet door stood open. She glanced toward it. "In the closet. I never thought about the significance of that until now. Here, look at this."

I sat on the floor beside her. Setting the box aside, she spread a photo album across our laps. It was one of the old breed—black pages interleaved with vellum, brass corners, fat brass hinges.

The first page contained, at its center, a five-by-seven of a young man in Navy crackerjacks. His crew-cut hair shone as burnished gold. He was posed to show red stripes on his black sleeve—and for that matter the robust girth of his shoulder. His smile was devilish, his bright blue eyes clear and happy. John Thomas Murray. My father.

"He was a handsome one," Barbara said. "I was in love with him for *years* before we met. I spent *hours* gazing at his photo in the high school yearbook."

She turned the page to deckle-edged black and white snapshots of a chubby blonde toddler with a tricycle. In one she stood beside the trike, her back straight, her head high. Pride of possession added inches to her height. Behind her, the clapboards of a house or garage—seemingly on the verge of rotting into squashy splinters—overlapped at crazy angles.

"You?" I said.

"None other," she said.

In another photo, she sat astride the tricycle and bawled, mouth open, head thrown back.

"What happened?" I asked her.

"I don't remember. Maybe I fell off it and they put me back on."

Wedding photos came next, black and whites on creamy paper, hand-tinted to show the bride's blushing cheeks and the groom's piercing eyes. "You have his eyes," she said. "The color's not the same, but the shape, the size. They're his eyes. Sometimes I almost can't look at you because of that." She touched his wedding portrait—the same pose as his Navy portrait, but now he wore a black suit. "Now for instance."

"Are you crying?"

"Don't be ridiculous."

Next, a fading gallery of our Polaroid years. I was a newborn in a receiving blanket, an infant in a jumper, a toddler in a baggy blue three-piece suit. My parents' waistlines spread inexorably. His hair thinned and grew sandy rather than gold. Hers got longer, darker, flatter. Everything took place, it seemed, on grass-green carpet with black paneling in the background, sucking up light.

The last photo was a family portrait. My father wore a pale green leisure suit with yellow stitching on the lapels. His crew cut hadn't changed, had never changed. Barbara's flat mouse-brown hair spilled over the shoulders of some black nautical dress or suit that recalled the crackerjacks of John's Navy picture. Fat and dimpled, carrot-orange hair neatly parted and pomaded, I wore a green leisure suit that matched my father's and a yellow shirt that matched the stitching.

Barbara cocked her head to one side, looking at the photo. She brushed her hand over it as if to whisk away a patina of dust. She said, "I suppose this is all my fault. We put you in Sunday School when you were practically an infant. We sent you to Vacation Bible School every summer. They drummed all that shit into your head before you could put a sentence together."

"I'm not some helpless pawn, you know," I said. My face grew hot. "I'm no longer practically an infant. I *am* capable of thinking these things through."

"Of course, of course."

She said this airily, lightly, as if she meant exactly the opposite, or as if it couldn't possibly matter either way. I twisted the hem of my sweater in my hands. I stared at the ceiling, my eyes crossing, my vision blurring. I did not quite know what to say next—not without profanity.

But perhaps she'd meant something completely different, or perhaps she'd been participating in the conversation without listening to either side of it; when she spoke next, her voice was slow, dreamy, distracted. "In the past, when I've not wanted to talk about this, about this part of our lives, it's not because anything so very traumatic happened."

She was silent for a long time. At last, I asked, "What *did* happen?"

"I settled. I married the first man who asked, and I lived where he wanted to live, and I did the things that he loved without loving them myself. Look at this hair. Look at this hair as brown as a mouse. I look like Karen Carpenter. Well, a fat Karen Carpenter. A version of Karen Carpenter that was never anorexic."

"I guess I ended up making the same mistake. Hopping the first train that rolled into the station."

She looked at me. "I never told you, but I always thought so."

"Tom was impossible. At the end, especially. He said he felt we were too young to settle down, but he couldn't quite get as far as leaving. Nothing made him happy. He spent all his time tearing around with these club friends of his. Late hours, coming home drunk, stinking of smoke."

"Do you think he was playing around?"

"I don't think so. That was another thing. He was jealous, weirdly suspicious. So if he ever—." My breath gave out on me. I let out a choked gasp. Barbara stroked my forearm. I patted her hand.

"Some of this sounds familiar," she said.

I cleared my throat. "Really, all along, he was maddening. Not just at the end. All along. He never picked up a sock. I mean, not even one sock, one time. He made up these weird jokes that weren't funny." I paused. "What do you get when you cross a chicken with a lamppost?"

"I'll bite. What do you get?"

"A chick-a-post."

"What?"

"Weird joke. Not funny. That's what I said." I peered into the box. It held some more photos that had never been put in the photo album or that had fallen out, a Bible in white leatherette, an orange diary with a broken lock, a few pencils, a few pink feathers. "He had a bizarre fixation with my bowel movements."

"Like—." Her upper lip curled. "Like a *sexual* fixation?"

"Nothing that adult. He just thought it was funny to talk about—. To talk about—you know—bodily functions."

"Your father had his faults. He couldn't hold onto a dollar if it was sewn into his pocket. He had a *vastly* inflated sense of his intelligence and talents—of which he had basically none. And of course he drank like a fish. But I think I can say without fear of contradiction that he never once mentioned my bowel movements."

I flicked the edge of our family portrait with my thumbnail. When had I last cut my fingernails? God, my hands were claws. I examined my long, curved, horny fingernails and stifled a wave of revulsion.

I said, "Sometimes Tom didn't shower for three or four days at a time. Whenever I was reading he had to interrupt me. He couldn't stand my attention being on anything but him. He hated my taste in music, so he had to have control of the stereo all the time." The words spilled out faster and faster. I took a breath to slow myself. "And there was this—this *thing* he always did."

It was easier to demonstrate than to explain. I leaned toward Barbara, so that my face came within a fraction of an inch of hers, and then I leaned back, and then I leaned toward her again. All the while, I bugged my eyes out and wagged my tongue.

After half a dozen repetitions, she hollered and pushed me away. "How on earth—? *What* on earth—?"

"I don't *know!*" I said, throwing up my hands.

"Did you ever tell him—?"

"*All* the time. Apparently I was the one who needed to make adjustments, not him."

She plucked one of the pink feathers from the box and stroked it along the underside of her chin. "I don't think I ever told you, I once met Sam Stinson."

"*Met* him? In person? Handshakes, introductions, conversation, all that?" I tried to imagine the parallel universe in which such a meeting would not obliterate all life on earth and send the moon hurtling into space.

"His ministry was not the multimillion-dollar business it is now. He had one or two books out—."

"*Love and Discipline.*"

"And others. I can't remember the others." She let go of the feather, and it fluttered into the box. "He came to our church. He sold most of his books in churches. His sermon was all about giving up your will for God, and how that was the only way to be happy. I was the chair of the hospitality committee, and your father insisted I invite him to our house for supper. Over dinner, he explained that for a woman there was the added happiness of submitting to her husband. The head and the body, the happy helpmeet, all that." She frowned. "Happy helpmeet? Do I have that right, or am I confusing it with the happy hooker?" She scratched her chin. "It doesn't matter."

"Isn't that what women have done for most of human history?"

"That's probably why I hate it so much."

She put the album in the box. "I reinvented myself, you know," she said. "I vowed I would never again be that mousy brown ... *thing*. And I never thought you would find yourself in the same situation. You're a male, after all."

"A gay male. The man wife."

She cut her eyes at me. "I knew Tom wasn't quite right for you, but I had no idea—."

"Why did you leave? What was the last straw? Something must have happened," I said. "You didn't leave him because of a hairstyle."

"True, true. I didn't leave him because of a hairstyle. Christ," she said. "I'm half starved. Come with me to the kitchen."

In the narrow galley kitchen, Barbara opened the freezer and took from it a pack of Virginia Slims. She tore open the cellophane and plucked a cigarette from the pack.

"Mother! You're smoking?"

"Medicinal purposes. It's an appetite suppressant." She sighed. "Where on earth did I leave my purse?"

She went searching. When she returned she had the silver lighter. Standing at the stove, she switched on the vent fan and lit the slender cigarette. She puffed and exhaled, her eyes glassy with pleasure. The fan inhaled the blue smoke.

I said, "I cannot *believe*—."

"Hush. I only smoke two or three a day. I've lost ten pounds, and it's taken me months. And since you didn't notice, you're out of my will."

A kitchen towel, pink and green, lay bunched in a corner. I picked it up, folded it. "Were you going to tell me why you left? Barbara?"

"It's another one of those weird jokes that's not so funny." Crossing to the sink, she ran water over the half-smoked cigarette and stuffed it into the disposal. "We didn't leave him. He left us."

I said nothing.

"It's a long story." She appeared to be addressing the faucet. "Not worth going into. Suffice it to say, I had the same problem your Tom did. I knew it wasn't right, but I couldn't get out."

"Were you never going to tell me this?"

"I hoped it wouldn't come up. I never know how much you remember, or how much you ever knew. I was—." With her index finger she made a twirling motion around her temple. She threw up her hands. "I wanted you to think I was stronger than I was."

In the scheme of things, it wasn't so much, really. We'd gotten rid of the bastard, one way or the other. Our life with him had been lamentable. Without him, our days had been resplendent, joyous. What did it matter how it had happened?

And yet—.

I went to the living room and sat on the couch. Rain rolled down the windows. When had the rain started? Hadn't the sky been clear when we left the restaurant, when we got to the apartment?

Barbara sat beside me. A fresh cigarette wafted smoke and the smell of ash. "Do you remember *Zelig?*"

"*Zelig?* What's that?"

"A Woody Allen movie. You saw it with me. It's made to look like a documentary, compiled out of a lot of old newsreel footage, or faked footage. It's about a man—Leonard Zelig—Woody. This man, Zelig, can transform himself into anyone he meets."

I sank back into the cushions of the couch. I hugged a pillow to my chest.

"He's a human chameleon. He has no personality of his own, only whatever personality he takes on from the people he meets. When he's with black people he becomes black. When he's with Nazis he becomes a Brown Shirt."

"We saw this together, you say?"

"I know we did. In the middle of the movie, there's this scene where he's being serenaded by Fanny Brice. I know we saw it together, because you said something about Fanny Brice and *Funny Girl.* I can't exactly remember what you said. It was very clever."

I stared at the black maw of the fireplace, at the gleaming brass andirons. "It was the actual Fanny Brice?"

"As far as I know, but there's some trickery. They somehow make it seem as if the song she's singing has the name 'Leonard Zelig' in it. Just after that, Zelig is alone in an empty hallway. All these people are streaming up and down this hallway, walking past him as if he's not there, and he sits there, all alone in a hard chair, eating something, some kind of bun or roll. He's at the height of his fame. His unscrupulous sister and her lover are exploiting him as a kind of sideshow attraction and living high on the proceeds. Zelig is known the world over. People flock to see him. But in that hallway, since no one is paying attention to him, he has no one to—to—*become*. He's nothing, no one. At his core he's nothing, a non-person."

I sat up, tossed aside the pillow, punched it down against the arm of the couch. "Mother, what does this have to—?"

"Hush." Her voice was even, calm. "I'm getting there."

I set my hands on my knees to keep them still.

She said, "The thing is, as you watch it, you get the feeling that it's not just Zelig. It's *Woody*. You're seeing a glimpse of how he feels about himself. Fame, money, respect. For fuck's sake he dated Diane Keaton *and* Mia Farrow *and* Charlotte Rampling—some of the most beautiful and talented women in the world—and yet—."

"And yet he feels like nothing. Or so it would seem if you read too much into the movie."

Her eyes narrowed. "You should still be hushing."

"Sorry, Mother. Go on."

"The point is, when I saw *Zelig*, I knew what he was getting at. I knew how he felt—Leonard Zelig—and Woody Allen. When your father left—Christ, for more or less the entire marriage—that's how I felt. I never wanted to feel that way again, and I never wanted you to know I had ever felt that way, be-cause I never wanted *you* to feel that way."

"Does this mean you dated Diane Keaton? Because that would rock."

She bit the filter of her cigarette and sucked it aggressively, as if punishing it. "Apparently you picked up a couple of Tom's bad habits."

Turning away, I stared at the rain-mottled window, orange in the gleam of the streetlights. I looked at her. Her jaw was set, but her eyes were soft and wet. "Not funny?"

"Sorry, darling. Not funny." Taking a ceramic bowl—a frog-green majolica cabbage leaf—from the coffee table, she rolled her cigarette along the stem end. A column of ash dropped into the bowl. "It was sort of a bastardy thing to say, actually." For a long moment she sat looking at me, her eyes heavy with sadness. Sighing, she stubbed out her cigarette. She stood. "I suppose I should get ready for work."

◆　◆　◆

Rain drummed the window. Far below, on the street, tires squealed. A man shouted. A car horn whinged. At a greater distance, blocks away, sirens keened.

I stood. The floor seemed to lurch beneath my feet. Perhaps there had been a tremor, a minor earthquake, or perhaps I'd only gotten up too quickly. For a couple of minutes I stood still and waited, my feet spread and my hands thrust out from my sides as if to balance myself. I felt nothing more.

Pacing the living room, I kicked over my tote bag, and the cigar box tumbled out. It tipped open, and the Walkman skittered across the floor. How like her to forget the damned batteries.

I ransacked the drawers in the kitchen. I poked around in closets. Surely somewhere nearby there was a bodega or convenience store where I could get batteries, but hard rain sheeted the windows now, and I knew that my mother and I shared an unfortunate inability to hold onto small necessary items such as hats, scarves, gloves, and umbrellas. If she owned even one umbrella, she would need it to get to work.

Outside the bathroom door I cocked an ear, listening to the spray of the shower on the tile. She would be in there forever.

I rummaged in Barbara's bedside table. No batteries. I closed the drawer.

As I turned to leave the bedroom, I tripped over Barbara's box of memorabilia. I remembered the diary I had seen at the bottom of it. I sat on the floor. I lifted out the photo album and set it aside.

The diary, it turned out, had been mine. My name covered the end papers in slanted, shaky, juvenile printing. On a half dozen or so pages, I had written a date—in each case I had misspelled "February" and had omitted the year—and a few mostly legible sentences. There was something about a dog. Had we ever had a dog? Someone—the name seemed to be "Silly," but that couldn't be right—had told me I was the last of the Murrays, and so it was very good that I had been born a boy. Just after that, I'd drawn a big crooked heart with an arrow through it, and in the middle of the heart I'd written, "Jody loves Silly." Here, the name was plainly Silly. What kind of a name was Silly? And who was Jody? In the final entry, I had written "I love Mommy" and had filled the rest of the page with X's and O's.

The loose photos at the bottom of the box were five-by-seven studio portraits of young children. A tow-headed boy in a sailor suit, with "Craig, Oct. 1973, 2 yrs" written on the back. A brown-haired girl in a pinafore, "Millie, 18 mos., 1974, Feb." An older boy, also brown-haired, in a green sweater,

"Andrew, Mar. 1975, 4 years old." There were others—two girls and a boy—ranging in age from six months to two years, all dated in 'seventy-three, 'seventy-four, and 'seventy-five.

Barbara appeared in the doorway. Her hair was damp. She wore a bathrobe, well-used, much-frayed, once-white. Patting her hair with a pink towel, she sat on the bed.

"Who are these children?" I asked her.

"You don't remember?"

I shook my head.

"Foster children," she said. "I had such a hard time giving birth to you. I just couldn't face another delivery. I just couldn't. Your father wanted more." Leaning over, she grasped Millie's picture by a corner and took it from me. She stared at it. "This was the compromise. I can't believe you don't remember."

How could I remember these children, when I remembered so little? My memories from that time were dim and few. Only the belt, my punishment for saying "fuck," even seemed important. The rest were scattered patches, random incidents, momentary flashes—riding in the car, trying on shoes, my father smoking a pipe. I didn't even remember that we'd had a dog, or the name of my best friend forever.

"I should go," she said. Still, she didn't move. Her towel lay in a bundle in her lap.

I stuffed everything—the diary, the photos, the photo album—back in the box. I left her to get dressed and went back to the living room. I lay on the couch.

It was a prodigally overstuffed velour beast, green and mauve, so long that I'd never understood how the movers had gotten it up the stairs. It clashed with the Art Deco décor—the cherry case pieces with their nickel accents and tapered legs, the doughy beige slipper chairs, the sleek porcelain statuary, the wood-framed Maxfield Parrish posters. But the couch was so soft that I couldn't help myself. I slept, my head covered with a pillow. For a long while, I heard nothing.

14 SMALL CLAIMS

My return flight, the following Saturday, was torturously early. During the drive to the airport, Barbara was strangely wired. I faded in and out of sleep while she recounted the details of Friday movie night. Most of the titles seemed to be in French or Portuguese or Czech. Her pronunciation was perfect, albeit stiff.

When she came to *Reservoir Dogs,* enthusiasm infected her speech with hushed tones and sentence fragments—"A masterpiece," she called it. "Perfect dialogue—gritty, but with this great wit to it. Almost poetry. The structure—. Like a visual fugue."

"Fugue?" I shifted in my seat. After six nights in the pillowy bed of the guest room, my hips and back ached.

"You have to see it to understand." She knocked her forehead with the heel of her hand. "I should have taken you to see it." She sighed. "Well, we had fun anyway."

As I remembered it, I'd spent the week more or less on my own—sightseeing during the day while she slept, prowling South of Market bars and clubs at night while she worked. For "fun," there had been only our lackluster tour of wineries in the Santa Cruz Mountains. Through twisting fogged-in roads she'd driven interminably, pausing at three hillside shacks, where, while she'd sipped wine and cackled with glee, I'd sulked and wished I'd brought along *The Seventeen Quartets.*

"Did we?" I said. I hadn't exactly intended to say it out loud. Luckily, she seemed to take it for a joke. Laughing, she batted my shoulder.

As we neared the airport exit, I insisted she drop me at the curb. "You must be exhausted after working all night," I said.

"I hope you'll reconsider," she said.

Had I missed something? "Reconsider?"

We sped by a row of taxis lined up for baggage claim. Their horns bleated. Their brake lights flashed.

"Moving here," she said. "It would do you good to get back in the game."

Oh. That.

Perhaps, I thought, I should tell her about Spike, that he'd lured—or forced—me back in the "game." Perhaps then she wouldn't be so inclined to think of me as a desolate widower, pining away in a cold-water garret. But I knew she'd say something about the absurd virility of his name. Whatever details I elected to share, she'd take too much pleasure in them, and she'd goad me for more. We'd trade Kinsey-queer double entendres, and the whole conversation would kindle some sort of weird hope in her while making me feel sleepy and forlorn.

I wrapped my jacket around me. Feverish and chilled, I leaned my forehead against the cool glass of the passenger's-side window. I promised her I'd mull it over.

◆　◆　◆

The plane was crowded and noisy, but almost as soon the pilot announced our departure from the gate, I nodded off. Mid-flight, I woke, restless and fidgety.

All week I'd been trying to get through *Command Performance,* but to my surprise I'd found it hard going. I fitted the Walkman's ear buds into my ear, rewound the cassette, and tried again.

The album began with "This Is Love." The piano chimed intricate changes. Karen dallied over the old familiar verse.

> Ev'ry night I find I sigh over him,
> And I might one day soon find I cry over him,
> But oh, how bittersweet is my plight,
> To pine for his kisses,
> And I love the very sky over him,
> Stars above, constellations that fly over him.
> If I know anything about love,
> Then I know what this is.

Even as she finished the last line, the accompaniment fired up into a nimble series of syncopated falling thirds. Karen lovingly prolonged the first words of the chorus—"This is love"—and then the phrase that followed—"if love is a state of confusion"—came so fast that it sounded almost like scat singing.

• ✦ •

On that long-ago night in the Algonquin Oak Room, Karen had also opened with "This Is Love." Patrick, her son and accompanist, had written a bluesy, downtempo arrangement. Karen had changed all the pronouns from "him" to "you," as if carrying a torch for the audience itself. The room had crackled with the joy of it.

Barbara had finagled us a table just a few paces from the piano, so that when Karen faced forward, her eyes seemed to meet mine. All the while I was keenly aware of Tom next to me, watching me with fond amusement. I tried to pretend I was wiping crumbs from my cheeks when in fact I was blotting tears from my eyes.

This—the *Command Performance* version—was yet another new arrangement. It was fleet and cheerful, but I hated it. What was wrong with either of the old arrangements? Why did everything have to keep changing?

As the first side of the cassette played on, Karen's voice grew husky, her diction sloppy. All of the arrangements seemed wrong-headed. "A Cockeyed Optimist" was too slow. "Easy to Love" was too fast. A strangely ponderous, convoluted chord structure backed "The Song Is You," so that it sounded like some kind of Mannerist recitative.

The new arrangements nettled and wearied me. Perhaps I was only sleep-deprived, or perhaps I was no longer one of Mason's pop-culture-obsessed "young people."

I switched off the Walkman and stowed it in my tote bag. McNamara's book brushed the back of my hand. I pulled it out. I'd hauled it all the way to California, but I'd never opened it. A slip of paper marked the beginning of chapter fourteen.

I skimmed over the parts I'd already read—Beethoven's fiscal disarray, his contentious relations with his brothers, the cattle stampede—and at length came to the composition of the sixteenth quartet. According to McNamara, the inscriptions—"*Muss es sein?*" and "*Es muss sein*"—had had nothing to do with incipient mortality, nothing to do with Beethoven's housekeeper. No, it had all begun as a dispute with a patron who'd questioned an exorbitant subscription price for a performance of the B-flat quartet. The patron had reluctantly paid the subscription to get copies of the parts, but not without complaint. "*Wenn es sein muss,*" he'd said—"If it must be." Beethoven, tickled by the aristocrat's exasperation, had written a trifling and, I thought, mean-spirited joke canon. "*Es muss sein, ja ja ja.*" Beethoven, it seemed, had been an asshole.

How banal it seemed. I wished I'd never sought out the true story. How much more interesting it had been to think it all stemmed from Beethoven's dread of his own death.

After the biographical details came the analysis of the quartet itself. McNamara quoted snippets of the score, but only a few, amounting to perhaps three or four dozen bars. In great detail he described passages that he neglected to quote. Without a recording to listen to, it was slow going. My eyes crossed and my vision blurred.

I dozed. I woke again when the landing gear bumped the tarmac in Minneapolis. The book had fallen closed in my lap.

As the plane taxied to the gate, I lifted the window shade and looked out onto the tarmac. In my absence there had been no new snow. All that remained of the last snowfall was a dirty crust and foamy black slush.

◆ ◆ ◆

After three hours shoe-horned between the window and a corpulent seatmate, after the trivial ordeals of fetching my duffel bag from baggage claim, after wandering the parking garage looking for my car, after my brief unfounded terror that—even with a new starter, less than a month old—the Chevette wouldn't start, I wanted nothing more than my own easy chair. But as I steered through the slick, wet streets of my neighborhood, I pictured the house covered in Sam Stinson bumper stickers, spray-painted with swastikas. I didn't want to go home.

It was just after noon. In my wallet I carried a few traveler's checks left over from my trip, and I hadn't even begun my Christmas shopping. The malls would be crowded. On a Saturday Saint Paul would be empty, abandoned, wind-whipped, the streets possibly clogged with bouncing tumbleweeds. Without even having seen the house, I turned around and set a course for downtown Minneapolis.

The Dayton's ramp was nearly full. I drove all the way to the top and parked on the exposed roof. The arcade between the ramp and the store was itchy hot. I pulled open my jacket and ducked into the store. Through the shoe department, past Papagallo and Charles David, past images of myself in sepia mirrors, I passed into the brilliant great hall.

Mistletoe dripped from the chandeliers. Pine garlands and golden bulbs decorated the cosmetics counters. Somewhere beyond the escalators, a pianist played "Winter Wonderland," a perfectly sensible, straightforward arrangement—not too fast but not too slow, not too jazzy but not too staid.

I walked around the escalators. There it was, in the center of a red carpet leading from the escalators to fine jewelry—a grand piano, shiny and black. The pianist was a gray-haired man in a tuxedo.

I paused at one of the cosmetics counters, partly to consider perfumes for Barbara and Christa, but really to hear more of the piano. I trailed my hands along the brushed chrome frame of the display case. Foil-wrapped boxes and chrome-topped bottles of cut and etched glass glowed like jewels.

I looked up. Before me stood Charlie Kent, dressed for work, it seemed, in a white shirt and striped tie and worsted slacks. In each hand he held a bottle of cologne. He hefted them as if gauging their relative weights.

God, the sheer hairy bulk of him—he was something out of mythology. I half-suspected he had a quiver of thunderbolts hanging on a hook in his entryway, back at his apartment atop Mount Olympus.

Charlie turned, and instantly his face broke into a smile. "Jonah?" he said. "Jonah Murray, right?"

"Exactly."

He set down the bottles and put out his hand. "Charlie Kent," he said.

"I remember perfectly." I remembered, too, the way brown hair covered the back of his strong hand, the way he had turned his hand so that mine was underneath it. Shaking my hand again now, he did the same.

"What have you been up to?"

"I just got back from San Francisco. I—." I looked around me. The tuxedoed pianist shuffled his sheet music. Cracking his knuckles, he launched into "Santa Claus is Coming to Town." I said, "I needed to do some Christmas shopping. What about you?"

"Same, same. Well, I came in to work today, but then I decided I needed a break. I was just considering some perfume for my mom." He walked his fingers along the tops of the bottles. He picked up two of them and turned them toward me. "What do you think? White Shoulders or White Diamonds?"

"You feel strongly that 'white' should be in the name, then?"

"It couldn't hurt." He grinned. "Which would you get for your mother?"

"I don't dare buy anything but Chanel Number Five for my mother," I said, "but my mother isn't like other mothers."

It had always been a point of pride—my mother wasn't like other mothers. Miserably, I realized that my mother was, in fact, a lot like other mothers— she was, in fact, probably a lot like Charlie's mother. More likely than not her political views were to the left of Mrs. Kent's—as they were to the left of al- most everyone's, except perhaps Ralph Nader's—and almost no one's mother ranted about politics and movies for a living, but for all that, Barbara was surely just as frozen in her habits and beliefs as anyone else's mother.

I tapped the rhinestone-crusted gold bow on top of the bottle of White Diamonds. "If she's ever said anything remotely appreciative of Elizabeth Taylor, that's the one," I said.

A clerk had appeared, a zaftig, sour-faced woman in a black smock. She wore a badge that read "Zany." I thought she must be the antithesis of zani- ness. Charlie showed her the bottle of White Diamonds. Grumbling, she set off to find the keys to the display case.

I said, "Did I understand you correctly? You work here?"

He tipped his head back, toward the escalators. "Upstairs. Corporate. It's our busy time, so I thought I'd catch up on some things. Have you eaten?"

"I haven't." I gazed up at a twinkling chandelier. "At least, I don't think I have." I put up my hands. "I think I'm a little jet-lagged."

Zany returned empty-handed. "Just a second," she said, grimacing. "The manager—."

Charlie shook his head. "Don't worry about it. I'll come back."

"Suit yourself," Zany said, and stomped off.

"Can I buy you lunch? I know just the place."

I nodded.

Charlie led me up the escalator and through men's wear. He walked quite fast. We came to a set of escalators, and for a second I thought we had some- how gone full circle. No, that narrow corridor to the left, between the escala- tors and a brightly lit display of sunglasses—I would've remembered that.

Charlie veered to the left. Slowing as he walked by the sunglasses, he turned back and said, "Let me pay for lunch. I'd like to make it up to you for what happened at group. I still feel badly."

Here there were floors of dark green marble, dark green display cases with brass frames. Rock music blared. In the corner of my eye I saw flashes of light and color. I turned. Enormous video screens played commercials—or maybe they were music videos. I couldn't bear to look at them for long.

To Charlie, I said, "You shouldn't. Feel bad, I mean."

We entered the skyway over Seventh Street. Christmas lights crisscrossed the outside of the structure.

"I needed to know eventually," I said. I looked at him. His eyes weren't as pale or as green as I remembered them. Perhaps it was that this time his shirt was blue.

"Eliot and I talked about you," he said. He rushed to add, "Don't worry. He didn't tell me anything personal. He just said that he felt badly about it, too. About what happened. He's terrified you think he tried to trick you."

I couldn't think of anything to say. I looked out the windows, up and down the street. Toward Hennepin there was another skyway, a pinkish shade of taupe. Toward Nicollet—beyond Nicollet—there was a brown skyway with row of pyramid-shaped skylights along the top. For an instant I had the sense that I was looking at a science-fiction cityscape, at a vision of a futuristic domed city of some kind, where it was unsafe to venture outdoors. "I'm sorry to hear that."

"He thought your lifestyle was causing you some pain."

"My *lifestyle?* I had sort of thought I was living a life, not a lifestyle."

"No offense," he said, "but isn't that worse? A life that's causing you pain, rather than a lifestyle?"

I looked down. Again he wore the tasseled chaussure of the pompous— brown, this time. "I see your point."

"In any case, Eliot only meant for you to see that there are alternatives."

"I see."

He said, "I thought you'd already—. That you'd already decided—."

"No hard feelings," I said, though I wasn't entirely sure it was true.

In City Center we passed Sam Goody. A slow-moving, rumbling escalator disgorged passengers. He said, "Everyone you met is still there. Still in group. Some of us are making remarkable progress."

"Progress toward not being gay?"

"That's the goal." He stopped. He stared at me, his face blank. "Do you really want to talk about this? I can't tell if you're really interested, or just humoring me."

We passed the entrance to Ward's. Next door, in front of a Radio Shack, a salesman rocked from heel to toe. Charlie waited for a chattering group of teenagers to pass.

"I'm interested," I told him.

"Why the change of heart?"

"I didn't say I wanted to sign up. I said I was interested." I regretted the crackle in my voice.

"Fair enough. I know this is a tricky subject for you." He stepped onto the escalator, and I fell in beside him.

"Why do you do this? Why did you set out to change everything you are?"

"It's not everything I am. It's just one small part of me. I learned it early in life, and I can unlearn it."

"I'm not sure I believe that. The impulses are insurmountable. For me they are."

His eyes searched mine. "Did you have any bad habits as a kid? Did you sneak smokes or eat too much junk food? Or maybe you had a friend who always knew how to get beer?"

"Would a Karen Holmes scrapbook count?"

He shook his head. He stepped off the escalator. Abruptly he strode off to the right. We'd already passed an Au Bon Pain and a sketchy-looking Mexican grill of some kind. Where the hell was he going? I scrambled to catch up.

"You know what I'm asking," he said.

Reluctantly, I nodded. "I do. You're saying it's no more than a bad habit."

He stopped. He looked at me. "It may feel like more than that, but it's just a bad habit."

"Why did you decide to do this? To change?" I cleared my throat, looked away. The teenagers had congregated in front of a GNC. Giggling, they poked each other. "Maybe it's none of my business."

"I was raised Foursquare Gospel. My daddy was a preacher. One Friday night, he caught me with a boy and disowned me on the spot."

I stumbled back, goggling at him as if he'd unexpectedly struck me in the face. "That's terrible. How old were you?"

Two blond boys, six or seven years old, ran by us, yelling, laughing. Charlie watched them, his eyes heavy. He folded his arms across his chest. "I was already out of high school, just screwing around—." He stopped himself, flashed a half-smile. "No pun intended. I was goofing off, putting off college. In a way, it was the best thing for me. I joined the Navy, and that taught me everything I needed to know about discipline and responsibility. Except sexually, of course. Like you said, the impulses seemed impossible to resist.

I prowled the streets of every city I found myself in. I took everything that came at me. I wasn't just promiscuous. I was cruel. It wasn't as good if the guy didn't want me to rough him up a little."

"Mean as shit," I said. I hadn't exactly meant to say it aloud.

"Exactly. Mean as shit." He gazed into the distance, as if a film of his old sexual exploits played on a screen behind me and to the left. "If I thought about how horrified my father would be to see me, it just made me want it more."

"Why the change of heart?"

"Daddy died. Six years ago, now. I wasn't there—couldn't be there—for him."

"I'm sorry," I said.

He waved his hand, as if batting an insect away from his face. "I couldn't be there because he didn't *want* me there. When he was gone, I realized how much I missed him and wished I could've said good-bye."

"He refused to talk to you, even on his deathbed? That didn't make you angry?"

"Part of me was angry, sure." He frowned. He stroked his beard. "But after I thought about it, I had to admire him for what he did. He didn't just hurt me, you know. An only son is a comfort and a pleasure to a man, especially in dying. He gave that up for what he believed in."

I wasn't sure I could see it that way. "And now? You're successfully changed?" Somewhere behind me there were shrieks. I winced. I turned. The two blond boys chased each other around a bench.

Charlie said, "Changed, but not cured. I never should have used that word before—'cured.'"

"Or 'victim,'" I said bitterly.

"*You* used the word 'victim,' not me."

I gave it some thought. He was right. I nodded.

"I've made peace with my dark side, and I've put behind me all the things it led me to do. But the darkness is still there. It'll always be there." He put his hand on my shoulder. "Come back. Start seeing Eliot again. Come to group. It hurts at first to think of it, I know. It hurts to consider giving up something that seems so much a part of yourself, part of your core being. But what are you really giving up? Sex with men you just met?"

I thought of the man at the beach, the white column of flesh standing up at the center of the shadowy form. I thought of Spike, alpha to my beta. I thought of Jose—*Aye, it's a wee little thing*. I blushed. To these men I'd just met, I'd given myself—not as a lover, not even as a sex partner, but as a thing to be used and discarded. And what had I received in return? Something, surely, beyond the raw physical pleasure, but what?

He leaned back. "I'm sorry. I didn't mean to embarrass you."

I shook my head. Tears pricked the corners of my eyes. "Not at all."

"Think about it, Jonah? Please?"

I nodded.

He jumped as if he'd been touched with a cattle prod. He looked down at a pager hooked to his belt. "I'm sorry. I have to get back. I have to pass on lunch." He stood a moment longer, looking at me. "Will you come back to group? Please?"

"I'll think about it."

"Can you find your way back?"

"Go ahead. I can make my own way."

•   •   •

From a block away I saw it. A sheet of white paper, it looked like, hung in the center of my front door. I glanced around the neighborhood—the ramshackle stucco duplex across the street, the green-trimmed rambler next door, the mock Victorian two houses down. On a few front doors there were wreaths, but mine was the only one with a sheet of paper on it.

It was handwritten—spidery blue printing. Biblical passages, four of them, the neatly copied text of each followed by its book, chapter, and verse. Sharp lines underscored portions of some passages. The vandal had nailed it—had *nailed* it—to the door. I tore the page free.

Standing in the entryway, I read the verses:

> Thou shalt not lie with mankind, as with womankind: it is abom-
> ination.
>
> Leviticus 18:22

> Know ye not that the unrighteous shall not inherit the kingdom
> of God? Be not deceived: neither fornicators, nor idolaters, nor
> adulterers, nor *effeminate,* nor abusers of themselves with man-
> kind, nor thieves, nor covetous, nor drunkards, nor *revilers,* nor
> extortioners, shall inherit the kingdom of God. Now the body is
> *not for fornication* but for the Lord; and the Lord for the body.
>
> I Corinthians 6:9-10,13

Thou hast set our iniquities before thee, our secret sins in the
light of thy countenance. Who knoweth the power of thine anger? even according to thy fear, so is thy *wrath.*

Psalm 90:8,11

Behold, now is the accepted time; behold, *now is the day of salvation.*

II Corinthians 6:2

The mail slot was full. Checking statement, credit card statements, electric bill, catalogues, fast food coupons, Christmas cards, and something from
the Court Administrator of the Ramsey County Conciliation Court. The post-
mark was nearly a week and a half old.

I was, it appeared, being sued for seven hundred and fifty dollars. The
plaintiffs were Rose Lynn Hill and Gregory Thomas Hill, Senior. Tom's parents.

What? What the fuck?

In blue ink, in a quivery childish hand, one of them had filled out the
statement of claim.

> Jonah Murray, the defendant, entered into an immoral sexual
> relationship with our son, who since passed away. They lived
> together in a house they rented together. The defendant seduced
> our son away from his good moral upbringing and the immoral-
> ity of this drove Tom to suicide by drink. He drank himself to
> death, literally. The least the defendant could do is give us back
> the deposit on the house so we can clear up the estate. We had
> called the defendant to demand this but he does not have an an-
> swering machine and he avoids our calls. We do not see we have
> any other choice but this.

What? What the fuck? True, I didn't own an answering machine, but if the
phone rang, I answered it. I'd never avoided anyone's calls. Never.

An immoral sexual relationship? Drank himself to death?

What the fuck?

For a long time I sat in the easy chair. In one hand I held the summons. In
the other hand I held the sheet of Bible verses. Where the nail had been, an
aureole of rust had bled into the paper.

Tom had been in pain. His drinking, his thrashing about with the club folk, had made that clear. But I'd taken him at his word. I'd believed that he'd only regretted settling down too soon. All along I'd thought that if one of us had mustered the nerve to make a break, then he, at least, could have been happy.

Now I wasn't so sure. Perhaps his parents were right. Perhaps his very *life* had been the cause of his pain. It had never occurred to me before.

Hell, it had never occurred to me that, as Charlie had baldly put it, my own lifestyle—or my own *life*—had been causing me pain. Certainly it wasn't far off the mark to say that my life of late had afforded me little pleasure. An hour of pleasure here, a night there. The rest was, indeed, painful.

I remembered how my crazy night with Spike and Jose had passed in a blur of adrenaline and euphoria, how I had been wolfish and insatiable, how I had craved and had literally begged for more, and more, and more—and then how, in the morning, I had regretted it all. Now, weeks later, recalling that crazy night filled me with shame and remorse.

I doubted that I'd driven Tom to drink, much less to drink himself to death. But perhaps it was true that his dissatisfaction had had less to do with me than with some deep-seated shame. Perhaps he hadn't even realized the true problem. His parents were Christians—he'd complained bitterly and often of their piety—and he'd been raised in a church. Maybe he'd drunk himself to death because, as they claimed, he'd chosen wrongly—not the wrong partner, as I'd thought, but the wrong life.

Both of us. Perhaps we'd both chosen the wrong life.

◆   ◆   ◆

The windows were dark. For hours I'd been sitting in the easy chair. At some point the pages had fallen from my hands to the floor. I picked them up, but in the room's twilight I could no longer read them.

I needed to piss. In the bathroom I switched on the light. As I passed the mirror I caught sight of my reflection. I stood at the sink and stared at myself.

God, I looked like shit. My beard was patchy, ragged, wiry. Whorls of orange whiskers filled the hollows of my cheeks. Beneath my lower lip there was a patch of pinkish-blond curls. A dark narrow streak marked one end of my mustache. My hair was wild, all split ends and frizz. With warm water from the sink I tried—and failed—to smooth it down. I switched off the light. I looked better as a silhouette, as the shadow of myself.

15 THE HARD-WON DECISION

In the white pages, I found Eliot's office number. I dialed. An electronic chime, then his voice: "This is Eliot Moon, family counseling. Leave your name and number and I'll get back to you. Or, if this is an emergency, please page me."

He gave the pager number, and I wrote it down, but I couldn't bring myself to dial it. This was scarcely an emergency. Again I dialed his office and left a message.

"Eliot," I said, "this is—. Hello, this is Jonah Murray. I don't know if you remember me. I saw you twice, a few weeks ago. And—. And there was a—a thing with—with your group. Anyway, you know all that. You were there, and—." I took a breath. "Never mind, never mind. I called because I need your help. I'm ready. Now is the day."

Twenty minutes later, he called back. "I was very excited to hear your message," he said. "Are you free now?"

"Now? Right—right now?"

"If not now, when? You said yourself, now is the day."

"I didn't mean—. That wasn't—. I had just been reading this—this thing—." I took a breath, held it, exhaled. "That's very kind of you, but I already chewed up one of your Mondays," I said. Something occurred to me. My face flushed. "I didn't even—. I never even paid you for those earlier—."

For a long moment, he was silent. "That's true," he said slowly. More quickly he said, "We can talk about that when you get here. Come on over."

"I can wait until you have an opening."

He paused. I heard paper rustling. "That's not until late next week. You're not getting cold feet, are you?"

"Not at all," I said.

"Come over, then."

"Now?" I said again. I was beginning to feel mentally inert. "It's Saturday, isn't it?" Perhaps I'd lost track of the days. No, no, it had to be Saturday. "I can't take up your Saturday, what's left of it. You must have better things—."

"I'm at home. You remember the way?"

"Sure," I said, and then, "That is to say—. No, I don't."

Speaking slowly and with great care, he gave me directions.

•   •   •

It was all as I remembered—the concrete stair, the stringy frozen grasses, the bare trees, the off-center porch. I climbed the stairs, followed the path to the front door. Snow began to fall. Great white gusts blew across the lawn. Crusts of grimy old slush lay in the corners of the flower beds.

I lifted the iron knocker and let it fall. Wind thrashed the trees and shrubs along the front of the house. I shivered. The muscles of my chest twitched and knotted. As I stood staring at the indistinct black lettering of the welcome mat, I wondered if I'd been hasty—calling Eliot, coming here—if I'd rushed into a course of action that I would come to regret. Certainly my last visit here had ended badly. On the other hand, perhaps my earlier escape had been the reckless course of action, and now I had at last come to my senses.

Eliot answered the door. He wore a pink Oxford shirt with the sleeves rolled neatly to his elbows. His collar was open. Patchy stubble darkened his cheeks and neck. He grinned and hugged me.

"Welcome back," he said. "I'm so happy for you."

I wrapped my arms around him, touched the lean, supple musculature of his back. His body was warm and hard against mine. Patting my shoulder, he stepped away.

"Are you ready to start? Come in."

He took my jacket and hung it on a hook in the entryway. I stepped out of my boots and set them beside a pair of thick-soled Nubuck work boots. A pool of snowmelt had dried to beige dust on the parquet floor.

In the living room, a fire burned in the grate. Eliot motioned me onto the sofa. I sat. He lowered himself into the nearest armchair. He slid it an inch or two closer.

"Before we do anything else, I think I owe you an apology for the misunderstanding at group."

"Charlie explained all that. He said you were thinking one thing, and he was assuming another."

"I'm afraid there was a lot of assuming all around."

"I was laboring under an assumption of my own," I said. "I thought that you and Charlie were—well, together." I looked around at the evidence I had so wrongly interpreted—the mismatched furniture, the practical but unlovely armchairs, the ornate side tables, the folksy Redlin print in its stark walnut frame.

Sinking back into his chair, Eliot crossed his legs. Gravely, he nodded. "I'm sorry to hear that. I've been working at this for a long time. I'd hoped that I wasn't still . . . giving off the vibe, so to speak."

"So you're—. You're going through this as well?"

"Of course. If I hadn't been through this myself I wouldn't feel comfortable leading others through it." Looking at the fire, he rubbed his nose. "I lived in New York for four years. I did my undergraduate work there. I hit the bars far more often than I hit the books. The bars, and worse—subway men's rooms, adult bookstores, the Ramble in Central Park. I always felt guilty afterwards. Six or eight men in a night. More, maybe—nights where I lost count. While it was happening, it all seemed so exciting. It was like I was drunk. It would all just happen in a blur. Afterward I always felt so small, so worthless."

I leaned forward. "I know just what you mean." I tucked my hands under my thighs. Another pair of gloves had gone missing—who knew where or when—and my fingers were sore with cold.

"Every night as I walked back or took the subway back to my apartment, I'd pray. I'd fall back on my convenient God, and promise that I'd be good, that I'd never sink so low again. And then the next night, I'd go lower."

Whatever specific things he'd done—I wasn't sure I wanted to know, and he didn't seem inclined to say—I was sure I knew how he'd felt. "It's like you watch yourself from a distance, watch yourself being—being used, being shoved down. And it feels wrong, but you can't get enough."

He nodded. "Exactly. Exactly. Finally, I decided I had to live up to all my promises. I couldn't string God along forever."

"All that guilt—. You were brought up to believe that being gay was—was—is wrong?"

"Absolutely. My parents were very devout. There was that, but also I *felt* that it couldn't be right. It just couldn't. The way I craved it so much, the way

I couldn't stop myself—. You can just *feel* when you're doing something that's not right, something that's bad for you, you know?"

"And so—. And so you just decided to swear off—?"

"In a way. I knew what the Bible said about it. I remember hearing a sermon in church, when I was a kid. A guest preacher. This young guy, one of our own, a seminary student back for a visit. He said that homosexuals would be the first into the lake of fire. So I knew it was wrong, Biblically speaking, what I was doing, what I was. But at that age, I thought I knew everything. I thought that, whatever the Bible said, the problem wasn't that I was with men, but just that I was with so *many* men. I stopped for a while—somehow I made myself stop—and I tried to find a boyfriend I could spend my life with. I thought if I could find a Christian man to spend my life with, then it would be all right." All at once his eyes reddened. "That didn't work out." By sheer force of will, it seemed, he made himself smile. "But we're not here to talk about me."

My forehead felt hot. Maybe I was coming down with the flu. Maybe it was the heat of the fire. I scooted forward, so that I sat on the edge of the sofa.

"I'm utterly clear on the point that the Bible takes a dim view of gay sex," I said. I thought of the Bible verses nailed to my front door. *Abomination,* one of them had said. *Abomination*—not an equivocal word, by any means. "But there's sex and then there's the—. There's the *act* of having sex with men, but that's not the same thing as the state of *being* gay. And maybe it's like you said, maybe it's the anonymous stuff—the casual stuff—that's bad. Maybe if I could be with one guy. Like a marriage. Like with Tom. I was happy with Tom."

"For a while."

I stared into the fire. "For a while. It was shitty at the end. But maybe—."

"In my experience they all end badly, gay relationships. It's not like a marriage. It's a more animal thing. Lust is the thing that holds you together, not love. When the newness wears off—."

"But maybe I just picked the wrong guy. Maybe with someone else—."

"You know that's not true."

I leaned back against the cushions of the couch. I closed my eyes. "Yes. I know. With Tom or anyone—." I choked down a knot in my throat. "I feel like I've picked the wrong life." I looked at him. "And since Tom died, it's like you said before, I've been trying to fill a spiritual gap with physical things."

"A lot of people do. I did."

"But at the same time, you know, the bare legal pronouncement—. The Biblical thing—. 'Abomination.' I'm not an 'abomination.'" Leaping to my feet, I barely avoided knocking my shin against the corner of the coffee table. I went and stood in front of the Redlin print. I stared at it, at its twilit, shadowed snow drifts, blue-white as china, gold where the light of a campfire touched them.

"Most men who go through this resist what they feel—what they know—to be true, simply because it's difficult to give up the physical pleasure and the thrill of the chase and all of the rest of it. That was a big block for me. The adrenaline rush of conquest." He coughed. His voice grew huskier. "That's exactly why it's so important to go through with this."

I turned, looked at him. "It's important to go through with this because I don't want to?"

"We often spend the most energy avoiding the things we most need, or desperately clinging to the worst of our bad habits, even knowing how bad they are."

"True," I said. "True."

Covering his mouth, he coughed again. "Sorry," he said. "I'm fighting a cold, and I think it's winning. I'd better get some water. Do you want anything? I could make some coffee or tea. Or some soda? I think I have some soda."

I shook my head. He disappeared into the kitchen and returned sipping from a tumbler of ice water. Again he sat in the armchair. He patted the couch. Obediently, I sat.

He said, "Think of it this way. You want to be happy, right? That's what all this is about?"

I shrugged. "Everyone wants to be happy."

"There are three ways of looking at happiness. There's the present, the past, the future. Present happiness is the immediate sensation of joy and euphoria. Past happiness is the satisfaction of a life well-spent. Future happiness is optimism for the course your life is taking."

"Okay."

"Most people focus on the present. The instant gratification. What feels good now."

"Okay."

"The thing is, the present moment is all about external circumstances, about what's going on around you. In the present moment, it's not really happiness, it more like—. It's all about pleasure or avoiding pain."

"Okay."

"Every moment of your life, a set of circumstances is set in front of you. You can react to those circumstances in various ways. Usually there's a way of reacting that will feel better in the moment, but will seem unwise in retrospect."

"Okay."

"Example. You just woke up. You could make a bowl of oatmeal and wait a few minutes for the water to boil, or you could eat the cold pizza that's in the refrigerator and wash it down with some beer. Cold pizza and beer would take less time and probably tastes better, but the oatmeal is by far better for you." He looked at me. "I've completely lost you. It would help if you said something besides 'okay.'"

"All right," I said. He gave me a stern look. I said, "I think I get it. Sacrifice immediate gratification for a sense of purity later."

"If you spend every moment trying to maximize your pleasure or minimize your pain, you're no better than an animal. That's what dogs do, what deer do, what ants and mice and lemurs do. Happiness—*real* happiness—is knowing that over time you've had a habit of doing the right thing—knowing that whatever life hands you, whatever you're facing right now, you'll act in good conscience—knowing that what you do right now, however difficult it seems, will make you proud of yourself later on, when you look back on it."

"I'm not so sure, at this point, that I can just accept the whole package, the changing or curing or whatever," I said. "I don't see myself—. For now, I think—I think I can accept that, for a while—maybe forever—maybe being celibate is the right decision. But I don't think I'm going to wake up one day and want a wife and kids."

He looked at the fire. He coughed. He sipped his water. Slowly, as if with reluctance, he turned his head, looking from the fire to me. "I think that's perfectly fine," he said softly. "One step at a time."

"When we met—. That day we met—. God, that awful day—." I felt myself flush. I rubbed my hairy cheek. "That day, you helped me a lot. I felt I could trust you."

"You can trust me."

"I—. I think I can." His hand on my shoulder, the way he'd hugged me, the way he'd seemed to understand—. "But what I wanted to say was—. I—. I felt betrayed after what happened at group."

His face fell. "I'm so sorry—."

"That wasn't right—. I didn't mean—. I was telling someone about it, and he made me feel—. I'm saying this all wrong. All I mean to say is, I understand about what happened. It was just a misunderstanding. I feel I can trust you, and what you're saying makes sense, but for right now—. I want to do this. I *need* to do this. But—. But I need to go at my own pace."

He nodded, visibly relieved. "I understand," he said. "One step at a time."

"I can accept that I've been—. I've been a little crazy lately. I've let some things happen that I shouldn't. I've thrown myself into some things that I shouldn't have. But I just can't get my head around the idea that what I *am* is wrong. That part—. That part, I just can't—."

"There are things we can understand, things we can't. We are small. God is big." His voice had grown rough. He gulped water. "Sometimes when something doesn't make any sense, you have to put your faith in God, in the fact that it *does* make sense, but in a way you can't understand." He hugged himself. "Does it seem cold in here to you?"

Rising, he went to the fire. Taking a brass poker from a rack on the hearth, he prodded the burning logs. "Sometimes," he said, "sometimes you do have to make a choice to believe things that seem counter to reason. Noah's ark, for example. If you think about it too hard, it makes no sense. Two of every species on earth, on one boat? Ridiculous. But you can just choose to believe it, even if it seems ridiculous."

"*Es muss sein*," I said.

"S-moose what?"

"This thing Beethoven wrote," I told him, "a string quartet. On his manuscript he wrote—in German, of course—'Must it be?' And then, 'It must be.' I always thought it had something to do with his fear and acceptance of death, but it turns out it's about some financial squabble. Maybe I get to decide, after all, despite all the evidence, it had to do with his fear and acceptance of death."

For a long moment he stared at me. "Maybe I'm not making any sense." He laughed. "I took some NyQuil before you got here. I think it's kicking in."

I stood and went to the hearth. I shook my head. "You're making perfect sense." I held my hands out to the heat of the fire. "I still feel kind of untouched by it all, though," I said. "On an emotional level. I feel like I'm just going through all the arguments, intellectually, and I'm going in circles."

He returned the poker to its place on the rack. His skin was golden in the light of the flames. "Maybe you're taking too much of an Old Testament view at the moment. For me, all the emotion is in the New Testament, in the Gospel." He paused, looked at the ceiling. "Well, there are the Psalms, of course. The Song of Songs. But never mind." He looked at me. "What I mean is, the Old Testament is all about the law. The emotion—the *love*—is in the Gospel. Jesus lived and died for us, out of love. The Old Testament is law. The Gospel is love. 'For the law was given by Moses, but grace and truth came by Jesus Christ.'"

"'For God so loved the world,'" I said.

"It's all about love. God's love for us. When it hits home, what Jesus did for us—for *you*—the passion will come to you." He laughed. "Passion," he said. "No pun intended."

I must have looked puzzled. With a fond, forgiving smile he said, "One step at a time."

I said, "Maybe I inherited all of my mother's opinions on the subject of religion, without really thinking through any of them."

He nodded. "That's probably true."

"Maybe I'm just considering all this as a kind of belated teenage rebellion."

"You have to make your own way, one way or the other. Whether your parents are among the faithful or not, at some point you have to decide what's best for you."

Again taking up the poker, he stoked the fire until it blazed. Sparks streamed into the flue. My forehead and my cheeks were hot, the skin tight. I turned away. My reflection in the gilt-framed mirror startled me. In the light of the fire behind me, my hair flared in a frowzy halo.

"Whatever your mother told you," Eliot said, "whatever you were brought up to believe, you have to find your own way."

•   •   •

We talked for hours, until I began to feel incoherent. Eliot offered me food and drink, but I was neither hungry nor thirsty. "I think I just need some sleep," I told him.

He walked me to the door.

"Group is still on Thursday nights, here, just like before. Come this week. Seven o'clock."

I said, "Thursday. Seven o'clock. Okay." Standing now on the porch, I took a step back from the welcome mat. "What does this say?"

"'Welcome, friends,'" he said, "only in Kanji."

"Kanji?"

"Japanese. My grandmother was Japanese."

I stared at the rush mat, at the ruined curves of the black calligraphy. The ink or dye had faded so badly that it might say anything, in any language.

"Thursday's a long way off," Eliot said. "Will you be all right till then?"

"I think so."

"Pray. Start now, on the way back. If you want a relationship with God, you have to talk to him. Pray."

"Pray. I will."

•   •   •

Pray.

Yes. Pray.

With the car idling at Fairview and University, I found that I simply didn't remember *how* to pray. I said "Hello?" to the air, hearing the tentativeness in my own voice, as though I expected—and perhaps feared—an answer.

"Hello"? That didn't seem right. What was it? "Dear Lord"? "Dear God"? "Our Father who art in heaven"?

The light changed. I drove on.

"Dear Lord," I said, "if you're there—." No, that was a bad start. "Lord, you must know what I'm about to try to do. Lord knows—." Another misstep. "*You* know—. It certainly *seems* that you've been trying to tell me something. All those Sam Stinson bumper stickers. The Bible verses. Spike. That business with Spike and Jose."

The skin at my temples tightened. At Snelling, as I entered the intersection, the light turned amber. Behind me there was a cacophony of horn-blowing. My heart skipped, but when I looked in the rearview mirror, the commotion seemed to have nothing to do with me.

I stopped behind a row of cars waiting for the light at Pascal. The driver who'd towed my car—Jaime, wasn't it?—sat in the driver's seat of his tow truck. I ducked my head, thinking I might catch his eye, but he watched the light steadfastly, single-mindedly.

How might things have been different if I'd taken him home? If I'd taken him home and made him supper and poured him a beer, would I now be trying to teach myself to pray? Or would we already be living together, smarting from my trip to San Francisco, from my recent week-long absence from our new life together?

No. No. My original impulse had been correct. It would have been a one-time thing, an endorphin-drunk afternoon followed by a hangover of regret. If Jonah had swallowed Jaime, the whale would have swallowed Jonah.

The light turned green. I pounded the accelerator.

16 SAVED

I was listening to Beethoven's C-sharp minor quartet, reading through McNamara's analysis. The piece itself so outpaced McNamara's pleonastic description of it that I felt a little bewildered.

> In both the exposition and the concluding series of *stretti* the answers come in the subdominant. This along with the prominence of Neapolitan harmonies and the masterful handling of thematic and rhythmic coherence across movements creates a feeling of tension and suspense, of massive forces marshaled and controlled in a marvelous and unprecedented manner.

The phone rang. I didn't feel like talking to anyone. I considered letting it ring, but then I remembered Greg and Rose Hill's claim that I avoided calls. Perhaps, occasionally, I avoided calls.

I set aside the book. I lifted needle from the record and answered the phone.

It was Tory. "How was San Francisco?" he asked me. His voice was strangely flat.

"Good," I said. "Good visit." In the easy chair I shifted my weight. My left hip pained me. My calves ached.

"I was thinking we might have brunch again. I've got stuff for a frittata—." He fell silent, for so long I thought the battery in my phone might have died, or the connection might have been broken. "What are you—? Are you free?"

I looked down. The brown-streaked stray sock still lay on the floor, where I'd left it weeks ago. "I should probably do a little—."

"I promise I won't burn the onions this time."

"Where's Christa?"

"Oh," he said. "You know Christa. Around somewhere."

They must have fought. They'd been together for—what?—four weeks? Five? For Christa, that was some kind of record. Surely, they had fought.

"I have something I'd like to give you," he said. "Can you come over?"

"I was just—. I really should—."

"Please," he said, in such a plaintive way that I couldn't bear to refuse him.

• • •

Tory greeted me at his front door. As before he wore his gray sweatpants, but this time with a blue T-shirt so pale and old and worn that I could see the skin of his belly through the fabric. He was unshaven, bedraggled. He wore grimy socks—there was a hole in the toe of the left one. On the top of his head his hair stood in a broad, greasy-looking cockscomb.

The house smelled of frying bacon and onions and of pine. A tall spruce filled a corner in the living room. At the base of the tree he'd draped a skirt of red velvet, but the branches were bare of ornament.

The stereo played some exquisite and sumptuous—almost luscious—piece. The orchestration was rich with overlapping melodies in the harp and woodwinds. "Debussy?"

"Ravel," he said.

"*La Valse?*"

"*Daphnis et Chloé. Première Partie,* I believe. The first *Danse generale* maybe? Fairly early on."

Of course. Of course he would know all of this—which composer, and which piece, and which part of the piece—and of course he would give the names in perfect French.

I followed him into the kitchen. In a skillet on the stove, onions and bacon hissed and popped in a pool of fat. Beside the cooktop, on the butcher block, there were mounds of ham and bell peppers—crimson, orange, and gold. Beaten eggs—a pool of creamy yellow foam—filled one of his ceramic bowls. A heap of shredded sand-colored cheese filled another, smaller bowl.

"Coffee?" He nodded toward the coffee maker, which burbled on the counter. In the carafe, ebony liquid quivered and bubbled.

I shook my head.

"Tell me about your trip," he said. He scooped up the ham and dumped it into the skillet. The purple cubes danced and browned in the sizzling fat.

I shrugged. "My mother took me wine tasting in the Santa Cruz Mountains."

"I didn't know you drank wine."

"I don't."

"Not so much fun, then."

With a snap of his wrist, he shook the pan. Grease splattered the cooktop and the floor. He jumped back; we both did. Tory dropped his hands and stared into the skillet. I thought he might weep.

I fetched paper towels and handed them to him. He tried to wipe away the spilled grease, but the paper towels only smeared it across the stainless steel surface of the cooktop.

"Are you okay?" I asked him.

"Fine, fine," he said. Nodding toward a cupboard to my left, he said, "Could you see if there's a jar of *fines herbes* in there?"

I opened the cupboard and searched through tidy rows of jars and bottles. I found a tiny corked crock with a hand-lettered label that read "FINES HERBES." I handed it to him.

"You know what's funny?" I said. "There was all that stuff in those sections of *Doktor Faustus*—. Beethoven was incapable of writing a fugue, all that. But I was just reading this morning that he turned to fugue more and more in later life. Fugue in the finale, fugue in the first movement—."

From the crock I'd given him, Tory tipped muddy-gray herbs into the palm of his hand. With the thumb of his other hand he ground them into powder. He sprinkled the powder into the skillet. "Have you talked to Christa lately?" If he'd meant the question to sound casual, he'd failed miserably.

"Not since before I left."

From a drawer he took a long-handled spatula. He rattled the skillet on the burner. With the blade of the spatula he stirred the herbs into the bacon and ham and onions.

He said, "She won't return my calls. I don't know what I did, or what I said, or why—." He sighed. "Maybe it was that stupid movie."

"What movie?"

"On our last date we saw *Reservoir Dogs*. I hated it, and she didn't seem to love it, but maybe—."

"My mother was telling me about that movie. It didn't sound like the kind of movie where nothing happens."

"Not a lot happens, really. There's a lot of blood, a guy gets his ear cut off, everyone swears a lot and pulls a gun at the drop of a hat, but really it's all just—." He banged the spatula on the side of the pan. "Never mind. Never mind. We went out to dinner afterward and I guess I got carried away, complaining. She just sat there, *watching* me complain, not saying *anything*. I just talked and talked—God, I *hated* that movie—and she just sat there watching me." His shoulders slumped. "She hasn't talked to me since. Maybe she—. Maybe she loved the movie, and I offended her taste?"

"I doubt it." I thought it over. I shook my head. I said, "No. That's not it. I suppose I should have warned you. She—. There hasn't been—. She's not—."

With great care he set the spatula on the butcher block. He looked at me with red-rimmed eyes. "Don't say any more, please. Let's talk about something else."

"Sure. Okay."

"I have something for you," he said.

He nodded toward the breakfast nook, where a slim notebook bound in black leather lay on the table. I sat and opened the notebook.

"I've been reading a lot of Whitman lately," Tory said. "He's my all-time favorite poet. I love his long lines, the sheer crazy exuberant freedom of those insane long lines, though I can't quite manage to make anything of that kind of free verse myself, in my own poetry."

The pages of the notebook were filled with a loose scrawl in violet ink. "Sullen and suffering hours!" I read. "(I am ashamed—but it is useless—I am what I am)."

At the stove Tory raked the diced peppers into the palm of his hand. He chucked them into the pan. "Whitman was gay, as I'm sure you know," he said, "and in his writing he was pretty open about it. His early writing, at least. I copied down some stuff I thought you might like."

I turned the page.

> Give me now libidinous joys only!
> Give me the drench of my passions! Give me life coarse and
>   rank!
> To-day, I go consort with nature's darlings—to-night too,
>   I am for those who believe in loose delights—I share the
>   midnight orgies of young men

That, I couldn't help thinking, was pretty open.

"Thank you," I said. I closed the notebook.

I stared out the window. Snow mottled the lawn. Delicate white palisades ridged the limbs of the oak tree. There was no sound but the skillet scraping the burner, the spatula scraping the skillet.

"I made a start on setting one of your poems," I told him.

"Which one?"

"'Fuck.'"

I looked up. He was smiling. He said, "I had a suspicion."

It wasn't exactly true, that I'd made a start. I knew precisely how the song should sound—a wallow of dissonant chords, a line of rising augmented intervals, a triple-stopped violin obbligato moving in contrary motion—and I could even picture the score in my mind's eye. But I had yet to commit a single note to paper.

"It's a little—. It's going to be a little cacophonous."

He said, "I'm not surprised."

He tipped the eggs into the skillet. The liquid hissed against the hot metal. He shook the pan.

"Fuck," he said. "I forgot to preheat the oven. Fuck, fuck, fuck." Sighing, he dragged the spatula's blade across the bottom of the skillet. He said, "You might consider having it start quietly, and sort of ramp up."

After a moment, I realized that he'd meant the setting of his poem, not the frittata. "I'll think about it," I said.

"One other thing," he said. "Don't get too far ahead of yourself. I know 'fuck' has a special kind of resonance—."

"True." All at once, I thought of the lines—*fuck hospitals—one more fucking day*—and felt the threat of tears. I looked out the window.

In the living room, the stereo now burbled some empty-headed Baroque piece. A concerto, it must be. The orchestra dropped back, and an ornate solo violin part came through.

"That's the—what?—third? fourth?—poem in the collection. I wouldn't get too far ahead in the sequence. You want there to be a progression, a sense of coherence. Descending, then rising."

"I'll think about it," I said.

A harpsichord clanked and jingled. The solo violin played an obsessive melody full of turns and mordents.

"Can you do me a favor?" Tory said. He stirred the contents of the skillet.

"Can you talk to Christa? I need to know what's going on." He looked at me. "I don't know what I did. It can't be about the movie, can it? It can't be."

I went to the stove and stood near him. I put my hand in the small of his back. "I don't think you did anything. That's what I was trying to say. I—."

He shook his head. "Just talk to her, please." With the spatula he prodded clots of cooked egg. "Please, just talk to her."

           ◆   ◆   ◆

Christa sat at her desk, typing. A bearded vulture—that is to say, Martin— leaned over her shoulder. As I entered, at the sound of the door, she glanced up from her keyboard and nodded in greeting. Straightening, standing stiffly, Martin watched me to my cubicle. I hung my jacket over the back of my chair. I sat at my desk and waited.

Soon, Martin appeared before me. He carried something behind his back. "Good morning," I said.

"Did you have a good trip? I hope you caught up on your sleep."

"Sleep?"

He dropped a red folder onto my blotter. My *Onslaught* book report. "You seem to have written this while very, very tired."

"That bad?"

"There were entire pages that made virtually no sense. Actually, very little of it made any sense."

"Sorry," I said. "I—."

He held up his hand. "End of the day tomorrow," he said.

Well after I heard his office door close, I said, "Yes, *sir*." I opened the folder. On the first few pages he'd made some notes in red ink—"More" and "What does this mean?" and "I'm not sure I follow." About halfway through, he'd taken to crossing out entire paragraphs. At the bottom of the last page, he'd written, "No! No! No!"

Christa ducked her head around the corner. "Lunch?"

I didn't look up from the report. "It's nine o'clock in the morning, Christa. A bit early for lunch."

"Ha-freaking-ha," she said. "You know what I mean."

At last I looked up, but not for long; her eyes were too soulful, the set of her mouth too anxious, to bear. In her hand she held a stack of pink Post-It Notes. She tweaked their edges.

I said, "I'm not sure. This is ages from being finished. I have to redo the whole thing. I should probably stay and work." I nodded toward the stack of pink Post-It Notes. "What are those?"

She dropped the stack onto my desk. "Phone messages. Michael Walton—."

"Walrath. Michael *Walrath.*"

"Whatever. He's been calling about once a day. He needs your paperwork on your shell."

I flipped through the stack of pink squares. Over and over she'd written, "Michael Walton," and "Boat Receipt," and a phone number. "Didn't you tell him I was out of the office all last week?"

She stomped her foot. "Lunch?" she said again.

"Okay, okay." I said. "Lunch. Where? Lagoon?"

"Vietnam*ese*?"

"El Bravo?"

"*Mexican*?" She said it as if I'd suggested a meal of spit-roasted kitten. She looked green. "Whatever. Whatever you want. It's not like I'm going to *eat.*"

"Let me get this straight. You're inviting me to lunch but not actually to—you know—eat lunch?"

She bounced on the balls of her feet. "I need to *tell* you something."

"Then *tell* me."

Anxiously she glanced at Martin's door. She turned her head and squinted. I turned. There was a shadow along the doorjamb, so that though the door was closed, it appeared that it might be an inch or so ajar.

She said, "Come out in the hall for a second."

I set aside the phone messages and closed the report and followed her. "What's going on?"

"I'm—. I need to ask you—." She took a breath. She wrung her hands.

"Christa, please. I'm a little—."

"In about eight months' time, do you think you might be available—?" She smoothed her hands down the front of her blouse, smoothing the fabric tight over her belly.

Whether or not she meant the gesture as a hint, it did the trick. "My God, you're pregnant."

"What I was going to say was, in eight months' time, do you think you might be available for babysitting?" She stared at her fingernails. Her nail polish was chipped, her cuticles ragged. "It sounded funnier when I was rehearsing it earlier."

"How long have you known? Have you told Tory? What did he say?"

She worried one of the pearly pink buttons of her blouse. Her foot patted the speckled blue-gray carpet. The heel of her shoe flapped against the sole of her foot. "That's just the thing. It's not his."

"It's not *his*? Whose is it?"

Throwing up her hands, she said, rather loudly, "Some *guy*." She took a step back. Her shoe skittered across the hallway. Quiet now, she said, "Just some *guy*. You never met him. I never mentioned him. It's not important."

I leaned over and scooped up her shoe. It was a strappy thing, black, stiletto-heeled. I handed it to her. "What are you going to do?"

Holding the shoe in one hand, she ran the thumb of the other along the sweat-darkened arch. "I'm in the process of moving to Hudson. My mother's going to help out."

Surely I had misunderstood her. I put my hand on her shoulder. The pinkish-white fabric of her sleeve was silky and cool to the touch. "I know you can't be saying that you're planning to move in with your mother."

Leaning on the wall for balance, she put on her shoe. "I don't know what else to do. I don't have room for a kid, and I don't have enough saved to move to a bigger place."

"And so—." I cleared my throat. Looking down, I smoothed the front of my shirt. "Is there a delicate way to ask—?"

"I'm thirty-four years old. I'm having it, of course." She stuck out her arm and jerked it a bit to coax her watch lower on her wrist. Staring darkly and perhaps a little blankly at the white face and black hands, she said, "Ticktock, tick-tock."

"What about Tory? You can't leave him hanging. He thinks—."

Her eyes narrowed. "You talked to him?"

"Yesterday. He invited me over for brunch."

She stared at me, hard. "Are you ever going to trim that ratty beard?"

I touched my cheek, my ratty beard. "That's awfully harsh," I said.

"You look like a mad bomber. Or an ayatollah." She laughed. "That's it. A baby ayatollah. Ayatollah Cockamamie."

"You *have* to tell him. He thinks it's something to do with some stupid movie. You have to tell him, Christa."

"Fuck," she said. Holding her stomach, she galloped down the hall.

•   •   •

When she returned, I was staring forlornly at my book report. I called to her over the wall between our cubicles. "Do you have time—?"

There was a rattle and a thump. "I'm going home," she said. "I can't take this any more."

I went to her cube. She had already put on her jacket and boots, had already slung her purse over her shoulder.

"If I barf one more time, I swear to God," she said.

"I need to get this—."

Sighing, she dropped her purse. It fell to the floor with a flump. "Sit. I'll show you."

I sat at her desk. She leaned over me. She flipped a switch on the side of her word processor, and the beige and sinister creature rumbled to life. The screen crackled. Somewhere in the depths of the machine, a fan whirred. Christa slid a floppy disk—it appeared to be roughly half a foot square—into a slot. She tapped a couple of keys, and the first paragraph of my book report glowed, white on black, on the screen.

"You just type, right?" she said. "Or in your case, hunt and peck. Every thirty seconds, press this button." She pressed a button marked "Save." Gears clinked and chattered. A word—"Saved"—appeared at the bottom of the screen.

"How do I print?"

She sighed. "Press this button," she said, and pointed to a button marked "Print."

"Is that all there is to it?"

She cut her eyes at me. She sniffed the air. "When was the last time you took a shower?"

I groaned. "This morning, if it's any business of yours."

"There are things growing in that beard." She reached for my cheek. Her fingers twitched. "I think there are mushrooms in there somewhere."

"Jesus," I said. I leaned away from her. "I hate it when you're sick."

"I'm hormonal. I've had sixteen hours' sleep in six days. I puke twenty times a day. Ten minutes ago I threw up *water*—freaking *ice* water, for God's sake. I have every reason to be cranky."

"Okay," I said. "Okay, okay."

"Every thirty seconds," she said again, "press the save button."

As she took up her purse and walked to the door, I turned to the screen. "Wait," I said. "How do I—you know—go to the next page?"

With her hand on the door knob, she stopped. To the door she said, "'Page Down.'" Over her shoulder she looked at me. "If you run into trouble, don't even *think* of calling me at home."

"Message received," I said.

I searched the keyboard. Gingerly I pressed the button marked "Page Down." On the screen the text leapt and shimmered. I lifted my finger.

> Stinson and by extension Thorstensen seems to believe that the sexes are disparately different genders. Flagmen are flagmen and females don't exist.

I paged down.

> Adherents to diversity are strip language of meaning. Examples including waitstaff and soldiers.

I was lucky Martin hadn't fired me.

I spent the rest of the morning rewriting and making corrections. Every so often, I punched the button marked "Save" and waited for the shining bold word to appear at the bottom of the screen. "Saved."

I found a rhythm. Type, type, save. Type, type, type, save. My fingers moved in flourishes, tapping the keys faster and with increasing confidence.

Somehow, while I was looking at the pages of the printed report spread out on Christa's desk instead of at the keyboard, I managed to press the wrong key. The text of my report vanished. The word processor droned. At the bottom of the screen there appeared a single ominous word: "Deleted."

"Holy shit," I said.

I searched the keyboard for a button marked "I Didn't Mean to Do That" or "Rescue Me" or "Save My Ass." No such luck. I found a key marked "Undo." It didn't do—or undo—anything.

"Holy shit," I said again.

I leapt up from Christa's chair. I paced the floor.

I approached Martin's door. It was ajar—actually ajar, now. Knocking, I pushed the door open. Martin stood before his desk on his bare right foot, his left leg thrust out to his side, his arms parallel to the floor. The thin fabric of his left pant leg had slid back to reveal his slim, hairless calf. He changed poses, drawing his arms and his airborne foot inward. Breathing deeply, he traced with both hands the axis of his body from navel to clavicle and back again. "What can I do for you?"

"Something just happened," I said. "I seem to have lost my report."

"I don't know anything about that infernal machine," he said. "Ask

Christa."

"She went home for the day. She's—. She's still sick, I guess."

"What is wrong with that girl? Her aura is as muddy as the Mississippi."

"You noticed it too?"

He looked at me askance. He touched forefingers and thumbs. His pinkies splayed outward. Closing his eyes, breathing deeply, noisily, he raised his arms above his head.

"End of the day tomorrow," he said.

"Here's the thing," I said. "The report was always meant just for internal use—just for *you*, basically. Maybe we could just sit down and I could *tell* you what the book said?"

He exhaled. "Very well. Very well. I'm listening."

"Well—." I slumped against his doorjamb. I had no idea what I wanted to say to him about *Onslaught*. It was only that I couldn't bear the thought of typing the whole report again. "It seems pretty clear—. If we—. If in the forums with Thorstensen's people, maybe if we give them a chance to vent about how society dumps on religious people—. Let them vent about how persecuted they feel—."

He nodded. "That makes sense. What else?"

"Maybe—." I sighed. "Give me a couple of hours. Okay? Or maybe—. Maybe in the morning?"

He dropped his arms, dropped his leg, stood flatfooted on his flat little feet, looked at me. "I had hoped, after so long a time away, that you would have developed a better attitude. A more positive aura. A smiling disposition. A habit of conscientious behavior."

"I'm sorry," I said. "It's been a bad couple of—."

He raised his hands. "Tomorrow morning, first thing. You'd better know what you're talking about."

Anything I might say next, I thought, could only make things worse. I said nothing. I backed out of his office and softly closed the door.

17 FORGIVEN

Thursday dawned clear and cold, but in the evening as I drove toward Prospect Park, a rugged wind rocked the Chevette. Clouds streaked the sky. An early moon, a half moon, shone clear and bright, high above the trees.

On Eliot's stoop there was a new mat, a thick rubber one bearing the word "WELCOME" in fat raised letters, in plain English. I rapped the knocker.

When Eliot answered, I realized how strongly I'd hoped for Charlie. I'd craved some small moment of privacy with him, for what reason—pure or impure—I could only guess. I met Eliot's smile with a smile. Again, as on Saturday, he hugged me.

With a hand on my shoulder he drew me inside. "I'm glad you're here," he said. "You won't regret it."

In the entryway I stopped to pull off my boots. I saw that he'd demoted, not discarded, the old rush welcome mat. In the corner, where before there had been a blot of gritty dried snowmelt, the old mat lay crowded with boots and shoes—Eliot's Nubucks, Tigger's Doc Martens, two pairs of hunting pacs with dingy white fur around the tops, a pair of slumped galoshes with pointed toes, a pair of loafers. Charlie's loafers? They were salt-stained, without tassels. An inch or so of stitching had come loose at the toe of the left shoe. They couldn't be Charlie's.

As we entered the living room, Eliot said, "I think you know everyone."

Fred, Jeremy, Tigger, Rob, Mason. I knew everyone.

A lacquer tray lay in the center of the coffee table. Crowded onto it were two carafes of coffee, a row of four mugs, and three silver bowls of chips, nuts, and pretzels.

As before, Mason sat in an armchair. As before, he wore a pilled cardigan. He gave me a thin smile and a small nod.

In the armchair opposite Mason, Rob slouched with his long legs stretched out before him, his ankles crossed. The other three sat on the couch, Fred and Jeremy close together on one end, Tigger leaning on the opposite arm.

I sat on the hearth, and Eliot sat beside me. The fire warmed my back.

"Charlie's not here yet, but why don't we get started? How did everyone survive the holiday? Rob?"

Rob hauled himself up and leaned forward with his elbows on his knees. "I made out all right," he said.

Eliot said, "And your father?"

"It could have been worse." Chuckling, Rob rubbed the palms of his hands together. "I guess it could always be worse."

No one spoke. I said, "I thought you were having an orphans' Thanksgiving at your place."

"Everyone had other plans." He looked at Tigger. Tigger shifted in his seat on the couch, running his hands down the length of his thighs. "Well, almost everyone did. So I went home instead," Rob said. "My parents only live a few miles from me."

"What happened?" Eliot said.

Sitting up, arching his back, Rob said, "Everyone else in the family is very supportive. They're proud of me for trying to change. But he—my dad— won't let it go. He makes these—these comments. I almost said 'subtle jokes,' but they're hardly subtle, and if they're jokes they're not very funny. Hairdresser jokes, AIDS jokes, all very junior high."

Eliot asked, "How did you respond to that?"

Rob crossed his legs, ankle resting on knee. Looking at Eliot, he said, "I ignored it as much as I could. We had a fire in the fireplace all day, and by five o'clock or so there was no wood left in the house. We went out together, my dad and I, to fetch some in, and I explained to him again what all this was about, what I was trying to do."

Tigger cleared his throat. He spun a pewter ring around the little finger of his right hand. His eyes, glassy and blind, fixed upon a narrow gap between Eliot and me. "I'll bet that didn't make a difference, did it?"

For a long moment, Rob studied Tigger. "It didn't make a difference at all."

Bending over the coffee table, Tigger set a mug right side up and poured coffee into it. He turned toward Rob. "I envy you," Tigger said. He lifted the mug, hugged it to his chest. "It may not be perfect, but at least your family welcomes you."

"Were you alone again this year?" Eliot asked. Tigger nodded. "Did you do anything to keep busy?"

Tigger swigged from his mug. Abruptly he stood. He paced the floor behind the sofa. "I went to the beach." He gulped coffee, grimaced. "There was no one there. I stayed all day, but no one else was there."

"Bare Ass Beach?" I said.

Tigger stared at me. He nodded.

I pictured him obsessively trudging the empty paths, tippets of mist and windswept snow curling around him.

Eliot said, "Tigger, maybe you should come sit down." Tigger returned to his place on the sofa. "If you hadn't been alone at the beach, what then?"

Tigger shrugged. "I suppose I would have taken what was offered," he said. He set his mug on the side table. Again he ran his hands down his thighs. "It scared me pretty bad. I couldn't seem to make myself leave. Not until dark, when I started to worry about bashers." He shook his head. "Bashers. As if that could be the worst thing." He swallowed dryly, stared wide-eyed into the fire.

"Tigger?"

Eliot's voice called him back. Tigger said, "Since then I've just gone to work and come home. Watching TV—that's all I've been doing. I've been wishing I could have another crack at that book. I haven't had the money to buy my own copy."

Book? What book?

Eliot said, "Charlie has it." He looked around, as if Charlie might be hiding in the folds of the curtains. "I wonder where he is."

Fred sat tall, his arms folded across his chest. Our eyes met. He looked at Eliot. He said, "Jonah doesn't know we're talking about *Hope and Healing.*" To me, he said, "It's a new Sam Stinson book that he wrote to help people like us. Eliot bought it, and it's been passing around the group."

Tigger looked at me. "There's a chapter called—what is it? 'Encouragement'? 'Tenacity'?"

Eliot supplied the name: "'Fortitude: Tenacity of Purpose.'"

"I've been trying to remember everything that's in it."

"Pray," Eliot said. "Make every thought a prayer."

Rob said, "Read the Psalms of praise."

"Take some physical exercise," Fred said.

Fred looked at Jeremy, and Jeremy added, "Sing hymns." I noticed, suddenly, that Jeremy's cheek was puffy, that there was a purplish swelling under his left eye.

Looking around at each of the men in the circle, Eliot said, "Enjoy the company of those who share your journey."

Holding out his hands, Tigger laughed, a genuine belly laugh. "Guys, guys. I think that'll hold me."

Eliot smiled. "It's good to hear that again," he said. "It seems I haven't heard you laugh in a month or more."

"The holidays always do me in," Tigger said. He rocked his head side to side. Bones in his neck popped. "I'm either dreading them, or—or *enduring* them, or getting over them." He groaned. "And there's Christmas yet."

Eliot scanned our faces. "Jonah? How did you do over Thanksgiving? You went to San Francisco?"

My skin burned. My hips and shoulders ached. If a case of the flu were coming on, as I'd suspected all week, I wished it would just come and go and be done with me.

They all watched me. I began to tell the story of my conversation with Barbara in the Vietnamese restaurant. Along the way, I fixed on a description of the food. I heard myself call the meat sauce an "offal slurry," and then I had to clarify for Jeremy the difference between "offal" and "awful."

Eliot cleared his throat and held up his hand. "I feel like you're avoiding something, Jonah. There's something you're not prepared to talk about?"

"I—I hadn't started all this yet. My mother works nights. I did some—some bar hopping. I did some things I can't be proud of now." I looked into my empty, chapped hands.

Eliot said, "There are no judgments here. You can—and should—talk about anything you need to talk about."

I looked at the faces in the circle, each in its own way welcoming me to open up, some—Eliot, Fred, Rob—by making eye contact, some—Mason, Jeremy, Tigger—by discreetly avoiding it.

There had been a few men. A slim blond in a USC sweatshirt I'd met on the street in front of Barbara's. A Latino boy with sparkling black eyes who'd cruised me in a men's room in the Embarcadero Center. A beefy black man in chaps who'd smiled at me in line outside the Lone Star, who'd yanked me out of line, who'd led me to his loft-cum-dungeon in the Mission.

"How much should I tell?" I said. I said, "You don't want intimate detail, do you?"

Eliot opened his hand: it was up to me.

Now the heat of the fire was oppressive. I stood. I edged away from the hearth. "I can't go into detail," I said. "I just can't. Suffice it to say, I spent the whole week wishing I'd put some condoms in my pocket."

No one spoke.

"Someone, anyone, please say something," I said.

Fred was the first to break the silence. He said, "We've all been there."

Tigger nodded vigorously. He said, "Totally."

"The crazy stuff I did when I was a drunk," Rob said.

Jeremy said, "It's purely by the grace of God I'm still here."

So there it was, just as Barbara had said. Men fear death, and so they cling to God. Was that why I was here? Fear of death? I didn't fear death—or I didn't think I did, not any more than anyone else. It was more a fear of life, a fear of fucking up, or that I'd already irrevocably fucked up. Maybe it was, after all, a fear of death.

"Are you angry with yourself?" Eliot asked.

Before I could answer, the door burst open to admit a whistling squall and Charlie Kent in a gray wool overcoat and boots. He stood on the threshold between the entryway and the living room. He saw me. He grinned.

"Sorry I'm late," he said. The tails of his trench coat whipped his calves. Under his arm he carried a hardcover book dressed in a cadmium-yellow dust jacket. "I got stuck at work. Be right back." When he returned he'd removed his coat and boots; underneath he wore houndstooth trousers and a white dress shirt. He handed the book to Eliot. "I finished this, finally," he said. He fetched one of the ladder-backed chairs from the far end of the room and set it next to Mason's armchair.

Flashing the title—*Hope and Healing*—in my direction, Eliot said, "Jonah? You're the only one who hasn't had it."

I returned to the hearth and sat next to Eliot. I took the book. All around the edges, the dust jacket showed the nicks and creases of much handling. Fingerprints blackened the edges of the pages. Opening the book across my knees, flipping through, I read the chapter titles: "The Cardinal Virtues,"

"Justice: Purity of Heart," "Prudence: Integrity of Mind," "Temperance: Sanctity of Body," and Tigger's chapter, "Fortitude: Tenacity of Purpose."

Eliot said, "Jonah was just telling us about his visit to San Francisco over Thanksgiving."

Dear Lord in heaven, would I have to say it all over again? I looked at Charlie. The oak chair creaked under his weight. His grin had not flagged. Could he really be that happy to see me?

Again I weighed words, tried to fit my mouth around a confession. But Eliot said, "I asked you if you're angry with yourself."

"It's not as though I've ever been any kind of stickler for safe sex. Tom and I—." I stopped myself. Eliot would be the only one here who'd heard me mention Tom. "My boyfriend and I—." Again, I stopped.

Eliot said, "You and Tom were monogamous. At least as far as you knew."

I nodded. "I suppose I never really got in the habit of thinking about protection, planning ahead. But still—. Still, it seems I should have taken better care of myself. Like I should have protected myself. I didn't—. There was this guy, a few weeks ago—. He had this sort of influence on me. A kind of *draw*—." I looked at Eliot. "I told you about him, but I didn't mention that—. Well, the condom broke."

"I see," Eliot said.

I looked around. Heads nodded. Perhaps it was a common excuse, *the condom broke*. I said to Eliot, "After the last group—. After the last group he showed up again, and then there was another guy. It was a crazy night. Some things happened that I—." I waved my hand. "I'm not going into details. It's embarrassing."

"Death by a thousand cuts."

It was Mason. I looked at him. He stared at the coffee table.

"Death by a thousand cuts." Except for the logs cracking in the fire and Mason's susurrous voice, the room was quiet. "It was a traditional Chinese punishment for treason or murder. A slow, humiliating, painful way to die. You're punishing yourself, self-destructing, killing yourself inch by inch."

I stared at Mason. He was motionless in his chair, his eyes cast down. He rarely spoke, it seemed, but when he did, his words were a stiletto slowly and gently piercing the gut.

"I—. I don't know what to say to that."

Now Mason looked at me. His eyes were wide and strange, the same eldritch blue as Spike's. "Say it's true."

For many minutes, it seemed, I looked at Mason, impaled on his weird blue gaze. I said nothing. I could not move my head, even to nod.

And did I want to nod? Did I want to say—or to show—that it was true, what he'd said? It felt true. More than that—it felt like a truth I'd been avoiding, hiding from myself.

Whether by accident or intention, Tom had killed himself. Long before his parents had written their accusations into a small claims complaint, I'd blamed myself, though only in some vague, inchoate way. I'd been punishing myself, obliterating myself, but—since, like everyone else, I feared death—I'd been doing it little by little.

It felt true.

I said, "I don't know. Maybe—. Like anyone else, I guess I—. I'm not in any hurry to—to get to the end of my life, or—or make it come sooner. I had—. Something Eliot said—. I had sort of been thinking that I was—like a lot of people—trying to hang on—. No, not hang on. Trying to feel alive by doing crazy things. Trying to fill a spiritual gap with physical distractions. There's a crazy kind of—of aliveness in doing things you know you shouldn't, right? Isn't there?"

For a long moment, no one spoke. Mason said, "There's physical death, and there's spiritual death. Sin is death. That's the worrisome one. You don't have a choice on the other, but you can choose eternal life over eternal death."

Eternal death? I swallowed hard.

"Sin separates us from God." Mason said. "Eternal separation from God, that is spiritual death."

Eliot set his hand on my knee. His touch startled me. He said, "I think the thing to remember is that what's done is done. The important thing is that you're forgiven of what you've done in the past, and you have the whole future ahead of you to prove that you've learned from your mistakes."

I took a breath. It seemed I had not taken a breath in thirty minutes. "Forgiven?" I said. "How do I know I'm forgiven?"

Charlie answered. "You've prayed for it, haven't you?"

My skin prickled. "I—I guess not."

"Haven't you been praying?" Eliot asked.

All eyes were on me. I blushed. "I *have*, but I haven't known what to pray *for*."

"Are you saved?" Fred asked.

"Have you at least prayed for Jesus to come into your life?" This was Jeremy.

He plucked at the gabardine of his trousers.

"Not in so many words."

A buzz filled the room. Eliot raised his hands, and everyone fell silent. Eliot turned to me. He said, "We usually end each group session with a prayer. Sometimes, when it's useful—when someone has a particularly pressing need or needs some comfort—we pause for our prayer in the middle, and then end with just a short prayer. I think this would be a good time to do that." He looked around the room. "All right with everyone?"

Heads bobbed.

Charlie said, his voice tender, "Eliot will go first, so you don't feel put on the spot. Just thank him for being there, then ask forgiveness, then invite him into your life to be your savior."

After a moment, I understood that he meant God, not Eliot. I should thank God. I should invite God into my life. I swallowed. I nodded.

As we bowed our heads, the air in the room seemed rarefied and hushed.

Eliot spoke. "Dear Lord our God, dearest Jesus, thank you for bringing us all together for the purpose of serving you and battering our lives."

Battering? Had I heard him correctly? Had he said *battering our lives?*

My stomach grew tight. I couldn't seem to keep my eyes closed. I watched Eliot. He sat hunched over his knees, his hands clasped between them.

No, not *battering. Bettering.* That's what he'd said. *Bettering our lives.*

"Lord," he said, "we are especially happy to have Jonah as a new member in our group. Thank you for the set of circumstances that brought him to us—and to you, however awful and painful those circumstances might have been. We understand that through pain sometimes we learn to feel joy. Lord, guide us in the rest of our work here tonight, and as we go our separate ways. Amen."

Amen. That was my cue. "Hello," I said, and earned a titter from Jeremy and Fred. "By now you must be wondering who I am and why I've been prattling on to you lately. Seems I missed a step." I peeked at the men around me. Charlie watched me; when our eyes met, I closed mine. "But I want to thank you for being there, and as Eliot said for bringing me here. Please forgive me for all of my sins. There are many, I'm sure, some greater than others. Forgive me for Spike—."

I paused, realizing that I'd mentioned Spike, but not by name, and that no one would know who he was. It was possible I hadn't mentioned Spike's name even to Eliot. But then, I was speaking to God, not to the men in the room, wasn't I?

I went on with my prayer. "Forgive me for Spike and for the others. For not taking care of myself when I was with Spike and Jose and when I was in San Francisco. Please forgive me for—for all of it." Now, how had Jeremy phrased that last bit? "Please come into my life and be my savior."

After I'd finished, Charlie said a few words, and then Rob and the rest—all but Mason. The voices droned on, at some point blending into a kind of chant that surpassed my understanding.

My heart filled unto bursting. All I could hear was a single word, over and over: *Forgiven. Forgiven. Forgiven.*

18 PRO AND CON

Forgiven.

Snowy drizzle dashed against my windshield. I drove down Seymour to the light at Franklin. Rain-blackened trees inclined toward me. The windshield wipers pulsed in the rhythm of a heartbeat. I saw, at the bottom of the hill, the pedestrian bridge over the highway, the handrails and fence glowing white.

I turned right. In the space of a few seconds I found myself near the river, near the University campus. All those weeks ago, after my first disastrous group session, when the way had seemed so unclear, I could have made a right turn, and in minutes I would have found myself at the river. Now, I took a detour through the campus; I needed buildings, lights, human activity around me, to hem me in.

Forgiven.

The word lightened me—*forgiven. Forgiven.*

It had disappeared, all of it—Spike, Jose, the guy in the USC sweatshirt, the Latino kid from the Embarcadero Center, the dungeon master. More: pot, beer, gossip, anger, sloth. It was as if none of it had existed, as if I'd never done anything worthy of regret.

Forgiven.

The rain and snow had driven all but a drenched few inside. All along Washington, the windows of empty shops and restaurants blazed with white and blue light. Turn the Page, my favorite used book store, was dark except for a single desk lamp on the counter. The tattered spines of books shelved behind it glowed in shades of ochre and russet.

Inside the door of an Arby's, half a dozen people stood looking out at the rain. The shining curve of a young man's shaved head, the ruffle of an old woman's hat, were all I could see as I drove by. Did they know this feeling? Had any of them known this unbearable liberty?

Liberty, I thought, because now all of time lay ahead of me. My future was brilliant white. My future and my past were no longer foxed like the pages of an old book, no longer marred and muddied by scratches and dust like the grooves of a ruined old record.

Yet it was unbearable, because it was so undeserved. What had I done for it, but ask? How could it be that I should care so little for myself for so long and yet have all of that washed away with a single sentence spoken on Eliot Moon's hearth?

Please forgive me.

Forgiven.

I pulled to the curb to make way for a fire engine. Its sirens were quiet, but its flashing red lights, reflected in the windows of nearby buildings, transformed the street into a brassy carnival. A firefighter rode clinging to the back of the truck, his coat wet and shimmering, his hat angled low to cover the nape of his neck.

Did he know? The firefighter—did he know what it was to be forgiven?

And what of my vandal? Did the hand that had written "GAF" in soap on my windshield, that had plastered bumper stickers on my front walkway, that had nailed Bible passages to my door—did that hand belong to someone who knew what it was to be forgiven? I could not fathom how anyone who had ever felt this gratitude—this freedom, this consciousness of absolution, this sense of radiant weightlessness—could possibly bear to accuse a stranger of wrongdoing.

But my vandal, too, deserved forgiveness—God's and mine. He, the vandal, was no more or less deserving than I was. And I was incandescent with forgiveness, brimful with forgiveness, bursting with forgiveness. Having received it, I longed to give it. Everything and everyone was forgiven.

For a long while I sat at the curb, watching the fire engine's lights recede. I felt as if I might float away, so much mist leaking out of the cracks and crevices of the Chevette, ascending into the sky.

◆ ◆ ◆

Forgiven or not, absolved or not, my vandal had visited again. My house again shouted my sins to the world. Block capitals—"GOD HATES FAGS"—contorted themselves around the windows and bushes, so that the message could be seen clearly from the street.

It was recent, this graffiti. Of course, it was recent. I'd stopped at home after work, and the house had been clean, its own bare, unadorned self.

Up close, I could see and smell that the paint had not yet dried completely. Rainwater and snowmelt had spotted the graffiti, had pockmarked the words. Serifs bulged at the top and bottom of each letter, where the flow of paint had started and ended.

At the side of the house, the garden hose hung coiled over a curved shelf. With numb, wet hands I lifted the hose to the ground. The stiff nylon loops fell to the brown lawn, crackled stiffly, scattered themselves in three directions. I tugged the nozzle free.

Returning to the spigot, I twisted it. It balked, then turned. The cold steel burned my bare fingers. Pipes inside the house squealed. At the hose's business end, the water came in a trickle. With my thumb, I reduced the opening to a crescent moon and aimed the flat stream at the house. To reach the word I most wanted to expunge, I sidled between the house and a holly bush. Glistening leaves dumped chilly water down my back, more water in a second than the hose had produced in all these minutes. Red paint rolled like clotting blood down the stucco, making the lettering more ominous, but no less legible.

I tightened the squealing spigot. Soaked now to the skin, I gladly went inside. I called Luther.

In twenty minutes—time enough for me to put on dry clothes and hang my damp jacket over a radiator—Luther emerged from the rain wearing a puffy down parka and carrying an unmarked plastic jug.

"It doesn't look good," he said. "You spread it around without really making it less readable."

"I'm sorry. I didn't know what else to do."

Shaking his head, he said, "Music majors." He lifted the jug a few inches. "I brought something that might take the paint off. It's probably too wet and cold out there now, though."

Reaching to take the jug from him, I said, "Leave it with me. I'll clean it up tomorrow."

"Wear rubber gloves or you'll burn your skin off." He let go of the jug. "It's damn cold out there, tenant."

I set the cleanser in the corner by the door. "How about some hot choco-late?"

"Erma never makes me hot chocolate. Is it the kind with the little marsh-mallows?"

"I only have the big ones." It occurred to me that I hadn't looked for or needed marshmallows in quite a long time. Tom had had a habit of eating them right out of the bag. He might have eaten them all.

Grinning, Luther pulled off his boots. "Even better."

In the kitchen I hunted the marshmallows. I found them—to my relief— in a corner cupboard. A few remained in the bottom of a tightly wrapped bag. I sniffed a carton of milk. It seemed okay. I filled a saucepan. "It's skim milk," I hollered. "I hope that's all right."

Luther appeared in the doorway, two or three audiocassettes in each hand. He'd removed his boots. His socks showed bluish circles of damp at the toes. He wore a white tank top tucked into blue jeans. The deep brown of his skin colored the shirt's thin fabric. A few gray hairs mingled with the black curls on his chest. "Milk? There's milk in hot chocolate?"

I fished a wooden spoon from the drawer. "How exactly do you think hot chocolate is made, landlord?"

"You pour powder out of a jar and add hot water. If you're really patient, you heat the water first in the microwave."

"That's how you make coffee, not hot chocolate. Let me just warn you well in advance." From the smallest burner, I coaxed a high flame. "Hot fudge sauce will make an appearance." I settled the saucepan in the center of the burner. I poured milk, stirred it with a wooden spoon.

"Do you really listen to all this dance shit?" He shuffled the cassettes.

I shook my head. "Tom did."

"Sorry, tenant."

I spanked milk from the wooden spoon and set it aside. From the refrig-erator, I fetched the fudge sauce, Tom's favorite, premium gold-label stuff in a Mason jar. I opened the jar. Tracks and ditches marked the surface of the thick brown sludge. With the wooden spoon I scooped out a dollop and stirred it into the milk.

"Pro and con," he said.

"Pro and con?"

"Real hot chocolate, big marshmallows—pro. No accidental pregnancies—

pro. Disco music—definite con."

How many more cons there were, he could never know. Skulking around in dark and smelly places or among cold dripping bushes, looking for "action"—con. Graffiti on the front of the house—con. Lifestyle, or life, causing you pain—con. Death by a thousand cuts—con.

Eking out a smile, I said, "So you think the disco music offsets everything else?"

"All by itself."

While I stirred and stirred, watching the fudge melt into the milk, he poked around some more in the living room. I heard things rattling. The television warbled.

I dipped a finger into the purplish-brown liquid. It was plenty hot. I turned off the heat. Two mugs from the cupboard above. Pour carefully. Plop in marshmallows, three for Luther, two for me. Add the crumpled bag to the overflowing trash.

In the living room, Luther stood before the television set, the VCR remote in his hand. I'd left one of Spike's videos in the machine. *Go Down on It,* it was called. It must have been the pinnacle of Spike's early career; he was in every scene. I'd left it at—or Luther had cued it to—the group scene at the end. Spike knelt, surrounded by erect penises, hub of a many-spoked wheel. Drunk or high or besotted with pleasure, his eyes heavy and hooded, he looked up at the men's out-of-shot faces. His lips curled in a sleepy smile.

Turning away, I handed Luther his mug. He sipped. Tipping the mug toward me he said, "Pro." He sipped again.

"And this?" I nodded toward the screen. "Would that be pro or con, landlord?"

"I haven't decided yet." He winked at me. Something seemed to snag his attention. Cocking his head, he listened. He raised the television's volume a couple of notches. "Isn't that a blatant rip-off of a Springsteen song?" He hummed along. "Down, down, down," he sang, "down, down." He laughed. "They just put it on a synthesizer and added a couple of extra downs. Not the words, of course, but notes where extra *downs* would go."

I set my mug on the eye-level shelf of a bookcase. Tom's porn, that was surely something I should not have around—especially Spike's videos. And the disco music was surely too bound up with the club scene, too much connected with the writhing of half-clothed male bodies. Too gay.

My Broadway LP's, though—? Were those bad influences?

"There wouldn't happen to be any more of this, would there?" Luther asked. When I turned, he was tipping the open mouth of his mug toward me. It contained only foamy brown dregs. He'd switched tapes, or maybe the video had run to the previews at the end. I didn't recognize the scene. There was a sling and an X-shaped wooden cross, men in harnesses of chrome and black leather, a preposterously large black dildo. I averted my eyes.

"I don't have any more milk."

Handing me his mug and the remote control, he said, "I should go anyway. You'll clean up that graffiti when the wall dries out?" In the entryway, then, he rocked his feet into his boots. "If you have any questions or problems, call me, tenant. Hear?"

"Sure."

"Are you all right, tenant? You're not mad because I was touching your stuff?"

Now that he mentioned it, it irked me that he'd started the VCR without asking. But I didn't want to quarrel with him. And even in my annoyance and embarrassment I still felt the glow of forgiveness—though by now it was an ember, not a blaze.

"Not at all. I'm—I'm just tired." I forced myself to smile. I glanced toward the television. In a jumpy freeze-frame image two men soul-kissed. One wore a thick, spiked dog collar. "And—and I suppose the homophobic graffiti has put me off a bit."

He chuckled. "I suppose it would. Sorry."

As I turned back to look at Luther, I spotted the small claims papers. They lay where I'd left them, on the floor beside the easy chair.

"There is something else," I said. "Something that's been worrying me."

I showed him the complaint. Frowning, he read. He clucked. "Shameful. They don't have a leg to stand on."

"Maybe so, or—or maybe not—but—. But what do I do? I just don't want to see them, especially not in court."

They would be dressed in their Sunday finery, of course—Rose Hill in a hat and some lavender polyester thing, and Greg Hill in the only suit he'd ever owned, likely also polyester and possibly machine washable. Whether or not they bothered to bring evidence of their claim, each would bring a Bible, and they would watch with glum incredulity as I—godless sinner, corrupter of their son—swore upon the Good Book.

"You have to fill out the answer. Unless you want to just pay them."

I shook my head. "It'd be worth it, just to be done with it, but you know—Christmas and all—. I just went on vacation—. I just don't have the money. Couldn't you—?"

He looked at me.

"Never mind."

Luther stood next to me now, so close that under the sweet scent of his cologne I could smell the innate spice of his skin. "I'll help you figure out what to say in the answer. Better yet, I'll write them a nasty lawyer letter and tell them to knock it off."

"What's your rate for a nasty lawyer letter?"

He waved away the question. "It'll take ten minutes. Have more marsh-mallows and whole milk next time, and we'll call it even." He raised the packet of court papers. "Can I take these?"

"Of course."

And he stood yet closer, so that I had to tip my head backward to see his face. He put his hand on my shoulder, and for a half-crazed moment I thought he might kiss me. But he said, "Take care. Get some sleep," and was gone. I locked and chained the door behind him.

Punching a button on the remote, I ejected Spike's video from the VCR. It must go. A cardboard box in the bay window held a few volumes from my last spree through Turn the Page—something about the Puritans, a collection of love poetry written by women, a history of sex in advertising—things I'd bought months ago, things I couldn't remember wanting. I left them where they lay and added *Go Down on It*.

And then Tom's audiocassettes—ABBA, Blondie, the Village People, all the rest, the whole lot, until his vinyl cassette case was empty.

I emptied the bookshelves of all of the books Tom had bought but had rarely, if ever, read. Christopher Bram, Alan Hollinghurst, Andrew Holleran, David Leavitt, Armistead Maupin, Anne Rice's *Sleeping Beauty* books and *Vampire Chronicles*, the *Men on Men* series.

But how far to go? Hart Crane? Oscar Wilde? Tory's collection of Whit-man quotes? The excerpts I had cribbed from Whitman and Crane to com-pile the text of *The River*? After a moment's reflection, I resolved to spare the poetry. I had bared enough shelf space as it was. On the top shelf, only *Tulips and Chimneys* remained. On other shelves, books leaned against one another into open spaces two, three, six, seven inches wide.

Tom's videotapes, though—. I would save none. I went to the bedroom and fetched the whole stack and dumped them all into the box.

• • •

At group Tigger had hinted that he wanted another crack at *Hope and Healing,* but since he'd read it and I hadn't, Eliot had given it to me.

The next day, Friday, I left the book in the back seat of my car.

On Saturday, I took the book with me into the Spin Cycle, thinking I might read it while I waited. Instead, I left it at the bottom of my laundry bag while I went across the street to the Rainbow Foods for a sandwich. No dryers were free when I returned, and—forgetting that the Stinson book was there—I set the laundry bag in a basket and piled my wet clothes on top of it. My damp shirts and jeans soaked the bottom edges of the front cover and the first hundred pages.

On Sunday I left the book propped against a radiator to dry.

Although I knew my Monday to be filled with meetings—three forums with DFL staff and a debriefing session with Martin—I carried the book with me as I left for work. Again, I left it on the seat of the car. There it stayed until the end of Thursday's workday.

To Eliot's I carried it, puffy but whole, under my arm. I arrived early. Only Eliot, Fred, and Jeremy were there. While Eliot busied himself in the kitchen, Fred and Jeremy bent their heads together, whispering. I opened the book. The pages parted at a chapter entitled "Why You're Homosexual."

There were bullet points. "Abandonment," one read. "Reinforcement," read another. "Defiance." "Narcissism."

Narcissism? I closed the book.

"What do you think of the book?" Jeremy asked. The puffy place under his left eye had faded to greenish-yellow. He moved his hand through the air, his fingers rippling like pennants. "Isn't it just *divine?*"

Eliot saved me from answering. He backed through the kitchen door carrying the lacquer tray. On it, the two carafes and the silver bowls and a half dozen mugs rattled softly.

Half-standing, I said, "Do you need a hand?"

"You could get the cookies from the kitchen."

"There are two kinds of people in this world," Jeremy said. He giggled. "To satisfy both, I made chocolate chip and oatmeal raisin."

Fred gaped at him as if he'd just said some uncommonly naughty thing.

I fetched the cookies. The oatmeal raisin cookies were larger by half than the chocolate chip and there were twice as many of them. Clearly, Jeremy was one of the oatmeal raisin people.

Charlie had arrived. He shook off his overcoat and draped it over a chair. He said, "What have we here? Jeremy's thousand-dollar chocolate chip cookies?"

"It's two hundred and fifty," Jeremy said. "Two-hundred-and-fifty-dollar cookies."

Charlie took a cookie, nibbled. "Mm," he said.

I sat in one of the armchairs. Charlie sat on the sofa, on the end nearest me. I opened the Stinson book and began reading the "Narcissism" passage.

> For some the same-sex desire is at the core a desire for the self,
> a diseased form of selfishness and self-centeredness, an erotic
> and infantile fixation on the self in both physical and emotional
> forms.

"What are you looking for?" Fred said. "I know the book almost by heart."

"Nothing. I was just glancing ahead."

"What do you think of the book? How far did you get?" Jeremy asked me. He couldn't seem to keep his hands still. "In a week's time I could just read and read and read."

Just then Tigger and Rob came in together, hugging themselves and stomping their feet. Mason arrived not long after. After a time of chatty crowding around the coffee and cookies, everyone found a seat. Mason pulled one of the ladder-backed chairs into the circle.

"What did you think of the book?" Eliot asked me. "Did you finish it?"

The way I held the book—with both arms, flat against my chest, as if it were a cherished object—earned beatific smiles from everyone. But after a moment of stammering, I had to say, "I haven't really started it. I meant to, but I just didn't get to it."

The saintly smiles turned glassy. Everyone looked at the floor. Everyone but Eliot. He said, "You didn't even read the foreword?"

"I skimmed some chapter titles last week during the session. And—. And then, just now—."

"Is there a reason?"

Rob said, "Didn't we make it clear that this book is the bedrock of this program?"

"I don't think you did," I said. The sharp corners of the book's cover dug into my forearms. "I just thought it was a helpful book you were passing around." I tucked the book between my leg and the arm of the chair. I leaned forward, elbows on knees, and glanced at Mason. His eyes met mine. I looked away. "Besides, Eliot said—."

Eliot had said that I was free to take this at my own pace, one step at a time. Now, his face was inscrutable. He said, "Did you read anything at all this week?"

"Outside of stuff for work? I read some—. Well, some, yes, I did some reading this week."

"What?"

"Beethoven," I said. "McNamara." I'd struggled through the latter chapters of *The Seventeen Quartets* to the end, and then I'd returned to the start. "A book about Beethoven's string quartets."

"Beethoven. You had time for Beethoven, but not for this." Eliot nodded toward the Stinson book. "Why is that?"

Sitting back, I set *Hope and Healing* squarely on my lap. I smoothed the glossy cover with both hands. Gray scuff marks marred the embossed letters of the title. With the tip of my index finger I traced the *H* of *Healing*. "I have a hard time with Sam Stinson," I said. "We talked about it a long time ago."

Frowning, Eliot said, "I remember." He might have said, "Why do you insist upon speaking Esperanto?"

"When I was a child, my parents studied one of his books in Sunday School, and my father took it too much to heart."

Eliot said, "And your mother took you away from your father?"

I shook my head. "The other way around. She told me—. When I was in San Francisco, I found out—she told me—it was the other way around. He left us."

Eliot nodded. He said, "Tell us about that."

My explanation rambled back and forth through time, taking in *Love and Discipline,* and Barbara's anti-Biblical tirade, and what she'd told me about her marriage, and the mysterious photos of the foster children. When I'd finished, each of the men sat at the edge of his seat, itching to speak.

Eliot said, "You really need to read *Hope and Healing,* Jonah. I think you'll see yourself in it."

Tigger said, "You were separated from your father at an early age. That's abandonment." He looked at Eliot. He seemed to expect some kind of prize. A gold star, perhaps.

"Abandonment," Eliot said to me, "is the idea that when a child isn't allowed to bond sufficiently with the parent of the same sex, it creates a hunger for same-sex bonding in other forms."

"And I think there is some reinforcement going on with that Barbara woman," Fred said. "Big time. Sounds like she did everything but *require* you to be gay."

"Barbara's always been unconditionally supportive of me," I said. "I thought that made her a good mother."

Eliot shook his head. "Reinforcement, in most cases, is an omission. Parents sometimes guess that their gay kids are gay, but purposely ignore the signs. They don't know what to do, so they do nothing, and the children take it for implicit approval. That's in *most* cases."

The men around the circle were nodding. Jeremy tucked his chin into his chest.

Eliot said, "In your case, it sounds like your mother was, and *is,* so 'supportive'"—he spat the word—"that she all but *pushed* you to be gay."

"And don't forget," Rob said. "Don't forget defiance. I think your mother contributed some to that too."

"That's true," Eliot said to Rob. To me he said, "Defiance is the idea that there's a perceived benefit in being unusual, in resisting the classical definitions of right and wrong. You just got done telling us your mother has a strong resistance to religion and traditional morality. And now—. Now. Just look at your reluctance to read Sam Stinson." He nodded toward the book. "If that's not defiance, I don't know what is."

"Surely no one's to *blame*," I said. "Surely I can't blame my mother for *making* me gay."

Charlie said, "It's not all her fault. She created the conditions, but *you* made the choice."

"When? When did I choose this?" I glanced round the circle at stony faces. "Do any of you remember choosing?"

Their silence was icy. Charlie said, "It's not an all-at-once choice. It's done in increments over years, until the habits form and become ingrained. It's in the book. It's in the chapter called 'Why You're Homosexual.'"

Narcissism. No one had said anything about it. I flipped pages again, toward the front where I'd seen the word. Now I couldn't find it. I closed the book and set it on its spine between my legs. My right leg quivered, my heel knocking the floor.

Eliot said, "Whether your mother left your father, or your father left your mother, it seems to me that she started running away from things when you were very young, and that you've been running from things ever since. You want to leave right now, don't you?"

Nodding all around. Was it that obvious? "I suppose I do."

"You ran from my office once when I started talking about God." He nodded once, emphatically, as if what he'd just said proved everything. "Don't run from this, Jonah. Read the book. It will help."

Looking at the floor, holding the book between the palms of my hands, I nodded. "I will. Shouldn't someone else get a chance to talk?" I said. "This has all been about me since we started."

Charlie put his hand on my knee. "That's another kind of running away, Jonah. We're all here for each other."

Eliot said, "Do you know what precipitated the break? The break between your parents?"

I shook my head. "I know what I thought it was. But I don't know what it actually was."

"What did you think it was?"

"My father hit me with a belt."

"Do you remember why?"

"I said a bad word. I was just repeating something I'd heard on the playground. I asked if it was a bad word, because I didn't believe it could be."

"'Fuck,'" Charlie said.

Mason shuffled his feet, shifted his weight in a way that made his chair creak.

Charlie said, "That had to be the word, am I right? I made up rhyming games. Duck, stuck, truck, muck, luck, buck."

"That was the word," I said. "And I made up the rhymes, too. Fuck, fuck, goose."

Tigger laughed, nodding. "My mother made me get a switch."

I looked at Tigger. "A switch?"

"Do you remember this?" Eliot said. I looked at him. He was talking to me. "Do you have a first-hand recollection of this incident?"

"I remember the punishment, not the crime."

"Then how do you know what happened?"

"Barbara told me."

"Do you think she told you the whole story?"

"Why wouldn't she?"

"Maybe because they had a big fight over it, and that's why he left. Or maybe at the time she also felt that punishment was justified."

I said, "What could I have done at four years old that would deserve a beating with the buckle end of a belt? Repeating a word I didn't know?"

Charlie put his hand on my knee again. "My father once broke my little finger because I misquoted a Bible verse. He bent it back until it snapped."

The pinky finger of his right hand—that must be it. Where it lay on my leg, it bent sideways a few painful-looking degrees. Charlie took his hand away.

"You win," I said. I set the Stinson book on the side table. To Eliot I said, "Is this where we implant a false memory?"

"I understand your hostility," Eliot said. "I understand that you feel some loyalty to your mother. But you have to wonder why a caring, Christian father would exact such a terrifying punishment for such a small offense." He spoke quickly. "Parents often go too far in the heat of anger and because of fear. Do you have any good memories of him? Did he ever hold you?"

"I don't remember him touching me except in anger."

"But he left when you were very young."

I nodded. "Six or eight, I think. There seems to be a lot of stuff I don't remember."

"Can you remember anything except the belt?"

I shook my head, then shrugged. "Not a lot."

"How would you know of anything that happened before that?"

"Barbara would have to tell me about it."

"Was it in her best interests to say anything kind about him, if by doing so she risked turning you against her?"

I leaned forward. I rubbed my temples. Looking up, I said, "It's not like she could turn me against her by saying he hugged me once."

"But if she could make you believe that you were better off without him, then—."

"I can't believe anything else, because I don't know anything but what she told me," I said. Soon after she'd told me the truth, I'd thought much the same thing.

Eliot said, "And do you suppose she told you everything? She misled you, didn't she? You thought she left your father, but he left her."

"True," I said. "That's entirely true." I looked at him. Still, he was inscrutable. "Barbara and I—. When I was growing up we relied on each other for everything. When I turned out to be gay, what was she supposed to do? Disown me?"

"Of course not," Eliot said. "Of course it's natural and healthy that a mother and son should be close. To a point. Your mother took a course of action that almost ensured you'd turn out homosexual." He rushed the word. He barely allowed it three syllables. "In that situation, I could hardly expect her to object to any great degree when you in fact did turn out to be homosexual." Again, he rushed the word, as if it were a profanity he could not avoid using.

"You're saying my mother set out to make me gay? Why would anyone do that?"

Fred said, "Your mother is Barbara Murray, right? I remember listening to her radio show fifteen years ago and hearing her talk about AIDS and gay rights and gay people. That's her audience. That's why she went to San Francisco, and she said as much before she left."

"My mother made me gay to improve her ratings?"

"Stranger things have happened," Jeremy said.

But Eliot said, "All of the things your mother did in raising you made it extremely easy for you to come to the decision that you were gay. No male role model, an utter lack of the opprobrium usually reserved for these behaviors, and on the contrary an atmosphere of approval and permissiveness. And an entrenched habit of defiance against religion and morality. Look how far she led you from the path you started out on. You knew you wanted God, but you didn't even know how to talk to him."

I remembered Barbara fleeing the hole-in-the-wall Vietnamese restaurant, the mad dash back to the apartment, the raven flutter of her skirt as she scurried up the stairs—all because I'd simply uttered the word *God*. I remembered her explaining how she'd reinvented herself, how she'd set out to do the opposite of everything she'd ever done. As a child, I could only have gone along for the ride.

• • •

When all the talking was done, I grabbed for my coat and, waving good-bye, made for the door. The chill of wet snow already fallen mingled with the smell of snow yet to fall. The stairs to the street were slick. I trod carefully.

Above me, at my back, Charlie barked my name. He stood, a crisp silhouette, on the lawn. He trudged down the steps. I waited on the sidewalk for him. He hadn't put on his overcoat. One hand was deep in his trouser pocket. With the other hand he extended the Stinson book toward me.

"You forgot this," he said.

I took it. As though it were a calf's bleeding liver or a handful of writhing leeches, I took it. "Thanks," I said. "You didn't have to—."

He put his hand over mine. "That wasn't easy for you," he said, "but don't run away. Don't give up. This is worth doing, and you can't do it alone." Taking the book from me, he unwrapped the bright yellow dust jacket. He kept the glossy paper and handed back the book. Nude, its true colors proved to be sand and olive, entirely respectable earth tones. The spine bore Stinson's name in tiny gold letters. "This keeps it from looking so much like a Joe Boxer ad. If you give the book a chance, if you just read one chapter, it will change your life."

"I'll read it. I promise."

He smiled. "You won't regret it." He hugged himself.

"Look at you," I said. "You're freezing. I'd better go and let you get back inside where it's warm."

Nodding, he took a step toward the concrete stairs. "I'll see you next week?"

I paused. "Okay."

He hugged himself. "I feel like we put you through the wringer. I can only imagine what you feel like."

I shook my head. "I think it was a bitter dose of truth, that's all." I'd said it merely to be polite, but then, after I'd said it, I realized it was true.

"It gets easier. I've been doing this a long time. It gets easier."

"What about the cravings, the—the desires?" I was thinking of the box of bad influences sitting in my living room. I'd looked at the box a thousand times, had thought a thousand times of slipping one of Spike's videos into the VCR. "Please tell me it gets easier."

He looked down. "I'll be honest. The temptations never go away. You have to—. You almost have to distract yourself sometimes." He laughed. "You have to have some damn good hobbies."

I smiled. "I have hobbies. I guess I need different ones."

"Probably so."

"Masturbation probably isn't a damned good hobby."

He frowned. He thrust his hands into his pockets, balled his fists.

"That was a joke," I said. "Not so funny?"

"Drive safely," he said.

"I have to," I said, "or I won't see you next week."

He grinned.

• • •

For a hundred hours, it seemed, I had worn the same wool slacks, the same blue oxford shirt, the same beastly boots with their prickly-hot felt lining. Tossing the Stinson book onto the easy chair, I stripped to skin.

I went to the bathroom to brush my teeth. Brush hanging from my lips, I ran the flat of my hand down my belly. I thought of Charlie, bringing the image of his sturdy body before my mind's eye. What would he look like, stripped of his business casual dress, divested of the chaussure of the pompous? My cock rose.

I looked at my shaggy reflection in the mirror. Suddenly I hated the freckles across my shoulders, the unabashedly auburn wisps surrounding my nipples, the raw throbbing pink of my penis. My dick looked embarrassingly pied and slender in its nest of ludicrous orange hair.

I spat and rinsed. My flagging erection led the way to the easy chair. I took up the book; it was time. I sat down. I began to read.

19 EQUAL AND OPPOSITE

Michael Walrath's door stood half-open. I peeked through the gap. Michael sat at his desk, his right foot tucked under his left hip. His hair hung down his back in a long pony tail—a frayed rope of satin strands. He wore shorts and a long-sleeved T-shirt. The muscles of his thighs and calves bulged in thick slabs and stout knots.

I knocked on the door. He looked up, smiled.

"Jonas?" he said, and laughed. "Just kidding." He waved me in. He untangled his legs and came toward the door to meet me.

At the foot of Michael's bed, his sheets and blankets lay in a puffy wad. He'd drawn the vinyl curtain across the wall of windows. He'd cranked up the heat. Baseboard registers ticked and pattered.

A pot of soup bubbled on the cooktop. Chunks of potato and carrot quivered in a thick greenish liquid. The whole apartment smelled of rosemary and of something flowery. Lavender?

"How have you been?" Michael asked me.

I smiled. "Great," I said. "Good. Not bad. You?"

He sighed. "Missing James."

"He's in Paris, right?"

I winced. Surely he'd never mentioned Paris. I knew that James was in Paris only because I'd snooped through Michael's things; that was the only way I *could* know.

To my relief, he seemed to think nothing of it. "You could use a shave, it looks like." With the back of his hand he rasped his own five-o'clock shadow.

He grinned. "Me too, I guess."

I touched my beard. The hairs had gone from wiry to soft. Curls bristled between my fingers. "Guess I do." I shrugged. "It keeps me warm on these cold winter nights."

"Speaking of cold winter nights, I haven't seen you since—. Well, you know."

I blushed. "I brought that receipt," I said.

It was in the inside pocket of my jacket. I drew it out, a flimsy pink sheet of paper, much wrinkled and creased. I unfolded it, handed it over.

He laid the receipt on the counter, smoothed it carefully with both hands. He read it over. "Thanks," he said. "You were the last holdout."

"Sorry. Did they find out—? The boathouse—. Who, how—?"

He shrugged. "A couple of kids. Just trying to get out of the cold, they said. They broke in, lit up a joint, tossed it into a corner where there were some rags stacked up."

"Happens, I guess."

"It happens?" He laughed. "That's a philosophical attitude if I ever heard one."

A couple of kids, he'd said. Suddenly I remembered the two denim-clad boys I'd seen at the beach, and then later on the river road.

"Have you see these kids? Were they like—? Did they—?" I was about to ask if they'd been wearing frayed black denim, if they'd looked strung out, if their eye sockets had been deep and bruised-looking, but of course if he'd seen them, it would have been on a different day, under entirely different circumstances.

And even if he could describe them perfectly, or if I could see them for myself, would I be able to say with any certainty whether they were the same two boys?

"Never mind," I said. "Does it seem—? It was really an accident? That's for sure?"

Crossing his arms, he leaned against the counter. "I'm not really handling that part of it. I'm just doing the insurance part." He glanced at the pot of soup, sniffed. Taking a spoon from a drawer at his hip, he moved to the cook top. He stirred the soup. "I guess I don't much care. It's sort of easier with the insurance if it was an accident." Leaning over the pot, he slurped soup from the spoon. He nodded appreciatively.

On the desk, where it had been before, the photo of Michael and James sat in its silver frame. Another, smaller snapshot leaned against it now. Blond, pale James stood before the Eiffel Tower, squinting into the sun.

"Why is he in Paris?" I tried to sound casual, as if we'd discussed James's trip to France a dozen times.

"Working on his thesis. Something about—. Fuck, who was it again? Ravel? Debussy?"

"Oh," I said. "He's a music major?"

He nodded. "Getting his master's. He started out wanting to write pop songs, ended up stuck on the French—. Fuck, what is it? French expressionists?"

"Impressionists."

"If you say so. You're sure you're okay?" Michael asked me. "Doing better?"

My shoulders and hips still ached. I shifted my weight. I pressed my fingers into the flesh of my right thigh. I sighed. "Got the flu coming on, or something."

"Flu?" He frowned. "Achy? Muscle aches? Feverish?"

"Achy." And right now, having come from the cold street into Michael's overheated apartment, I did feel feverish. I resisted an impulse to test the heat of my forehead with the back of my hand.

His frown deepened. Stepping closer, he squinted at me. "When were you last tested?"

"For the flu?"

He rolled his eyes. "You know what I mean."

I cleared my throat. "Oh, you know . . ."

"Never?"

I shook my head.

"That's what I thought. You've been playing safe, right?"

"Well—. I—." I couldn't say to him that I hadn't used a condom in years— literally years, not since my first days with Tom. But what could I say instead?

"I know, I know," he said. "Rubbers stink, literally. They don't feel the same. Blah, blah, blah."

"It's not that. I—." I shrugged.

"You should come in sometime."

"What?" I said. "Come in where?"

He went to his desk, searched it, found a box tucked away in a corner, under some papers. He plucked a card from the box. He handed it to me. In pink, in wavy, curl-seriffed letters, it read, "The Pink House." Below that, in block letters, "Walk-In Clinic." Below that, also in block letters, but in smaller type, an address in Minneapolis, a phone number, and hours of operation.

"Starting next week, I'll be there on Thursdays," he said. "Six to ten. I've been doing Wednesdays forever, but—." He plucked the card from my hand. "Here. Let me write it down." He took the card to the desk and scribbled something on the back of it. Handing back the card, he said, "Thursday, six to ten. Starting next week."

I flipped the card over. Even if none of his other talents or attributes fitted him for the medical profession, his handwriting certainly did.

"It's flu season and all," he said. "Could be the flu. But you can't be too careful. Better to know than not to."

◆　◆　◆

In a cold sweat, I drove to Eliot's. I stopped for green lights. I coasted through stop signs.

That twitch in my right eyelid—a symptom, a sign?

I laid the back of my hand across my forehead. Warm. Fever?

That gland under my chin, on the left side—was that swollen?

It must mean something that my hips and calves and shoulders had been bothering me for weeks. My muscles ached. My joints ached. It must mean something.

It was flu season, after all, as Michael had said. But—.

Early in the week I'd dubbed the C-sharp minor quartet onto cassette, and as I drove, I plugged one of the Walkman's ear buds into my ear. I pressed play. The tape was cued to the beginning of the second movement.

A slender tune whispered in the violin. The melody meandered in circles, a puppy chasing its tail. An accompaniment of block chords in the lower strings gave way to mimicry, imitation, counterpoint—a whole litter of puppies chasing their tails.

It was all so playful, so lively. And I couldn't bear it. I switched off the Walkman.

Maybe I should skip group altogether. Last week's group had been uncomfortable. I'd had a bad week. I'd had a bad day. With a couple of squinty looks and a couple of nosy questions, Michael Walrath had nearly guaranteed I'd have a bad night.

Michael's bedside manner was—. Well. It was fortunate that, as a researcher, he wouldn't *need* bedside manner.

By habit or muscle memory, somehow, I got myself to Eliot's. I parked in front of his house and switched off the ignition. I reached into the back seat and felt around for *Hope and Healing*. I laid the book in my lap. For a time I stared at it, stroked the cool ochre cloth along the spine, traced with my thumb the cooler gold letters of the title and of Stinson's name.

Charlie had been right—somewhat right. I couldn't say the book had changed my life, but reading it had helped. At times it had helped only to fill the hours. But sometimes—over time, as I'd read deeper—it had helped me to feel less lonely, less rootless, less adrift.

And it had helped, certainly, to reform my opinion of Sam Stinson. Most recently I'd read the chapter in which he outlined the merits—yes, the merits—as well as the detriments of being gay. In some shamanic traditions, he explained, homosexuality was considered a gift, an elevated state of consciousness. I might have expected Stinson to scoff at such an idea, but he gave credence to it. Gay men and women, he wrote, possessed characteristics of both sexes, and so they also were endowed with a unique outlook on the world.

Pity, then, that in our modern, fallen times, homosexuals had become alienated from spirituality of any kind, focused on carnality as a political statement—almost as an article of faith. Shamans had once enjoyed a kind of transcendent connection with the divine, yes, but that was virtually unthinkable for most modern homosexuals.

Homosexuality was both an opportunity and a burden—a special kind of challenge that God entrusts to few. According to Stinson, if I could quell or alter my carnal desires—if I could achieve purity of heart, integrity of mind, sanctity of body, tenacity of purpose—then great riches would be mine. Eternal life, yes—but all Christians gained that simply by asking for it. Oneness with God, yes—but also a rare communion with both sexes. Holiness of the highest and best kind—that which is hard-fought and well-earned.

The book had helped. Charlie had been right. It had helped, though in fact I'd tried few of the techniques Stinson prescribed. I'd not had much luck making every thought a prayer, because my thoughts—prayerful and otherwise—always seemed to wander from one subject to another. I didn't own a Bible, and I hadn't read a word of the Psalms of praise. I couldn't sing hymns, because I didn't know any. I hadn't taken any physical exercise since the loss of my boat.

One technique, though—enjoying the company of those who shared my journey—was available, freely and easily available. Right now, as I sulked in the car, men who shared my journey already enjoyed each others' company at the top of the concrete stairs, at the end of the brick walk, in Eliot's fire-warmed living room.

The book had helped. Group would help. Seeing Charlie would help.

I got out of the car.

•   •   •

I'd never heard Rob speak so ardently, so rapidly, as he did now. As I hung my coat in the entryway and kicked my boots onto the mat, I caught a few words. "Lovely" was among them. "The one." "Can't believe—."

Charlie patted an empty chair next to him. It was my turn, this time, to sit in the ladder-backed chair, but Charlie—or someone—had dragged it into the circle for me. He leaned over. "I thought you were skipping," he whispered.

I looked at him. "Traffic." Plausible, right? Traffic?

Eyes were on us. I said, "Sorry I'm late, everyone. The traffic was beastly."

Tigger was absent, I saw now. Maybe he had actually gotten caught in traffic.

Eliot said, "Rob was just telling us about a relationship he's thinking of pursuing."

"Her name is Chloe," Rob told me. He sat across from me, in one of the armchairs. "She has the loveliest green eyes. I met her just—oh, just at random, at a Christian bookstore. We went for coffee and had the nicest talk. We see eye to eye on so many things."

"Are you planning on seeing her again?" Fred asked Rob.

"Of course, of course," Rob said. "I'm visiting her church this Sunday."

"Which church?"

Soon, I lost the thread of the conversation. I froze my face in a smile. I looked at Charlie. He kept fidgeting and shifting his weight in his chair.

Eliot addressed the group. "Any other good news? Charlie? It looks like you're itching to say something."

Charlie cleared his throat. "I—." He winced. "Never mind."

"What do you want to say, Charlie?"

Charlie looked at Eliot. He looked at Rob. He looked at me. He looked at Rob. "No disrespect, Rob, but is this really good news?"

Rob looked stricken. He raised his hands, as if to cover his mouth in shock or plug his ears in horror, but he stopped them halfway. They dropped, limp, into his lap.

Charlie held out his hands. "No offense," he said. "No disrespect, but—." He looked around the circle. *Everyone* looked a little stricken, now. "I don't believe a leopard can change its spots."

Rob's face was a pile of ash. "Wh—? Wh—?" He didn't seem fully capable of speech.

"I made it a good long way down that road and almost wrecked two lives with my selfishness," Charlie said. He stroked his bearded chin. "I'm not attracted to women. I never will be. I'm satisfied with my own company, and the company of good friends." He looked around the room. His eyes brimmed.

No one spoke.

I said, "How close did you get?"

Charlie looked at me. "A ring and a date."

"You broke it off?"

Nodding, he leaned back into his chair. He looked around. "You all know this story." To me, he said, "We were registering at Marshall Field's. In Chicago. I lived in Chicago then. We were registering, and laughing, goofing on all the useless junk we were putting down on the form, all the trash we knew we'd never use. I put my hand on her shoulder, just lightly laid my hand there and squeezed, like I'd done a thousand times before."

To demonstrate, he placed his hand on my shoulder. Through the fabric of my shirt, his skin was warm, perhaps slightly damp. He squeezed lightly, almost not at all, but even so I sensed the potential strength of his grip.

"But this time it struck me how slender it was," Charlie told me. "I could feel her bones." He took his hand away, flexed it as if it had been injured. "It was like holding a kitten. You feel the bones slipping around under the skin, and you know how frail and vulnerable they are."

Raising his chin, as if turning his face to a light above him, he drew his thumb and forefinger down the length of his nose.

"We'd never slept together," he said. He spoke into his hand. "We were waiting for the wedding night. I hadn't thought much about it, hadn't thought about it at all, really. Right there in the Marshall Field's, for the first time, I imagined what it would be like, and I realized that it wouldn't be the same at all as with a man." He looked at each man in the group, then at me. "The position wouldn't be the same. The feeling—the sensation and the emotion and the intensity—. It would all be entirely different. With two men, sex—when it's good—it's the collision of two equal and opposite forces. It's explosive."

I pictured him as he'd been in college, mean as shit, a young buck riding roughshod over some submissive young man he'd picked up.

Rob said, "But men and *women* are opposite forces. More so than two men."

Charlie shook his head. "Not sexually. Yes, of course, men and women represent opposites, and in every other arena, they can complement each other. They can enlarge each other, enrich each other, by contributing their different perspective on things. That's the whole plan God had in mind, right? That's the grand scheme." He cleared his throat.

Eliot frowned. "That's correct."

"But sexually, it's always on the woman's terms. A woman has a slower fuse, so a man, when he cares anything for a woman, he'll tone things down. I know this isn't always the way it is. There are women—. I'm talking about a *good* woman. With a *good* woman, a man will start easy and build slow. That's how it has to be. With two men, that's one way to go, but, well—speaking for myself—I liked to fuck like an animal."

Around the circle, everyone stiffened, sat up straighter.

Charlie blushed and cleared his throat. "Sorry," he said.

"What's going on with you tonight, Charlie?" Eliot said.

Charlie glared at Rob. "Every other week Rob claims he's found the woman of his dreams. I don't see it happening." He cocked his head. "I don't mean that. I mean to say that if he does—. If you do, Rob—. If any one of us finds a woman and tries to make a go of it, it can only be half a marriage. To some of you I'm sure it's even the better half."

Eliot clenched his fists. I scooted my chair back an inch or two. Eliot said, "Charlie—."

As always, Fred and Jeremy sat together on one end of the sofa. Charlie turned his head, looked at them, glowered at them. He said, "You two. You two concern me most of all. Here, in group, you rarely say anything, but at any kind of social function you cut up like—. Well. You snip and snipe like a couple of queens. You *live* together, for God's sake."

"In separate rooms," Fred said.

"On different floors," Jeremy added.

The two men had, if anything, drawn closer together. Fred lifted his arm as if to wrap it around Jeremy's waist.

"You were lovers for *years*," Charlie said. "How do we know—?"

"Charlie!" This was Eliot. He had stood. On the rack on the hearth, the poker and shovel and tongs clanged against each other. "This is not an appropriate—."

All at once Charlie seemed to sink into himself, to slacken, to go from a hulk of muscle to a puddle of muck. "I'm sorry," he said. "I'm sorry, everyone. It's just—."

Softer now, Eliot said, "What's going on, Charlie? What is this about?"

Red-eyed, Charlie looked at Rob. "I'm happy for you, Rob. I am. But for me—." He looked into his hands, open on his lap. "For me, it doesn't feel like it's ever going to happen." Again he looked up. "I hope it happens for you, for you and for—for Zoe."

"Chloe," Rob said.

"Chloe. Sorry."

I said, gently, "I think Charlie has a point." I looked around. On the sofa, in the chairs, the men held themselves quite still. They might have been characters in a slasher movie, waiting, waiting, waiting to hear whether some ominous sound turned out to be a tree limb brushing the side of the house or a serial killer with a machete. "I'm new here. I'm sorry if I'm getting this all wrong—. But—. But I was just reading *Hope and Healing*, and Stinson says some people are able to change, but most are not."

Everyone was nodding.

I looked at Rob. "If you're able to change, that's fantastic, but it's rare. And—and you have to be honest with yourself, and be really sure that it's a change, and not wishful thinking." I looked at Charlie. "And if you're not one of the ones who can't change, it—. It's nothing to be ashamed of, but—but it's not uncommon for—for people like us. It means—."

I was about to say that Charlie was one of the chosen few, with a life of hard-won, well-earned holiness to look forward to. But I glanced at Rob, and I saw that his face had fallen. The corners of his mouth drooped. His gelled and pomaded hairline seemed to have slumped halfway down his forehead. Somehow even his nose seemed to have lowered itself a fraction of an inch. My mention of "wishful thinking" had been too accurate for his comfort, perhaps. I thought awhile, choosing my words carefully.

How had Stinson put it?

Again I turned to Charlie. "You have to continually do your best to subjugate your carnal nature."

Eliot smiled at me. "Exactly," he said. He resumed his seat on the hearth.

Charlie stared at the floor, at a point somewhere beyond his feet. He rubbed the nape of his neck. "I apologize, everyone. Long day. Meetings all day. I'm sorry." He turned to me. Almost in a whisper, he said, "Sorry." Again, as if I—more than all the others—desired, deserved, or had demanded an apology, he said, "Sorry."

·　·　·

After the prayer, the men pounced like famished dogs on the leftover coffee and cookies. I stayed where I was, next to Charlie. We sat a while in silence.

At last I said, quite softly, "I've heard there's a restroom at Dayton's, on the second floor—."

Eyes wide, he looked at me. He shook his head. "It's in the basement. Behind the shoe repair."

"What happened?" I asked him.

With one hand he kneaded the knuckles of the other. "Nothing," he said, looking at me sidelong. "Essentially nothing. But it was—. A boy offered, and I got as close to him as I am to you now. He was—. He was attractive." He exhaled, as though he'd been holding his breath for hours or for days. "Very attractive, and everything out there for the taking. His pants down around—."

He stopped. He drew himself up. I looked over at the knot of men gathered at the opposite end of the coffee table. Rob stared at Charlie.

"Never mind that," Charlie said. "I had my hands almost on him. After all these years. I was this close." A wave of his hand took the measure of the distance between us. He shook his head. "I've been trying to figure out how I could have such a false ideal of my own tenacity of purpose."

"Didn't you tell me that the desires never go away?" I looked up at him. He nodded. "Didn't you tell me that you almost have to *distract* yourself to avoid them?" Again he nodded. "And don't we all recognize that we can't do this alone?"

"You're right," he said. "Of course, you're right." He opened his mouth to speak further, but I interrupted him.

"Maybe you've depended too much on your distractions and not enough on your—." I glanced up. Eliot was watching us. I dropped my voice. "That is to say, not enough on God."

Stung, he looked at me. "Maybe you're right." Turning to me, he said, "After Rob went on like he did, and everyone piled on, congratulating him on his success—."

"Today was a bad day for it. You had a bad day, that's all. Like Eliot said—."
A spasm in my shoulder. I kneaded the muscle. "Like Eliot said—. I'm para-
phrasing, but he said that the past is fixed. The present is all about external
circumstances. You have to do what you know is right, and in the future
you'll look back and know—. You'll know you behaved correctly, and you'll
be proud and happy."

Again, Charlie stared at the floor.

I said, "Last week you said we all choose this, but that's not what Stinson says. That is to say, I may have read it wrong, but in *Hope and Healing,*
I thought it said the circumstances that—that cause us to have these desires—. Those are beyond our control, early in life. The choosing is all in
how you handle them—whether you act on them or not. You did what you
were supposed to do. You were tempted—you can't help being tempted—but
you walked away."

Charlie looked up. He looked at Eliot, but Eliot was talking to Jeremy and
didn't notice. Charlie said, "I'll make an appointment with Eliot. I haven't
seen him privately in a long time. I'll start seeing him every couple of weeks."
He looked at me, smiled wanly. "I'll get through this. I've been through
worse."

Stroking his beard, he stared into the fire. I looked at him, followed his
hand with my eyes as it ruffled his whiskers. I longed to hold him, to feel
his thick arms around me, to touch the slabs of stony muscle on his back. I
forced myself to look away.

In Martin's office, above a bamboo fountain and a tiny sand garden, next to the white board, a poster of Ravi Shankar hung in a cheap plastic frame. Always it had fascinated me. Shankar bowed over his sitar with a look of perfect concentration, pure whole-hearted joy. But it was not all joy, I was sure. There must be supplication as well, subservience to his gift, obeisance to his Muse, or to whatever analogue his culture recognized.

Now that I found myself once again at Martin's conference table, in the chair that faced the poster, I could not move my eyes from it. Absently I rubbed my hands along the smooth curved edge of the wooden tabletop. The placidity, the quiescence, of Shankar's pose moved me. For a couple of hours, maybe—thirty minutes here, fifteen minutes there—I had felt what I saw in Shankar's enraptured expression—the joy, the gratitude. The sense of being small, inadequate, flawed—but cared for, protected, loved.

Sometimes, when I had a sheet of staff paper in front of me and a pencil in my hand, and ideas seemed to come faster than I could write them down—sometimes, when it was all going perfectly—I felt as if the music wrote itself, or rather as if it came from some source outside of myself, or perhaps from some part of my brain that could not be touched by logic or speech. There was nothing to do, then, but listen, obey, transcribe. I hadn't experienced that rarefied state of inspiration in months—not since Tom had died.

Christa sat across from me. She nudged my shin with the neb of her shoe. Impaling my eyes with hers, she said to Martin, "Jonah and I were talking about that just this morning. He made a very good point. The phrase has become a kind of joke."

Which phrase? What the hell had we been talking about? The last minutes were a blur.

Martin stood at the white board. He held a Dry-Erase marker, wiggled it, beat it against the palm of the opposite hand. We'd started early. Cramped and cryptic green lists joined the rainbow cicatrices of last week's lists and the lists of a month before.

Martin said, "We're off the subject. The forum starts in less than two hours. Thorstensen will be there, watching like a hawk."

Christa rolled her eyes. "Gasbag." Quickly she added, "Thorstensen, not you, Martin."

"We're not just the political correctness police. This has so little to do with political correctness, and yet everyone thinks that's what we're all about. How do we get this across?"

I said, "What about the idea that we're trying to prevent *all* sorts of discrimination, including discrimination against people who hate political correctness? Did you mention that to Thorstensen?"

Looking down, Martin capped and uncapped the marker. "It has seemed impolitic to approach the subject directly. If I had to conjecture based on his behavior, I'd have to say that that approach would go far. Or maybe we're off his radar entirely, now. It's hard to say. His attitude has been as—well, as *hail-fellow*—as ever."

Christa had slouched in her chair. I looked down. She cradled her belly in her hands as if she were months along instead of weeks, as if her belly had swollen enormously. But for four weeks I'd watched her carefully, and she'd gained no weight that I could see.

Hauling herself upright, Christa turned toward Martin. "'Hail-fellow'?" she said. "I never heard that."

"Cordial," he said. "Congenial. Friendly in a man's-man sort of way." Looking at me, Martin said, "I mean 'man's man' in the hetero sense, of course." He watched his fingers fidget with the marker. "There's always the chance he's being disingenuous. I'm not the judge of character I aspire to be."

One of his infamous silences followed. Christa poked me again with her shoe. I popped my eyes at her; I had no more idea than she where these jaunts of Martin's took him.

I said, "We'll know more at the end of the forum, I suppose. Until then it's all conjecture."

• • •

Christa and I left Martin to copy his green ciphers onto index cards. In the outer office, I filled my tote bag with books and journals. Leaning against the edge of my desk, Christa scrutinized her fingernails. Occasionally, randomly, she handed me a book. I set aside the tote bag and flopped into my chair.

"It's not even remotely time for lunch, and already it seems like it's been a long day."

"True," she said. Her tone suggested that she had no idea what she'd just agreed to.

The phone rang. Christa went back to her cube. I answered the phone.

Eliot. "I owe you an apology," he said.

"What on earth for?"

"I still haven't done something for you that I promised a couple of weeks ago. I promised to clear an evening appointment for you."

"You did?"

"For most people the group sessions are only supplemental. *Most* of my clients, in fact—the majority—don't even participate in group. Group sessions provide extra support to help keep on track. Private sessions keep group from focusing on just one of us. Do you want Tigger's slot?"

An unfortunate choice of words, I thought. "Tigger's, um, slot? What about Tigger? Doesn't he need his slot?" Barbara would have chortled at all this, had she been there to hear.

"Tigger's giving up."

I stopped cold. "Giving up?"

"He called me a while ago. He and his ex-lover are moving in together."

"That's horrible." Wasn't it? Mostly I thought so, but another part of me—I was still new to all this, after all—envied Tigger. In my mind's eye, I saw him in a summery loft in downtown Minneapolis, sharing a futon with another twenty-something in jeans and Doc Marten boots. In my mind's eye, they looked happy. Hard-fought, well-earned holiness be damned—they looked happy.

"Monday at six o'clock. That was his standing appointment."

"That's fine. In general, that's fine, but I'm not sure I can make it tonight. My boss and I have a meeting. It might run late."

Eliot cleared his throat. "I'll wait until six-fifteen. If you can't make it by then, I'll count on you for next week. Well, for Thursday and then for next week."

Almost the second I rang off, Christa appeared. "What's so horrible?"

"Nothing. An acquaintance has decided to ruin his life."

"Any thoughts on lunch?"

"You're eating now?"

"Like a horse." Her hands smoothed the shimmery bronze fabric of her blouse over her belly, framed it as if it bulged hugely. "Everything except for milk. Cheese is okay, oddly enough, but the very idea of milk turns my stomach." She grimaced.

I spun in my chair so that I faced her. "Nothing ambitious, please. I don't feel like driving, and I'm certainly not riding with you."

She clucked. "You're just being difficult. I've never had an accident or a ticket in my life."

"I'm sure you haven't," I said. Rising, I took her by the elbow. "Not since you faked your own death and changed identities."

In the hallway, she tugged on her skirt, an ankle-length sheath of tawny suede. "Does it show that I had the surgery?"

"The Oslo surgery?" I closed the door behind us. "When you go to the gym, don't do any more shrugs. Those shoulder caps betray your deepest secret, my brother."

She sighed. "I'm tired of that game now. Are we going to DOT?"

I shook my head. I was weary of the Department of Transportation's cafeteria, and of the crowds of beleaguered motorists and would-be motorists who took refuge there after a long morning's confrontation with the state bureaucracy. "Let's do the cave."

It was her name for the cafeteria in the nethermost vaults of the Capitol. To reach it we walked through passages of glossy ceramic tile and gray concrete. It was early. We had the cafeteria nearly to ourselves. Near the door, under a groined vault, we crowded our Reuben sandwiches and Diet Cokes onto a square oak table.

"So tell me about this mysterious acquaintance," she said. "Is he ruining his life by sleeping with you or by swearing off sleeping with you?"

I swallowed. "Nothing like that. I barely know him."

"What is it, then? Drinking? Drugs? Green stamps?"

"Green stamps?"

"Lottery tickets? Obsessive chess playing? Kleptomania? Dipsomania? Beatlemania?"

"Like I said, I barely know him." I swigged my Diet Coke. "Let it run."

Chewing, she looked around. A few people occupied nearby tables. Everyone wore a suit. A woman guffawed.

Shifting in her seat, Christa said, "We have to talk about something harmless. Talk about rowing. That always absorbs time."

I sighed. "I miss my boat." Three quarters of my sandwich remained, but my appetite had gone. I shoved my plate aside. Flexing my shoulders, I said, "I feel all slack and soft lately."

She grunted, nodded. "I see what you mean. Maybe *you* should have the Oslo surgery. Man up a bit." She blotted her mouth with a paper napkin. "You wouldn't be rowing now anyway, though. Isn't the river frozen over already? What about a gym?"

"I had a membership. I had to cancel it. Tom was paying half the rent, and now—you know—he's not."

Crinkling her nose, she said something I didn't catch. Thorstensen had walked by. Through an open doorway I could see him standing in the food line. He was in shirtsleeves and a vest of puckered gold silk—why could he never buy his clothing in the correct size? Tray in hand, he elbowed the ribs of a chum. They threw their heads back in laughter.

"He can't see us as anything but a bunch of nosy, bossy liberals butting into everyone's private beliefs," I said. "He won't stop until we're abolished." That had been the message he'd delivered with a thud, all those weeks ago when he'd dropped *Onslaught* onto his desk.

Christa frowned. "What? Who?" Turning, she saw Thorstensen. "Oh. Gasbag."

"He's not going to stop till we're abolished."

"God," Christa said. "I want a cigarette." She took a bite of her sandwich. No, it was my sandwich; she'd finished hers. At her elbow her plate lay empty, dotted with pumpernickel crumbs. She chewed carefully. "I haven't wanted a cigarette since my drinking days in college."

"This is hardly the time, with Peanut coming and all."

"Peanut? Where did you get that?"

I shrugged. "Just came to me, just now."

"That's cute. I've been thinking of it—excuse me, him or her—as The Blob, which is accurate but not what you'd call adorable."

I stared at Thorstensen, watched him as he moved through the line, as he stacked enormous quantities of food on his tray.

Christa leaned forward, so abruptly that she shook the table. Plates rattled.

She was suddenly avid, if not slightly manic. "Is he stalking Barbra Streisand?"

"Thorstensen?"

"Your friend who's ruining his life."

"Barbra *Streisand?* I don't think Barbra Streisand has anything to do with it, or any other topic of conversation, for that matter, unless I missed something and we're suddenly talking about raging egomaniacs in desperate need of rhinoplasty."

Christa stared at me.

"Everyone treats her like some kind of goddess," I said. Now I was avid—if not slightly manic. "*The Broadway Album. The.* Not *a, the.* As if there's never been another Broadway album. Karen Holmes has been making Broadway albums for twenty years."

"Note to self," Christa said. "Never mention Barbra Streisand again."

"Sorry," I said. I calmed myself by tearing a paper napkin into tiny perfect squares. "Have you talked to Tory?"

She groaned, so loudly that people at nearby tables turned to look at her. "Weigh 'nough. I'm not going to tell Tory. I'm just not." She poked at the remaining half of my sandwich, tentatively, as if it might poke her in return. "It's *embarrassing.* I just can't. It's not *his.*"

"You keep saying that."

She looked at me. "It keeps being true."

"Let me tell him, then. He's crazy about you, you know. For reasons I cannot begin to understand, he thinks you're marvelous. He deserves to know why you won't talk to him, at least."

She sighed. "I'll think about it. Maybe I could write him a letter." The idea seemed to fill her with sudden hope and joy. "Could I do that?"

"I don't think so." On the other hand—. What would be the harm? If she wrote the letter, maybe I could convince her that mailing it would be a tacky, chickenshit thing to do, that she needed to deliver it in person. And if not, at least Tory would know what had happened, why she had vanished from his life. "You could," I said. "You *should.* You can work on it while we're at the forum."

She stared off into space, flicking the tip of her index finger with her thumbnail. If she'd heard me, she gave no sign.

◆　◆　◆

Roughly ten minutes before the appointed time of the forum, Martin and I crept into the powder-blue third-floor conference room. Roughly ten minutes after the appointed time of the forum, the IR staffers we had invited appeared en masse. Three women, four men, each chin, each mouth, each eye creased and furrowed more deeply than the last. The staffers sat on the opposite side of the table from us, in a row of squeaky, high-backed blue chairs. Thorstensen ambled in and took a beige tweed side chair in a corner of the room.

I looked at Martin. He was looking at me. I set my legal pad before me. Martin cleared his throat.

"Good morning. We're here to—"

But Thorstensen stopped him. "If you could introduce yourself for the record?" His tone was glacial.

Record? What record?

"Of course," Martin said. He tried a smile. Gray blank faces stared at him. "I'm Martin N. Maddock, director of the Office of Workplace Tolerance."

He looked at me, and I said, "Jonah Murray, analyst for the OWT."

Thorstensen leaned back, and his chair reared up on its hind legs. With interlaced fingers he cradled his head against the wall behind him. "Please proceed, Mr. Maddock."

"Perhaps," Martin said, "perhaps we should *all* introduce ourselves?"

The staffers tersely, tensely introduced themselves—names only, no titles. On my legal pad, I made a map. I drew an oval: the conference table. Around the oval, I wrote in the staffers' names: Betty Moseley, Bill Merton, Jasper Ulema, Burt Nichols, Sarah Lincoln, George Crocker, Sally Farrow. In ten minutes' time, I thought, Martin would have forgotten every name, and the map would come in handy. I snapped the page free of the pad and set it between us.

Martin said, "As I'm sure you all know, our office is taxed—pardon me, *tasked*—with creating a comprehensive legislature-wide policy concerning all forms of tolerance and harassment binding all the many offices of the legislature. This policy cannot be—cannot instantly be—*consummated,* let us say."

Consummated? Why not *completed,* or *created,* or even *drafted?*

Sally Farrow stiffened, holding her straight back inches from the curved back of her chair. She was a study in gray—gray curls of hair piled atop gray folds of skin draped in gray pleats of flannel. She removed her glasses and, folding them, laid them before her on the table. Perhaps she could no longer bear the sight of us.

Martin forged ahead. "We've divided the process into a number of overlapping intervals. We are conducting a series of forums like this one, through which we will determine the extent of the problem."

Thorstensen cleared his throat. "Mr. Maddock, I'm going to stop you there for a moment. Can you tell us how much time and money has already been spent to conduct these forms?"

While I dug through my notes, Martin said, "At this time we have only been able to conduct the forums on the DFL side. You yourself have—."

"That's not what I asked."

I wrote a couple of figures on a blank sheet of my legal pad. Sliding the pad toward Martin, I tapped the numbers with the butt of my pen. He shook his head. "That's not right," he told me. To Thorstensen, he said, "Rest assured, the cost is small, but we have attempted to be thorough, so a fair number of hours—. Excuse me. One moment."

I covered my mouth, whispered to Martin. "That's the closest I can get. I never even tried to—. Christa would be able to—."

Thorstensen said, "Mr. Maddock, if you don't have it, you don't have it."

Again Martin said, "Rest assured, the *cost* is small. No more than the typical office supplies and what-have-you that any legislative office would incur."

Thorstensen smoothed the folds of his vest; instantly the fabric puckered again around the buttons. "Somewhere along the line, someone thought it was a good idea to go around letting people vent about their petty qualms. But at what *cost?* That's what I'd like to know."

"Qualms?" Martin said. "Not at all. We're only saying that—."

"Just a moment." This was Jasper Ulema, a youngish man with flaky skin and a black pompadour. He tugged at the lapels of his blue blazer. "I think this is all ridiculous. I don't know why I have to be here. Aren't there harassment policies in place already?"

"When this project began—."

Ulema said, "Yes?"

"Mr. Thorstensen—," Martin said. "*Representative* Thorstensen, rather—. Mr. Ulema—." Then, "Excuse me. It's my understanding—."

Around the table, the faces were stony. Arms were folded. No one seemed inclined to speak.

◆ ◆ ◆

On University Avenue the evening traffic crawled. I reached Eliot's office at twenty after six, as he was locking up. When my car swung through the parking lot, he waved and smiled. By the time I'd made my way through the barbarous cold to his door, a warm yellow glow lit the windows.

The warm glow was deceptive; the office was frigid. Eliot sat at his desk, shivering in a gray cardigan sweater over a blue V-neck sweater over a red pinstriped shirt.

Half-rising, he shook my hand. "Sorry about the cold. The ventilation system in this building is a disaster. It's either freezing or boiling. I guess the furnace—or the heat pump or whatever it is—just can't keep up when the temperature outside dips below ten degrees."

I slid my hand from his and, hugging my arms to my body, settled into a chair across from him. "You won't mind if I keep my coat on?"

"Not at all." He rubbed his hands together. "It gets colder in here by the minute. We won't go too long."

"As long as we stop when we can see our breath."

"That could happen at any moment." He laughed. "Some business first, if you don't mind." In front of him on his blotter lay a sheet of white paper. He slid it toward me. "I found an assistance program that will help defray the cost of our sessions."

"Thank you," I said. "I—. I appreciate that. How—how much will my part of it be?"

He grinned. "Twenty dollars per session."

"That's—. That's—." I felt my jaw drop. "Where do I sign?"

"Fill this out and bring it next time," he said.

He handed me the sheet of paper. At the top, in blue, it read "Twin Cities Mental Health Assistance Program."

"I will," I said. I folded the form into quarters and slipped it into the inside pocket of my jacket.

"Enough about that." He rounded the desk and sat next to me. "How are you feeling?"

"Cold." I blew warm air into my fist.

"Seriously, Jonah."

I looked away. I looked at the baseball bat in its cradle. I let my eyes go slack, out of focus. The bat fattened, whitened.

"When I started this," I said, "it seemed easy. I didn't do it on a whim. I did it for good reason, because I was—. You know how I was. Everything had come to seem so difficult. This—. This seemed easy."

I said, "Weekends are hard." The empty hours to fill. The call of nightlife going on all around me. A box of Spike's old videos in the living room, and his pager number in every drawer in the house. "Every day is hard. There are—. I see men everywhere, and—. It's all willpower now."

Eliot nodded. "I understand. What have you been doing to keep on track?"

"I've read most of the Stinson book. I've gone over some of it three or four times. It helps. It really does, but—."

"What else have you been reading? Besides your Biblical readings."

I flinched.

"You haven't been reading the Bible?"

"I don't own one," I said. "I didn't—. That is to say—." Rocking forward on my hands, I fell silent.

"This is an active process, Jonah. You have to participate. The emotions you first felt, the relief of having your burdens lifted, you can't count on feeling that way forever. Everyone has difficult days. I have difficult days. I'm sure Sam *Stinson* has difficult days."

I leaned forward. "Wait. What? Is Stinson—? Was Stinson *gay?*"

"No, no, of course not. I just meant we all have our temptations, our trials. Everyone has some thorn in the flesh. Whatever Stinson's is, I'm sure he has difficult days. We all have difficult days. Everything you need to get through them is in the Bible."

He said, "You have to learn, study, develop your relationship with God. You have to work at it much of the time. You can't wait around for beams of light to come down from heaven and make you feel divinely inspired. You have to read. You have to study."

Laying my hands on my knees, I stared at my knuckles. All were raw, winter-chapped, denim-scraped. Tiny red beads of scab studded the second knuckle of my left hand. "I wouldn't know where to start."

"Romans. Start with Romans. It's my favorite."

I nodded. "Thanks. I would have started with Genesis."

"Don't. You'll never make it past so-and-so begat so-and-so."

"I do feel I've made some progress," I said. With some pride, I remembered the last group session. It had helped to be some comfort to Charlie after his near miss in the Dayton's men's room, but I didn't say anything to Eliot about that. Instead, I described how I'd packed away all my books and videos, as though I'd packed them away just yesterday, not weeks ago.

"That's very good," he said. "What did you do with them?"

"Nothing yet."

He leaned forward. "Then don't you see that you're still holding on? Part of you is still holding on."

My thumbnail was ragged. In lieu of cutting my nails I'd taken to chewing them, though I couldn't remember precisely when I'd started. "You're right."

"What will you do tonight?"

"I'll buy a Bible on the way home, and I'll throw away the books and videos."

• • •

He saw me to my car and waited by my open window until I'd started the engine. Even through gloves, the steering wheel was stinging cold.

"Until Thursday," he said.

"Christmas Eve? Group meets on Christmas Eve?"

"The holidays are hardest," he said. "There's no better time. Call me if you need anything. And don't forget to fill out that form. And actually—you know—bring it next time." He smiled. "Take care. Be well," he said.

He plodded away, hunched over in the cold. I waited to see his car's exhaust. After some minutes, bluish smoke curled into the air.

As I drove by, he waved and smiled.

• • •

The front windows of Turn the Page were steamy. Droplets of water rolled down the glass. Ceiling-mounted furnaces blasted and parched the air. Overstuffed shelves towered over narrow aisles. The warmth, the closeness, were entirely welcome.

I dawdled in the music section, kicking a stool along in front of me. I considered and rejected a Ravel biography and a survey of Britten's operas. On the uppermost shelf, I found a slim paperback entitled *Beethoven in London.* Had Beethoven gone to London?

McNamara was the book's author. *That* McNamara?

I tipped the book forward, and it dropped into my hands.

Above a portrait in oils of a scowling, black-maned Beethoven, the title scrolled across the cover in ornate white script. At the bottom, also in white, but in a blocky white font, "A Novel by Terrence McNamara."

Yes, then. *That* McNamara.

On the back, a short blurb read:

> In 1954, preeminent Beethoven scholar Terrence McNamara turned his immense knowledge of Beethoven's life and work to an ambitious work of fiction. His novel, *Beethoven in London*, long out of print but presented here with new endnotes and an expanded bibliography, asked "What might have happened if Beethoven, like Haydn before him, had undertaken a concert tour of London?" McNamara's deep understanding of the historical record concerning the composer's life, and of the psychological underpinnings that formed ...

Et cetera, et cetera, et cetera.

I glanced around me. On the stool I stood on tiptoe, craning my neck to see over the shelves. I felt furtive and undeservedly lucky. Surely a horde of Beethoven fanatics lay in wait somewhere, waiting to seize the book from me. But the store seemed to be empty of people, and certainly—except for me—of Beethoven fanatics.

I opened the book. End paper, title page, dedication. "To Jesse," the dedication read, "*mein unsterblicher Geliebter.*"

Geliebter—that would have something to do with love. *Lover? Beloved?*

Unsterblicher, though—. I had no idea what that might mean. Something about stars, perhaps? Unstarry lover? No, probably not.

McNamara had dedicated the book to someone named Jesse. Not a woman, surely. It was possible, I supposed, that some woman, somewhere, at some time in the history of the world, had been named Jesse. But it seemed far more likely that Jesse—McNamara's *unsterblicher Geliebter*—had been a man.

I flipped to the back of the book, looking for some kind of biographical blurb about McNamara. I found one, a single paragraph that shared a page with a colophon explaining that the book had been printed in Baskerville, a font designed in 1757. The description of the font and its designer was twice as long as the blurb about McNamara.

> Terrence Alan McNamara was born in London in 1904. For his entire career he was a respected Professor of Music at the prestigious Barton School of Music in Manhattan, and the preeminent Beethoven scholar of his day. His explications of the Beethoven

String Quartets, Piano Sonatas, and Symphonies are regarded
as the seminal works on those subjects. He died in New York
in 1973 at the age of 69. *Beethoven in London* is his first and only
novel.

Died how? Died of what? Died where, exactly? In the arms of Jesse, his—
his what?—unstarry lover?

•   •   •

The Bibles must be on the second floor, in the Spiritual Studies section. I
climbed the creaking stairs, forgetting as ever to avoid touching the sticky
blue paint on the banister.

The Gay Studies section was at the top of the stairs. When Tom and I had
come here together, he'd always crouched there, browsing the novels, the an-
thologies of erotica, paging through a copy of *The Joy of Gay Sex* that for some
reason never seemed to sell.

I couldn't help glancing at the low shelf where *The Joy of Gay Sex* was kept.
It wasn't there. Someone had finally bought it.

I made straight for Spiritual Studies.

I had expected to find very few Bibles—who would sell a Bible? But there
were many, almost enough to fill an entire system of shelves. I walked my
fingers along the spines, looking for the least abraded and creased among
them. King James Version, Revised KJV, New International Version, The Living Bible, The Way.

I took down two or three different versions. The modern translations were
full of exclamation points and prosy fourth-grade-level sentences.

I found something called a "Tyrone Study Bible," a King James Version
bound in floppy maroon vinyl or Naugahyde. It was in perfect condition,
except that a previous owner had penciled tidy glosses on many of its pages.
Inside the front cover, a bookplate bore a watercolor image of flowers and
ribbons and the name of the previous owner: Elizabeth Weitzel.

I turned to Romans, where Elizabeth's handwriting filled the gutters and
margins. A sentence across the top of a page bridged chapters six and seven:
"Slaves to sin are free from righteousness, but slaves to righteousness are free
from sin."

Further into chapter seven, beside a bold heading—"The Law: Good or
Ill?"—Elizabeth's meticulous hand had written, "Law exposes sin and its

deception. We know we are sinful because of the law, but the law does not *cause* sin."

A curved arrow connected chapter fourteen, verse ten—"But why dost thou judge thy brother? or why dost thou set at naught thy brother?"—to a small phrase—"Me, then, why *do* I?"

The archaic poetry of the King James Version appealed to me. The chatty annotations only added to the allure—I wanted to read them, to see what my predecessor had thought and felt while reading this Bible.

Hugging the Bible and McNamara's book to my chest, I made for the stairs. Along the way I noticed that *The Joy of Gay Sex* had not sold, after all. On a hard wooden chair tucked away into a niche beside the stairs, the book lay open to an illustration of two men having sex. The bottom was on all fours. The top knelt behind him, between his legs, grasping his hips.

I stopped. I stared. I couldn't help myself—I stopped, and I stared.

We all have our temptations, Eliot had said. We all have our trials. Some thorn in the flesh.

21   SLAVE TO THE RHYTHM

Side seventeen of the Guarneri Quartets—the C-sharp minor quartet—had not been off my turntable in weeks. In all that time I had seldom allowed the needle to travel beyond the first movement, the mournful fugue.

I switched on the stereo, turned up the volume, set the needle. Settling into the easy chair, I opened the Bible across my lap. Again, as in the bookstore, I turned to Romans.

In Turn the Page, the King James Version had seemed romantic, poetic, somehow more authentic than the other versions. But I had only glanced through a couple of passages. Now, after a few of the antique verses—the chapter opened with a circuitous, rambling salutation—I found myself regretting my choice. My mind began to wander. My eye began to wander.

Elizabeth Weitzel had underlined a passage early in the first chapter:

> For this cause God gave them up unto vile affections: for even their
> women did change the natural use into that which is against nature:
> And likewise also the men, leaving the natural use of the woman,
> burned in their lust one toward another; men with men working that
> which is unseemly, and receiving in themselves that recompense of
> their error which was meet.

Miss Weitzel's underscoring was obsessively tidy—the lines absolutely regular in length, perfectly straight, entirely consistent in their placement beneath the lines of text.

An arrow connected "recompense" to a word written sideways in the margin: "DEATH!" A dire, forbidding word, and Elizabeth had written it in an unusually ominous way. Instead of pencil, she'd used blue ink. Instead of her customarily trim printing, she'd outlined fat, three-dimensional letters, had hatched and stippled and shaded them. Her heavy pen had dimpled the page.

I flipped ahead. Again I found the page I had first seen in the bookstore—"Slaves to sin are free from righteousness" along the top.

In the following chapter, on the facing page, more underscoring:

> For I know that in me (that is, in my flesh,) dwelleth no good thing:
> for to will is present with me; but how to perform that which is good
> I find not.

"In me—in Lizzie—dwelleth nothing good!" Elizabeth had written. Her exclamation point was wavy and twice as tall as the adjacent "d" of "good."

A lump formed in my throat. What had Eliot said? The Old Testament was all about the law, but the New Testament was all about love? I wasn't, as yet, feeling the love.

I closed the Bible and set it aside. I took up *Beethoven in London*, opened it. It opened with Beethoven standing in the bow of a boat.

> The wind was cold. The boat surged over the waters of the Channel, through foam and chop. He turned to Schindler, whose heavy cape flapped in the wind.

> "You asked me where I get my ideas," Louis said. He laid his hand on his breast. In his coat pocket he felt the conversation book, the very one in which Schindler had written his question.

> Louis went on. "They come unsummoned, directly, indirectly. I could seize them with my hands. Out in the open air, as now, with the wind off the water, the surging of the surf. Or in the woods, walking in the silence of the nights. Early in the morning. The very moods a poet translates into words, I translate into tones that sound and roar and storm about me until I have set them down in notes."

The open air. The wind off the water. The silence of the nights. Yes. The woods. Yes.

I longed, suddenly, to be at the beach, to sit on the dock, to hear the ice crack in the river, to hear the trees rustle in the wind. Even in the cold, even in the snow, I would go—except that I knew only too well that the sounds of the night and the smell of the river had little to do with my desire. It was an excuse, a ruse. If even one other lonely soul walked the paths, I would be tempted. I would take whatever was offered.

I set the book aside and went into the workroom. In this room, at least, all was tidy. My sketches for *The River* lay stacked in boxes. The boxes sat stacked in a corner. The surface of the card table I used for a desk was bare except for Tory's poems. The sheaf of onion skin paper lay in the center of the table.

I found a packet of staff paper in one of the boxes. I sharpened a pencil. I opened *Grieving Songs* to "fuck." I sat down to work.

Snapping a ruler down along the left side of a page I drew bar lines, divided the staves into systems. Piano, violin, voice.

For some time I'd been thinking that, for "fuck," there was only one possible key. C-sharp minor. I scribbled the key signature—four sharps—onto each staff.

I needed a halting, jagged time signature. Seven-eight. Each bar would contain seven eighth notes, grouped in fours and threes.

Tory had suggested starting quietly. I liked the idea. I liked, also, the idea of starting low in another sense—setting the accompaniment low on the piano, anchored in the bass clef, both hands playing below middle C. The violin obbligato would start on the G string.

To start, then. I stared at the nearly blank page. I wrote in a C-sharp minor chord, low on the piano. Too plain. I added a minor seventh. Next—in honor of Beethoven, in honor of the C-sharp minor quartet—I put in a Neapolitan sixth. For a few bars at least, the two chords would alternate—a club-footed, hobbling figure. I drew in the chords in fat half notes and slimmer dotted quarters.

I hummed the jagged obbligato line I'd been carrying around with me for weeks. I scribbled and sketched. The violin argued with the piano, striking B-sharps against B-naturals, E-sharps against E-naturals.

I looked at Tory's typescript. I hummed, then sang, the melody, transcribing as I went. The melody leapt and fell in awkward intervals.

The song inched forward, measure by measure.

"Fuck all of this," I sang. "Fuck life," I sang. "Fuck death."

*   *   *

In the morning, the phone woke me. It was Martin. "Bad news and worse news," he said. "Which would you like first?"

I stared at the ceiling. I'd been dreaming, and though the dream had already faded, I had the sense that Martin had been in it—that the real-life Martin had interrupted the dream Martin mid-sentence.

"Jonah? Are you there?"

"I'm here. I'm trying to decide. Can you say them both at once?"

He cleared his throat. "Bad news first, then. After the forum yesterday I had occasion to speak with Thorstensen. He told me he plans to fight for the abolishment of OWT. The phrases 'tooth and nail' and 'at all costs' were used."

"And the worse news?"

"Christa's been in a car accident." I sat on the edge of the bed, already reaching for the socks and sweater I'd cast off last night. "She called a few minutes ago. She called in 'broken.' 'Broken' instead of 'sick.' Can you imagine that?"

"You talked to her? She's all right?"

"She's in the hospital for observation. Saint Joseph's, downtown."

I cradled the phone between my shoulder and chin. I snapped one of my socks in the air to turn it right side out. "And Peanut? Is Peanut—?" I swallowed hard. Had Christa told him about the baby?

"What's this about a peanut?"

I stopped. I kept very still. Maybe if I kept quite still, if I waited long enough, something would distract him—something shiny, some movement at the periphery of his vision.

"Jonah," Martin said. "Peanut?"

I said, "She never—? I can't believe she never—." I took a deep breath. "Christa's pregnant, Martin."

"I see."

"Like I said, I can't believe—."

"No matter," he said. "Obviously I don't know anything about any peanut."

"I won't be in until late morning or early afternoon. You know that, right?"

"I assumed as much."

*   *   *

Christa had a room to herself. On the left side of the room an empty, stripped bed lay flat and low. Chairs crowded around it in a half circle. Gray light and a view of a concrete parking ramp filled a narrow window.

Behind a curtain of rumpled blue cotton, Christa lay in a navel-high bed, in a nest of white sheets and beige blankets. A white plaster cast encased her right leg from the knee to the knuckles of her toes. Another window, same as the first, looked out on the same austere parking structure and the swath of pale, empty sky above it.

She opened her eyes, looked at me dimly. Abruptly, though, she grinned and giggled. She wriggled the bare toes of her uninjured left foot.

"Ayatollah Cockamamie," she said, and giggled again.

"Exactly how high are you?" I said.

She wrapped both hands around my forearm. "All they'll give me is codeine, the bastards." She relaxed, leaned back. "But still, it ain't bad."

"What happened?"

"I don't actually remember. I sort of remember. I'm a little foggy. I was turning left. Some guy plowed into me. Bastard."

Her head dropped back onto the pillow. Her body seized and shook. Her mouth folded in on itself. I let her grip my fingers. I waited.

"Drugs must be wearing off," she said. After a few deep breaths, she said, "They're keeping me because of Peanut. They want to make sure it's—." She covered her mouth with her hand. "Oops. I mean, they want to make sure *he* or *she* is okay."

"Sensible, I suppose."

She clasped my hand in both of hers. "Can you go to my place and pick up a few things?"

"All the way to *Hudson?*"

"*My* place, not my *mother's*. I'm not moving. My mother and I—."

"You had a fight."

She wagged a finger at me. "This is no time to say you told me so."

"Don't be silly. This is the perfect time to tell you I told you so."

"Can you go? Please? You'll be saving my life." She blinked limp-lashed cow eyes at me.

"Let's make a list." I pantomimed writing on my hand. "Number one: mascara."

"Bring me my glasses." She dropped her voice. "These idiots lost my contacts. Brand new gas-permeable hard lenses."

"Where are they?"

"I don't *know*. They *lost* them." I rolled my eyes. She said, "Oh. The glasses.

In the bathroom, in the vanity. In a black case. And I need clothes. They had to cut my jeans off me. Freaking hundred-dollar jeans."

"The bastards."

"A nightgown, some underwear. Maybe a T-shirt? What they say about these hospital gowns is true." With a curled finger she beckoned me closer. In a stagy whisper, she said, "Completely bare in the back."

"Don't knock it. I hear it's all the rage in Paris."

"And something to read. Stat. I'm already dying of boredom." Clutching the sleeve of my jacket, she dragged me toward her. "I was thinking." Her eyes slid off to one side, toward an unplugged heart monitor. "Maybe—." She paused for so long that I thought she might have drifted into sleep.

"Maybe what?"

She looked at me. "Maybe I should move in with you," she said. "Don't look at me like that. I'm completely lucid."

Completely lucid, I thought, was a stretch. She was giggling and saying "bastard" a lot—uncharacteristic habits, drug-induced, I was sure. Still, though she seemed foggy, she *was* more or less coherent.

"I'm listening," I said.

"You're struggling to make rent, right? And I need more room, right? It's perfect."

"I think you're having a Sally Bowles moment," I said. I lifted her hand. I examined her fingernails, to see if it so happened that she'd painted them green.

She yanked her hand back. "Think about it. I actually clean house." She nodded sagely. "I do dishes. I have houseplants. That's worth thinking about." She tried to wink, but didn't quite manage it.

"Clean dishes *and* houseplants? That's a sweet deal, indeed."

She sighed. "I'm serious."

Behind me the door opened with a snick. A nurse in blue scrubs bustled in. She was a tiny woman, older than seemed quite safe for a nurse to be. Lines and folds crazed her face. She wore her hair in a lofty blue-rinsed bouffant.

"Good morning," the nurse said, cheerful as daisies. According to a tag pinned to her breast, her name was Viola. She smiled, and her cheeks smoothed and plumped. "How are we feeling?"

"Almost as if we got hit by a car," Christa said.

"Keeping our sense of humor, I see. That's a good sign. We can have a pain med now if we'd like."

"Excellent news," I said. "I'll take two."

Viola shook her finger at me. "Naughty, naughty," she said.

"I would dearly love a pain med," Christa said. She shifted her weight, slipped her hand into the small of her back. The bed creaked.

"Back in a flash," Viola said.

Once the nurse had gone, Christa said, "You're going crazy from loneliness. I can tell just by looking at you. That beard, my God. You look like you're about to invade Kuwait."

"Weigh 'nough," I said, without much conviction.

"I'll bet you haven't done laundry in weeks. If you can't even take five minutes to shave ..." She grimaced, kneaded her shoulder.

"I did laundry just last—." Just last week, I was about to say, but that wasn't true. It had been a couple of weeks at least. I wasn't sure, exactly, how long it had been.

"When was the last time you cleaned your bathroom or did dishes?"

"I—."

The nurse returned, carrying a tiny paper cup and a larger Styrofoam one. "Here we are," she sang.

"Just in time," Christa said.

Viola handed Christa the paper cup. Christa upended it over her open mouth, and two white tablets landed on her tongue. She washed them down with water from the Styrofoam cup.

Viola, I thought. What if I used a viola obbligato instead of a violin obbligato? Dr. Benton had said once, in orchestration class, that a melody played high on a viola always sounded more intense, more urgent, than the same line played on a violin.

"Thank you," Christa said, but the nurse had vanished.

"She's swift for a centenarian," I said.

Christa closed her eyes, exhaled, sank into her pillows. "Better already," she said. "Hard to believe. Maybe it's the placebo effect."

"I should go," I told her. "I'll pick up your stuff and drop it off on my way to work."

She opened her eyes. She peered at me, her eyes wide and watery. She said, "Think about what I said."

"I will."

At the door, I stopped, turned. "I nearly forgot," I said. "I—. I did something you're probably not going to like."

"You told Martin about Peanut."

My jaw dropped. "How did you—? How—?"

"He called. Don't worry. I'm not mad." Propping herself on one elbow, she punched and fluffed her pillow with the other hand. "Plenty of time for that when the drugs wear off."

I opened the door, then, again, I stopped. A janitor in khaki twill pushed a cart down the hall. One of the cart's wheels squeaked. I gritted my teeth.

"There's one other thing—."

"Gasbag wants us abolished," Christa said, her voice heavy and thick. "He told me that, too. Tooth and nail. At all costs."

I sighed. "I guess there's no need to panic. It'll take a while. There's plenty of time before we—. He might not even—."

I turned. She'd fallen asleep.

◆ ◆ ◆

From a pay phone in the lobby I called Martin. "She's fine," I told him. "A broken leg and traumatic bluntness."

Seconds passed. He said, "I don't know what that means. That doesn't sound very medical."

"Never mind. She asked me to pick up some things from her apartment. After that, I'll be in."

"It's the twenty-second of December." He sighed. "I don't expect any of us will be much in demand. Do what you need to do."

◆ ◆ ◆

I drove west on Summit Avenue with the first movement of the C-sharp minor quartet pouring into my right ear. Somber, portentous music for a gloomy, ill-fated day.

Over time I had come to understand what McNamara had written—I had come to hear and feel the tension and suspense he'd described. My ear was not so refined that I could identify the Neapolitan harmonies McNamara had found so important, but even so, as I listened, I had the sense of—how had he put it?—massive forces marshaled and controlled. It was as if the entire movement existed only to keep the rest of the quartet at bay.

Heaps of snow lined the curbs and boulevards, but the streets were dry. The slow-moving traffic and Beethoven's plaintive fugue drew me forward. Ever forward, and in the right direction, and yet I had the sense that with every spin of the tires, my destination grew farther away.

• • •

Christa's apartment was tucked away in a remote corner of the apartment complex, far removed from the street. For any visit lasting more than three minutes, I had learned, it was easiest and safest to park in the neighboring lot, behind the Lund's and the Carson-Pirie-Scott. I turned right at Ford Parkway, left at Finn. I drove to the back of the lot and parked at the end of a row of empty spaces. Hunched against the wind, I walked through a row of shrubs, across a strip of lawn, along the paved pathways, among the squat brick buildings.

In summer, when ivy cloaked the walls and sheer drapes crowded the open windows, I sometimes stood on the sidewalk to hear the racket of televisions and stereos, to breathe the scents of fresh lemon and burned steak, to spy on these miniature worlds of mothers and sons, fathers and daughters.

But now, in the bloodless morning light of the second-shortest day of the year, the ivy hung in brown and black shreds. The yellow-mullioned windows were sheets of hoarfrost. Girls in parkas and plaid skirts waited for a school bus, their laughter purling and plashing. Women in long robes waved their children from their doors.

Christa's key burned my palm with cold. Slipping it into the lock, I gripped the curved brass handle with my other hand. Pull, turn, wiggle, push. In.

Always in this place the sweetest of fragrances, some combination of lavender and apples and cedar. No wonder Tory had preferred Christa's three cramped rooms to his own gaunt, odorless palace.

An entryway, the size of a small closet—too small for a coat rack or a boot mat—gave onto the narrow living room. Along the longest wall a tweed sofa sat facing a pine cabinet, an entertainment center. The cabinet doors were shut tight; walking past it would hardly be possible otherwise. Houseplants—a big leafy fern hanging in the window, glossy ivies trailing down the frame of an étagère, and lavish, hairy African violets erupting with blooms—imparted a green tinge to the room's white walls and beige carpet.

Half a dozen magazines lay scattered across the glass coffee table. Two issues of *People*, two of *Us*, a year-old *Rowing News*, a recent *Entertainment Weekly*. I shuffled them into a pile on the corner of the table; I would take them with me. Clothing—a T-shirt, a pair of sweatpants—lay over the slumped back of the sofa. I hung them over my arm and tossed them into the bathroom hamper on the way to the bedroom.

The bed was a disaster of twisted linen. It was a small bed—full-sized, surely, not queen-sized—and I couldn't believe Tory had ever slept in it comfortably. After sharing this narrow thing with Christa, sleeping in his enormous platform bed must feel like lying in the middle of a sweeping plain.

In the closet I found a nylon duffel bag. I searched the chest of drawers. Underclothes in the top drawer, nightgowns in the bottom drawer, T-shirts and socks in the middle. I grabbed two of everything and stuffed it all into the duffel.

A paperback book, a romance novel, lay on the nightstand. *Her Majesty's Folly.* On the cover a brutishly muscular, bare-chested man embraced a busty woman in a heavy violet gown or robe trimmed in gold. The colors were vibrant, saturated, nearly chimerical. A slip of paper marked a spot in the middle of the book. I tucked it into the duffel bag.

Carrying the bag into the bathroom, I propped it on the edge of the sink. I put in everything I could lay my hands on: toothpaste, toothbrush, shampoo, cologne, comb, brush, blush, lipstick, eye shadow, mascara, styling gel, and finally the glasses in their black case.

What else? I looked around. I kept my gaze low, avoiding my reflection in the mirror over the sink.

Thick towels hung in tidy green rectangles. On the toilet tank, pink pisciform soaps lay in a white china dish. Even in Christa's bathroom the sweet scent of an orchard in springtime filled the air. My bathroom always smelled of mildew and stale laundry. In my house, decorative towels and soaps—had I bothered with either—would all wear a patina of dust.

I closed the duffel and zipped it.

But wait. What about leaving the hospital? She'd need street clothes. I set the duffel in the hallway and returned to the bedroom. In the closet I tugged a string, switched on the overhead light. A skirt, it seemed, would be just the thing. But which? This red wool plaid I'd never seen her wear? No, she'd look like one of the Catholic school girls. This gauzy beige dirndl? Too summery.

Shoving aside denim and twill and corduroy and suede, I spotted a pile of magazines on one of the shelves. The stack had toppled; the glossy covers were as slick as oil. *Playgirl.* I had not seen a *Playgirl* since high school.

On the cover a blond man grinned and flexed. He was brawny, tan, shaven, permed—groomed almost to the point of asepticism. I opened to the centerfold, where the blond man reclined on a chaise. Behind him shone the blue water of a swimming pool. Naked, prodigiously erect, he thrust his head back as if in unendurable pleasure. His tan lines were perfect, so sharp and clean that they might have been drawn in with drafting tools. It was unseemly, somehow, the way the narrow band of white skin framed his pale, hard cock.

One tug at the top button of my jeans, and my fly opened. My erection sprang free and strained for its final inch. I studied the blond man. I stroked myself. On the next page he stood in profile, his arms hooked behind his head. His thighs were enormous, the curve of his ass white and ample.

I turned the page and found the Fantasy Forum. In sepia photographs sprinkled among the columns, nude men wrapped their lean and tawny limbs around the china-white bodies of faceless women. Each tale bore a bold, lower-case title:

> alyssa/all work and no play
> marianne/up on the roof
> joanna/slave to the rhythm

Slave, I thought. *Slaves to sin are free from righteousness, but slaves to righteousness are free from sin.*

This was wrong, what I was doing. A sin.

"Wrong," I said aloud. "Wrong."

I tossed the magazine atop the pile, grabbed the dirndl, switched off the light, and backed out of the closet. Now, along with Christa's potpourri of flowers and fruit, I smelled my own sweat, my own lust, my own stench. Stuffing my irrepressible erection down the right leg of my jeans, buttoning my fly, I made for the door.

"Slave to righteousness, free from sin," I chanted. "Slave to righteousness, free from sin."

On the way out I gathered everything into my arms—the skirt, the duffel bag, the magazines from the coffee table. I took no time to put on my jacket. Instead, I tucked it under my arm.

I stumbled through the door, closed and locked it behind me.

The wind slapped my cheek. I breathed the freezing air, letting it sting my lungs.

22 THE DISTANT BELOVED

Someone had parked in the space next to mine. A scrim of white exhaust at first hid the car from my view. A breeze kicked up, and the mist trailed away, and I saw that the car was a silver Mercedes. Tory's Mercedes. The driver's side window slid down, and Tory leaned out.

"I *thought* that was your car," he said. He nodded toward the Chevette.

"None other."

"Get in," he said. "It's cold out there."

"I can't right now. Sorry. I have to—."

"Please," he said. It sounded more like a demand than a plea. He leaned across the seat and opened the passenger's-side door.

No letterman jacket today, I saw. No sweats or madras plaid. Today, he was dressed for work. Charcoal gray suit, crisp white shirt, paisley tie, houndstooth overcoat. He'd gotten a haircut since I'd last seen him. Where he'd parted his hair, slightly left of center, I could see a straight white line of scalp.

I settled into the passenger's seat. Torrid air blasted my face. Tory closed his window. I set Christa's duffel bag on the floor between my feet. I laid my jacket across my lap.

"How have you been?" I asked him.

He shrugged. "Fair." He stared straight ahead, through or at the windshield. There was nothing to see, except for a row of leafless shrubs. Their limbs swayed in the breeze.

With the windows closed and hot air blustering from the heater, the car became stuffy, arid. "Are you sick?" I asked him. "A cold? The flu?"

He looked at me. "Sick?"

"The heat. It's really hot in here. I wondered if maybe—. A fever? The chills—?"

"Sorry." He tapped a button on the dash, and the heater tailed off. "Wasn't paying any attention."

For a time we sat in silence. I watched his expressionless face, watched him stare at the shrubs, or at the windshield itself, or perhaps into infinite space. Cold air oozed through my window. I hugged my jacket to my chest.

Almost at the same moment, we both said, "What are you doing here?" I laughed. Tory didn't.

He beat his thumb against the steering wheel. "Why are you coming out of Christa's apartment at eight-thirty in the morning with an overnight bag?"

"I was just—." I stopped myself. It hit me, all at once, what he meant, what he suspected. Dumbfounded, I stared at him. "Tory, you can't be thinking—."

Again, more softly, he said, "Why were you coming out of Christa's at eight-thirty in the morning, carrying an overnight bag?"

"She's not here, Tory. She had a car accident. She's in the hospital. I came to pick up a few things for her."

His eyes widened. His jaw snapped shut. "Car accident? Is she okay? What happened?"

I told him. Christa turning left, the bastard hitting her. The broken leg. Twenty four hours for observation. I didn't mention Peanut.

He reached for the gearshift. At first I took it for an unthinking act. The news of Christa's accident had knocked him senseless, I thought. He must be grasping for something—anything—solid. He must be trying to steady himself in any way he could.

But then he popped the gearshift into reverse. The car lurched backward and to the right. He braked so hard that the car shuddered. He shifted into drive. Seconds later we were out of the parking lot, on the street, weaving through traffic. At Cleveland, he paused, and then—in plain defiance of a sign that read "NO TURN ON RED"—he rolled around the corner and tramped on the gas pedal. We were headed toward the river road.

I was insensible now. I grasped for something—anything—to steady myself. The armrest, the dash, the seatbelt. I dug my heels into Christa's duffel bag, as a rider might thoughtlessly, reflexively dig his heels into the flanks of a runaway horse.

"Which hospital?"

"Tory, my car—. I—."

"I'll take you back to your car. Which hospital?"

"Saint Joe's."

Abruptly he cut the wheel to the left and turned down Montreal. At Saint Paul Avenue, where there was a four-way stop, a baby-blue Cadillac coming from our left had stopped. It crept into the intersection. Tory pressed the center of his steering wheel, sounded the horn. The Cadillac halted and fishtailed. Tory rolled, then bolted, through the stop sign.

"You say they're keeping her for observation?" he said. "For a broken leg?" The leather of his gloves creaked against the leather of the steering wheel. "That's kind of unusual, isn't it?"

"It's because she's pr—." I clapped my hands over my mouth. His driving was erratic, but not so erratic that I should lose my mind and—for the second time in a day—blurt out something stupid about Peanut. I pretended to yawn. I dropped my hands. "Christa's probably—." What? Probably what? "She's probably got a slight concussion or something."

He punched the accelerator. I clutched my armrest.

Tory said, "Concussion?"

"I don't know," I said. "Just a guess. No one said anything about—."

He interrupted me. "She drives like a maniac. I'm not surprised this happened. She was turning left?"

"That's what she said. She was hazy on the details."

He pounded the steering wheel with the heel of his hand. "Her fault, then."

"But what if—?"

He cut his eyes at me. "If she was turning left, it's almost certainly her fault."

At Snelling, he sped through a red light. Behind us, the caterwaul of horns erupted and receded.

I remembered that Luther and Erma lived at Snelling and Montreal. I looked back and saw their house, a modest Craftsman bungalow cut into a small hill. White Christmas lights—burning in the daylight, apparently forgotten—outlined the many large windows and the front door. Luther's white pickup truck sat in the driveway.

It reminded me, passing Luther's house, that if his nasty lawyer letter to

Tom's parents had gotten any results, I had yet to hear about it. Maybe he was still working on the letter. Maybe he'd forgotten about it. Surely he had more pressing concerns.

We passed fields of snow, vast white blanks—Highland Park on the right, the golf course on the left.

On the other side of Edgecumbe the street sloped sharply. At the bottom of the hill a line of cars sat waiting for a red light at Seventh. Clouds of exhaust rose and fell all around them.

Tory stopped a few yards behind the last car in the line. He gunned the engine. He muttered, sighed, shifted his weight.

"I'm sorry for what I said back there at Christa's," he said. The light changed. Traffic rolled forward, and he eased the car along. He looked at me. His eyes were wide and watery. He raked his fingers through his hair. "I don't know what I was thinking."

I knew what he'd been thinking; I didn't know how he could have thought it. I cleared my throat. "Why were you there? You never told me."

He swung the car in a wide left turn, onto Seventh, into the right lane. The cars ahead of us moved slowly.

"Did you ever see a movie called *Say Anything?*"

"Is that a movie where nothing happens?"

"You keep saying that, like I'm supposed to know what it means. Is that a reference to something?"

"It's nothing. Never mind."

A few dozen yards ahead of us, in front of a Burger King, a brown Volvo slid sideways into the curb. Its hind end blocked our lane. The car behind it—a Volkswagen Beetle, a crumbling and noisy thing that appeared to be constructed mainly of rust and Bondo—skidded and struck the Volvo's right rear corner.

"Fuck," Tory said, stretching the word to three or four syllables. He sank back into his seat.

"*Say Anything,*" I said. "What about it?"

"There's a scene where John Cusack serenades—sort of serenades—his girlfriend. Ione Skye, I think. They were dating, but her father doesn't approve, and he's broken them up. John Cusack is beside himself. He gets a boom-box and stands out in front of her house and holds it up over his head and plays 'In Your Eyes.'"

Tory steered into the left lane, into a narrow gap between two panel trucks.

As we passed the Volvo and the VW, I watched out my window. It appeared that the Volvo had barely been scratched. The Bug, though, had lost its front bumper. Its hood had popped open. The drivers climbed out of their cars, shouting and waving their arms.

Tory said, "That Peter Gabriel song, you know. 'In Your Eyes'?"

We started to move again at a tolerable pace.

"So what does—?" But then I understood. I turned and looked over my left shoulder. On the seat behind Tory, a boom-box lay on its back. "You were going to stand out in front of Christa's and play a Peter Gabriel song?"

"Not a Peter Gabriel song. Not 'In Your Eyes.' It's a great song and all—." The truck in front of us slowed for a left turn. Tory grunted. "It's a good song, but I was thinking of playing *An die ferne Geliebte.*"

"*An die ferne*—?"

"*To the Distant Beloved.* It's a song cycle Beethoven wrote—."

"I know what it is," I said, though I hadn't known, until he'd begun to explain. "I don't think it's something Christa would—."

We came to a red light. Tory stopped. "Not even the Dietrich Fischer-Dieskau recording?"

"Fischer-Dieskau? How likely is it that Christa has heard of Fischer-Dieskau? And it's in German, isn't it? The song cycle is in German?"

"I wrote out a translation," he said. "Made a little booklet out of it."

It was sweet, really, what he'd planned—so sweet and so foolish that I nearly laughed. I bit my lip. At length I said, "I don't think it's the best choice."

He dropped his chin to his chest, dropped his hands into his lap. "You're right."

"Does it work?" I asked him. "In the movie? Holding up the boom-box, playing 'In Your Eyes'—does he get her back that way?"

He clenched his jaw. He said, "Come to think of it, she hears the music, but just sort of rolls over in bed. They get together again, of course, but not right then."

The light changed. Gripping the wheel tightly with both hands, he drove on. We passed the old Schmidt's brewery. A square, crenellated tower of red brick rose above a complex of other red brick buildings. A long skyway bridged the gap between the brick tower and a slightly taller structure, an ugly column of plain gray concrete.

"What does *unsternlicher Gelieber* mean?" I asked him.

"*Unsternlicher Gelieber?* Those aren't real words. Do you mean *unsterblicher Geliebter?* Immortal beloved?"

"Immortal beloved. Ah."

"But that's a male beloved. *Unsterblicher*, with the *r* on the end. *Geliebter,* also with an *r*. There's that famous letter Beethoven wrote to the immortal beloved, his *unsterbliche Geliebte. Unsterbliche Geliebte,* without the *r*'s, that's the female beloved."

So. Jesse had been McNamara's immortal beloved. Remarkable, that in 1954 he'd dedicated a book to a man, to his immortal beloved.

Just past Jefferson, the street climbed. Far ahead and to the right, mostly obscured by a power plant, the Smith Avenue High Bridge appeared. Plain, unadorned—nothing more, really, than a highway overpass, a roadbed on tall concrete pilings and steel arches painted rust-red—and yet in the misty cold or at twilight, seen against the high snow-covered bluffs on the other side of the river, the bridge was majestic in its way. Whenever I saw it, I craved an excuse to drive over it. Now, I caught just a glimpse of it, and wished I could see more.

"You know," I said to Tory. "ABBA would be a good choice. 'One of Us' maybe? 'Take a Chance on Me'? No, 'One of Us.' Definitely 'One of Us.' Tom had a bunch of their stuff. I'm sure I have a cassette somewhere with that song on it." *Somewhere,* I'd said, but I knew full well where the cassette was— in the box of bad influences. I'd told Eliot—I'd promised him—that I would discard the contents of the box, but I hadn't done it. "I don't—. I can't—. I haven't been listening to his music lately. Tom's music. You could have any or all of the ABBA stuff."

He shook his head. "Thanks," Tory said, "but it was a stupid idea, the *Say Anything* idea. I haven't had the nerve to do it, anyway. I've been by there at every hour of the day. There's never been any sign that she's there. She *does* still live there, doesn't she?"

"She's been staying with her mother recently."

"Her *mother?* Why? What on earth for?"

I could tell him anything but the truth, but the true story was the only one I could think of.

"It's weird," he said. "Staying with her mother. What's going on? Have you talked to her?"

"Things have been—. It's complicated, I think. I don't know all the—."

Tory smiled—a doting, tolerant smile. "You're an incredibly bad liar, Jonah."

"I—. I think that's a compliment?"

"You're hiding something. Covering for her. That's fine. I'll get the story from her. I can't go on like this. I just can't."

* * *

Another patient had been brought into Christa's room. In the bed on the room's left-hand side, a young woman lay sleeping, open-mouthed, snoring softly. A straggle of dark hair lay on the pillow around her head.

Christa was out of bed. She sat in a green recliner in the corner, her bum leg in its linen-white cast propped up on the leg rest, her good leg tucked underneath her. A sheet and blanket covered her from knee to chin. She dozed, her head drooping to one side.

I set the duffel bag on the bed. I went to the chair and crouched down beside it. I touched her arm. She woke.

"Did you think about what I suggested?" she asked me. She spoke urgently, as if, in all the time I'd been gone, the question had been the crux of her thoughts and even of her dreams.

"I'm still thinking about it," I said, though I'd given her suggestion barely a moment's thought since she'd made it. "You know who has a lot of space, though?"

She blinked at me, said nothing.

"Tory," I said. "His house is *huge*. Have you seen it?"

"What the hell?" She narrowed her eyes.

I stared out the window. "You're going to kill me," I said.

She hoisted herself up and slid her good leg out from under her. "What are you talking about?"

"Tory. He's here. He's out in the hall."

Slumping against the back of the chair, she said, "Did you tell him about Peanut?" Her tone was as sullen as the bare white sky outside her window.

I shook my head. "I almost slipped, but I caught myself. You have to tell him, though. He won't go away until you talk to him."

She groaned and leaned back in the chair—or tried to. The chair was not tall, and her head dropped back and knocked against the wall behind her. "You're right," she said. She rubbed the back of her head. "I'm going to kill you."

"I couldn't help it," I said. "He was just *there*, at your apartment. Well, not your *apartment*. In the parking lot. When he heard you had a car accident, he more or less kidnapped me."

"You poor thing. The torture you must have endured."

"You *have* to talk to him."

She glared at me. "And how's *that* conversation going to go? 'Hey, Tory, I got really wasted one night at a bar and slept with the first guy I saw—and I *do* mean the first—and now I'm carrying his baby. Want to shack up? Oh, let's do!'"

I toyed with the hem of her blanket. "This was before you met Tory? The guy at the bar?"

Nodding, she said, "A couple of days."

"I thought it was weeks and weeks. If it was only a couple of days, then how do you know—?"

She yanked the blanket, pulled it out of my hand. "Because Tory and I always used protection."

"Oh." I stared at the floor between my feet, at the beige linoleum, at its green speckles and streaks. When I looked up again, the set of her jaw was ominous.

"Where is he?" she asked.

"Right outside."

"Shit," she said. "I must look like utter garbage. Did you bring me makeup?"

"In the bag."

"Give it."

With the aid of a small rectangular mirror in the drawer of her bedside table, she applied powders and paints. I sat on the edge of the bed and watched her. After many arduous minutes of grooming, she put all the pots and tubes back into the duffel bag. She looked up at me.

"Okay?"

It was on the tip of my tongue to say that it was obvious how badly she needed her contact lenses or her glasses, but I thought better of it. Not a good time for jokes. "Gorgeous," I said.

She spread her fingers, examined them. She sighed. "I wish you'd brought nail polish. Never mind." She waved toward the door. "I'm as ready as I'm going to get. Bring him in."

In the hall just outside the door, Tory fidgeted and paced. "How is she?" he said.

"See for yourself," I said. I stood aside to let him pass. "Good luck," I said.

"Thanks." His breath came in short gasps.

"Somehow 'break a leg' doesn't seem appropriate," I said, but he didn't seem to hear. Not a good time for jokes.

Standing tall, he smoothed the folds of his overcoat. He cinched his tie. Buttoned, then unbuttoned, the jacket of his suit. It occurred to me that at this early hour I'd already spent an unusually large proportion of my day watching people primp themselves.

Tory slid past me. As the door swung shut, I watched through the slowly narrowing gap. Tory knelt beside Christa's chair. He put his head in her lap.

Tentatively, she reached for him, pulled back her hand, reached again. She stroked his hair.

●　◆　●

Nurses and aides scuttled in and out of Christa's room. I sat on the floor, slouching against the wall opposite her door. Christa's roommate must have been the recipient of all the medical attention; I could see, whenever the door opened, that Christa still sat in the armchair, that Tory still knelt beside it. In relative privacy, with the blue curtain partially drawn to divide the room, they talked on and on. Tory held Christa's hand in both of his. He leaned in close, so that the top of his head nearly touched her forehead.

After thirty minutes or so, the nurses and aides disappeared. Christa's roommate's problem, whatever it had been, must have been corrected or resolved. For another thirty minutes I stared at the closed door, humming new melodies for my setting of "fuck." I wondered if a viola could somehow be made to sound like a heart monitor. Harmonics, perhaps?

When Tory emerged at last, he was pale, and his hands shook, but when he saw me he smiled. I stood.

"How did it go?"

"I'm a daddy," he said.

Mouth open, I stared at him. For some reason, I could think only of the scene in *Chicago* in which Amos—Mister Cellophane—cries out, unheard, ignored, "Hey, everybody! I'm the father! I'm the *father!*"

"What?" I said at last.

"Oh, not technically," he said. "I know, I know. Not *technically* a daddy. She told me everything." He frowned, mock-stern. "No more secrets."

Until the muscles in my gut slackened, I hadn't realized how tight, how tense, they'd been. All morning, since Martin's call, my belly had been a tangle of knots and snags.

Tory said, "We still have stuff to work out. We're not getting *married* or anything, but we're going to try to do this together."

"This is a lot to take in. Are you *sure* you're okay with—?"

Before I quite knew what was happening, he wrapped his arms around me and hugged me tight against him. Slipping my hands between his warm body and the cool silk of his jacket lining, I hugged back. I lay my head on his chest and breathed deep. He smelled of something clean and summery, of green apples and sweet pinesap and fresh water.

He whispered into my ear. "Yes," he said. "Yes. Yes. Yes."

PART THREE

23   DEEP WATER

"We're not getting *married* or anything," Tory had said, as if getting *married* were the most outlandish or inconceivable course of action anyone could have suggested.

It became a theme.

When, early in January, Christa returned to work, hobbling on her cast and a pair of crutches, she told me that she'd given her landlord notice, had given up her apartment, had begun to pack her belongings and sell her furniture. By the end of the month, she'd be living at Tory's. She said all of this in a rush, her face flushed, glowing. But, she said, it wasn't as if they were getting *married* or anything.

The following Sunday, while Christa was visiting her mother in Hudson, attempting a reconciliation after their quarrel, Tory invited me for brunch.

Standing barefoot at the stove, wearing short denim shorts and his madras plaid shirt, whisking a bowl of frothy, creamy-white pancake batter—he claimed he'd forever given up on frittatas—he described with agonizing specificity the difficulty he and Christa had had in finding baby furniture. I sat in the breakfast nook, listening, watching.

They'd been to a dozen boutiques and easily as many department stores and discount stores and furniture stores, he told me. He rolled up his sleeves. He whisked and whisked, the thick muscles of his forearms flexing. He poured batter onto a sizzling griddle.

They'd comparison shopped, he said. They'd sent away for catalogs, had consulted friends, acquaintances, and interior designers. The search continued, and they were enjoying every minute of it.

I realized I'd never seen his bare legs, had never seen him barefoot. I couldn't take my eyes off his meaty thighs, his chunky pear-shaped calves, the long, blue-veined insteps of his bare feet.

They couldn't wait, he told me, for the racket of a baby in the house, for the nightly grind of two-o'clock feedings, for the drudgery of diaper changes and baths.

◆　◆　◆

Christa's birthday fell on the first Sunday in February. On Monday I took her to lunch. She chose Lagoon. To my surprise she ordered hot and spicy chicken, extra hot and spicy, and she asked the waitress to bring a bottle of chili oil to the table. Though she'd had her cast off for nearly a week, she sat with her right leg thrust out to one side, her foot and calf blocking the walkway between the tables.

While we waited for our food, I handed over my gift, a set of Prince albums and twelve-inch singles I'd spent weeks collecting. She tore open a corner of the wrapping paper, and then for fifteen or twenty minutes the package lay in her lap, mostly wrapped, while she recounted the seven-course meal Tory had cooked for her, the music they'd danced to, the dozens of roses, the white candles, the antique diamond brooch and bracelet he'd hidden in a hollowed-out book. It had been the single most romantic evening of her life, she told me, all the more so because it had all taken place in her own living room.

But it wasn't as if they were getting *married* or anything.

◆　◆　◆

When Christa invited me to join the two of them for brunch on the following Sunday, I knew that something was coming. For weeks the lady and the gentleman, both, had been protesting too much, I thought, and I knew that something was coming.

For Tory and me there were mimosas, for Christa, sparkling cider. Christa brewed coffee in a French press. We had to drink it black; the very sight—the very *idea*, it seemed—of a jug of milk or half-and-half or cream in the fridge could make Christa queasy. Even black, unsweetened, the coffee was delicious, rich and velvety on the tongue.

We sat at the table in the breakfast nook. Snow fell, deepening the drifts in the back yard.

Tory and Christa sat opposite me, barely inches apart. They were dressed as if for church, he in khakis and a starched blue shirt, she in a silk blouse and skirt. It must be for my benefit, surely. The very idea—Christa attending church—. Impossible. Absurd. The two things were mutually exclusive—Christa and church. Preposterous.

Tory made a frittata. If he remembered banishing the frittata from his culinary repertoire, he gave no sign. It was perfect, the frittata—fluffy, creamy, exquisite in texture, studded with chunks of bacon and flecks of spicy red and orange peppers.

Tory ate and drank one-handed, with his left arm wrapped around Christa's waist. "What's going on with that court case?" he asked me.

I looked at Christa.

She blushed. "Sweetie, he's an *attorney*," she said. "I thought he might have some ideas."

"It's still pending," I said. "Luther—. That's my landlord." I cut my eyes at Christa. "Also an *attorney*."

"Weigh 'nough," Christa said.

To Tory, I said, "Luther talked to Tom's mother. Weeks ago now. He tried to get her to drop the case, but she has this strange notion that it will be a life lesson for George. That's Tom's little brother—George."

"A life lesson?"

"He's been in trouble lately. Cutting school, vandalism, smoking pot. Luther said she went on for quite a while, describing all his shenanigans. She thinks it's all because of his grief about Tom. She thinks if he sees the justice system punishing someone who really deserves it—that is to say, me—he'll come to understand that the authorities aren't out to get him."

Tory said, "That makes no sense."

I shrugged. "Couldn't agree more."

After that we ate in silence—or rather, Christa and I ate. Tory set his fork crosswise on his plate. He gazed at Christa with an expression of uxorious bliss. When we'd finished, Christa looked at Tory. He looked at her—but of course he'd never stopped looking at her.

"Is it time?" she said.

He nodded. "It's time."

Christa looked at me. She held up a finger. "One sec."

She scooted her chair back. Giggling, she scurried from the room.

"What's going on?" I asked Tory.

Quivering with joy or anticipation—nearly throbbing, in fact—he kept his eyes on his napkin. He laid it across his lap. He folded it, creased it, folded it again. Shrugging, smiling, he said, "Guess you'll have to wait and see."

Christa returned, her hands behind her back. She shuffled toward the table, came to a stop inches from my chair. I looked up at her. Her face was incandescent.

"What have you got behind your back?" I asked her.

She grinned and showed me her right hand. On the ring finger she wore a platinum ring. It was brand new—spotless, shiny, entirely free of scratches or nicks. A spray of tiny diamonds girdled a pink pearl the size of a golf ball.

"I don't know how he knew," she said. She seemed to be speaking to me, though she looked at Tory. With her free hand she held her belly. She was showing now, I saw. There was a swelling, a firm, full mound below the waistline of her cocoa-brown skirt. "I don't know how he could *possibly* have known, but I've always *dreamed* of a pearl engagement ring."

"Engagement ring?" I said. I tried to sound surprised.

Tory yelped with laughter. He doubled over, arms held tight across his ribs, as if assuaging a deep ache there. He laughed and laughed. I stared at him.

Wiping tears from his cheeks, Tory said, "Jonah, I just love you to pieces."

"I—. I—. I—. What?"

He said, "I have *never* in my whole *life* met such a bad liar."

• • •

Later, in the living room, the two of them sprawled arm in arm on the sofa while I sat in an adjacent loveseat. Through the front windows I watched a flock of black birds rise and fall on currents of air above the icy lake.

The slow movement of a Beethoven symphony—the Eighth, I thought, though I didn't dare say so aloud—muttered on the stereo. The woodwinds sang a sweet melody against a hesitant, dotted-rhythm accompaniment in the strings. The theme swelled in a crescendo, and the brass joined the accompaniment, and then everything dropped back to a whisper.

Tory said, "I'd like you to be my best man."

I looked at him. "Your best man?" I couldn't be the closest thing he had to a friend, could I? He must have other friends, coworkers, buddies from that bar—what was its name? Players? Victors?

"It'll just be a small ceremony," Christa said. "Just us, and you, and my mother as my matron of honor."

"I—. I don't know what to say."

Tory said, "Say yes." He sipped his mimosa.

"When? Have you set a date?"

"Valentine's Day," Christa said. She giggled. "Isn't that kitschy?"

I finished my drink and set the glass on the floor at my feet. "That's—. That's one word for it."

"Will you be my best man?" Tory said. "You haven't answered me." He leaned forward, elbows on knees. He watched me intently, as if it meant more to him—more, even, than marrying Christa—that I consent to stand up with him.

"Haven't I?" I said. "Sorry. Of course. Of course I'll be your best man."

He grinned. "Fantastic."

Christa said, "You have to get rid of that ridiculous beard, though, you know. There will be pictures. I don't want Ayatollah Cockamamie showing up in my wedding album."

• • •

By the time the icy streets of Saint Paul led me home, the sky had just gone dark. Still, the words on my front door—the leaning white letters my vandal had painted there—shone like foxfire in the glow of the humming streetlights. Reflective paint?

I approached the house slowly, my eyes searching the street and the snow-covered lawns. When I reached the door, I found that the paint was more or less dry. The bulbous beginnings and ends of the letters were gummy, but the paint left no traces on my fingers.

So. My vandal had come to my house in daylight, had spray-painted graffiti across the front of it, and no one had noticed—or at least no one had done anything about it. In the plain light of day, this had happened, and no one had done anything about it.

Turning, I glanced up and down my street. Neighbors' houses just opening their eyes to the night, a few still and ice-crusted cars along the curb, the neon glow of University Avenue—nothing out of the ordinary.

Nothing, that is to say, except for the two words painted on the front of my house.

DIE FAGGOT

I sorted through my keys. I slipped the door key into the lock. But before turning it, I pulled my hand away. What if my vandal had broken in, and he now waited inside for me? What if he'd rigged the door in some way? What if "DIE FAGGOT" wasn't just a coward's hollow threat? What if—?

I pulled the key from the lock, backed away from the door. The street was too quiet. I needed to be where there were people. University Avenue.

At the corner I passed a Ford Festiva, parked crookedly with one wheel against the curb. On its back bumper there was a Sam Stinson bumper sticker, also crooked. "Love Is All Around." I hadn't seen—or hadn't noticed—one of those in a while.

At the traffic light in front of the Rainbow parking lot, a Chevy van idled, its engine chuckling, its tailpipe rattling. On its rear doors, it bore the familiar "Love Is All Around" sticker and an older, much-begrimed sticker that read, "This Is The Day." Even a bicycle, locked to a light post, sported a pair of "Love Is All Around" stickers on its salt-spattered panniers.

A stretch of empty curb, a yard or so long, lay at my feet. I sat down. The cold of the concrete bled like water through my jeans.

Forgive, I thought. *Everything and everyone is forgiven.*

Christa and Tory were expecting a child. They were getting married. Tory had asked me to be his best man, which surely made me his best friend. I had a family. I was wanted, loved.

There was paint on the front of my house. So what? It meant nothing. I was forgiven, and I could forgive. I was a child of God. We were all children of God, weren't we?

I could put aside some graffiti. I could wash it off my house with the magic potion Luther had given me. The house could be spotless. So could I. I could be spotless. I could be clean. I could be happy—if I tried hard enough. Love was all around.

"Enough," I said aloud, rising. "Enough." Passersby stopped, turned, stared. Ignoring them, I set off for home. On the stoop, I turned and shouted to the street, to the neighboring houses. "I will not be driven from my home," I shouted. But the words at my back, glimmering pinkly out of the darkness, robbed my voice of its force. I raised my voice, cried out, but the round painted words spoke louder.

The wind gusted, blade-sharp. My nose and eyes were running, and I shivered in my leather jacket. As before I found the key, but now when I slid it home, I turned it. The deadbolt released with a hollow snap. I opened the door on solid darkness. I went from room to room, switching on lights. Everything was just as I'd left it.

From the entryway closet I fetched my parka and Luther's graffiti potion. The viscous, milky liquid, I knew, would make short work of "DIE FAGGOT."

◆ ◆ ◆

Short work. Not quite. With a wire brush and the dregs of the jug, I scrubbed and scrubbed. When my nose and fingers and toes grew numb, I went into the house to warm myself. Once warm, I bundled up again and went back to work.

At last only a trace of the paint remained. If I stood close, I could see faint white outlines and smudges in the crannies of the brick, but from the street I couldn't see a thing.

I took a hot shower to warm myself. I put on the C-sharp minor quartet. I sat in the easy chair. I opened *Beethoven in London*. For weeks I'd been trying to get past the first chapter, but in nineteen-fifty-four McNamara's powers of obfuscation had apparently been at their apex. There were arcane details of boat construction, magnificently specific and precise descriptions of garments and conversation books and luggage, page-long conversations in untranslated French.

After just a few words—a sentence or two toward the end of the first chapter, a description of Beethoven's cab ride from London Bridge Wharf to his lodgings in Saint John's Wood—I plunged into a dream. Dark, heaving, foam-beribboned water churned around me. Or perhaps it was not water— it seemed thicker, heavier, than water. I paddled to stay afloat. Fog or haze wafted and swirled around me, and I could not see the shore. Exhausted, chest heaving from exertion, I stopped paddling. I sank.

As I descended, the water grew warmer, not colder. But it was dark, and growing darker. Around me I felt the movement of big slick fish, or perhaps of kelp floating in the black undercurrents. I looked up and saw light far above me, the sun breaking across the still, blue surface of the water.

I woke. *Beethoven in London* had slipped from my fingers, had slid to the floor. A couple of pages had folded themselves over against my foot. Creasing the bent pages to straighten them, I closed the book and set it on the side table.

Barefoot, naked, I padded to the bathroom. I switched on the light and squinted at myself in the mirror. I looked like utter garbage. My beard was long, curly, skewbald. My hair was wild, kinky, mangy.

I understood, all at once, in a flash, why I had resisted trimming or shaving for so long. It was a disfigurement, this mess of orange hair. I'd decided—or, no, *decided* was the wrong word—. I'd *allowed* myself to look ugly, to show the ugliness I felt in me.

More than that—I'd submerged myself in ugliness. I'd used this disfigurement as a screen, something to hide behind. How often had I seen passersby take notice of me—of my wild hair, my crazy beard—only to look away as if they'd just seen some kind of freak, some object of pity or disgust?

But that was done with, over. I was clean, now. Forgiven. No longer ugly.

On a glass shelf above the toilet tank lay an electric shaver. I stared at it. My eyes were open now, wide open, and I was old enough to know better. But here were my hands, switching on the shaver, lifting it to my forehead, raking its chattering teeth backward along the center of my scalp. Again. Again. Folding forward one ear, again. Reaching for the back, easing into the nape, again. Again, again.

In a few upward strokes, I removed the beard, too. Whiskers fell onto the orange haystack in the sink.

Only stubble remained, brilliant, shimmering like copper. Funny, how something so simple could change everything, how I could remake myself with a few passes of the clippers. I looked more intense, somehow, my eyes sunken, dark.

In the top drawer of the vanity, a few disposable razors rattled their yellow plastic bodies among boxed soaps, loose cotton swabs, combs, and the remnants of a manicure kit. No shaving cream. I found a fresh razor and set it on the counter. Squatting, I poked through the mess beneath the sink. No shaving cream.

Leaning toward the mirror, I ran water until I could barely stand its heat. In the soap dish on the wall there was half a bar of white soap. It slithered wetly between my fingers. From ear to ear, from forehead to nape, I spread the glistening lather.

Slowly, almost reverently, I scraped the cheap blade backward along my scalp, downward along my cheek, upward along the curve of my neck. The stubble came away in rusty flakes.

Head in the sink, I scooped water over my skin. With splayed fingers I hunted for hangers-on. A recalcitrant patch in the folds of skin behind my left ear: I lathered and scraped it away. A nearly single-file row at rear center: gone, without even soap to help the going.

So. It was finished.

No. Not quite. Down below, still, the rust remained.

As I spread warm suds around it, my cock stretched suddenly to its full length. Holding it aside, I shaved away the orange whiskers. Gradually, while

I took care to stretch tight and shave bare, my erection sank.

But when I stepped into the shower, and the hot spray engulfed me, I remembered the *Playgirl* I'd found in Christa's closet, the muscular blond man on the cover. I remembered his tanned skin, the girdle of white around his middle. He wasn't my type—too blond, too plucked. Even so, I imagined him standing over me, imagined his strong hands around my throat.

I remembered that old video of Spike's, *Go Down On It.* I remembered him kneeling in the circle of men. I imagined myself in his place, looking up, mouth open, receptive, waiting.

In the tub I knelt. Eyes shut tight, tight grip.

Tan line. Pale, curved ass. Chunky pink erection.

Stroke. Tight grip.

Spike. Hairy thighs, white chest, black whiskers. Hands around my neck.

Stroke. Stroke. Tight grip. Stroke.

Tory. Yes, Tory. That hug in the hospital. His body warm and solid against me.

Tight grip.

Those short shorts, those heavy, muscular thighs and thick calves shaped like upside-down hearts. His bare feet. The blue veins. I imagined myself crouching before him, before his long veined feet. My tongue darting.

My erection thumped in my hand.

The smell of him, the fresh smell of him as he'd hugged me. The fresh, juicy bite of apples. The cinnamon scent of pinesap. The clear water of a mossy brook.

My breath came hard. Hot water poured down the bare skin of my scalp. I felt dizzy.

If I could only—. If I could only have one kiss, one long kiss—. If I could touch him, kiss him—. If only—.

Tory.

◆　◆　◆

When I'd finished, the guilt swept me. Silently, thoughtlessly, senselessly, I dried myself, switched off the light, and felt my way through the dark to my bed. I pulled the covers up to my chin, tucked pillows around me.

Tory? I thought. Where had *that* come from? Christa's *fiancé*, for God's sake. *Tory.*

"Forgiven?" I whispered, hoping for the old sense of relief to flood my heart. It never came.

24 KISS AGAIN

The next morning, when I saw myself in the bathroom mirror, I did not quite regret my late-night barbering. It pleased me to see the shape of my head, the sudden smoothness of scalp and crotch, the strange and unexpected transformation. And yet, the intensity—.

How it could be, I did not understand, but by removing my hair it was as if I had revealed not merely some additional square inches of skin, but all the dark places in myself. Without the frame of hair and beard, somehow, my eyes seemed deeper, darker, stranger.

After the deep-water dream, after I'd shaved and had gone back to bed, I'd had no more dreams—or none that I could remember. But I looked as if I'd just awakened from a night of prophetic, fevered visions. I looked as if I'd spent the entire night dreaming the Book of Revelation.

◆　◆　◆

Just before nine o'clock, Martin passed my desk on his way to his office. He gave no sign of having seen me, but then he called out to me through his open door.

"Could you join me in here, Jonah?" As I fumbled for a legal pad and pencil, taking his question for a genuine request, he added the punch line. "My desk lamp has burned out, and I'm certain you'll fit the bill nicely until Central Stores can replace the bulb."

Ha-freaking-ha, I thought, tossing my pad and pencil onto my desk.

When Christa arrived, she looked at me, cocked her head, stared, grunted. Without a word, she went to her cubicle.

I followed her. I stood before her desk. "You *said* to trim."

With barely a second's glance at me, she tossed her purse into a drawer, slammed the drawer shut. "What does it matter?"

"Beg pardon?"

"There's not going to be any wedding."

I knew there were things I should say, comforts I should offer, but I couldn't think what they might be—or rather, I could think of nothing but ridiculous bromides, corny as Kansas in August.

"Tory's wretched preacher—. Preacher, reverend, minister, priest—whatever he calls himself. He won't marry us without six weeks of counseling. Six *weeks!* In six weeks, I'll be five months pregnant."

"So you're calling it off?"

She glared at me. "Of course not. What's *wrong* with you? We're *postponing.*"

My knees trembled. I steadied myself against her desk. "You just *said*—."

"First he insists on getting married in this giant freaking church of his, and then it turns out—." She flung her hands in the air. "It doesn't matter. We'll figure something out. *I'll* figure something out."

"I'm sure it'll be fine."

Spinning her chair, rolling it to the shelves at the back of her cube, she fetched the entire stack of phone books she kept there. She slammed the whole lot onto her blotter. She looked up at me. "Are you still here?"

No, I wasn't—not for long. I fled to my own cubicle.

Christa spent the entire day on the phone with chapels and churches, with frequent calls to Tory in between. I strained to hear. I gathered that he could not or would not consider the simplest, quickest option—a civil ceremony.

• • •

As the hour of my appointment with Eliot drew nearer, I grew anxious. Surely he would see my shaved head as something more than simple grooming, as a shave that was not just a shave.

In *Hope and Healing,* in the chapter called "Temperance: Sanctity of Body," Stinson explained that the trappings of the gay lifestyle—body piercing, tattoos, leather clothing, dance music—often hindered the recovery process. For many, he wrote, it was difficult to change inward things—desires, emotions, thought processes—if the mirror continued to show the unchanging outward self.

I *had* made a change. Of course. The mirror did not show my unchanging outward self. But maybe I'd gone too far. It might be narcissism, the shaving. Self-indulgence? Ostentation?

I couldn't stop thinking I'd gone too far.

◆ ◆ ◆

On my way to lunch in the cave, I stopped in the men's room to wash my hands. Buzzing fluorescent fixtures over the sink cast weak, discolored light. Always in this place, my skin looked pasty and jaundiced—and now there was just so much more of it, so much more skin. My head was an immense, bulbous globe of gleaming icterus. Maybe I hadn't made such a very big change after all. Perhaps I'd simply gone from one kind of freakish disfigurement to another.

◆ ◆ ◆

I slunk through Eliot's door expecting a lecture of some kind, a sermon, a Biblical reading assignment, or at least a disapproving look. Instead, Eliot greeted me with a smile, and followed the smile with a hug. He waved me toward one of the armchairs.

Dropping into the chair next to mine, he said, "How are you, Jonah?"

"All right," I wanted to say, or, "Can't complain." But I forced myself to give the real answer. "I've never done anything so difficult."

Crossing his legs, frowning, Eliot said, "Tell me about that."

"There are days when I want every man I see." A *Playgirl* model, Spike, Charlie, Tory. Tory, Tory, Tory. I stared at the ceiling. "My fantasies can be—. These are fantasies I'm trying not to have. They just arrive in flashes of heat and light. Intense—. Sometimes kind of—kind of rough."

"What do you do about them?"

"I pray. I try to think about something else. I read the Bible. I spend a lot of time in Second Corinthians," I told him.

He nodded. "'There was given to me a thorn in the flesh,'" he said.

Had this been Paul's thorn—this constant unwanted wanting? Lizzie Weitzel had thought so. In the margin alongside Second Corinthians, chapter twelve, she had written in her usual fastidious way, "Probably an illicit sexual attraction, possibly homosexual. No cure. Only control."

I had come to picture Lizzie. Whenever I read her Bible—*my* Bible now—I imagined she sat next to me, watching. She never wore makeup, not even mascara. She wore her hair in a long brown ponytail. Always she wore the same clothing—a pale gray cardigan buttoned high against her throat, a plaid skirt, Mary Janes, bobby socks with frilly lace cuffs.

Suddenly I felt sleepy, heavy as granite. *No cure. Only control.* I sank into my chair.

"Give me an example."

"An example? An example of a fantasy? Isn't that counterproductive?"

Eliot shook his head. "Not at all. By simply trying to ignore these fantasies and circumvent them, I think you're giving them more power than they deserve. If you face them, and understand them, and are fully conscious of them, you'll have the tools you need to explain them away. More than likely, they'll evaporate all on their own." He flattened his hands on his thighs, ran them down to cup his knees. Grime blackened the thumbnail of his left hand and the nail of his right index finger.

He said, "Imagine someone accidentally and repeatedly stepping on your heels as you walk. If you ignore the person, you get angrier and angrier, and hate the person more and more. But he might not even know he's doing it. If you turn and face him, chances are he'll throw up his hands and back off." He picked at his thumbnail—the right one, the clean one. "See what I mean?"

I nodded. Eventually, I would have to tell him about Tory—the fantasy I'd had about Tory. But I said, "Something from today?"

"Recent, but not necessarily today. Is there something in particular you're thinking about? Something you don't want to tell me?" He gave a wry smile. "Because that's the very one I want to hear."

My shoulders slumped forward. I nodded. In a halting rush, I told him about the previous day. Tory and Christa's engagement, the graffiti, the dream, the shaving, the shower.

Saying nothing, he sat, his left elbow resting on the arm of the chair, his chin resting on the heel of his left hand. At last he nodded. "This Tory fellow, he's a good friend?"

I gave it some thought. "My best friend. My best *male* friend."

"You see a lot of each other?"

"Not a *lot,* no."

"But you enjoy his company."

"Very much," I said. "We have a lot in common. We can talk about—. About music, Beethoven, poetry."

"Poetry?"

"He's a poet. Writes poetry. Loves Whitman."

"*Walt* Whitman?"

Was there another Whitman? "Do you think it's dangerous?"

"Not entirely dangerous," he said, but he said it with a deep frown. "He's getting married, after all."

On my right hand, the chapped skin of my palm had started to flake away at the base of the middle finger. I picked at it. "It's true. He's entirely taken with Christa. I'm just a friend."

"Do you love him?"

Tears welled at the corners of my eyes. I did love him. I loved Tory—inaccessible, spoken-for, heterosexual Tory. Tory the wearer of a letterman jacket. Tory the know-it-all. Tory the maker of frittatas of inconsistent quality. How had this happened?

"I think it's a peculiar part of our sickness that we seem to confuse the thrill of every illicit attraction with love."

"I can see that happening. That is to say, I've felt so swamped by someone that I thought I might be falling for him." Eliot knew about Spike. If I uttered that single syllable—*Spike*—Eliot would know what I meant. But I couldn't bring myself to say Spike's name.

"Moving forward, what's your strategy for dealing with these temptations?"

I shrugged. "I don't think I can do much more than I'm already doing." I reached up to run my fingers through my hair. To feel stubble instead surprised me. A small thrill passed through me. "I can pray and wait it out. That's about all."

"Do something else for me," Eliot said. "Get yourself a small notebook. Just a little spiral notebook, something you can carry around with you, nothing fancy. Whenever you're attracted to someone—a man, I mean—or whenever you have a fantasy, write it down. Just enough information so that when you go back to it, you'll remember what you saw and what you thought."

I frowned. "If I go back and read it again, won't that be inviting the temptation to return?"

"I think you'll find that it won't. First of all, when you recall these incidents at some distance, you'll likely see how unjustified the attractions were. In the case of Tory, for example. Don't you already feel foolish about fantasizing about Tory?"

It was true, I did. I nodded.

"Second, before you look at them again, you'll pray and get yourself into a reverent mood. You'll read them aloud as the confessional part of your prayer. When you're done, you'll write 'forgiven' crosswise on the page, over and over, until you feel that it's true."

Forgiven. I looked down at my hands. How empty—how ordinary—that word, *forgiven*, had become. Once it had filled me with joy. I remembered feeling like a wisp of smoke, a current of air. That word, *forgiven*, had lightened me that much. Now it had all the force of any other word—*white* or *short* or *redhead*. "Are there sins so horrible that they can't be forgiven?"

Eliot put his hand on my arm. Through my sleeve his skin was cold. "What could you have done that would be so heinous?"

I shrugged, shook my head. "Not any one thing, I guess." Taking his hand in both of mine, I rubbed his chilly skin.

Eliot chuckled. "I don't think it's possible to lose your right to forgiveness, or to lose your salvation."

"Not even if you renounce it? Not even if you turn into a worshipper of Satan?"

"Were you thinking of doing either of those things?" He chuckled. "If so, I'll have to ask for my hand back."

Laughing, I let go of his hand. I scratched above my left ear. A fringe of whiskers had hidden in a divot in my scalp, and I'd missed them when I'd shaved. "I guess I just like to know where the boundaries are."

"I'm not God," Eliot said, smiling. "I'm not fit to judge. I suppose if you entirely turned your back on God, he might be"—here he paused, staring at the ceiling—"a little less friendly. Anyone who doesn't love God loves Satan. We are either with God or against him."

"Do you believe that the devil exists, then? That there's some being at large in the universe who's only purpose and fondest desire is to lead God's children astray?"

He squinted at me. "Of course. What else?"

I blushed. "In college when we talked about the Bible we discussed the devil as a literary device, as a metaphor for evil, not as an actual being."

Squeezing the bridge of his nose between thumb and forefinger, Eliot shook his head. "And I suppose in ethics class you talked about how outmoded ethics have become in a technological society."

"How did you know?" I giggled, picturing Mr. Pepper—never Dr. Pepper, thank you kindly, despite the oak-framed PhD on his office wall. I remembered him raising his small arms from the sides of his little round body. Most lectures ended with him railing against the backwardness of Christian ethics. I'd joked about his class along with all his other students, but now as it turned out, I'd taken much of it with me.

Smiling, Eliot said, "I took the same class, or a similar one, rather. There is no black and white, remember? Whether something is right and wrong depends on motive. The whole world's a gray area."

That sounded like Mr. Pepper. I remembered his tiny voice, breaking with passion. How very strongly he'd believed in—what?—nothing?

•   •   •

At Thursday's group, from the moment I stepped into Eliot's living room, Charlie could not take his eyes off me.

Mason wasn't there. He hadn't been to group in a couple of weeks, and there was some discussion about his absences. Was he sick? Had he taken on a new schedule at the library? Had he decided to leave group? Eliot waved away the questions. "I'm sure he'll be back soon," he said. "Let's get to it, shall we?"

Charlie barely spoke. All the while the others talked, he watched me.

Jeremy's boss was playing some kind of passive-aggressive game, sending him the stingiest and surliest customers, and then complaining that Jeremy's sales numbers had declined. I'd had no idea that Jeremy was a salesman. It wasn't clear from his story what he sold.

Charlie watched me.

After a few awkward dinner dates, Rob's fledgling relationship with Chloe had fallen through. He wept for a while, choked his way through the story of her gradual withdrawal from him, of his repeated attempts to win her affection. Eliot hugged him, comforted him, patted his back, stroked his shellacked hair.

Charlie watched me.

Fred had gotten fired. Though he'd sent out dozens of resumes, he couldn't find another job. He'd been struggling with a temptation to bind Jeremy with nylon rope—to beat him, spank him, torture him with alligator clamps and wax dripped from burning candles. When they'd been a couple, I gathered, all of this profligate activity had been the stuff of any old weeknight. Mouth hanging open, I listened to the details of Fred's elaborate, vicious, and very specific fantasies. Jeremy listened, too, with an oddly affectionate half-smile.

And all the while, Charlie watched me.

At the end of the session, after Eliot disappeared into the kitchen and as the other men gobbled Jeremy's heart-shaped sugar cookies, Charlie leaned over and said in a whisper, "You look good. I like the—." He brushed the top of his head with the palm of his hand.

"I was overdue," I said. "I was thinking maybe I went from one extreme to the other, though."

"Not at all." He glanced across the room. He licked his lips. "Do you—? I was wondering, do you belong to a gym?"

"A gym?" I blinked. A random question, to be sure. "I did. A long time ago. I had to quit."

"Do you want to work out together some Saturday?" He was still whispering. "I can get you a guest pass. My treat. It's only five bucks or something."

"Well. I—."

"You'd be helping me out. I'm in desperate need of a spotter."

Given Charlie's size, I doubted I could usefully spot him on wrist extensions; the idea of spotting him on something like a bench press was patently ludicrous. What on earth could he be thinking? I cleared my throat. "I don't think—."

"Please."

"I guess—. I guess so."

Across the room, someone—Rob, I thought—said, quite loudly, "If you don't ask, I won't tell." It could have been Rob. His eyes were red-rimmed, puffy from crying, but he was smiling. Everyone laughed.

Fred said, "I'm certainly not planning to pursue," and again, they all laughed.

Urgently, Charlie said, "This Saturday?"

"This Saturday?" I pretended to think it over. "Not this Saturday, no."

I looked at him. Again, he licked his lips. He wore a green silk shirt, the color of a golf course or of a field of new wheat. In the firelight his eyes shone more greenish than usual.

More laughter. Guffaws. I looked. Fred stood with his left hip thrust out to the side, with the back of his right hand resting on the opposite hip. His left hand dangled limply from his wrist. Belatedly, I realized that he had said something bawdy, that he had said it in an effeminate way, with a lisp. Had he said something about having sex—anal sex—"on the pulth of morning"?

Rob said, "I can always feel my pulse in the morning."

And again, they all laughed. Fred—still keeping his wrist limp—slapped Rob's shoulder.

Charlie touched my elbow. I looked at him.

Something in his eyes—the jade shimmer, the intense stare—told me that I wouldn't be able to put him off forever. He wouldn't stop asking, inviting, pressing me to join him at the gym.

And if we went to the gym together—. If we ended up in the locker room together, stripping, showering, sitting in the steam room, what then?

"Next Saturday?" he said.

He leaned toward me, his eyes glowing, intense. It was unseemly, the way he leaned in, the way he stared at my mouth.

"I'm not sure," I told him. "I'll let you know."

• • •

Christa and Tory settled on a date for their wedding. The twenty-eighth of February—a couple of weeks away, but—as Christa put it—not six whole freaking weeks.

The date moved again, though, and then there was no date. Certain delicate negotiations with Tory's parents were proceeding in fits and starts, Christa said. He'd decided they should come to the wedding. They lived in Phoenix and hated to travel north of I-40 between October and May. They hated to fly. Talks had broken down, Christa told me, as if Tory were negotiating with a sovereign nation and not his own parents.

She told me all of this in the cave, over sandwiches and bowls of soup. She didn't seem upset. I began to worry. The phrase "cold feet" kept running through my mind.

"You're taking this with a surprising measure of equan—equanim—." The word escaped me for some reason. "You're awfully calm. You're going to be four and a half or five months pregnant, after all, by the time you set a date."

She shrugged. "*Que sera,*" she said.

"Have you started meditating or something?" I asked her.

She laughed and batted my shoulder. "You're funny," she said. "Confidentially—." She leaned closer and looked over her shoulder, as if prying ears were all around. "Confidentially, I just hated that wretched Lutheran guy, that preacher or priest or whatever of Tory's. I don't give a shit how pregnant I am, as long as my water doesn't actually—you know—break during the ceremony."

Relief washed through me, and then I felt silly for feeling so relieved, and then I felt silly for having worried in the first place.

Christa tugged a leaf of lettuce from her sandwich and munched on it. "God, that guy's a dick," she said, staring off to her left.

I turned to see what she was looking at—surely at Thorstensen, I thought. But there was only a television set tuned to the Senate session. I realized, then, that she meant the wretched Lutheran guy. The wretched Lutheran preacher or priest or whatever of Tory's—he was the dick in question.

• • •

Eventually, they set a date, a final date. March fourteenth. Christa promised me, no more postponements. Tory's parents weren't coming. Instead, Tory and Christa would spend a week in Phoenix on their way back from their honeymoon.

On the day of the wedding, as I stood at my bathroom sink—all the while I shaved my head, my chin, my pubic stubble—sleet pecked at the window. I edged aside the blinds. The streets were coated in ice. Power lines and tree limbs sagged under the crystalline weight of dripping icicles.

Three or four times that morning I called Tory's house. There was a chance, surely, given the weather, that the wedding would be postponed yet again. Each time I called, the answering machine picked up.

I left the house at three o'clock, allowing two hours for travel time. The sky had cleared. The sun shone bright. Streets, sidewalks, lawns, trees, utility poles—everything glimmered and dripped, bright as glass. Meltwater streamed in the gutters and silvered the streets.

As it happened, it was crazy to allow two hours for travel time. The streets were clear. I-94 was dry. Traffic moved quickly. In thirty minutes, I reached the church. It was easy to find in the tidy grid of streets below Lake Street— at Lake and Thirty-Second, not far from Tory's favorite bar—what the hell was its name? Competitors? Champs? Heroes?

Alterations to the building's façade and roof line—the addition of a pair of spires, of a gothic arch above the doorway, of an enormous placard bearing its name, The Word of the Spirit Church—had more or less failed to disguise that it had begun life as a Kentucky Fried Chicken restaurant.

I sat in the Chevette, reading *Beethoven in London*, until in the rear-view mirror I saw Tory's silver Mercedes slip into the lot, and then until I saw Christa and Tory step from the car. She wore a puffy orange parka over a lacy cream dress, and she carried a small bundle of white lilies. Tory wore a black suit, a shirt that matched her dress, and his houndstooth topcoat.

We hugged all around, grinning. Suddenly I was near tears.

Christa plucked at the lapel of my suit coat. "Don't you look lovely," she said. She flicked my tie. "No sign of the ayatollah."

"Are you nervous?" I asked her.

She laughed and waved away the question, as if it were the most ridiculous thing anyone had ever asked her. Tory said, "Holy fuck, yes."

The officiant greeted us at the front door. Her white robes shimmered like dew. She was tall, dark-haired, slender. She looked familiar—the oval shape of her face, the cleft chin. She shook our hands—Tory's, then Christa's, then mine. To Christa, she said, "Your mother's here."

Christa's mother, Alice, sat fidgeting on the edge of a folding chair. Rubbing her hands on her sleeves, she stood. Her crisp gray suit must be brand new. The collar of her blouse was pure white and priestly stiff. She'd polished her flat-soled, sensible shoes as if for military inspection.

"I'm sorry I'm so early," Alice said. Creases folded and smoothed themselves alongside her mouth. "I was so afraid I'd be late. This weather." She touched her blue-rinsed hair. To Tory, she said, "You look so handsome."

He did look handsome, in his princely suit and his shiny, tassel-free chaussure. A hank of hair had come loose and hung down on one side of his forehead. I fought the impulse to reach up and tuck it back into place.

"Thank you, Alice," he said. Alice turned one cheek toward him. Bending stiffly at the waist, he kissed her. From the pocket of his overcoat he produced a red tie, held it up. "Excuse me," he said. "I need to find a mirror."

Christa turned, looking for the officiant. "Jonquil?" she called. "Jonquil?"

Jonquil. Jonquil? Could it be—? How many women named Jonquil could there be in the world?

From a back room Jonquil appeared, her robes flashing and coursing like water. It *was*. It was *that* Jonquil. Much about her had changed, it seemed—her clothing, her posture, the color and cut of her hair—but she was, without a doubt, *that* Jonquil.

"Yes?" she said.

"Almost ready," Christa said. "Just waiting for a Windsor knot."

• • •

Jonquil arranged us around a makeshift altar—a card table, it looked like, with a white cloth spread across it and some candles lined up along its surface. Christa and Tory stood in the center, Alice and I on either side.

Jonquil pointed a tripod-bound camera toward us, looked through the viewfinder, made adjustments. She pressed a button. A red light on the front of camera glowed. Gears clicked and whirred.

Placing herself between Tory and Christa, facing them, the altar at her back, Jonquil said, "We begin with a reading from the good gray poet, Walt Whitman." From the folds of her robe she drew a crackling sheet of onion-skin paper. She opened it. She read.

> When I heard the learn'd astronomer,
> When the proofs, the figures, were ranged in columns before me,
> When I was shown the charts and diagrams, to add, divide, and
>   measure them,
> When I sitting heard the astronomer where he lectured with
>   much applause in the lecture-room,
> How soon unaccountable I became tired and sick,
> Till rising and gliding out I wander'd off by myself,
> In the mystical moist night air, and from time to time,
> Look'd up in perfect silence at the stars.

Jonquil tucked the paper under her arm. She laid a hand on Tory's shoulder, a hand on Christa's. "So it is with the love between two people. An attempt to quantify it or explain it, or to force it down one road or another, can kill it." She folded her hands. "We all know that there have been rough spots in the last couple of months. There have been breaches. There have been crises. But there is an unshakable bond between these two. There is a truth between them that has existed since the moment they met, and that will continue to exist until they are separated by death." She paused, looking first at Alice, and then at me. "To symbolize the infiniteness of this connection, we use a simple platinum band, a shape with no beginning and no ending."

Alice and I gave over the rings. Alice's eyes glistened. I wiped a tear.

"Tory," Jonquil said, "place the ring on Christa's finger. And I believe you have something to say?"

Holding Christa's hand in his, Tory slid the ring onto her fourth finger. "Nothing I can say can capture the depth or the breadth of what I feel for you, or encompass the strength of my commitment to you. For millennia, poets have used metaphor to express these things that are felt but not seen, known but not heard. 'The obscure moon lighting an obscure world of things that would never be quite expressed.' I love you, more than I love myself. I need you, more than I need breath. And I promise you that for as long as I live, I will be yours." Bending at the waist, he kissed the place where the platinum band—narrow as a thread—nestled against Christa's skin.

I looked up at Tory's handsome profile, at the rugged line of his jaw, at the good, high bones of his cheeks, at the wet glint of his black eye. God, I loved him. How had it happened? How had it come to pass, that I'd fallen in love with my best friend's fiancé? Two minutes more, and he would be her husband.

"Christa," Jonquil said.

Christa—weeping openly, I saw, her mascara beginning to run—pushed the ring onto Tory's finger. The ring snagged on the loose skin at the last knuckle. She twisted it, gently forced it into place.

She said, "I used to think that I was a mostly self-sufficient person, and that if I could have a few houseplants and Peanut"—here she touched her belly—"and a place of my own, I could weather anything. But you came along and showed me different. For one thing, you showed me that I don't have to go through life being named Christa Kristiansen."

Christa paused, and we all looked at her in stunned silence. And then Jonquil laughed—a warm, robust, musical laugh. And then we all laughed, except for Alice. Alice wore the expression of a woman whose shoes were two sizes too small.

Christa said, "I love you for loving me, for wanting me more than you want anything else. I promise you that, no matter what happens, we will be together. This is forever."

Forever, I thought. Forever, he would be hers. My heart hammered in my chest.

Jonquil said, "Beloved, I believe that constitutes a marriage vow."

They kissed, Christa and Tory. A tender kiss. A fierce kiss. A soul kiss. A kiss between newlyweds.

Jonquil waited. She said, "For our final word, let's turn again to Mr. Whitman." From the fragile page she read.

> Fatigued by their journey they sat down on Nature's divan whence they regarded the sky. Pressing one another's hands, shoulder to shoulder, their mouths opened, without uttering a word they kissed one another. Near them the hyacinth and the violet marrying their perfume, on raising their heads they both saw God who smiled at them from his azure balcony: Love one another, said he, it is for that I have clothed your path in velvet; kiss one another. Love one another, love one another and if you are happy, instead of a prayer to thank me kiss again.

The newlyweds kissed again.

•   •   •

Winners. That was the name of the bar. We went there for the reception. Tory led the way. The sun had warmed and dried the streets, and we had only a handful of blocks to go, but Tory drove the Mercedes at something like twelve miles per hour, so that Alice could follow him. I followed Alice, and Jonquil followed me.

Basketball and hockey games played, as before, on muted television sets. Half-sloshed sports enthusiasts sat on stools all along the bar, cheering or groaning over their mugs of foamy beer. From the back room I heard the bump and crack of billiard balls.

We claimed a big round table in the front window. Tory and I fetched drinks from the bar—Guinness for him and me, club soda with lime for Christa and Alice, Long Island iced tea for Jonquil.

"I'm famished," Christa said to Tory. "You know what I'd love?"

"What would you like, my bride?"

"A big platter of those super-atomic chicken wings."

Tory smiled at her. I didn't think he'd stopped smiling since Jonquil had read the first line of the first Whitman poem. The muscles of my jaw ached in sympathy.

"It's buttons," Tory said. "I'll be right back."

The four of us sat around the table, looking off in every direction. I sensed movement at my elbow. Jonquil. She'd leaned sideways, toward me. She'd outlined her eyelids with thick streaks of kohl. Tiny black specks dotted her cheeks and the sharp bones beneath her eyebrows.

She'd left her white robes at the church. Now she wore jeans and a man's white V-necked undershirt.

"You look so familiar," she said. "Where do I know you from?"

"Doctor Bell's office."

"Of course," she said. She slapped her forehead. "That's where I know *everyone* from." She gulped her drink. "What was your name again?"

"Jonah," I said. "Jonah Murray."

Frowning, she shook her head.

"Something about a boat," I said.

Her eyes widened. "That was you?"

"None other."

"I can't believe I didn't recognize you. *That* was my most fun day of work *ever* at Doctor Bell's."

"Fun?"

She held her hands out in front of her. "Sorry, sorry. That sounded simply awful, I'm sure."

"Not so—."

"It's just that, what you don't know about Doctor Bell is that he's *boring*." She rolled her eyes, tipped her glass, took a big swallow. "Not Doctor *Bell*, necessarily, but his patients. Old, old, *old*."

Jonquil cut her eyes at Christa's mother. She seemed to be gauging whether she now needed to add a disclaimer—"no offense intended," perhaps, or "no reflection on you." But Alice didn't seem to have heard. She sipped her club soda, her eyes following the wedge of lime perched on the rim of the glass.

Alice looked at Jonquil. Their eyes met. Alice flinched, startled, as if Jonquil had just materialized in a cloud of pink, kohl-tinged smoke.

"What did you think of the ceremony, Mrs. Kristiansen?" Jonquil said.

With great care, Alice placed her half-empty tumbler in the very center of her cocktail napkin. She laid her hands on the table, on either side of the napkin. "Oh, you know," she said with an air of apology. She sighed. "I'm a more traditional sort. I didn't understand all that stuff you read about astronomers and balconies."

I looked at Christa. With an affectionate and—I thought—somewhat lascivious expression, she stared at her new husband, who leaned over the bar, speaking with the bartender. Tory's suit coat had ridden up—the vent had fallen open—and his trousers hugged his narrow hips. Christa watched him and watched him and watched him.

"So how have you *been*?" Jonquil asked me.

I shrugged. "How did you get from Doctor Bell's to this?"

"I was just working there to get through seminary," she said.

"Seminary?" I said. The word had such a Catholic flavor to it. It conjured images of priests, of celibate men in black tunics and high collars, of Gregorian chant and stony chapels.

Jonquil sucked on an ice cube. She looked at me over the rim of her glass. "Seminary."

"You don't strike me as the seminary type."

She grinned. "Because I'm a woman?"

I wondered if she'd gone to seminary more or less because women didn't generally go to seminary. "No. Of course not."

She raised an eyebrow. Perhaps, as Tory kept pointing out, I was an inept liar.

"And this church? What is it? Word of the Spirit? Spirit of the Word? Did you start this church?"

"Yes. Yes, I did." She grinned. "But you never answered my question," she said. "How *are* you? Better since all that stuff about—about the boat?"

"Never better."

I wondered what she would say if I told her about Eliot, about the group, about *Hope and Healing*, about my box of bad influences. Of all the things she might not understand, I was sure that forgiveness was the one thing she *would* understand.

She leaned closer. "Can I tell you a secret?"

I was sure she would tell me in any case. I said, "Of course."

"My real name is Janice."

"I'm sorry? Janice?"

"You can be anything you want to be. I decided to be Jonquil, not boring old Janice. Then I decided to be the Reverend Jonquil, not just a receptionist in a dentist's office."

"What if I wanted to be the Zodiac killer? Or—. Or what if I wanted to be Sweeney Todd, the Demon Barber of Fleet Street, and make meat pies out of self-righteous beadles?"

"Ha. That's very funny. Fleet Street." She said it a few more times, clipping the syllables, biting them off between her teeth. "You know what I mean. As long as you don't harm anyone, including yourself, you can be anything you want to be."

"I—. Why are you—? I don't know what—."

Just then, Tory returned to the table with a platter the size of a manhole cover. In the center of it, a six-inch-high mound of chicken wings glistened, red-orange. Christa swept away the salt and pepper shakers and a napkin holder, and Tory set the platter in the middle of the table. The wings smelled of vinegar and hot peppers.

I hadn't eaten all day. I'd been famished, I realized, and now I was ready to devour the better part of an entire chicken.

◆　◆　◆

We ordered more drinks, more chicken wings. Christa made many trips to the jukebox to play ABBA and Prince and Gloria Gaynor. Jonquil and Tory played a round of pool. Christa guzzled club sodas, but giggled and slurred her words as if she were growing very, very drunk. Alice sat in her chair, looking prim and disobliged. As the hours wore on, Alice seem to fold into herself, to shrink and wrinkle like an apricot drying in the sun.

And then she vanished. All at once, I realized that Alice had gone. Perhaps to the ladies' room? But no, after thirty minutes, it was clear—she'd gone home.

Jonquil left, too, slipped out while I was in the men's room.

Tory slid into the chair next to mine. He wore the same broad grin he'd been wearing all day. "I never got a chance to say how good you look," he said. He stroked my bare scalp. His fingers were warm, his grip strong. "I like it. You should keep it."

"I—. I will," I said.

"And thank you for standing up with me," he said.

I leaned toward him, hoping to catch that smell, the apple-pinesap scent he'd worn in the hospital. Now, though, he smelled of nutmeg and tobacco—not of smoke, but of rich, earthy, pipe tobacco.

"I know it's not exactly traditional—the groom and the best man dancing—but how about a dance?"

"A *dance*? Here? Do you feel like getting knifed out back on your wedding day?"

Christa leaned over, grinned, poked my ribs. "You *dope*. This is a gay bar."

At the bar, two men sat side by side. One laid his head on the other's shoulder. The bartender had removed his shirt, and his muscles bulged and rippled around the straps of a leather harness. I could see, through a narrow gap, that in the back room two of the men playing pool stood arm in arm. There were no women in the bar, other than Christa.

Tory laughed. "You never noticed?"

How could I have noticed? The first time we'd come here, I'd been too busy getting drunk, pining for Spike, and popping in and out of the phone booth. This time, I'd spent the entire afternoon and evening watching Tory, staring at him in his spruce black suit.

"I guess I—." I rubbed the top of my head. "This is *your* bar? The—the bar you come to most often? A *gay* bar?"

"I came here a lot with Adam," Tory said. "So?" He stood, held out his hand. "Dance?"

Christa dropped a couple of quarters into the jukebox. She selected a Streisand song, of course. "If I Loved You." Wasn't that from *The Broadway Album*?

I cut her a look. She stuck her tongue out at me.

There was no dance floor. Right there in the front window, alongside our table, Tory took me into his arms. I tried to keep some distance, but he pulled me tight against him. We swayed, each trying to lead.

"I liked all the Whitman you used in the wedding," I told him.

He grinned. "He was Adam's favorite, for obvious reasons. That last bit—'fatigued by their journey' and all that—it actually refers to two men. It was something Whitman wrote in his journal. God giving his blessing to the love that dare not speak its name. I trimmed it, so it fit us better."

Instead of a prayer to thank me, I thought, *kiss again.* I looked at Tory's mouth, his beautiful full mouth, and wished that I could kiss him.

Tory leaned down, whispered into my ear. "Thank you," he said.

"For what?"

"For everything. Mediating. Getting us back together. Being such a good friend to both of us. Being my best man."

I started to say, "It was nothing that—." But there was nothing to say, really. Nothing more useful than, "You're welcome."

Again as on that morning in Saint Joseph's, I laid my head on his chest. He cradled my head in his warm, damp palm. I snuggled myself against him, held tight to him.

The music played on. "If I Loved You" had always been a favorite of mine. Streisand sang it beautifully—I didn't want to let myself think so, but it was true. She sang it beautifully.

Tory and I danced.

I let him lead.

25 A MAN OF GOD

The evening air was balmy—relatively balmy, that is to say, in the forties, surely. The sky was clear, deep, starry.

A few blocks down Lake Street, I plugged the Walkman's earphones into my ears. The C-sharp minor quartet, of course. I fast-forwarded past the first movement, into the second.

I didn't feel like going home to my empty house. As I drove, I avoided the freeways. I turned left, onto a street I didn't recognize, made another turn, another. I let myself get lost in the streets of Minneapolis.

The C-sharp minor quartet played on—the second movement, the third, the fourth.

In time I came to the river road. I told myself I'd found it by accident. I *had*, hadn't I?—found it by accident?

I slowed, looking into the lawns on my left. I couldn't say, now, which house was the little gray-haired man's. His lawn signs were all gone, the election lost, America's goose well-cooked.

Near the main entrance to the beach, cars—a few cars—lined the street. I rolled past—the steep asphalt ramp on my right, the Shriners Hospital ahead on my left.

At first I shook off the impulse to stop—"I don't do that any more," I told myself—but past the train trestle, past the three-way stop just beyond it, I pulled to the curb. It was too early to go home—I didn't want to go home.

The clarity of the moonlit sky filled me loneliness and longing. How long had it been since anyone had held me the way Tory had held me as we'd danced? Before Christmas, and that had been Tory, too, in the hospital corridor. Sitting, still, behind the wheel of the Chevette, I hugged myself. I hoped to recapture, somehow, the sensation of Tory's body against mine, but I felt only that my arms were empty.

Pocketing my keys, I descended dark ledges of stone, past a thick, rough-barked tree, past a slender, smooth-skinned one. Bare branches swayed against the luminous sky, tickled the moon.

The last step was the steepest, a drop of eighteen inches or so. Standing on the brink, I curled my toes, as if they could, through the stiff soles of my dress shoes, grasp the sharp stones. I let myself rock forward and landed silently on both feet.

In a semicircle of young trees, on a rough-cut stump, a man sat, his twill-clothed legs splayed wide, one hand in his pocket. The night reduced him to his brightest colors, the white of his long beard and narrow fingers, the pale blue of his shirt, the orange firefly of his cigarette. "Evening," he said in a voice cracked by age and smoke. "How are you?"

"Can't complain," I said, and hurried past.

Further along the path, a black shape rustled the limbs of a sumac. The shape might have been one man standing alone or a pair of men huddled together. I didn't stop to see.

At the bottom of a two-foot drop was the park's official entrance. I made the small leap and stood on the asphalt plateau. On the right, the steep climb to the street. On the left, the steeper drop to the picnic area and the central paved trail. I hiked downward, into the river-fed chill of the park.

Crossing a squarish patch of concrete at the foot of the hill, leaping over a border of rough rock, crunching through sand, I went to the water's edge. The river licked the soles of my shoes. Up above, on the street, the air had seemed almost warm, but here the wind whipped through the thin fabric of my trousers as if they were mesh or gauze. I breathed deep, letting the cold burn my nose and throat, taking in the clean watery scent of earliest spring—sap, bark, peat, budding greenery.

Above me half a dozen parallel curves of cloud stretched across the sky, delicate wrinkles in taut velvet. To the west, Orion stood tall, one foot—or was it a hip?—already below the horizon.

From behind me and to the left, where a small path stumbled upward among bamboo stems and oak burls, a figure appeared. The moonlight was clear enough, bright enough. I saw the fireplug, brick-shithouse shape of him, the silver sheen of his shaved head, the bristles of his goatee. He wore baggy knee-length shorts and a black T-shirt. A sudden breeze off the water rippled his clothing.

Seeing me, seeing me watch his approach, he stopped. He paused a moment, looking around him. He came and stood next to me.

"Damn cold down here," he said. As he turned his profile to me, moonlight glinted along a ring in his septum.

Tigger? I squinted at him. Yes, it could be Tigger. "Tigger?"

The bluish whites of his eyes grew large. He leaned forward. "I'm sorry," he said. "I don't remember your name."

"Jonah. From group."

"From group. I remembered that much." He cleared his throat. "Are you still in?" He chuckled. "Obviously, you aren't, or you wouldn't—."

I stopped him. "I am. I'm still in group. I thought you were with someone."

He stuffed his hands into his pockets. "We broke up again."

"Are you coming back to group?"

Shaking his head, he looked out across the river. His eyes climbed the height of Orion. "What's the point? I'll only wash out again."

"Isn't it worth it to try?"

Turning, he looked me up and down. "The whole time I was in group, I was coming here. That's the real reason I left. Bobby wanted to get back with me, sure, but I was already a goat among sheep. Why stick around?"

"Why didn't you ever say anything? Couldn't we have helped?" I studied the river-slicked tips of my shoes. I stepped back from the water. "Not me, in particular, but Eliot and the group? Aren't we supposed to help each other out, hold each other accountable? If you'd just been—."

Backing off a step, he swung his arms out. "If I'd just been, if I'd just been. I'm queer. That's all I've ever been. That's all I'll ever be." He poked my shoulder. "You too. You're queer too. That's why you're here and not home genuflecting or sacrificing or reading your fucking Bible. The sooner you get over yourself and be who you are, the better off you'll be."

He strode off, toward the heart of the beach, toward the sumac-covered dunes. To the back of him, I said, "Are you better off, Tigger? Are you happy?" He couldn't have heard me over the sounds of the wind, the tree branches knocking together, the river washing the shore.

My feet ached with cold. In my jacket pockets, in my gloves, my fingers were nearly numb. And yet I could bring myself neither to leave the park nor to penetrate further into it. I lay instead on top of a picnic table above the beach. Its surface was oddly warm.

The ripples in the sky, the six wavelets of cloud, had slumped together. Above me they formed a set of rounded and uneven tiers, a stairway to heaven, impossible to reach and climb. Or an ancient eye shut tight, folded in on itself, blind.

Wind rattled the trees behind me. With a start, thinking that someone new had emerged from the path, I looked around me. No one. Again I lay back.

Poor Tigger, I thought. So lost. But then, here we were, searching in the same place for—*admit it, Jonah*—the same thing. In his case, though, a passing resemblance to Tory wouldn't be a requirement.

"Wasn't this supposed to get easier?" I said aloud. "Wasn't the loneliness supposed to go away? Wasn't that the whole idea?" I listened. My only answer was the slurp of river water on the sand.

Group. The group was an integral part of Stinson's plan. We all had the same struggles, we all had the same desires. By participating in the group, each of us bound himself to the others. If one of us went astray, the others brought him back. If one of us struggled with temptation, the others helped him resist. If one of us made progress, the others praised him.

Once, long ago, Tigger had come to group, had confessed that he'd spent an entire day cruising here. Eliot and the others had comforted him, had encouraged him. To confess another day spent cruising, though—? And another—?

It was one thing to confess a fantasy, an impure thought—even thought as deeply, deeply impure as Fred's—but an *act*—a repeated act—the act of coming here, of seeking a physical connection—that was another matter.

Could I, would I, sit in group on Thursday night and admit that I'd come here?

"Lord, forgive me," I whispered. I closed my eyes. "I'm weak. You know how weak. I want to do right. I want to be a part of your plan."

Out of the night air, a spot of warmth. A hand. Bare fingers caressed my thigh, feeding my senseless flesh with their heat. Another hand snaked its way inside my jacket, walking its way up my chest. It palpated the muscle. A finger flicked each nipple. My dress shirt and undershirt muffled the sensation, so that I felt his touch as something apart from me, at a remove.

I felt the bulk of a head between my legs and hot breath through the taut worsted of my trousers. Slowly the fingers tugged at my zipper.

"No!" I shouted. In an instant I stood on top of the picnic table. The man knelt in the sand at the table's end, looking up at me, an apotheosis of supplication and fear. "No!" I said again. My voice returned to me on a watery echo. "You will not have me, darkness," I said. I said it more or less to the gray-bearded man who crouched below me. And that was so absurd—he wore a Helly Hansen jacket and a heavy twill trousers, not a cloak of darkness—that I began to laugh. Laughing, I said, "You will not make me your whore." Turning, I addressed the beach at large. "You will not capture me, and use me, and make me your whore. I am a man. A man of God."

By then the gray-bearded man had disappeared, leaving only a rustling of branches as evidence that he had been there at all. Others—surely only one or two, in this cold, on this night—hid in those bushes, other men wrestling shadows, other ears craving truth. Thickets and dunes might conceal them from me, but I had only to raise my voice to reach them. "My weakness brought me to this evil place. I am in this evil place, but I am not of this evil place."

I paused. The whisper of leaves underfoot, the clicking of branches against themselves, gratified me. And then a voice, from afar, said, "Bug the fuck out, Jesus freak."

My voice boomed out over the river: "By the power of God, by the blood of Jesus, I will be rescued from the demons that lured me here." These words, it seemed, came not from me, but from heaven itself. I lifted my head and my hands to receive them. My eyes fixed on Orion's belt.

I felt drunk. How many glasses of Guinness had I had?

No, the Guinness had nothing to do with it.

I said, "If on the third day the Christ rolled away the stone and rose from the tomb, surely he will lift this burden from my shoulders, and I shall rise from the stinking grave, the prison of my sinful nature. I shall be of a holy heart and a pure mind. I shall be the beautiful thing I was meant to be." And here the tears rolled freezing down my cheeks. "I shall be like Christ."

A hand caught mine. I looked down. It was Tigger. "Are you crazy?" he said through lips stretched tight across his teeth. "Are you completely bug-fuck insane?"

Smiling, I squatted on the edge of the table. I clasped both his hands in both of mine. "Brother, I have never been more sane."

"You have to come with me," he said. He tugged on my hands, and I leapt off the table.

My feet plunged into soft sand. I knew, somehow, that my shoes were ruined.

Suddenly Tigger's knit brow smoothed itself. His worry collapsed into laughter, and for a second I thought he was laughing at my ruined shoes. "You're in serious danger here, man. You're about to be reverse-bashed."

Laughing still, hanging an arm over my shoulder, Tigger led me to the concrete ramp. At the plateau, Tigger steered me toward the pink stain of light at the top of the hill. As we climbed, I felt that eyes were on us, hostile eyes. The idea was oppressive at first, but by the time we emerged onto the sidewalk above the park, I was laughing again.

I looked at Tigger. Here, under the bright streetlight, I saw for the first time the outlandish proportions of the jewelry he wore in his septum piercing. A five-gauge—or perhaps four-gauge—bent barbell. The two beads nearly touched his upper lip.

We stood on the sidewalk, panting from the climb. Neither of us was laughing now.

"Thank you," I said. "I don't exactly know what came over me down there—." I glanced down the path. Waving shadows filled the chasm.

Tigger touched my hand. I looked at him. In this light his blue eyes paled nearly to whiteness. "If you don't know, I'm sure I don't know."

"Will you come back?"

He shook his head. "I can't." Shivering, shifting his weight from one booted foot to the other, he hugged his arms to his body. He stared into the sky. "I do feel kind of lost, but I can't come back. I can't see Eliot."

"Did something happen? Did he—?"

Tigger looked at me, stared at me. His eyes were fierce. I hadn't noticed, before this, that pale stray hairs stood up from his eyebrows, curly and wild.

"You're some kind of special case, you know. Eliot's favorite. You've never seen how he can get."

"What do you—?"

He interrupted me. "Every one of us, except you—. When someone's not doing what Eliot thinks they should do, he's—. He's fucking *mean*, man. Mean as shit."

I flinched. *Mean as shit.* "What—what does he—?"

"It's all just talking. But fuck. Holy shit. You've never heard anything like it. He can make you feel—."

"Like nothing?"

He nodded, chewing his thumbnail. "I can't see Eliot again."

"I just can't believe—."

"You haven't seen it happen. He's done it in group. He made Mason cry one time. And this one time, with Charlie—." He threw up his hands. He turned his head, squinted into the distance as if the striped façade of the Shriners Hospital suddenly fascinated him.

"It's cold out here," I said. "Let's go—." I nodded toward my car.

He walked with me to the Chevette. We both climbed in. The air inside was cold, but when I started the engine, the heater still blew warm air.

Eliot. Mean as shit. He could be stern, yes, as a father could be stern. But mean as shit? I thought—I could only think—that Tigger must be hypersensitive. Perhaps his father had been abusive, perhaps Eliot's sternness triggered some kind of overreaction. Of all of us, Tigger had always seemed the most fragile. Even Mason, in his quiet way, was stronger than Tigger.

And how long had it been since Tigger had come to group? November? December? Maybe Eliot had mellowed since, and Tigger had washed out too soon, had missed a gentler Eliot.

"If you ever need to talk," I said, "if you ever find yourself headed here, you can call me. Please? Three o'clock in the morning, four o'clock in the afternoon, call me."

I fumbled around for a pen, for something to write on. I took a pen from the ashtray and a dollar bill from my wallet. I wrote my name and both my phone numbers—work and home—on the single. I handed it to Tigger.

"I might take you up on this," he said. He stared at the dollar. "I need to stop coming here. I'm sick of it, but it's like an addiction. I can't help myself."

"We have to help each other," I said, "or we're doomed to fail."

26 ASSISTED LIVING

Early in the morning on Thursday, just before seven, the phone rang. Eliot. "We have to talk," he said. "Meet me at my office in an hour? Eight o'clock? Can you make it?"

"Okay," I said. I was barely awake. I might have said anything.

"Eight o'clock," he said again. "My office."

"Okay."

Only after he'd hung up did it occur to me to ask why I was meeting him.

If I didn't get out of bed, I knew, I would roll over and go back to sleep and miss our appointment. I climbed out of bed and went to the bathroom.

I lathered for a shave. When I'd finished, a mask of white foam covered me from the neck up, everything but my eyes and nose.

The warmth of the lather, the scrape of the blade. I couldn't help thinking of Tory, his hand on my head—on the top of my head as he'd complimented me, on the back of my head as he'd danced with me. I ignored my growing erection.

I showered, but only long enough to rinse away the soap. Anything more, I felt, and I would be on my knees again, my slick hand moving swiftly.

Dressed in my work clothes, carrying my leather jacket, I hurried for the door. Under skies of deep blue, the wind whispered a promise of warmth in the crisp air. Swift clouds, moving east, covered the sun. Crocus dotted my lawn with lavender and yellow.

By the time I reached the Midview Center, though, clouds had slumped in from the west. Rain fell in gallon drops that exploded against my windshield.

I pulled into a parking space near Eliot's door. An Acura Vigor, the color of a new-minted penny, glided into the space next to mine. A blotch of grayish salt spray darkened the passenger's-side fender. From the driver's seat Charlie looked at me, a long look, a longing look. Leaning sideways, he unlatched the passenger's side door and shoved it open. I dodged raindrops—or tried to—and dashed from my car to his. With the flats of my hands I swept chilly water off my scalp.

Over a T-shirt of mottled gray cotton, Charlie wore a rumpled shirt, unbuttoned, tails free. Over that, a navy blue Helly Hansen jacket—brand new, it looked like. The jacket—the white logo, the two side-by-side H's near the zippered breast pocket—reminded me of the bearded man at the beach. Charlie's black jeans and blue sneakers had frayed and frazzled themselves at the edges. Mousse or gel darkened and stiffened his hair. The short hairs behind his ear stood on end. A musk of sweat and tobacco filled the close air of the car.

"What's going on?" I asked him. "Eliot called me—."

"I called *him,* asked him if we could all get together. We need to talk."

"About what?"

"If it's okay, I'd rather wait till—." He looked down at his gloved hands. They lay limp in his lap. He didn't seem inclined to say more.

His eyes darted briefly toward me. Then, seeming all at once to sink into himself, he turned his head. For a long moment he looked at me, his eyes gray in the cloudy morning light. He blinked, looked down at his hands, said again, "If it's okay, I'd rather wait—."

I nodded. "Sure. Okay."

◆　◆　◆

Eliot's office was muggy and close. Throwing off our jackets and gloves, Charlie and I sat in the armchairs. Eliot sat behind the desk, his back bearing-wall straight.

"Charlie has something he needs to tell you," Eliot said.

I looked at Charlie. Mournful, disconsolate, he stared at Eliot.

"Charlie?" Eliot said.

Again as in the car, Charlie looked at his hands. Mumbling, he said, "I have feelings for you."

"Feelings?" I said.

"He thinks he's in love with you," Eliot said.

"In *love* with—?"

Charlie said, "I don't know how it happened. Something about the new—." He touched the top of his head.

I looked at Eliot, at Charlie, at Eliot again. "Something about the shaved head?" I said.

We'd spent so little time together, Charlie and I, and so little of it alone. In group, at the end of the session, yes, we'd talked sometimes. In something akin to privacy—if it could be called privacy, with the rest of the group on the opposite end of the room—yes, we'd exchanged a few words. But—. But for something like love to be built on that—. How—?

"I don't know how it happened," Charlie said again.

"It doesn't matter how it happened," Eliot said. "These things happen. It's a danger we all face. I don't think you two should see each other any more."

I looked at Charlie. He was already looking at me, his eyes deep and watery.

"Never? Not for a minute?" he said.

"What would you do with a minute?" Eliot said. His voice was hard and coarse. "Lust after each other?" He blew into his fist, shook his hand. "Kiss?"

I wanted to say that I was in no danger of lusting for Charlie, not if I had a minute or an hour or a year. I wanted to say that I was in love with Tory— that Charlie was in no danger from me, that he posed no danger to me. But of course, it wasn't true. I *had* lusted after Charlie, after all. When we'd first met, I'd imagined us living together with two cats and a pair of matching Hondas. Since then I'd watched him in group, had longed to touch him, hold him, kiss him. More than once, and not so very long ago, as I'd stroked myself in the shower, I'd called up an image of him—the sheer hairy bulk of him.

What difference did it make, really? Charlie or Tory—or Spike or Jose or Jaime or the plucked and tanned model from *Playgirl*. What difference did it make? Lust was lust.

"You have to decide," Eliot said, looking back and forth between us. "I'm only advising."

Again, I looked at Charlie. Already he was looking at me. He nodded, a small motion. "We have to," he said. "I can't look at you without—." He stopped, shot a furtive, guilty glance across the desk. He looked at Eliot as though Eliot had caught him jacking off. "You know what I mean."

Now he stared at the floor beyond his feet, at the leg of the desk, and I wasn't sure who he'd meant. Eliot knew what he meant, or I did? I wasn't sure.

"What about group?" I said. "We shouldn't even see each other at group?"

Tucking his hands into his armpits, Eliot said, "Again, I'm advising against it. One of you will have to leave group. I'll supplement with another private session."

Head bowed, Charlie clasped his gloved hands together.

Eliot said, "Again, this is just my advice, but it seems to me that Charlie should stay in group." He looked at Charlie. "You have a longer history, and until now you've served as something of an example to the others."

Without looking up, Charlie nodded.

To me, Eliot said, "Jonah, I don't think group ever clicked for you. Am I right?"

I was ashamed of the relief I felt. I tried not to smile as I said, "I won't miss it."

"Then it's settled." He slapped his hands together. "Shall we pray?"

The prayer was all about lust and shame, forgiveness and purity of heart. I sat stiffly in my chair, trying hard to shake the notion that I'd been unjustly accused. In truth, I *was* guilty of lust—I *did* feel the shame of it. But still—in the past few days, at least—Tory had been the object of my lust, not Charlie.

After the prayer, we all stood. I felt hollow, shell-shocked, numb. For a moment Charlie and I stood looking at each other. In twenty minutes, it seemed, he had aged twenty years. Back hunched, eyes sunken, lips moving soundlessly, he made to pass me. He stopped, looked at me again, looked me up and down. "Bye," he said at last.

I started to say that I was sorry—sorry that I'd shaved my head and caused him trouble, sorry that he would have to find another spotter at the gym. But I said nothing.

"I'll miss you," he whispered.

And so Charlie had gone. Smiling at me, Eliot arranged the papers on his desk. "It's for the best," he said. "It's for the best."

He stood over his desk, paging through his calendar. "I have Fridays free. Six o'clock? For your second weekly session?"

"Sure, sure," I said.

Leading me from the office, Eliot switched off the light.

We stood together at the front door. Light streaming through the blinds cast bars of shadow across the floor and desk. When Eliot opened the door, the pure yellow glow of sunlight streamed through the gap. The rain had passed.

Charlie plodded away toward his car, hunched over in the chill air, Atlas shouldering the planet's whole mass and weight.

• • •

I drove to work with the third movement of the C-sharp minor quartet singing in my ear. Not yet nine o'clock, and already it had been an odd, odd day.

Strange, how the heart worked. All the while I was busy falling in love with Christa's husband, Charlie had been falling in love with me.

Or no—not love. Lust.

Lust, of course—for what could have made Charlie love me—really, truly love me? He barely knew me. His so-called love seemed to be based more on the workings of my electric shaver and my disposable razor than on any particular aspect of my personality.

And what, really, could have made me love Tory? The certainty that he was off limits, out of bounds? Before that, to be sure, I'd had no great affection for him. As a friend, perhaps—yes, I'd come to think of him as a friend. Yes, that was true. But as a lover? Only after he'd committed himself to Christa, had become unapproachable, had I come to believe I loved him.

It hardly mattered. I might never see Charlie again—or, more to the point, he might never see me again. And by now Christa and Tory were on a plane, on their way to Hawaii. Three weeks in Hawaii, a week in Phoenix. In four weeks' time, who knew? I might have fallen in love with someone else—anyone else.

I craved the Great Fugue, the goblin march. Its sharp edges and precipitous leaps would be well-suited to my mood. But I'd never dubbed the Great Fugue to cassette. Weeks and weeks ago, after my crazy night with Spike and Jose, I'd sworn off it.

• • •

All morning, in Christa's absence, her twittering phone destroyed my concentration. Martin had decreed that it should never go unanswered. If we failed to answer the phone, if we scrimped on rudimentary office procedure, he'd said, a legislator might decide that we cared little for our jobs and that we might as well be abolished.

Fine for Martin. When the phone rang, he sat in the bunker of his office and ignored it.

By one o'clock, I could stand it no longer. I knocked on Martin's door. He sat at his desk, staring over the top rim of his glasses at his poster of Ravi

Shankar. He had the *Pioneer Press* spread out across his desk.

"I need to go to lunch," I told him.

He waved toward the paper. "Did you write in to the Bulletin Board?"

"Bulletin Board? What? No. Why?"

He leaned over his desk. His finger flitted up and down the page, fell on a column in the upper right-hand corner. "Where have you gone, Mrs. Malaprop?" he read. He cleared his throat. "'Red' of Saint Paul writes: Anders Thorstensen, Minority Leader of the Minnesota House of Representatives, is Mrs. Malaprop. In a recent committee meeting, Thorstensen referred to the DFL's long-standing habit of championing entitlement over meretricious-ness." He looked at me over his glasses. "That happened in our forum. He said that in our forum."

I shrugged. "I didn't do it. It's nothing to do with me."

"Who would it have been? You were the only redhead, if I remember rightly."

"The forum was a while ago, and you just read that it was a recent committee meeting. A committee meeting, not a forum. Maybe he said the same thing again."

"I suppose it's possible."

"I didn't do it. He's said much dumber things. I wouldn't have picked that one." It occurred to me that I wasn't helping my case.

He picked up the paper, rattled it, folded it. "Hm," he said.

"I need to go to lunch," I said again. "Can you handle the phones?"

I didn't exactly wait for an answer. I fled to the cave.

•   •   •

Session must already have adjourned for the day. A line of staffers and legislators, all in suits, stretched from the cashier stand to the main entrance. I waited in line for twenty minutes for a chef's salad that I didn't really want.

I roamed the cafeteria, searching for an empty table. In the far corner, Thorstensen sat munching a sandwich, reading a book. He looked lonely, somehow, and smaller of stature than I remembered.

His vest, though—the color of a robin's breast or a cockscomb—that was entirely familiar. The buttons bulged as always, enough to put a hand through each gap.

I steeled myself, approached his table.

"Representative Thorstensen?" I said. "I wondered if I might join you?"

Grunting, he closed his book. *Love and Discipline*—in hardcover, surprisingly. A new edition?

"Have a seat," he said. "What can I do you for?"

I did not sit. I nodded toward the book. It *was* a new edition, I saw. Near the bottom edge of the front cover, in stark sans-serif type, there was a slug that read, "Newly Revised and Updated—*The* Resource for the Modern Parent."

I said, "I haven't read that one."

He raised his eyebrows. "I wouldn't have thought you would."

"*Hope and Healing,* though," I said. "That's an awfully good book."

Leaning back in his chair, he dropped a crust of bread—all that remained of his sandwich—onto his plate. He brushed crumbs from his fingers. With a paper napkin he dabbed daintily the corners of his mouth.

"Do you know that book?" I asked him. "Are you aware of its subject matter?"

He frowned. Slowly, in eight or so syllables, he said, "Yes." The last syllable—call it the ninth—transformed the word into a question.

"Then if I ask you for a favor, you'll know that I'm asking as a brother in Christ, a born-again Christian, and a reformed—a *reforming*—homosexual."

Hauling himself upright, he said, "Young man, I am not accustomed to having people come up to me in public for the purpose of being so—so pertinent. I'm pleased to hear you saw the light of day, but I'm afraid that that simply isn't resonant to—."

Where have you gone, Mrs. Malaprop? I thought.

"Mister Thorstensen, I'm asking you as a brother in Christ. Leave the OWT alone."

He guffawed, so suddenly, so loudly, that I flinched. All around us, heads turned.

"That's entirely out of my hands, my boy. Entirely out of my hands."

"As far as I know, you haven't introduced a bill yet. All I'm asking is—. I'm just asking you, please—. If you haven't introduced a bill yet, don't."

For a moment he seemed suspended in deep thought, his head lolling, his lips smacking. He said, "It's a trifle more complicated than that."

Gingerly I edged an empty chair toward his. "May I, sir?"

A foolish question—he'd already invited me to sit. But he took no notice. He nodded, gestured toward the chair. I sat on the edge of the seat. I set my salad on the table. I caught a smoky whiff of the ham. I edged the bowl away, into the farthest corner of the table.

"I'm sorry. I didn't intend to be rude." I gave a short, self-conscious, self-deprecating laugh. "Maybe I thought I could win your respect if I affected a certain—a certain bravado. Please forgive me."

He nodded. I caught him eying my salad. He sucked his teeth.

"There are many things in my life that are changing now, as you can imagine. My friends, my habits—." I swallowed hard. "My *filthy* habits, my whole way of thinking and being. I've had to give all of those things up to God in the hopes that he'd change them."

With a kindly smile he leaned forward. "And he is, isn't he?" Falling backward again, he barked, "He is, isn't he?"

"Yes, sir, he is." I couldn't manage to return his smile, not quite. "He most certainly is."

"I have always said that my God is a just and powerful God," he said. He jabbed the table with his index finger. "I have *always* said it."

Edging my chair forward, I said, "But then you can see how burdensome it would be for me to find other work, especially when OWT has a worthy purpose. It may not be the highest purpose in the world, but it's not unwholesome. And I—. You remember what we said in that forum, about protecting against anti-religious harassment. I can do some good as part of OWT."

He nodded. "I see what you mean. I do. But there are so many other factors—. This is not just about you. There are budgets to consider, and office space, and—well, and any number of things."

I slid backward into my seat. "I understand that," I said. "I've been here long enough to know that no decision is made in a vacuum."

"For example," Thorstensen said, clearing his throat, "I've *heard*—. I've *heard* that there is to be a provision in your policy concerning specific protection for homosexuals." He tipped his chair back, balancing it on its hind legs. His vest opened its half dozen mouths. "I've heard that in one of your *forms,* someone was complaining because a coworker objected to a book. A pornographic book left out on someone's desk."

I had no idea what he meant. A pornographic book? Which book? To Thorstensen, *Leaves of Grass* would be pornographic. *Ulysses* would be pornographic. For all I knew, the classic comic book of *Moby-Dick* might, to Thorstensen, seem pornographic.

"I've *heard,*" he said, "that the *objection* to the book would be classed as harassment, but not the book *itself.* I think it should be quite the obverse, don't you?"

I felt my face grow hot. I swallowed. "Nothing's set in stone." Had my voice sounded as foreign to him as it had to me? "The policy is still in its beginning stages. Adjustments could be made. There are things we've been considering that could be—. That could be altered or eliminated."

He nodded. He smiled. He licked his lips. "That's what I thought." He cleared his throat. "There is much business before us this session," he said. "I think it's probably a little late now for proposing a lot of new and trivial legislation."

I smiled. I tried to make it a broad and happy smile, but I felt queasy. "Thank you, sir. I'm glad to hear you say that."

◆　◆　◆

Martin sat at Christa's desk. He wore her phone headset. As I ducked toward my cubicle, he shot me a vituperative look. "I'll look into that, senator," he said. "Of course, you have every reason—. No, not at all—. My assistant will—. Yes, good—."

I had barely enough time to sit at my desk before he appeared at my side. "I know I was gone for a long time," I said, "but trust me when I say it's worth it."

He folded his arms across his chest. "'Worth it'?"

"I ran into Thorstensen in the cave. I convinced him to leave us alone."

His eyes grew large. "'Us'? 'Us' meaning the OWT?"

Smiling, I nodded.

"You're joking. How?"

My smile disappeared. "If I tell you, you'll lose all respect for me."

Chuckling, he reached out as if to pat the top of my head. "That already happened, when you shaved your head." Beaming, winking, he drew his hand back. "I won't inquire, then." He rubbed his hands. "But we have a lot of work to do, don't we? We haven't accomplished a thing in weeks." He backed out of my cubicle. "Come see me when you've settled in. We have a policy to create."

He disappeared into his office.

I had already settled in. I had no more settling in to do.

So. Legal pad and pen. I summoned up my blood. I stood at the door of Martin's office. I set my teeth, held my breath, and stretched myself to my full height. Into the breach.

◆　◆　◆

Decades later—or so it seemed—when I returned to my desk along the trail of stones I'd left for myself, a light on my phone blinked, showing that

I had voice mail.

Tigger. "Sorry to call you at work." He spoke in a hoarse whisper. "I had—well, I had a bad night last night. Tonight's bound to be worse, I know it. I really need to talk to someone. Call me." He counted out his phone number, twice, slowly. I copied the number at the top of the top page of my legal pad. I dialed.

At first, the line was busy. When I tried again, after about fifteen minutes, he answered on the fourth ring. "I can't seem to keep myself away from that place," he said. "I went last night."

"Why didn't you call?"

"I didn't want to bother you."

"You're *supposed* to call. We help each other."

"Days are getting longer now. I feel like getting some air after work, and—. I know I'll go back tonight. Last night I was only there a few minutes. Tonight I might not be so lucky."

Martin, on his way out, gave me a small wave. I returned it, waited for him to go. To Tigger I said, "Luck has nothing to do with it. You make these things happen, and you can make them not happen."

He made a small sound, a whimper, a sigh. "You're right. I'm sorry."

"Let's do something tonight."

It was Thursday. Thursday, and yet—and yet!—I didn't have to go to group. I felt it again—the joy, the relief. Thursday, and no group.

"Let's get your mind off it," I said. "Let's see a movie or something." A movie where nothing happens, perhaps. With a pang, I thought of Tory. "Or we could just hang out and watch television. Anything that might help. Where are you?" Hadn't I written down his phone number? Yes. Here. Two-nine-two was the exchange. "St. Paul?"

• ◆ •

Tigger gave me directions to an apartment building next door to the Fitzgerald Theater, across the street from the science museum. I knew the street well—in summer, when I often went to the library at lunch, I walked by it at least once a week—but I'd never noticed this tall, tiny-windowed structure. Two colors of brick formed a basket-weave pattern up the front of it—red on the vertical lines, yellowish-tan on the horizontal.

Opposite Tigger's building, along the street, a half dozen metered parking spots stood empty. Tigger's street ended at a cross street, at the front door of a church, Central Presbyterian. Against its red stone façade, a green banner read, "SAM STINSON IS COMING! ARE YOU READY? MAY 3." I waited for a red light, made a U-turn, pulled into the parking space nearest the corner.

A narrow strip of grass, winter-browned, lay behind an iron fence. In a few weeks it would be filled with sunlight and laughing children. Now it was a desolate place. As I passed, an icy breeze whipped through it, stirring the damp carcasses of dead leaves and slicing through the fabric of my khakis.

Tigger waited in his building's vestibule, looking through me, it seemed, not at me. Crossing the empty street, I waved. Double-taking, staring at the top of my head, he held the door open to me. In the lobby, along walls the color of linen and among vinyl furniture the color of mud, men in bathrobes shuffled their slippered feet. The warm air smelled of hospital disinfectant.

Tigger led me to the elevator. "I'm glad you could come," he said. He wore a blue and red flannel shirt, cut-off fatigues, and the familiar, much-scuffed Doc Marten boots. His nose was bare—no septum piercing. I took it as a good sign.

"This is all about being there for each other," I told him. "Say," I said. "You mentioned something about Charlie and Eliot—."

Tigger looked at me. "It was—. You just don't know—."

Just then, the elevator doors rattled open. A bony man in a pale blue bathrobe leaned against the carpeted wall. I stood aside for him. When he didn't move, Tigger stepped into the elevator and pulled me after him. Mumbling, the man in the blue bathrobe stroked his long yellow-white beard.

Just as Tigger and I stepped out onto the fifth floor, the old man cried out. "Bean sprouts," he said. His eyes—wide as pennies, the same washed-out blue as his robe—held mine. "Don't ask, don't tell," he said. "Government waste."

Tigger tugged my sleeve. The elevator door slid shut behind me. "That's Mr. Graves," Tigger told me. "He's not supposed to watch the nightly news, but he always finds a way."

He led me through narrow hallways, along walls covered in blistered paint, past baseboard heaters pouring their swelter into the air. At apartment five-fourteen we stopped, and Tigger fumbled a thick featureless key into the doorknob. Standing aside, he waved me through a tiny hallway and into a living room. Sepia walls seemed to lean in on an unmade futon, a square table of unfinished wood, and a waist-high bookcase of incongruously rich cherry.

I stepped to the table. Some drawings lay in the yellow light of an ancient desk lamp. In the drawings, squarish, random objects scattered themselves across narrow, hand-drawn grids.

Beyond the table lay a galley kitchen. The narrowness of the space accounted for the counters' lack of depth, but not for their lack of height. Tigger saw me looking.

"This apartment is really intended for someone in a wheelchair," he said. Leaning forward, he pointed to the base of the kitchen cabinets. Underneath the countertops there was leg room for someone wheelchair-bound. "See?"

"What is this place? Some kind of nursing home?"

Blushing, stuffing his hands into his pockets, he walked across the futon. "Assisted living," he said. At the window he turned. "I have these seizures. Sometimes I need to have someone around, in case." Jumping as though someone had poked him, he returned to the futon. "I'm being a bad host. Let me make a place to sit." With a few deft motions he slid the futon's frame into the rough outline of a couch. The pine frame scraped across the linoleum. "Have a seat," he said.

But by then I had found more drawings. Line and shade represented in hyperrealistic detail a male form. In one drawing the subject stood erect, holding his erect penis while tweaking his left nipple. His angular lips were parted, his eyes shut tight. He reminded me of someone.

Tory. He looked like Tory. The square jaw, the high cheekbones, the straight, slender nose. Having felt Tory's chest against my cheek, I could say with some certainty that his bare chest would be similar to this man's—broad, somewhat flat, with a deep cleft down the middle. I wondered if Tory were as well-hung as this fellow, if his cock would be as well-proportioned, as long, as thick, as perfect.

In another drawing, the man lay on his stomach, his legs spread, his scrotum sprawling in vein-shaded fullness. In a third, his thick fingers explored—something, a pair of sketchy curves—a second man's ass? In a fourth, he stood over the slender, prone body of a man whose hands had been bound with rope.

Joining me at the table, standing on the other side of it, Tigger blushed. He tapped the standing figure, the man who reminded me of Tory. "Bobby," Tigger said.

He slid a drawing from the stack. It showed two men fucking. The bottom, the man on all fours, was clearly Tigger.

I raised my eyebrows. "'These are from life? Not fantasy?'"

"Some of both. He didn't pose or anything, but that's him."

Somewhere beyond the walls of the apartment, pipes squealed and clunked. Water gurgled and surged. I imagined that I could hear it striking a surface of tile or porcelain. The walls must be very thin.

I said, "Is that the neighbors' shower?"

"What?" Tigger cocked an ear. "No, that's Bobby, taking a shower. He works nights."

"Bobby," I said. Laying my finger on the last drawing, I said, "Bobby?"

Folding his arms across his chest, Tigger nodded. He frowned as if in concentration, as if trying to surmise where my question might lead.

I said, "You're still living with Bobby? I thought you broke up."

Tigger dropped his arms. "Sure, sure, we did break up."

"But he's living here?"

"Where else could he go?"

"Do you mean to say this whole time you've been in group, trying to transform yourself, you've been living with your lover?"

He turned toward the futon. "I sleep here." He pointed toward a green door behind him. "He sleeps in there."

"You don't see a problem with that arrangement? You live with this man, you draw him tying you up, and you wonder why you can't keep yourself from the beach?"

His frown, now, was one of displeasure. Taking a drawing from the table, a drawing in which Bobby carefully and methodically aimed his erection at a bent-over bottom, Tigger traced with his finger the shape of the buttocks. "This isn't me. See? This guy is much narrower in the hip than I'll ever hope to be."

With the same screech and bang that had announced its starting, the water stopped.

"Maybe I'd better go," I said.

"I don't understand."

Softly the green door opened, and the subject of the drawings appeared. He wore a damp towel slung low across his hips—nothing else. In life, Bobby was softer than he'd appeared in charcoal, softer and hairier. Before he saw me, he said to Tigger, "Got some grub for me, boy?"

With his eyes he expressed that superiority, that cockiness, that I'd seen before in Spike's eyes. His voice, too, reminded me of Spike's. It was if in this one man I had found a combination of Spike and Tory. My heart splashed in my chest.

Bobby saw me at last, acknowledged me with the barest hint of a smile.

"No, sir," Tigger said. "I've been entertaining my friend, Jonah."

Sir?

Bobby's eyes grew wide. "*This* is Jonah. Jonah with the shaved head."

Tigger said, in a small, urgent voice, "He's from group."

"From group," Bobby said, and his smile grew positively salacious, the grin of a satyr. It took only a flick of his finger to drop the towel. The white terry cloth fell to his feet, revealing narrow hips and a growing erection. Stepping toward me, taller than I had realized, he placed his hand on the side of my head, so that it covered the curve above my left ear. "I like a challenge." He chuckled. "I will say, though, that none of Tigger's little Christian friends have been much of a challenge."

His grip was strong. It forced my head downward. I saw a trail of ebony curls dwindle toward his navel, then flare into a spade of glistening obsidian at the root of his cock. And I saw that the thick brick in Tigger's drawings was, in life, more of a narrow arrow.

"Like the looks of that?" Bobby said. He placed a hand on either side of my neck and pushed downward. "You'll like the taste even better."

Bobby's resemblance to Spike—and to Tory—vanished. This close, I saw how wrinkles crowded his eyes and framed his mouth, how his arms carried the bulk of fat rather than muscle, how the absence of both lateral incisors from his lower jaw debauched his smile. Ducking out of his grip, I laughed.

To Tigger, I said, "I'm going now. You ought to come with me."

Bobby's face crumpled in anger. Still naked, his erection pitifully shrinking, he stalked toward me. "What are you laughing at?"

"Tigger?" Tigger stood nearly motionless, his fingers clutching at air, his jaw working. "You're crazy to breathe the same air as *this*." I waved in Bobby's direction.

Still, Tigger stood rooted to the floor.

Bobby lunged, swiping at me. I dodged him easily, and in the same motion I had the doorknob in my hand.

Following me into the hallway, still naked, Bobby said, "You don't know what you're missing, boy."

Turning, calling over my shoulder, I said, "I've seen what I'm missing. It's not much."

•   •   •

As the elevator sank—empty, now, of Mr. Graves—my spirits surged. My chest lifted, my back straightened. I had withstood temptation. Face to face with Spike's personality married to Tory's features, I had blinked, it was true. I had, at first, been tempted.

But upon opening my eyes, I'd seen Bobby for what he was. And I'd resisted him, easily, with little effort.

But what about Tigger? I'd left him, abandoned him. If I could withstand Bobby for a minute, could I not also have withstood him for five, or for ten, or for a hundred, while I lured Tigger away? What if Bobby now turned violent? Or worse, seductive?

I stood at the foot of the building. I counted the windows—five rows up from the sidewalk—but I had no idea which might be Tigger's. Indeed, I had no idea, even, if his window faced the street. In every window the blinds were the same. Every ceiling, every wall, was the same yellowed shade of taupe. For some minutes I stood watching, waiting for some telling shadow. None appeared.

• • •

Victory was short-lived. As I drove home, I began to feel nibbles of regret. *What if?* I thought. What if Bobby's attitude had been more than bravado, more than posturing? Close inspection had revealed him to be—what?—not a beast, after all, but rather an ordinary middle-aged man. A man not much older than Tory, and a man who bore a strong resemblance to Tory. And, yes, Tigger's drawings had exaggerated certain of Bobby's physical attributes, but even so—. Even so, frankly, his cock was bigger than mine.

What if?

That night, as I lay in my bed, I imagined the three of us. Tigger and I side by side on our knees, Bobby our lord and master—.

And then—. And then, somehow, Tigger disappeared, and Bobby disappeared, and it was Tory who stood over me. In the bed I arranged myself in the position I'd seen in Tigger's drawing, the drawing in which the bottom had been bound.

On my belly, my legs spread, my hands clasped behind me, as if bound, I humped the mattress.

In my mind's ear I heard Tory's voice. *You want it? I think you need it pretty bad.*

Aloud, to the empty room, I said, "I do. I need it bad." And to the imaginary Tory I said, "Please—. Please, sir."

BONDAGE AND DISCIPLINE

On Friday morning, Eliot called me at work. "I'm giving up my office space in the Midview," he told me. "I'm tired of burning up or freezing to death through every session."

"Where will you go?"

"There's a small addition at the back of my house. I've been working on it for a couple of years now, turning it into an office. It's finally ready."

A couple of years? I thought. I said, "So I should meet you there tonight?"

"Would you? I haven't moved the furniture yet, but I'm just not up to having heat rash today."

•   •   •

The new office had once been a lean-to porch, its length more than three-quarters the width of the house's backside. We surveyed it from the kitchen, through a narrow door. He'd painted the interior walls the same sesame color as the walls of his office in the Midview Center. The room smelled of paint and spackle. Except for a torchére lamp and an aluminum ladder draped with a drop cloth, the room was empty.

"You did all this yourself? I had no idea you were so handy," I said.

"We all have our diversions." Smiling, he laid his hand on my shoulder. "Mine just happens to be drywall."

Slender heaters lined the baseboards of three walls, but, as Eliot told me, he had not fired them up in some days. He closed away the room's chill. "We'll be more comfortable in the living room." He led the way.

"It makes sense," I said, "having your office here. You have group here

anyway, so why not see clients here?" Again I felt the shameful thrill of freedom—I would never have to go to group again. I could not help grinning. I
hoped my smile was not too broad.

"My thoughts exactly."

We settled in front of the hearth, where a small fire crackled. Eliot took an
armchair. I slouched in a corner of the sofa.

"How goes it? On the phone you said you had good news."

"I saw Tigger last night."

Eliot grimaced. He slumped in his chair. "*That's* your good news?"

"I—. I—. What?"

"Tigger is lost. Entirely lost."

"I—. I suppose he's *somewhat* lost, but—."

"I could tell you things, but—. Well, no, I couldn't tell you anything. It was
all said in confidence. Never mind. What happened?"

I told him about Tigger and Bobby, about my victory over temptation. I described the sense I'd had that Bobby embodied the most attractive features of
both Tory and Spike. For the first time in weeks, I invoked Spike's name.

I hadn't meant to tell Eliot about what happened afterward, at home. But
once the story was underway I got caught up in it. Without thinking, I said,
"If only I hadn't—." I stopped myself, but it was already too late.

Eliot raised his eyebrows. "If only you hadn't—?"

"If only I hadn't gone back to it, in my head. Later, when I got home, I—.
You know."

"You *were* tempted, then, after all?"

"Part of me—the old nature—regretted passing up an opportunity. But if I
had it to do over again, I'd make the same choice. I still wouldn't *do* anything,
but if I could go back—. I wouldn't think about it afterward, either. Or at
least I wouldn't—. You know."

He smiled. "We talked before about keeping a journal. How are you doing with that?"

My face grew warm. The skin at my temples tightened. I cleared my throat.
"I haven't been."

I'd found a small spiral notebook in a drawer, and I'd ripped out the used
pages. For days I'd carried the notebook in my breast pocket, but then I'd
forgotten about it, and it had gone missing. I could not even picture where
it might be. On the table beside my easy chair, maybe, or on a shelf of the
bookcase. Perhaps, even, in a drawer of my desk at work.

Eliot said, "It's well worth doing, Jonah. It's counter-intuitive, I know. You're thinking you'll just reinforce the thinking you want to stop."

"That's not why I haven't done it."

"We can start tonight, even without the journal. First, let's talk about how you fantasize."

"How I—?" I said. "I'm not sure what you mean. I just—well, I just do."

"Everyone fantasizes differently. Some are more visual, some more verbal."

"When I see a man on the street, or when I go—when I used to go—to the beach, for example, I might picture us together. I might try to imagine him naked. But that's always brief, just a flash, a picture in my head. When I'm alone, I sometimes tell myself a story, or I'll imagine what we'd say to each other."

"Give me an example."

I blushed.

Leaning forward suddenly, Eliot said, "That one. I want to hear that one. The one you just thought of, that made you blush."

I told him, at last, in full, the fantasy I'd had about Tory. I told him how I'd lain on my belly, how I'd kept my hands behind my back as if they'd been bound there.

Again I heard Tory's voice in my mind's ear. *You need it pretty bad.* It was, I realized, something Spike had said that first morning, so many months ago. *Looks to me like you need it pretty bad.* My cock stirred.

"This can't be helping," I said. "I'm turning myself on."

Eliot lifted his head. "Remember what I told you. It's counter-intuitive. At first you'll be aroused, but after we've done this enough, you'll find you make yourself sick. Go on. You're not *having* this fantasy. You're *telling* it."

My throat had filled with cotton. I swallowed. "I told him—. Tory, in my fantasy—. I told him I'd do anything he wanted."

"How far did you take it? Did you try to stop yourself?"

"A hundred times. I kept hearing him, kept imagining his voice. Tory's voice. 'Take it, boy. That's it. I said you'd like the taste of it, didn't I, boy?'"

It was not the kind of thing Tory would ever say, I was sure. Bobby had said it—*you'll like the taste even better.* It was not the kind of thing Tory would say. I felt queasy.

"What else? What else did you imagine him doing to you?"

I laid a hand on each knee. The fire, though small, had warmed the cotton of my trousers until it was almost painful to touch. Opening my eyes, I slipped off my shoes and tucked my legs under me. I said nothing. I couldn't say anything. It was too humiliating.

For a long time Eliot was also silent. Then, "You masturbated."

I nodded.

"I'm glad we talked about this."

"I was intending to talk about Tigger," I said. My voice was weak, reedy. "I was thinking I might be able to help him."

"Tigger is lost," Eliot said, and he waved away the whole topic of Tigger.

I stared into the fire. "Or I thought we might talk about this court case—this thing Tom's parents started. They think that—."

"I'm absolutely sure that keeping a journal will help you with this. Jonah, please look at me." I did. "When this happens again, I want you to get to a place where you can sit and write for some time. Write down every thought, every desire, every bodily reaction. Analyze it. If something moves you particularly, write down why you think it affected you so much. Stay with it until it stops."

"What if it doesn't stop?"

Abruptly, with some alarm, it seemed, he looked into the fire. He squinted into it for a moment. Shaking off whatever he'd seen, or thought, or thought he'd seen, he said, "That's a possibility. The journal won't do the work for you. You do have to have some measure of willpower." He looked at me. He smiled. "Don't look so sad. You must have some willpower in you somewhere. Right? Everyone has *some* willpower, right?" He chuckled. "If not, we'd all weigh four hundred pounds and work twenty-minute days, right?"

In spite of myself, I laughed with him. "That long? Twenty minutes?"

◆ ◆ ◆

On the way home, my fantasy plagued me. Already it sickened me, just as Eliot had promised. Still, it would not let me be.

NPR could not expunge Tory's voice, or rather the masterly caricature of Tory's voice that I had conjured. One of the pundits crooned in the same throaty way. Every pop station, it seemed, had devoted its play list to the quiet storm; every song preached the gospel of eternal arousal.

As I entered the house I made straight for the easy chair. Without even removing my jacket, I sat.

A pile of books and papers covered the table. I tossed everything aside that was not my journal—that is to say, everything.

The notebook had not found its way to the bookcase. I searched for it to the point of pulling books off the shelf.

Perhaps the bedroom, I thought, but no. It was neither on nor in the bedside table.

In a shirt pocket? In the pocket of a shirt I'd dumped into the laundry hamper? Perhaps, but could it be worth the effort now?

Returning to the living room, I at last shrugged off my jacket. Where it fell, I let it lie. It came to rest, as it happened, on a pile of dirty clothes beside the couch. I added my shirt and trousers to the pile. I hung my tie over the nearest doorknob.

Back to the easy chair. From the debris I had just sent crashing to the floor, I chose the envelope of my latest bank statement. I smoothed it, laid across the back of *Beethoven in London*. I took up a ballpoint pen.

Where to start? The date, the time, the place. "After session, in the car," I wrote. Should it be a narrative? A list? Right. This wasn't a term paper. No one was grading this exercise. Whatever form it would take, so be it. "After session, in the car, I had the now recurring fantasy about Tory."

Now recurring? No, *now-recurring*. I squeezed in the hyphen.

This was impossible. As long as I put pen to paper, I would worry more about spelling and grammar than about substance. I thrust away the envelope. It fluttered away, briefly came to rest on top of my jacket, and fell to the floor.

I paced the room. I needed some alternative. What, then? Act out my fantasies for a video camera? Absurd. Draw tableaux of my fantasies, as Tigger had done? No, I couldn't draw.

Perhaps, now that I thought of it, Tigger's drawings had been *his* journal. If Eliot had counseled me to keep a journal, then he had counseled Tigger to do the same. Maybe Tigger was, in some small way, still keeping the faith. Maybe he was not entirely lost.

I went to my workroom. I cleared the card table and set a blank sheet of staff paper in the center of it. I took up a pencil.

"March 19, 1992," I wrote.

"On the way home from a session with Eliot, my fantasy about Tory recurred, or, in a sense, resumed," I wrote. "The bondage fantasy."

I wrote and wrote, describing the fantasy in every detail. The shape and size of Tory, the hyperbolical version of him I had imagined. The tightness of his hands around my throat. The texture of the rope he used to bind me.

The smack of straps and paddles on my skin. All of it.

Somehow in spite of myself—in spite of the tightening of my belly, or per-haps because of it—my cock stiffened.

"This is giving me an erection," I wrote, "and it's very difficult not to want to do something about it."

Stop. Breathe.

"I don't understand where this comes from," I said. "It's Tory in the fantasy. It's clearly Tory, and yet it's also Spike, and also Charlie." Yes, there was a hint of Charlie in the way I pictured Tory's shoulders and biceps—overgrown, puffed up with muscle. "And I guess it's also Bobby. I can't imagine Tory do-ing any of the things I've been thinking of."

Something had changed. All at once, I realized, something had changed. My erection had flagged. I sat for a moment, trying once more to conjure the image of the bulked-up Tory standing over me, the feeling of Tory's big hands around my neck. Tory's, or Spike's, Charlie's, or anyone's.

It had seemed so clear before. I had imagined it so clearly that I could *feel* it. Now I could not picture anything—could not feel a thing. It had all faded away.

"Just as Eliot said," I wrote, "the fantasy has faded, just from dwelling on it. But now I seem to be trying to goad myself into having a different fantasy, almost as a test." I yawned. "It's not worth doing. Enough."

Enough. I went to bed.

I slept like a Jonah-shaped stone.

*   *   *

On Monday morning the sky was perfectly cloudless, uncannily blue. I be-gan the day with a heart just as clear and clean. As I drove to work, I found myself humming.

When I arrived at the office, Martin was already there. He poked his head around the wall of my cubicle. "Your enthusiasm is infectious," he said. "What's the occasion?"

"Oh," I said, "just—you know—spring has sprung?"

"I see," Martin said. "Don't get too excited. March is a capricious month." He cleared his throat. "I was thinking, we'd better procure the services of a new assistant. I'll write the posting."

"A new—? What about Christa?"

"She's on her honeymoon, and then she's going right into maternity leave."

"She—? What? She never said—. Is she not coming back?"

"I'm thinking someone temporary," Martin said. "I don't relish the idea of answering phones for weeks or months."

"Excellent point. Let's write it together," I said.

His forehead puckered, but he nodded and said, "In my office."

Again I sat facing Ravi Shankar, my legal pad set out before me. The white board still bore the marks of our last briefing: "Harassment," and "PC," and "Stinson," and above it all, "Don't Panic." Martin wiped it all clean—as clean as he could. Scrubbing could not budge the outlines of some long-standing letters. He left Christa's "Don't Panic."

"The successful candidate will," I said, pretending to write on my legal pad, "be able to clean any white board."

"You laugh," Martin said, "but I think cleanliness and organization would be very good qualities to have."

"We can say 'organization.' Let's not go so far as 'cleanliness.'"

On the board, he wrote, "Organized."

"Let's not skip over basics. Phones, typing, meeting minutes, proofreading, fact-checking, research. What else?"

But by then Martin had just come to write "Minutes." "What came after meeting minutes?" I repeated the list, giving him more time for each word. "What else will she do?" he said.

"Why *she*? Some legislative assistants are men. At one time they were all men."

"This is not a dating opportunity for you, Jonah."

I felt my mouth turn downward at the corners. I tasted bile at the back of my throat. "I don't do that anymore, Martin."

Frowning, he capped his marker and set it in the trough at the bottom of the white board. He sat across from me at the table. "You don't *do that* anymore. What do you mean by *that*?"

"Men, Martin. I don't see men anymore."

"Did something happen? Do you have AIDS?"

I blinked away the suggestion. "It's complicated."

"In my experience, when someone claims a situation is complicated, he usually means he doesn't want to talk about it."

"Fair enough. I don't want to talk about it."

Stroking his beard, twisting together the hairs under his chin, he nodded. For a long, silent moment, he stared past my left shoulder. Abruptly slapping the arms of his chair, he rose. "Then let's get back to the matter at hand.

What comes after meeting minutes?"

Leaning forward, I brushed my fingertips along the edge of the table. There was a crack in the veneer, a sharp place where some ragged strips of wood had peeled away. I stroked the ruined place, letting the edges prick the pad of my index finger. "Research," I said. "Proofreading. Fact-checking."

Martin wasn't writing. He stood, wagging his blue marker, staring at—or perhaps through—the board.

"It's just ordinary administrative assistant stuff," I said. "Maybe we can copy another posting."

In a rush Martin returned to the table. As he settled into a chair next to me, the marker still clattered in the trough at the bottom of the white board. "I know I haven't always been—or haven't seemed to be—supportive or accepting of your—well, your lifestyle, as they say." Clearing his throat, he pinched the skin below his Adam's apple. "But if that has anything to do with—."

A laugh bubbled out of me. "I'd hardly go to the trouble of reinventing my entire personality to win your approval."

Swallowing—with difficulty, it seemed—he nodded. He turned to the white board. "Ordinary administrative assistant stuff, then. Such as what?"

"I'm sorry, Martin. I didn't mean that the way it sounded. I only meant that—. There's a lot more at stake than any one person's disapproval."

"This is a religious thing, then."

Lucky guess? Or was he more perceptive than I usually gave him credit for? "You could say that." I folded the top sheet of my legal pad in half, creased the fold, creased it again. "It's about time I believed in something, don't you think?"

"This wouldn't be my first choice." He smiled. "Actually," he said, stroking his beard, "it *was* my first choice." He sighed. "So many of us in this country have Christianity thrust upon us as children."

I shook my head. "That wasn't the case with me."

He raised his eyebrows. "You never went to Sunday school as a child, not once? You got off scot-free. Why would you willingly—."

"When I was very small, yes, I went to Sunday school."

He clapped his hands. "I *knew* it." He pointed at me. "I *knew* you were smarter than that."

My stomach tightened. "Smarter? I like to think I'm just now wising up."

"You're answering to messages that were placed in your head when you were an infant. Listen to that still, small voice. Sit and listen. It's *your* voice."

For a time he stared at the white board. Turning, he narrowed his eyes. "Would this have anything to do with Thorstensen's sudden change of heart concerning the OWT? Or rather, would his change of heart have anything to do with this?"

I let the torn strip of veneer slip between the nail and the flesh of my thumb. I flinched in pain. "As a matter of fact—." I couldn't bring myself to say more.

"What did you promise him?"

· · ·

"He told me to sit and listen to the still, small voice," I told Eliot. "He said, 'It's your voice.'"

Eliot's reply was neither still nor small. Sitting on his hearth, he slapped his knee and guffawed. "Truly, things like this just make my day. People allow themselves the most insane and vapid rationalizations and delusions." He wiped a tear from each eye. "What did you say?" he asked me.

"After that, things took a turn."

He pulled a face. "A turn?"

When, at length, after much cajoling on Martin's part, I'd described the vague deal I'd made with Thorstensen, Martin had been very cross with me. I wasn't sure we were still speaking. I told all this to Eliot.

"You're free to find another job, aren't you?"

After I'd begged Thorstensen to spare the OWT? After I'd risked—and suffered—Martin's disapproval to save my job? Never. To Eliot, I said, "Martin's hopeless without me, and I'm sure he'll forgive me in time. The money's decent. My resume is—. My resume has one thing on it. I can put up with a few minor frustrations."

Nodding, he stood. He shook his hips to straighten the legs of his trousers. He moved to the chair on my right. "How has your journal been working out?"

"It worked. Just as you said it would. That fantasy about Tory wanted to resume itself on the way home, but after I wrote it out, I just got tired of it."

"Did you bring it with you?"

I nodded. I had it in my jacket pocket. I drew it out—a tiny knot of paper, folded over itself many times—and handed it to him. He opened it. I'd used any sheet of paper I'd found at hand. Staff paper, spiral notebooks, legal pads. He sorted it all out, spread it across his lap. He read.

"Are your fantasies often so fierce?"

"The bondage? The spanking and stuff? It's entirely new." Not entirely new. Spike had spanked me. Spike and Jose had taken turns spanking me. I didn't say so to Eliot.

"Why do you suppose it's coming up now?"

"I don't know."

Tipping his head back, he frowned at the ceiling. "As you sit here now"—he looked at me with widened eyes—"what distinguishes you from an object?"

"From an *object*? I—. I'm—. I'm breathing, moving, talking."

His mouth curved upward. It couldn't properly be called a smile. "And from an animal? Besides talking, what separates you from a dog or an orangutan?"

"I—. I guess—. The way I think. I know about cause and effect. I can reason."

He nodded. "And?"

My turn, now, to examine the ceiling. Soot or shadow filled the innumerable shallows and depths of its craggy surface. "I have emotions and preferences." I looked at him. "I can make choices."

"And if you were a—for lack of a better word—a slave? Tory's slave?"

"All my choices would be made for me."

He said, "And that's an attractive idea, suddenly?"

Was it? Was that what all these fantasies had been about? Someone—Tory—making choices for me? "I—. I guess."

"Why do you suppose that is?"

My hands lay in my lap. I looked down at them. "I haven't given this a moment's thought till now," I said. "Off the top of my head, I'd say it'd have to be because I've been doing a rotten job of it." I frowned. I shook my head. "But that's insane. Shouldn't I want someone to force me to do the *right* thing, rather than the *wrong* thing?"

He crossed his legs. "I'd like to meet the man who could get his jollies that way. Besides, in real life, in the situation that started all this—this particular fantasy, I mean—did you make the wrong choice?"

I smiled. I couldn't help it. I smiled so broadly that it hurt. "I didn't, did I?"

"Now you see why this journal is a good thing."

He set aside the staff paper, turned to a sheet torn raggedly from my legal pad at work.

He read it aloud.

> When I got back from lunch this afternoon I stopped in the re-
> stroom. A guy, a tall guy with short dark hair and a slender body,
> looking good in a tailored white shirt with monogrammed cuffs—
> JPG was the monogram—stood at the urinal next to mine. He
> pulled out a very big uncircumcised penis.

Eliot looked at me. Blushing, I shrugged.
He went on reading.

> I didn't mean to look, but it was the biggest thing in the room. I
> couldn't help but look at it. And then, without ever having peed,
> he started to stroke it, and it got bigger, until finally it stood
> straight out from his body. By then I was also fully erect.

Eliot looked up. "You had sex with this man? Why didn't you—?" He
stopped. Somehow my facial expression must have made it clear.
He read on.

> That's not what happened. In reality, he came in, he took his piss,
> he shook himself toward the bowl a couple of times, he left. I
> stood there pawing my erection for another ten minutes, or so it
> seemed.

"You didn't finish telling the fantasy," Eliot said.
"I got bored with it."
"Tell me about it."
"I don't remember most of it. It's the same old nonsense."
"Let's go back. When you imagined him enticing you by touching himself,
what else did you imagine? Did you picture a particular facial expression?
Did you imagine a smell? Did he reach a hand into his shirt and play with
his nipples?"
"Yes, and no, and no."
"What was the facial expression?"
"He was smiling. An arrogant, self-satisfied kind of smile." The kind of
smile Spike might wear.
"Interesting. Did he say anything?"
"Nothing."
Just so, and yet my evanescent men's-room daydream turned into another

thirty minutes by Eliot's hearth. After that, the journal offered up more men—butts, goatees, forearms, more of the things that had lured my attention as worms lure fish. Another men's-room peek at JPG and his uncircumcised monster. Another fantasy, another half an hour plumbing every nuance.

28 BROTHERS IN CHRIST

On the last morning of March, I woke an hour before my alarm. A dozen times or more I rolled over and pounded my pillow and tried to sink back into the dreams I'd been having of rowing on bright water, of stalking through cool woods. But something kept me awake, some sense that this day would be too good to squander on sleep. For a time I lay face up with my eyes closed, watching my eyelids brighten, until my aching bladder at last broke my inertia.

The sun filled the bathroom with diamond-sharp light. Too bright. I closed my eyes. Even as I peed, even as I fumbled among the bric-a-brac on the vanity, I kept my eyes closed. At last I had to open them to aim the toothpaste tube at my toothbrush. As I scrubbed my teeth, I paced the floor.

I found myself in the kitchen. Its windows faced west, so that the room was a cool shadowy place of dimly glinting surfaces.

Wait. What? There were marks of some kind on the windows. Lines, scratches.

With my toothbrush hanging from my lips, I inched toward the windows. Each of the three bore a word in ragged, deeply cut letters. Together they formed a rudimentary sentence:

FAG HAS AIDS

Trembling, I touched the glass. Smooth. The etching must be on the outside. Of course, it was on the outside.

I remembered the "GAF" written in soap on my windshield. Many months ago, that had been, time enough, it seemed, for my vandal to practice and to acquire the knack of writing backward. Leaning forward, I peered out the window. I could see my car, but a blue minivan, a Lumina, blocked my view. I couldn't see if my vandal had marked or harmed the Chevette in some way.

Early sun glinted on the Lumina's windshield. That shadow, inside, on the driver's side, was that a person, sitting behind the wheel? Someone wearing black?

And in the passenger's seat? Another figure, this one wearing blue—or was it gray?

I returned to the bathroom and tossed my toothbrush—still foamy—into the sink. The bathroom window, too, had been etched:

COCK

I went to the bedroom and lifted the window shade. It, too, bore some carving:

SUCKER

On the opposite side of the room, in the window to the right of the bed:

PACKED

"Packed"? Oh, yes: here on the bed's left was the rest:

FUDGE

Here the letters were tall, filling the window pane. On the outside the sashes bled white splinters.

Numbly I pressed my fingers to the "E" of "FUDGE." What tool could gouge glass so deeply, so angrily, without poking through it or shattering it?

I hated to see—but I had to see—what my vandal had done to the picture windows in the front of the house. I tugged the blinds, and they snapped open. The larger canvases had given him room for dependent clauses. The westward-facing window read:

IF YOU LOVE GOD HATE EVIL

And the southern-facing window read:

IF YOU HATE EVIL KILL FAGS

While I'd slept, this had happened. While I'd lain oblivious in my snug bed—perhaps not so long ago, perhaps even while I'd lain awake, relishing but postponing the promise of a spring day—my vandal had stood feet from my head, scouring my windows with some sharp implement. Perhaps some noise he'd made had awakened me.

I flew to the bedroom. Yesterday's clothes—.

No, I could spare an extra minute to find something new. Denim and flannel came first on the rack. So be it. During the legislative session there was a dress code—business casual, no jeans. Fuck the dress code. Fuck the legislative session.

I pulled boxers, undershirt, and socks from the dresser drawers, left the drawers hanging open. Jeans on but unbuttoned, I stepped into a pair of running shoes. I had neither worn them nor put them away, it seemed, in months.

On the way to the front door, I tucked my T-shirt into my jeans and buttoned them. I slid my arms into the flannel shirt. Wallet. Keys. Leather jacket. Out.

Outside there were dewy lawns, budding trees, singing birds. The sunlight was bright and warm on my face. The street was empty of people. I dashed for my car, as though snipers crouched on nearby roofs, training their rifles on me.

The minivan had gone. The Chevette stood at the curb. It looked lonely, somehow, and exposed.

As I'd feared, the vandal had scratched my windshield. This was no "GAF." Sitting behind the wheel, I read with perfect clarity, "DIE FAGGOT."

As I neared the State Office Building, my heartbeat calmed. What could touch me within the marble walls of the capitol complex?

In the comforting bland smallness of my cubicle, I reached immediately for my phone. The green light blinked. Voice mail.

The dial tone stuttered. I dialed. Eight new messages. A fuzzy whisper. "Shit-eating cocksucker," one said. I deleted the message.

The voice rasped, "You die tonight, faggot." I deleted the message.

Another: "There's no place in this world for people like you. You are corrupt and evil. God turns his back—."

I deleted the message. I deleted the rest of the messages without listening to them. Anyone who had left an authentic voice mail, I thought, would call again, eventually.

The voice had sounded familiar. Deep, thick. Spike? No, not Spike. I'd never given him my work number. I'd told him I worked for the legislature, though, hadn't I? My office number was a matter of public record. He could have tracked me down. But why? Why, after so much time? Why, indeed, at all?

No, the voice must belong to Bobby. The plosives of "cocksucker"—the sound of a padlock snapping shut—were his. The vowels of "faggot"—the stretch of a yawn on a velvet night—were his. And I had given Tigger my work number. It must be Bobby.

My stomach turned. I placed my hand on my belly, as if by pressing on it I could settle its roiling.

I dialed Eliot. I got his answering machine.

"Eliot," I said. "Jonah. Something's—. A number of things have happened, none of them good. Could you give me a call when you get this? Thanks. I—. I hope to speak to you soon."

Almost as I set the handset in the cradle, the phone rang. Trembling, I lifted the handset to my ear.

"You can't have forgotten me." My mother, in her best radio voice. "I've been too good to you."

"Barbara—." Funny, how alien it sounded now, to call her Barbara. "Mother," I said, though that didn't sound right, either. "I'm kind of—. That is to say—."

All at once her voice slumped. "We haven't talked in three months."

Three months. Had it really been that long? I counted on my fingers. No. Two months, not three. It had been two months since we'd spoken. She'd called me in January, a few hours after Clinton's inauguration. She'd told me she wished she'd taped it. She'd said it would make a great drinking game. To play the game, I remembered, you would take a shot every time one of the pundits made a reference to John Kennedy.

Thinking of this again now, I remembered that Tom had made the same joke in the first days of the Gulf War. In Tom's drinking game, though, the trigger word had been "sortie."

I'd distracted myself. I hadn't spoken in some few seconds.

Barbara was saying, "And I know session is on, but—."

I said, "You called me in—." I shook my head to clear it. I'd fallen behind a topic. I said, "Session is—. As a matter of fact, I do have some things right now that—."

"Nothing could be more important than this conversation." Her diction was precise, a little stiff. She paused. While I searched for a reply, she said, "Are you angry with me?"

Weeks had passed since we'd talked about Barbara in group. "Her course of action almost guaranteed you'd turn out homosexual," Eliot had said. "She led you so far from the path you started out on that you didn't even know how to talk to God," he'd told me.

"Why would I be angry?"

She sighed—with effort, it seemed. "You'd have to tell me that in order for me to know, don't you think?"

"Mother, there are things—."

She cut me off. "Good Christ, you've done it, haven't you?"

I lifted my hand to run it through my hair and instead found only three days' stubble. My scalp itched. "Done what, Mother?"

"You've gone Christian."

"I've—. That is to say—." From the back of my head, I peeled away a scab from my last shave. I looked at my hand. Brown blood stained my fingernail. Instantly, as if at the sight of my own dried blood, I boiled with rage. "I've gone quite Christian. Enormously pious and hypocritical. I read my Bible by candlelight into the wee hours of every morning. I've stopped believing in protons, DNA, and the existence of orangutans. I'm thinking of changing my name to Zacharias. Oh, and I think gun control is a sin. And—."

But by then I was speaking to a dial tone.

Just as well, for now Christa's phone was ringing. I picked it up. Martin, calling from home. Unusually bristly, even for him, he said, "Conference me with the house session number." I checked my watch. Could the house be in session already? It was just now eight o'clock. "Quick," he said.

With jumpy fingers I put him on hold. I pressed the speed dial button marked "House." Instantly, without a single ring, I connected. The chief clerk's Klaxon voice startled me. "—in accordance with the recommendation and report of the Conference Committee. Said Senate File—"

But I'd forgotten what buttons to press for a conference call. I thought about it for a moment, twirling my fingers above the phone's keypad. Flash. Line one. "Martin?"

"Conference committee report on Senate file number twenty-two-seventy-six. A bill for an act relating to the financing of state government."

"I'm here," Martin said.

"It's the appropriations bill."

"It's *an* appropriations bill, not *the* appropriations bill. Hush."

The Chief Clerk had finished, and now Thorstensen said, "—since the good people of Minnesota haven't yet seen fit to place an IR majority in either house. Along with most of my colleagues on this side of the aisle I have become accustomed to seeing things much changed once that venereal body, the Senate, has finished with them." After a moment's pause and a word growled out of his microphone's reach he said, "Pardon me, ladies and gentlemen, I meant to say venerable body."

"Martin, what is this? What's going on?"

"In its sense," Thorstensen said, "this bill makes minor adjustments to certain expenditures related to the legislature. We're proposing a few changes, a few cuts. Nothing to contend to about that."

"*Martin*," I said. "What's going *on*?"

Martin said, "What is it Christa used to say? Weigh enough."

Thorstensen was saying, "The contention centers around a provision that somehow slipped in regarding the Office on Workplace Tolerance."

"You see," Martin said.

Thorstensen said, "The affect"—by stretching the *a*, he made it brutally clear that he intended to say *affect*—"of the Senate amendments was to commission a policy prohibiting"—he rattled papers—"certain forms of harassment. As most of you know, I and my colleagues on this side of the aisle never approved of the creation of the OWT, and my personal displeasure with it has grown ever more strident. Especially when I saw this." There was a great thump.

I jumped. My chair rolled back a few inches. "What the hell?" I said.

"This is a book that purposes to describe new and modern standards for gender-free language. Ladies and gentlemen of the House, this book recommends—and I am not joking—the replacement of 'men' with 'fem.' Yes, you heard right. Anywhere in the English language where the letters M-E-N occur, this book recommends replacing them with F-E-M. I, for one, do not relish the notion of taking up 'ay-fem-femts' on the floor of this distinguishable body."

"Hush up and listen," Martin said, for I had begun cursing.

"But what book is he talking about? I've never—."

"Hush up and *listen*," Martin said again.

Thorstensen cleared his throat. "Now, to all of you who have worked with me during this long session—."

Something now muffled Thorstensen's voice; he must have dislodged his microphone. A triangular button on my phone raised his voice and the hiss of static surrounding it. "—And pay for them we must," he was saying.

"What are we paying for?" I said. "I didn't catch it."

"For the LCC to do a study," Martin said.

Thorstensen said, "So we propose to move the work of the OWT to the Legislative Coordinating Commission as well and pay for the new position there by eliminating OWT altogether."

"Reprehensible son of a bitch," Martin said.

"What can I do?" I said. "Anything? I could go to the floor and—and lobby some of the—."

"Forget it, Jonah. It's over. It's a conference committee report. They can't amend it, and they can only vote yea or nay. They're not going to scuttle the whole bill to save us. If you have any vacation time coming, I suggest you take it."

Gently I pressed the button that connected us to Thorstensen's voice. His voice stilled. Static cleared from the line. "Thanks. I will."

"Thank you for everything," Martin said. "It's been a pleasure working with you."

Tears pricked the corners of my eyes. "Same here. I wouldn't change it."

Gingerly I replaced the handset. For some lost length of time I sat staring into empty space. *Brothers in Christ,* I thought. *Brothers in fucking Christ.*

Again I dialed the session number. Busy.

I kept a name tag in my pencil drawer. It was all I needed to get onto the House floor. I pinned it to my breast pocket. My footsteps echoed darkly in the dark tunnel. I ran. How long since I had run? As I mounted the last long hill into the Capitol, my heart pounded and my lungs fought for air.

In the short corridor to the elevators, I launched myself into the midst of a gaggle of tiny blue-haired ladies. Backing out, I dodged a bewildered-looking page with a Rubbermaid cart full of manila folders. I ran for the stairs.

I found myself on the Capitol's ground floor. All around me, above me, voices echoed against stone and plaster. The voices of people talking, of televisions playing the session debate, of someone speaking—no, preaching—through an amplifier or bullhorn.

"God takes a hand in the affairs of men and the governments of men," I heard. "This is a critical time, but we have confidence that God will prevail. What is right will prevail."

At the top of the stairs from the ground floor to the first floor, I stumbled headlong into the rotunda. In frescoes high above me, Greek demigods discovered and settled the land of ten thousand lakes—or so I had always guessed. I paused a moment, looking at painting of a pale blond man. Except for a sash of blue cloth, he was completely naked. It seemed that the blue sash had, however improbably, blown in on a breeze to wrap itself around his leg and cover his genitals. The man reached his hand out to a woman clad in a filmy green shift. Was she levitating above the grass? What the hell—?

I shook my head. "Focus," I said aloud. "Focus."

On either side of the rotunda, curving marble staircases rose to the chambers. But which—? No matter. I took the nearest.

Columns of marble—white and reddish gray—rose to a barrel-vaulted skylight. At the top of the stairs, a door stood open on the Senate chambers, a study in shades of red. Red carpeting, red seats in the gallery, red and pink marble columns on either side of the dais.

The stone hallways buzzed with whispered conversations. Men and women in suits and clattering hard-soled shoes milled about with briefcases and Day Runners and cellular phones as big and heavy-looking as cement blocks. They smelled of money, these men and women.

I slipped into the House chambers the back way, past the House Desk. I knew some of the staffers from our forums. Ignoring faces smiling in recognition and frowning in bewilderment, passing the huge whirring dumb waiter that served up the thousand latest versions of a thousand different bills, I placed myself at the threshold of the chamber. On the green carpet the representatives' tiny pulpits spun themselves into a semicircular web.

Someone from the majority—a tall, gaunt black man in a tight brown suit—held the floor. I didn't know him. He spoke in the breathy whisper of flute and fife. All he seemed to get from his microphone was feedback.

No sign of Thorstensen. I ducked my head in further. The Speaker, a slim and dapper man named Packer, held the gavel.

A page carrying an enormous stack of green-jacketed bills brushed past me. His eyes narrowed, his jaw worked itself. Of course, of course. I was dressed like a truck driver, like a convenience store cashier, like an off-duty janitor. I didn't look like someone who should be standing here at the door of the House chambers.

Either my glower overmatched the page's or he saw my name tag; without a word he scurried to the dais at the front of the chamber.

And there. There stood Thorstensen, to the right of the dais, laughing with some crony in a wide orange-checked tie. The page approached the trademark red vest with something like awe. The small boy tendered to the great man the green jackets. Thorstensen waved him away. In doing so, somehow, Thorstensen's eyes found mine. He grinned. He waved.

I said, quite aloud, "Brothers in Christ."

Thorstensen put his hand to his ear, made a show of not hearing.

But suddenly the floor was abuzz. The chief clerk brayed the House into order.

"A roll call vote has been requested," Packer said. "Seeing twenty hands—." Covering his microphone, he leaned forward to hear the chief clerk. "Representative Gertz, a roll call vote is automatic on a conference committee report. There will be a roll call vote."

Gertz, the man in the tight brown suit, said, "Thank you, Mister Speaker."

"The clerk will call the roll."

Thorstensen had returned to his chair. He pressed a button on his desk that lit his name on the tote board. "Brothers in Christ," he said—or rather, that's what I thought he said. I couldn't hear him.

The board was green from top to bottom. Beside Gertz's name stood the only nay.

We were abolished.

◆　◆　◆

Eliot's number again rang through to the recording, to his answering machine.

I called Luther. I heard paper rattling in the background. "What's wrong?" he said. "You sound upset."

"The vandal again. A night raid."

He cleared his throat. "What happened?"

"I'm sorry to say this, but I think I need to just move on. This kind of thing will keep happening until I do. Of course I'll pay for the windows—. You can take it out of my half of the deposit, and send Tom's half to—."

"Tenant, tenant, tenant." With each repetition his voice grew louder. "What happened to the windows?"

"Someone scratched graffiti into them."

"What does it say?"

"You don't want to know."

"Have you called the police? Do you want *me* to call the police?"

"I don't know what they'll be able to do. I doubt they'll put a couple of detectives on it."

"Let me try, at least. I'll call. Give me your number at work, in case they want to talk to you."

An hour or more passed, and I heard from neither Luther nor the police. There was no point in staying. I might as well go home.

Many papers and books covered the surface of my desk. Reports, forum notes, academic journals, drafts and revisions and revisions of revisions of our harassment policy. I couldn't envision wanting any of it.

Someone would have to clear it away, eventually. I should, at least, clean my desk before I left. I sat staring at the mess, wondering if—and why—I should bother.

The phone rang. I wondered if—and why—I should bother answering.

I answered.

"Success, my boy. Success." It was Thorstensen.

"*Success?* What—? What was that stuff about M-E-N and F-E-M? No one ever—. And you just eliminated my *job.* How is that—?"

He chuckled. "Quite the contrary. We *moved* your job. The LCC position is for you."

"For me? The LCC position—. What about Martin?"

"Isn't he some sort of *Hindu?*" He pronounced "Hindu" as if, loosely translated, it meant "ravenous eater of excrement."

"I believe he's a Buddhist."

"Well, son, is there a difference?"

He gave a hearty laugh. I waited for him to stop.

"I only have a freshman-year survey course to go on," I said, "but I believe it's like this. The Buddhists believe that suffering is inseparable from existence, but that a state of enlightenment beyond suffering can be attained through the extinction of the self and bodily desires. The Hindus believe that you will be a cockroach in the next life."

I slammed the phone down.

I took my jacket, and I left.

• • •

From a distance nothing seemed to be amiss. In the slanted light of afternoon, the scarred windows appeared normal. I saw no signs of further meddling. I wondered, for a second, if I'd somehow imagined the whole thing.

But no. No, I hadn't imagined it. Up close, the windows showed deep scratches.

DIE FAGGOT
IF YOU HATE EVIL KILL FAGS

With exquisite care, as if it might give way, I mounted the stoop. I opened the front door. The air inside was dark and chill and stale. Normal. Everything appeared normal.

Shrugging off my jacket, I stole further into the house. Kitchen—clear. Bathroom—clear. I took a piss.

Bedroom. Not clear.

The windows on either side of the bed were jagged mouths of broken glass. Shards lay in the bed, carefully arranged, it seemed, in a circle pointing inward on a broad, flat rock and a crudely lettered scroll of cardboard. "DIE TONIGHT," it said.

I charged from the house. I left the front door banging behind me. I patted my pockets. Keys. Thank God, I still had my keys. I had neither my wallet nor my jacket, but I couldn't go back for them now. I just couldn't.

Thank God, too, I had filled my gas tank. But where could I go? It would be better to stay, to call 911 and wait for the police to do—what?—something—anything. But I couldn't. I just couldn't sit in that house and wait for my vandal to throw his next stone.

Eliot. I had to talk to Eliot, and from his house I could call Luther, and Luther could call the police.

It was by no means certain that Eliot would be home, I told myself. I hadn't been able to reach him yet today. There was no reason to believe that he was at home.

He *was* at home, though—or rather in his front yard. When I pulled to the curb in front of his house, he stood at the top of the concrete stairs.

Seeing me, he smiled. "I'm glad you're here," he said. "I've been expecting you."

29   DIRTY

Expecting me, he said, because of the messages I'd left on his answering machine. He led me into his living room—his front door stood open—and sat me on the sofa in front of the fire. The coffee table had disappeared, and he'd moved the sofa so that it sat barely a yard from the hearth. Tugging his pant legs, he sat on the stone to face me. Our knees nearly touched.

"I'm sorry I wasn't here when you called," Eliot said. "I had a doctor's appointment, some other errands."

One of the errands must have been fetching things from his office. A stack of file boxes, I saw now, sat against the wall, just inside the entryway.

Smiling, he laid his hand on my knee. "Doesn't it help just to get next to the fire? That's why I moved the sofa. Do you like it?"

An odd tangent, I thought, and in truth the heat of the fire was oppressive, but I nodded. He couldn't seem to stop grinning. Maybe it made him very happy indeed to have a fire in the hearth.

He said, "You said on the phone something happened. Tell me about it."

Where to begin? I'd started the day with a keen sense of its glad possibilities. So far it had, instead, been a thoroughgoing disaster. I told him the story, ending with the glass in my bed.

By then Eliot had turned to stoke the fire. "Do you expect to go to heaven?" he said.

Heaven. I'd heard so little about heaven, so much about hell. And this seemed like a very odd time for the topic to arise. "I suppose so. Why?"

He looked at me over his shoulder. "If you're going to heaven, rather than staying here, wouldn't it be better to go tonight rather than twenty years from tonight?"

"Is that supposed to comfort me?" I heard the hardness in my own voice. "If so, it's not working."

Eliot laid aside the iron poker. He turned once more to face me. "It's supposed to make you think, Jonah Thomas Murray." As he spoke each of my names, he touched the center of my chest. "You're thinking of today and tonight. I'm trying to make you think of a thousand years from now, and a million." Leaning back, he flung his arms wide. "A trillion years from now, when you're at God's right hand"—he showed me his, Eliot's, right hand, landing it on my thigh, nearly in my crotch—"singing his praises in the golden light of countless days, will you even remember the glass in your bed? What will it signify?"

"When you put it like that—."

He took his hand away. "Who will decide when it's your time to go? Some skulking vandal, or the Lord and Creator of all?"

"Certainly when it's my time, it's my time, but—."

Turning to one side, so that he sat with one hip along the edge of the hearth, he looked into the fire. "Still, having said all of that, I don't think you should go back there."

How many hours had I spent here, by this fire, talking to Eliot? The two of us alone, or in group—how many hours? I couldn't begin to count the number of hours, and yet none of them had been as odd as these five or ten minutes had been. He might almost be speaking a different language—Swahili, Esperanto, Romanian.

He said, "There's no point in staying where you know there's danger."

"But all that stuff about—. What you were just saying—."

He rolled his eyes. "Let me start again. You drive every day?"

"Of course."

"You know there are risks? An eighteen-wheeler could come barreling out of nowhere and flatten your little Chevette and you along with it."

He waited. Looking at him askance, I nodded.

"You don't stop driving, because you know that whatever will be will be. If today is the day God calls you home, and he sends an eighteen-wheeler to do the work, so be it."

"I'm having trouble following this. What does this have to do—?"

Laying his hand on my shoulder, he leaned forward. "My point is this. You don't stop driving, because you have faith that you are being watched over. But you also don't drive into brick walls just to see if your guardian angels are on their toes."

"I have nowhere else to go. My mother probably isn't speaking to me now, so I have no family. As of today, I have no job."

"You have a place to go. To come. You can come *here*."

"*Here?*" I looked around. Baroque mirror, humble ladder-backed chairs, ro-caille side tables. "With you? I can't impose on you like that."

I stood. I slid past him. I went to look at the Redlin print. It was like a dream, that print. The happy figures posed happily around a happy fire on a happy snowdrift at the edge of a happy forest. It was a scene from a world that had never existed.

"It's not an imposition, not at all. I have plenty of room." He pointed to a door behind me. "The spare bedroom's right there. It even has its own bath-room."

"But it can't be appropriate for a client and—."

He raised his hand. "We are brothers in Christ before we are counselor and client."

"Brothers in Christ," I said. I couldn't help thinking of Thorstensen's glut-tonous smile as he'd mouthed the words at me from the House floor.

"Just till you can find something new."

"I'll pay you rent."

He grinned. "So it's agreed."

"Sure," I said. "Okay."

I had nothing with me but the clothes on my back. I had to return to the house. As hungrily as my heart cried for Eliot to accompany me, I refused him when he offered. "I think I have to do this alone," I told him. "If I can't do this, what can I do? How can I face a job interview if I can't walk into my own house and pack my own belongings?"

He had not moved from the hearth. "I don't disagree."

"I need to have enough faith for that, at the very least."

"You're absolutely correct. While you're gone, I'll go and have a key made."

He walked me to the door. We stopped in the entryway. The file box on top of the stack was open. The box contained books, loose papers, a scattering of baseball cards. At the bottom I saw something familiar—a sheet of white pa-per that read, along the top, in blue, "Twin Cities Mental Health Assistance

Program." The form had been filled out. In the space marked "Last Name," there was a name. My name, in my own handwriting.

I leaned toward the box, reaching for the form. "Eliot, what—?"

Placing his hand in the small of my back, he nudged me toward the front door. "Everything's going to be all right, Jonah. You'll see."

◆ ◆ ◆

I studied the house with exquisite care. It was just as I'd left it. No new graffiti, no bumper stickers, no nails in the door, no new mischief. But it had seemed so the last time, and then I'd found the broken windows.

I walked along the street on the westward side of the house. Here they were, then, the broken windows, hidden somewhat by an unruly boxwood. At the base of the hedge, where no grass had ever grown, footprints gouged and marred the soft earth. The wounds had scabbed over during the day, so that the craters were crusty and dark here, soft and slick there.

Standing on my toes, I stretched to see something through the windows' breach, some sign of movement or change. I saw shadows and gleams, nothing distinct.

A neighbor, walking her schnauzer, scowled at me as she tugged the quivering gray puppy across the street. It occurred to me that I should smile, that I should make some greeting, that I should assure her somehow that I belonged here. I couldn't—I couldn't bring myself to do any of those things. I ignored her.

I went inside. I'd left the front door unlocked. Of course, I remembered— I'd dashed from the house, I'd left the door open. Why not engrave some invitations? *Jonah Thomas Murray is pleased to announce the availability of his humble abode for acts of vandalism and theft.*

No dawdling. I needed clothes and a toothbrush. Everything else could wait. In the bedroom I averted my eyes from the bed. Through the broken windows I felt a breath, a chill, of evening.

Dumping my gym bag onto the floor of my closet, I reached for clothes— shirts, jeans, sweaters. I stuffed them into the bag. I went to the dresser, scooped underwear and socks into the duffel. Good. Zip.

In the bathroom I added to the bag my toothbrush and toothpaste, deodorant, shaving cream, razors, a bar of soap still in the box. The mirror showed a wildfire of red stubble across my scalp.

Enough. Eliot would have all the toiletries I would need. Or if not, toiletries were cheap. I needed to get out of here. I trembled. My heart pounded.

I could hardly breathe. I needed to get out of here.

The phone rang. I froze. On and on the bell jangled, bright and loud.

I made for the door. Stopped. Turned. Answered the phone.

"You killed him." It was the same deep voice that had left all those voice mails on my phone at work. "As sure as if you put a gun to his head, you killed him."

"Who—?"

"My brother," the voice said. "You killed him."

Dial tone.

I stared at the handset. George? Tom's brother, George? All this—the bumper stickers, the paint, the scratched windows, the voice mails—. It had all been George's doing?

He was just a kid—true, just a kid. But clearly he was capable of violence, of evil.

I needed to get out of here. I unplugged the phone, and I left.

Just as I reached the curb, a car rumbled toward me. An old Cadillac, a behemoth, greenish-blue. Its grille had been busted out or kicked in, so that it appeared to be grinning toothlessly, malevolently. Much of the vinyl had peeled away from its roof, and strips of it waved and shimmered in the failing sunlight. The windows and windshield were all tinted black, so that I could see the driver only as a vague silhouette.

The Cadillac's horn blew. I jumped, faltered, backed away from the street. The car veered, its vicious grin aimed directly at me. It came to a stop with its fat front tire against the curb. All the driver had to do to leap the curb, I was sure, was tap the accelerator. To get to my car, to flee, I would have to enter the street, walk or run out into the open. But by the time I reached my driver's-side door, slipped the key into the lock, and climbed in, I knew, the Cadillac's driver could have run me over four or five times.

I turned and bolted for the house.

As I ran, I fumbled in my hip pocket for my keys, fished them out, dropped them, shuffled through them, dropped them again. I found the door key. I stabbed the key into the lock. Turned it. Opened the door. I crashed through it, and then I heard behind me—realized that I had been hearing all the while I'd been running—a voice. A deep male voice.

"Beta! Beta! Beta Murray!"

◆   ◆   ◆

Spike wandered through the house, looking at all the ruined windows, tracing the letters with his thick fingers. He wore a full beard now, bushy and black. He stroked it.

"What the hell?" he said.

"My vandal."

"*Your* vandal? You have a pet vandal?"

He stopped at the box of bad influences, stooped over it.

"Are you moving?" he asked me.

I shook my head, but then I said, "Yes. Soon. Now."

"My videos are in here," he said. He smiled. "Are you throwing these away?"

"I was going to—. It's hard to explain."

"I brought you a new one to add to your collection." From the inside pocket of his jacket he drew a videotape. It came free with some difficulty, snagging on the corners of the pocket. He waved it in the air. He grinned. "Hot off the duplicator," he said.

He slipped the video into the VCR. He pushed play.

After all the disclaimers, the FBI piracy warning, and an advertisement for lube, the screen faded to black. An electric guitar crunched fat chords. It sounded familiar—the dotted rhythm, the predominance of minor sevenths. The goblin march? The Great Fugue, played on an electric guitar?

A title swam up from a single point of light to fill the screen.

A single word. The title was a single word. *Dirty.*

Suddenly Spike stood quite close to me. He'd been smoking pot. I could smell it on him. He reeked of it. The bottom dropped out of my stomach.

Spike kissed my ear. "I think it turned out pretty well," he said. "All things considered."

It took me a second to realize that he meant the video.

His credit—he was still John Bambrick, I saw—flashed across the screen.

Taking my hand, he drew me closer. Fred and Ginger. He wrapped his arms around me. He'd lost weight. There were deep clefts on either side of his mouth. Veins—the channels and distributaries of a river delta—stood out at his temples.

I struggled to pack into one sentence the events of four months. "Things have changed," I said.

Letting go, he stepped back. "Are you with someone?" He looked around him. If he expected to see signs that I'd taken up residence with another man, he saw instead the wreckage of my lazy and solitary life. Shirts, towels, books, papers—a broad jumble of junk on either side of a small path to the hallway. The brown-stained sock still lay in the middle of the floor.

"No, I'm not, but—."

Smiling, he again drew me close to him. In long smooth strokes his hands caressed my back. "What then?" Before I could answer, he kissed me.

His mouth was cool and tasted of the pot he'd been smoking. His whiskers chafed my chin and cheeks. Plunging my fingers into the starling-darkness of his hair, I pulled him against me. He pressed his hips to mine. He crushed me against him.

Together we worked the buttons of his clothing. Together we stripped away his shirt and jeans. Underneath he was nude—no underwear, no socks. I touched him everywhere. I nibbled the smoothness of his chest. I squeezed the hard curves of his ass.

Pushing me back, onto the floor, he lay on top of me. He linked his fingers with mine, pinning my hands to the floor. He kissed me roughly, like a man staking a claim. Letting go my hands, he tugged the hem of my T-shirt and in one sharp move pulled it and the flannel overshirt from my body. Meanwhile I yanked open my belt and fly. With one firm yank he laid me bare.

He flipped me over. He spread himself across my back. Tucking himself in at top and bottom, he nuzzled my neck.

Wrapping one hand round my neck, he turned my head. "Bed?"

"There's—. There's glass in it."

"Glass?"

"My vandal."

"Right. You have a pet vandal. I have a pet redhead, you have a pet vandal."

"I—. I don't mind the floor," I said, and I lifted my hips, thrust myself up into him. "But could you—? Could you—?"

He kissed the back of my neck. "What?"

But I couldn't say it. Instead, I moved my hands, moved them into the small of my back, clasped them as if they were bound. I craned my neck, looked at him.

He grinned and reached for my jeans, for my belt.

•　•　•

I lay underneath him, my hands bound with my belt, my head spinning, my cock humping the rough carpet. He fucked me. It hurt, but I wanted it to hurt. I wished it could hurt worse than it did.

"I have the best line in the whole movie," he told me.

I grunted. I was incapable of speech, and in any case, this was no time for a chat.

"You'll see. It's coming up. Look."

I looked. The scene began without preliminaries, without dialogue. A bodybuilder—a giant, a god, far bigger even than Charlie—stood in an empty room. Naked, erect, he stroked himself. From knees to navel he was slick, wet with lube. Spike appeared, also naked. He kissed the bodybuilder, tweaked his nipples. Yanking on them, yanking hard, yanking downward, Spike brought the other man to his knees. The bodybuilder looked up, worshipful. He held hands behind his back.

Groaning, I lifted my hips. Spike thrust himself forward and down, buried himself in me, held still. His beard scoured the back of my neck.

He said, "Here it comes."

Spike—the onscreen Spike—said, "Let's see if we can get you pregnant."

Everything stopped. My heart thumped, hammered, threatened to burst. I turned my head, saw him in the corner of my eye. "Pregnant? What does that mean—pregnant?"

He shoved in deeper. He said nothing.

On the screen, the bodybuilder said, "Fuck yeah." His voice was thinner, higher, than I'd expected.

"*Pregnant*," I said. I tried to force my hands apart, tried to wriggle free of the belt, but he'd cinched it tight. I tried to lift him off me, but he was too big, too heavy. "You said you were clean."

With his mouth against my ear, he said, "Things have changed."

"Things have—. What the fuck are you—? You weren't going to—?" The leather dug into my wrists.

"You hate rubbers as much as I do. You're obviously pretty slutty. By now, I figured—."

I raised my hands, shoved against him. I looked at him over my shoulder. "Get off."

"That's what I'm trying to do," he said. He stirred his cock around inside me. It hurt.

"Let me up," I said. My throat felt scratchy, my voice sounded hoarse. Had I been yelling?

Yes. Yes, I'd been yelling. Less than sixty seconds ago, I'd been howling, urging him to fuck me harder.

"What the fuck?" he said. But he rolled off me and set about freeing my hands.

I rubbed my wrists. "You have to—. I have to go," I said. I reached for my jeans.

"Chill out, Beta."

Since I'd seen him last he'd started a pot belly. I hadn't noticed it before. His shoulders had narrowed. His hips had narrowed. His skin seemed to lie uneasily over his shrunken muscles. Everywhere—on his legs, on his arms, on the caps of his shoulders—his veins popped and snaked along the curves of his body.

"Don't call me that, please." Already I was in my jeans. I buttoned the fly. I searched for my shirt, the flannel shirt. I found it draped across the box of bad influences.

He sat cross-legged on the carpet. "I have a few days off," he said. "I figured we'd—."

"I have to go," I said again.

I found my wallet. I stuffed it into my back pocket. I found my jacket. I put it on.

"The ironic thing," Spike said, "is that the line was a fiction at the time, or we all thought it was." He leaned over and pulled a joint from the pocket of his jeans. It was a crumpled, twisted thing, already half-smoked. He said, "I was just playing a part."

He turned toward the television. He lit the joint and toked. Glassy-eyed, he watched the video, watched himself trying to impregnate the bodybuilder.

•   •   •

I drove like a lunatic. University, Snelling, I-94.

The card Michael Walrath had given me—The Pink House, 1362 LaSalle, LaSalle at Grant—had been, all this time, in the ashtray of my car.

LaSalle at Grant. LaSalle at Grant. It sounded familiar.

Of course. Tom's favorite Thai restaurant, King and I Thai, was at LaSalle and Grant. Though Tom had loved the restaurant, had loved the atmosphere, had loved the food, eventually he'd refused to go there with me. Throughout the process of getting there, ordering, eating, and getting home again, I'd been almost entirely unable to utter a sentence without adding "Et cetera, et cetera, et cetera."

As I drove with one hand I held the card in the other. I-94 through downtown Minneapolis. I swerved from lane to lane, dodging slower-moving traffic. A red Ford Mustang—brand-new, bearing temporary tags—poked along in the left lane at fifty miles an hour. I laid on the horn, darted around it on the right.

Lyndale. North on Lyndale.

On the back of the card, Michael had written—something. "Thu, 6-10" perhaps? I hoped so. It was Wednesday. I hoped it wasn't his night to work. I hoped he wouldn't be there.

Walker Art Center on my left, Loring Park ahead on the right. I turned right on Oak Grove Street. Loring Lake was milky gray, as if the thinnest skim coat of ice lay on its surface. Oak Grove forked to the right. I veered left, onto Fifteenth.

Pregnant, I thought. Who would ever—? How could—? What kind of sick mind would confuse a virus with a baby? *Christa* was pregnant. A life—an entire person—was growing inside her belly. The thing growing in Spike—the thing that might be growing in me—. Yes, it was life, a kind of life, a living thing. But, no—really, it was death.

Fuck. LaSalle was a one-way street, a one-way going the wrong way.

Flu-like symptoms, I thought. I remembered my aching hips, my sore shoulders. *I should have known.* But then, I *had* known, hadn't I? *Just because you're a hypochondriac,* I thought, *doesn't mean you're not sick.*

The traffic light at Fifteenth burned red for what seemed minutes, hours, years. Cars sped by on Fifteenth—hundreds of cars, it seemed. I became certain that this light was the longest, most ill-timed traffic light in the universe. I pounded the steering wheel. I shouted at the light. I begged it to change.

At last, it changed. At Nicollet I sailed through an amber light, turned left.

Nicollet and Grant. Another long light. Fuck.

The Regency Athletic Club and Spa, a big block of grayish-white concrete, lay ahead of me on the left. All or part of the building had been given over to restaurants and bars. One of the lighted signs along the front read, "Spike's Sports Bar."

Pregnant. Fuck.

My stomach lurched. I thought I might vomit.

Grant. At last. LaSalle and Grant. I didn't see a pink house. King and I Thai. The Loring Municipal Parking Ramp. A strip mall with a SuperAmerica and a pub and a bookstore. Some kind of red brick apartment complex. No pink house.

On the right, past King and I Thai, LaSalle dipped into a tunnel or under-pass. It must be to the left. I signaled. I turned left.

I passed it three times—circled the block, sat through the long lights three times—before I found it. Between the SuperAmerica and a fenced parking lot behind the Emerson School, the Pink House sat at the back of a narrow, deep lot. Only the door and the window frames were pink. Otherwise, the building was plain and rather ordinary, a beige stucco house not unlike my own, with a foundation of red brick and a low front porch. The sign out front was discreet, unobtrusive, the size of a sheet of notebook paper.

After all that rushing around, after driving like—well, like Christa—to get to The Pink House, I sat for a long time in the Chevette. I couldn't bring my-self to go in, couldn't bring myself, even, to get out of the car. I sat with my hands on the steering wheel, the car in reverse.

In the rearview mirror, at the edge of my vision, I saw something move. Something—. Someone—. A man on a bike rode up behind me, came along-side.

Michael Walrath. Of course. He knocked on my window. I rolled it down.

"Here you are at last," he said.

I showed him the back side of the card he'd given me. I still had the card in my hand. The sweat of my palm had dampened it, darkened it.

"I thought you were here on Thursdays."

"It *is* Thursday."

"It's—. It's *not*. It's Wednesday, March—."

He shook his head. "April Fools'," he said.

I stared up at him. Was he messing with me? An early April Fools' joke? Or had I missed a day? Had I been thinking, all day, that it was the last day of March, when it was really the first day of April? How could that be?

And if it *was* Thursday, wouldn't Eliot's group be starting about now? Why hadn't Eliot mentioned it? Wasn't I supposed to stay away—stay away from group, away from Charlie? Why hadn't Eliot been in the midst of his usual frantic preparations—chilling bottles of soda, dumping bags of nuts into sil-ver bowls, wiping down the lacquer tray?

I looked at Michael, studied him for some hint, some sign, that he was teasing me. He was inscrutable.

"You rode your bike all the way here from the U?" I said. "Isn't that some-thing like—?"

"I ride my bike everywhere. It's only four or five miles. Not far," he said. He said, "Come on in."

"You don't have a car?"

He shook his head.

"Is it because all that carbon monoxide makes the earth weep?"

He squinted at me. "Don't be a dick. It's because I'm poor."

"What about when it's fourteen below?"

"I presume you've heard of buses," he said. "You're trying to dodge me. Come in, please."

"I don't think I can."

"Come on. You got yourself here. That's half the battle."

The corner of the business card pricked the skin of my palm. I looked at it. Softly, I said, "Michael, I think I know what the results are going to be."

"Everyone says that. It's not always true." He nodded gravely. "It's not always true. And if it is, it's better to know, don't you think?"

"Is it?"

Reaching through the window, he put his hand on my shoulder. "It is. It's better to know. If you're positive, there are things you need to start doing, and you need to start doing them right now. It's better to know. Trust me. Come inside."

I looked up. His black hair streamed around his face. His face was pink, after his bike ride, flushed from effort and from the wind whipping his skin. He smiled, showing his fine white teeth. God, he was beautiful.

"Michael, have you ever heard of something called the Twin Cities Mental Health Assistance Program?"

He looked at me as if I'd just sprouted a third arm.

"Never mind," I said.

"There are breakthroughs every day," he said. "New drugs. New treatments. It's better to know, so you can take action." He held out his hand. "Please," he said. "Come in."

I got out of the car. I followed him into the clinic, through the pink door.

30 FIRE

Eliot greeted me at the door. Like a fretting house-mother he stood in the open doorway, his arms folded across his chest.

I slipped off my boots. One foot was bare. Fuck. In my rush to get away from Spike, I'd forgotten one of my socks. I removed the other sock and tucked it into my boot.

"It was dark hours ago. I was about to call the police. Where've you been? Where's your stuff? Your clothes and stuff."

Fuck. In my rush to get away from Spike, I'd left my gym bag.

I stammered. "Something—something happened. Something came up." I said, "Sorry. It's—. It's hard to explain." I took off my jacket, draped it across the back of the sofa.

"What happened?"

"Spike happened." In my rush to get away from Spike, it seemed, I'd left behind one sock, my undershirt, my belt, my boxers, my gym bag, and my better judgment. I told Eliot everything. The car, the video, the bondage, the Pink House, the HIV test, everything.

He stood in lithic silence, his fingers kneading the flesh of his forearms. At last he said, "I can smell him on you. Lube, ass, pot."

I blushed. Had Michael Walrath smelled it on me? Pearl, the sweet-tempered phlebotomist who'd taken my blood—had she smelled it on me?

In a flash Eliot leapt the gap between us. Clutching my wrists, he dragged me toward the fireplace. His fingernails dug into my flesh. I saw that on my left arm, where wrist met palm, there was a deep red crease where my belt had notched my skin.

Eliot sat on the hearth and dragged me down to sit beside him. A fire blazed at our backs.

"I fear for you," he said. He spoke in a bare whisper—the crackling of the fire was louder—as though he meant to impart some great secret. "I'm not talking about the results of the HIV test. I'm talking about your *soul*. How long have you been working at this? How long have you been engaged in this struggle, only to throw away months of abstinence for a moment's pleasure?"

"I weakened. I know, I was weak, but—."

"I have watched you sin and sin and sin. You beg for forgiveness, but you never change your behavior. Forgiveness without repentance. You are holding on by your fingernails." As if to illustrate, he jabbed his own fingernails into my flesh. "You will stand or fall tonight. I intend to see you stand."

His eyes were wild. Brilliant spots of color shaded the sharp ridges of his cheeks. His fingers were translucent, bloodless from the tightness of his grip.

My left hand was going numb. I tried to shake free, but he held me fast.

"Eliot—."

"Do you love God?"

"Of course. Of course, I do. Eliot, you're hurting me."

"Do you intend to renounce the sin of homosexuality?"

In sudden and perfect stillness our eyes met. Blood rushed in my ears. I should deny him, I thought, curse him, throw him off. And yet—. I bowed my head. "I intend to renounce that part of my life, yes."

"Tonight, once and for all, I intend to purge you of it. Will you do what I say?" Letting go, finally, of my hands, he stood facing me. He lifted my chin. "Will you do what I say? Everything I say?"

In the light of the fire his eyes were amber. His pupils were enormous.

I cast my eyes down. I nodded.

"I'll be right back."

I stood. I turned to face the hearth. I stared into the fire. Orange flames lapped the charred bodies of half a dozen logs lying in the grate. Sweat dampened the back of my shirt. I reached back, plucked the sticky flannel away from my skin.

Behind me I heard a door open and close. Eliot set a box on the hearth, directly in front of me. It contained books, cassettes, videos. I knew the titles. *Go Down on It. Streets of Los Angeles. Interview with the Vampire. Men on Men.*

ABBA Gold.

"What is this? Where did you get these?"

"From your living room."

I felt myself faltering. I fell back and landed on the sofa. "You? You broke into—?"

Eliot sat next to me. "Don't be absurd. You went away for hours. When you didn't come back, I went looking for you. You left the door open, did you know that? I walked right in."

"Was—? Was Spike there—?" Spike and Eliot in the same room—. The idea alarmed me.

Eliot didn't answer me. He shook the box. "You were supposed to throw all of this away, Jonah, not save it as some kind of altar to your sinful nature."

I looked at him. In the firelight his face was a mask of gold.

His hand squeezed my shoulder. "It's time, you know. You have to throw every bit of this trash into the fire," Eliot said.

He stood, stepped toward the fire. He held his hand out.

I reached for him. Fingers intertwined, he pulled me toward him. Fred and Ginger.

We stood very close to the fire now. My face burned.

He squeezed the knotted muscles on either side of my neck. "The box."

My hands hung heavy at my sides. I felt the sore places where my belt had dug into my flesh, where Eliot's fingers had dug into my flesh.

He said, "It hurts to remove a tumor. Even something that can kill you becomes part of you, until you tear it out of you."

Strangely easy, to throw away the audiocassettes and the videos—even Spike's videos. They contained only sex and music, after all. *ABBA Gold. Command Performance. The Best of Blondie.* I cast them into the fire.

Black smoke oozed from the slots and crevices of each tape. Beige plastic, black plastic, clear plastic. The tapes puckered, shrank, collapsed. I watched them burn.

Streets of LA. Go Down on It. Into the flames.

I breathed the smoke. It stung my nose and the back of my throat.

Tom's books next—Rice, Leavitt, Holleran, Bram. Though they had belonged to Tom—or perhaps *because* they had belonged to Tom—it was liberating to destroy them, to rip them apart page by page and watch the ink and paper curl and blacken and burst into starry brilliance.

But Walt Whitman—. Walt Whitman in Tory's handwriting—that was something else. I held the notebook Tory had given me, caressed its leather cover, squinted at the beige stitching along its spine.

Eliot stabbed his thumbnails into my back. "I should have made you take that one first. That's the most dangerous of all. Tory gave that to you. I looked at the first page, the inscription. You don't love him. He's nothing to you. He's not a lover, he's a friend. You said so yourself. After tonight, he won't be anything to you."

I looked at him. "After—?"

"Rip it up. Every page."

I peeled the cover from the notebook. I crumpled the first page, on which Tory had written, simply, "Whitman." I tore free the blank pages at the back. I ripped away the second page, the page on which Tory had written his inscription.

> To Jonah, my good friend and fellow Beethoven enthusiast, my
> fellow lover of poetry. I hope this inspires you as much as it has
> inspired me, and I hope when you read these lines, you will
> think of me with fondness and friendship.

Below that, Tory had signed his first name in sprawling cursive letters.

"Don't make the mistake of doing this mechanically, unthinkingly. It shouldn't be easy. Every single page should feel like it's ripped from your own heart. Do you feel it?"

Not yet, no. I hadn't yet torn away anything of substance. I hadn't yet consigned a single line of the good gray poet's writing to the fire.

Eliot told me, "I should have brought *all* of your poetry. All that metaphor. Not one line that means what it says. It's distorted your whole way of thinking." His voice twisted in on itself, mocking me: "Does heaven really exist? Isn't it just a metaphor for happiness? Does evil really exist? Isn't it just a metaphor for dissatisfaction?"

Here, finally, the first page of poetry. It came away with a ragged sound. I glimpsed a few words as they sailed into the fire.

> Do not remain down there so ashamed ... I have long enough
> stifled and choked.

"You think a few bombastic lines of Whitman stand for something real, and the Bible is a collection of symbols and indirections. It's precisely the opposite."

A page, and another page, only sheets of paper. Words, only letters strung together. Nothing of substance. Just a poem, just words, nothing real. And yet as the pages, the lines, the words vanished in the fire, I found myself weeping.

> To escape utterly from others' anchors and holds!
> To drive free! To love free! To dash reckless and dangerous! . . .
> To ascend, to leap to the heavens of the love indicated to me!

Words, only words.

Eliot said, "Until you stop this cycle of sin and shame and begging for forgiveness, you'll never be free. Until you learn to keep your eyes fixed on the final goal, the final prize, you're a dead man. Dead in the eyes of God." Standing close, wrapping himself around my back, he stroked the stubble on the top of my head. Into my ear, he said, "Lost."

Lost, like Tigger. Lost. Lost and dead, like Tom.

"Don't get me wrong," Eliot said. "Faith is the key to salvation, but what kind of faith can you profess to have, if it doesn't transform you into the beautiful soul God wants you to be? If it doesn't free you from the stink of your own bodily desires? The stink of it's on you right now. The stink of fucking."

I ripped a page from the notebook. On it, Tory had written:

> the live-oak glistens there in Louisiana, solitary, in a wide flat
>   space,
> Uttering joyous leaves and its life, without a friend, a lover, near,
> I know very well I could not.

Louisiana? Why *Louisiana?* I pictured a marshy seaside plain, a bruised sky hanging low over it, and a lichen-stained tree, chattering to itself in its native language of creaking branches and scraping leaves.

Walt's words vanished in the flames. The bruised sky, the trembling oak. The page—words, only words—rose as smoke into the flue.

"Think how you've sickened yourself," Eliot said. "How many times have you thought you were finally turning a corner, only to be dragged back into the mud by your own filthy and selfish desires? Faster now." Leaning over my shoulder, he tipped the book. "See how all these little booklet-like things are sewn together?" I saw. "Take a whole section at a time."

Balancing the open book across my thighs, I tore a sheaf of pages from it.

"I know it's difficult to think of a life without these desires, without this sickness at your core, but it's within your power. You can be free."

He leaned against me, a hand on each shoulder. I was trembling. I clenched my teeth.

"You'll be surprised," he said, "how rich and happy your life can be, without the constant struggle to snag a man, without the constant futile prowling and hunger."

More pages into the fire.

"It will be difficult," Eliot said. "This may not be the last time we do this." His lips were near my ear. As he whispered I felt the moist warmth, smelled the apple-sweetness, of his breath. "You'll have to learn to live in a new way, to think in a new way. But I'm here to help you. I'll be here for you every minute."

Eliot's hands crept down my spine. "You'll be new-baptized," he said. "You'll breathe, sleep, eat, talk, and dream the Holy Spirit." His hands girdled my hips.

Here it was at last. The last remaining page of the notebook, the words that Jonquil had read at Tory and Christa's wedding.

> I have clothed your path in velvet; kiss one another, I am not
> looking. Love one another, love one another and if you are happy,
> instead of a prayer to thank me kiss again.

Into the fire. It was done.

Eliot thrust into my hand a sheaf of onion-skin paper. *Grieving Songs.* My fingers trembled as I held the delicate paper.

"Eliot," I said. I couldn't raise my voice above a whisper. "This doesn't belong to me. This is borrowed. It's not mine. I can't—."

"Burn it, Jonah. Cast it into the flames. It's filth."

> Far beneath in the earth's deep flesh,
> In the flanks, in the cavities and bones,
> As Eve was hidden in Adam's rib,
>
> The spring is hidden. The promise of summer's
> green is hidden under the white snow,
> under the blue ice.

The fire made short work of the onion-skin paper. The page flashed and flared and in a second was ash.

Eliot nuzzled my neck. "You'll walk through fire."

> Along the path the leaves are crimson, orange, and gold,
> Like crackling fire beneath our feet.

"When you fall, I'll punish you. I'll set you right."

> Against the sky, the leaves of crimson, orange, and gold
> Are trembling flames upon the wind.

Eliot wrapped his arms around me. He laid his cheek between my shoulder blades. Softly his fingers stroked my belly. He lifted my shirt. His lips brushed the nape of my neck.

"I'll be with you all the time," he said. "I'll keep you in line, keep you on the straight and narrow."

I held a page in my hand, half-crumpled.

> I am no priest. I cannot absolve him.
> There is nothing to absolve. The body
> is salt and water, seeks water and salt.
> It hungers, hungers for other than food.
> Hunger must be fed, and thirst must be quenched.
> He is an animal. So are we all.
> Animals. There is nothing to forgive.

"We'll be together forever," Eliot said. Through my shirt, his hot breath burned my back. His hands roamed my shoulders, my arms, my belly, my chest. "Forever. Now, and through eternity."

With one hand Eliot grasped the top button of my fly. The buttons popped open. He tugged my shirt free.

A single brutish shove sent me sprawling forward. The rough stone of the hearth chafed the heels of my hands. I cried out. My face—inches, now, from the fire—burned. The skin of my face tightened and smoothed.

All at once he bent over me, curved his body against mine. He yanked at the waistband of my jeans, pulling them down.

I shouted his name. I struggled, pressed myself back against him, forced him away.

He slumped away from me, and I rolled away from him. I stumbled, fell, landed on the carpet.

"What have I done?" Eliot huddled in front of the sofa, weeping, his head buried in the tangle of his limbs. His fly was open. His cock—a small thing, as purple-red and shiny as a dog's phallus—stood erect. It was flagging, shrinking. "What have I done?"

I stood. I hiked up and buttoned my jeans. I lifted the box of my belongings—what few remained. I saw that the Guarneri *Quartets* lay at the bottom of the box, alongside *Beethoven in London* and *The Seventeen Quartets*.

Eliot hugged my ankle. "Don't go," he said. He choked, his voice thick with sobbing. "You're the only one. You're all I have. They all left me—Tigger, Lowell, Rob, Mason, Charlie. They're all gone. Stay. Stay and we'll work together. You can help me. I can help you. It's all about helping each other, being there for each other."

I yanked my foot away from him. "Get away from me, or so help me God, I'll tear you apart."

He let go. I walked to the front door, opened it, walked out into the night.

A crisp breeze stirred the tails of my shirt. My skin puckered in the chill air. The bricks burned my feet with cold. I left the path and let my toes sink into the wet blades of grass.

EPILOGUE

THE RIVER IN WINTER

       It's bright red, my new shell—or, no, not so new, now. It's four months old, more or less the same age as Christa and Tory's pink-cheeked, blue-eyed daughter—darling, plump Ruby, who will, I suspect, forever be called Peanut. I named the shell *Ruby*, in Peanut's honor. They were delivered a week apart, in late July.

The shell lies in its rack in the new boathouse. It's a thing of beauty—this jewel, this *Ruby*, this new shell—far lovelier than my lost, unnamed boat. Candy apple red—red and red and red in beating leagues of monotone. Its fiberglass body is sleek, slender as an arrow. I've rowed in it many times, and it's nimble and swift.

I lift it from the rack, carry it out the broad steel-framed door, tip it into the drying sling on the porch.

The sky is clear, starry black to the west of me, icy blue to the east. The air is still and cold. The river laps the planks of the dock. Above me, somewhere on the riverbank, birds chatter and whistle.

I strip off my jacket, my jeans. I lay them aside. I tug my shoes off. I peel my socks off my feet and tuck them into the leg of my unisuit. That's new, too, the uni—also ruby red, to match the shell.

I drop my shoes into my duffel bag. Something crackles—paper, some kind of paper. I bend over the duffel, open it, look in.

Christa has packed me a lunch in a paper sack.

I open the sack and peek inside. On a couple of sheets of notebook paper folded together, in Tory's handwriting, a poem. A new poem.

Share the midnight orgies, dance with the dancers, drink with
   the drinkers.
Create and destroy. Depart and return. Fall and climb. Love your
   sins, regret your sins. It is all profane, it is all sacred.
Water and salt, salt and water. Each seeks its own.
Spirit and flesh, flesh and spirit. Each seeks its own.
To be holy is to be human. To be human is to be holy.

I find that I'm smiling.

So Tory, then, not Christa, packed the lunch. Of course. I see now that there's a thick sandwich of shaved ham and Swiss cheese, a slice of tomato and a leaf of curly green lettuce in a separate Ziploc bag, a packet of mayonnaise and a plastic knife, an apple, thin spears of celery and carrot.

Irrefutably, Tory packed this lunch. Christa would have made me a peanut butter sandwich—with or without jelly, it's impossible to predict. At the bottom of the paper sack there would be a bag of potato chips, ground to dust underneath the sandwich—that much is altogether predictable.

I read on. There's a second page, a second poem.

You pass over it on the freeway in the sealed space of your car.
It's a flash of light, a rippling reflection of setting sun.
You put your visor down, you ignore it, you can't see it for what
   it is.
You can't see the river for what it is.

◆   ◆   ◆

Tory fibbed. When he told me he had other copies of *Grieving Songs*, he fibbed. He gave me the only copy. I burned it in Eliot's fireplace.

Eliot put my scores and sketches into the box. He planned for the fire to claim them, but we never got that far. Everything that I set to music remains. All of "fuck" remains, a few lines of "The River in Winter" remain, a couple of stanzas of "Crimson, Orange and Gold" remain. The verses I read as I pulled apart the pages and tossed them into the fire—they remain, as if the fire burned them into my memory. The rest is lost. More than a dozen pages, hundreds of lines—dead, vanished, lost.

After a few weeks of grieving for the *Grieving Songs*, after many tears, after a tense time when he couldn't bear to look at me, couldn't bring himself to speak to me, Tory set about recreating the poems. But of course he couldn't recreate them, not precisely as they were.

And something strange happened. The new poems turned out less sad, less angry, than the originals. They are celebrations, not elegies.

Lately, Tory's been experimenting with free verse, with long lines of chaotic, Whitmanic exuberance.

I read on.

> From the bank it's a sliding current, a big puddle of mud.
> Leaves, twigs, the occasional ripple of a fish's mouth claiming an
>   insect skating on the surface.
> The trees arch over it, bending their limbs toward it.
> You see the trees, the forest, the twigs, the mud, but you can't see
>   the river.
> You can't see it for what it is.

I can hear a melody. A crazy, vigorous melody turning in on itself—eighth notes, sixteenth notes, the words coming fast. A piano thumping chords underneath, a viola in counterpoint.

I am still smiling.

I put the paper sack and the poem back into the duffel, shove the duffel into a corner. I close and lock the door.

I carry *Ruby* to the dock. The planks are dry underfoot but chilly. The rough, cold wood bites the bare soles of my feet. I put my socks back on.

Over the disordered chuckle of the current, I hear a rhythmic slap—the sound of oars stroking, scooping water. Out in the channel there are two singles, two rowers side by side. Lifting their oars, turning, they make for the dock. The two men wear sweatshirts, gloves, and stocking caps. They face downstream, away from me, but I know at a glance who they are. The long black hair, the shoulder-length white-blond hair. Michael and James.

I set my boat on the dock and wait. As he turns his boat—port forward, starboard back—Michael sees me. He grins. "Jonas!" he calls.

"Michael Walton," I say. "You're out early."

"Always."

They pull to, James first, and then Michael. I crouch on the dock. I hold their boats fast against it as they climb out. We lift the boats out of the water—Michael's first, and then James's.

They're handsome boats, matching Staempfli cedar shells, glossy, the color of cinnamon. Water streams off the hulls, darkening the dock. I feel the damp rising through the soles of my socks.

Michael hugs me. James hugs me. James says, "How are you doing?"

"Fantastic," I say.

Michael frowns. "Still having the headaches?"

"Don't have one now," I say. I smile.

"And the nausea?"

James pokes Michael's arm. "Hey. Doctor Walrath. Knock it off."

Michael groans. "I'm not a doctor *yet*." The way he says it, I know that he's saying it for the four hundredth time.

James laughs, showing straight white teeth. He hasn't shaved. Peach fuzz shimmers along his jaw line. "You don't have the degree, but you are most definitely a doctor."

To me, Michael says, "Don't stop taking it again."

The AZT. He means the AZT.

• • •

Three days. Seventy-two hours. One hell of a pregnant pause.

I waited for three days, for seventy-two hours, knowing all along what the results would be, but hoping I was wrong, hoping I was just a hypochondriac, a paranoiac, a worrywart.

No.

No. I wasn't wrong. I wasn't just a worrywart.

When the news came, when Michael sat with me in a small, dark room at the back of the Pink House and showed me a dot-matrix print-out and told me the news, I saw nothing, heard nothing. He pointed to some numbers on the page, explained what they meant. He spoke, but I couldn't hear, couldn't understand. He might have been speaking Swahili, Esperanto, Czech. Blood sang in my ears. I ran out.

He followed.

"Every day," he said. "Every day there are new breakthroughs." He'd said it before. Now he said it again. And then he said it again. "Come back tomorrow or the next day. There are things you need to start doing."

I stood in the parking lot, staring at the grimy hubcaps of my car. Had I ever washed my car, in all the time that I'd owned it? On University, I remembered—not far from Eliot's, not far from Michael's—there was a car wash. What was the name of it? Squid? Anemone? Octopus? I should take my car there, I thought. I should get it washed.

Michael stood next to me, so close that I could feel the heat of his body. It was a warm day—a gorgeous day, a plucked-and-shaved *Playgirl* centerfold of a day—but I felt cold. I shivered. Michael hugged me, tightly, as if he could still the quivering of my muscles.

"Come back," he said again. "Come back tomorrow or the next day. There are things you need to start doing."

Over and over Michael said the same few things. He held me fast, held me tight, smoothed and calmed my trembling limbs.

"There are breakthroughs every day. New drugs. Come back tomorrow or the next day."

I said nothing. I kept thinking that my car was in urgent need of a wash. When had I ever washed it, after all? It was filthy.

• • •

The next day, I went back to the Pink House. Michael wasn't there. I saw a doctor, a slim, entirely bald man in a white jacket. It was bad news, of course, the doctor said, but it was better to know. Every day, there were new breakthroughs, he told me—new drugs, new treatments. His name was Doctor Bell, but I couldn't make myself see that as a good sign.

There were things I needed to start doing, he said. Diet, exercise, safe sex. AZT.

"Safe sex?" I said. "But what if I'm with another guy who—?"

"We believe there are multiple strains of the virus. There is the possibility of—."

But by then my attention had faded. Spike hadn't been the only one, after all. Jose, the men in San Francisco. If there were multiple strains—.

"We'll start you on AZT right away," Doctor Bell said. He took a pad from his pocket, wrote out a prescription. "AZT is a drug that's commonly prescribed—."

My mind wandered again. I held the prescription in my hand. I stared at the three big letters—the only three letters that were legible. AZT.

From the beginning, I hated it. The headaches were bad, the nausea was bad. After a few weeks, I stopped taking it. When Michael found out, he did everything he could think of to get me back on it, short of sitting on my chest and injecting the drug into my neck.

• • •

Michael says, "I know the side effects can be—."

"I know, I know. I won't stop taking it." I try to show, by my tone, that I'm making him this promise for the four hundredth time.

James says, "Have you found a place yet?"

I glance out over the river. Curls of mist wave above its surface. "I'm going to stay with Tory and Christa. They don't mind—or at least they *say* they don't mind. I have the whole basement to myself. I have my own bathroom." A small and mildew-smelling bathroom, true, but I'm used to mildew-smelling bathrooms. "And there's a piano down there." An old out-of-tune spinet, it's true, but I've found that it's easier to compose on an out-of-tune piano than on no piano at all.

◆ ◆ ◆

I moved into Tory's house even before he and Christa returned from Arizona. By chance, Christa called from Tory's parents' house, to check up on me, and I told her the story—what had happened to the OWT, what had happened with Eliot. She put Tory on the phone, and—by then I was weeping—I told him the story.

"There's a key in the garage," he said.

"What?"

"In the garage," he said. "The shelves at the back. Under a clay pot. You'll find it. It's the only clay pot there. Stay at my house—at *our* house—till you find a place." He gave me the combination for the garage door opener. "There's a keypad on the door frame. Did you write down the combination? Do you have a pencil?" He reeled it off again, a series of four digits.

"Tory," I said. "I—. Thank you, but I can't. I—."

I thought it would be difficult to live with them, difficult to see them together. I thought I would moon over him, pine for him, that I would become the lovelorn heroine of one of Christa's romance novels.

"I'm not going to argue," he said. "There's a key in the garage. The shelves at the back, under the clay pot. You'll see it. If you're not at the house when we get back, I'll never forgive you."

◆ ◆ ◆

At first, it *was* difficult to live with them. Around the house Tory more often than not was—*is*—catch-as-catch-can about what he wears, especially in the morning, before he's had coffee. He owns a pair of tight and obscenely short shorts—red nylon gym shorts with an R above the hem of the left leg, shorts that he may, in fact, have worn in junior high school. In the morning, that's all he ever wears. At first, the sight of his bare chest and bare legs could make me tremble with longing.

One Sunday morning in late spring, not long after he at last forgave me for burning *Grieving Songs,* Christa and Peanut were off visiting Alice in Hudson. Tory made pancakes. He flipped them onto matching plates. He poured coffee into matching mugs. He sat across from me at the table in the breakfast nook. Taking up our matching silverware, we ate in companionable silence. I watched a flock of silver-white birds dip into a hedge and crowd its leafy branches.

"What are you going to do next?" he asked me. "For work, I mean."

I'd been doing temp work—filing, reception—"light clerical," they called it. "Light clerical"—it was a nice way of saying that I couldn't type for shit. When I didn't have an assignment from the temp agency, I volunteered at the Pink House. For a couple of weeks, I'd been answering phones at a law office in downtown Minneapolis.

"I thought I was doing it," I said.

I looked at him and saw that he was frowning at his pancakes. His fork lay in a pool of buttery amber syrup. "What if you went back to school? Got a master's? There are places that hire resident composers. Churches, maybe the Saint Paul Chamber Orchestra. Or you could teach. Theory, history, composition."

"I never thought—."

"You're too good for this temp stuff," he said. "You deserve better. Think about it."

He looked up. His eyes met mine. The set of his jaw was firm, resolute, as if he'd been planning to say this—had been rehearsing it—for some time.

All at once something shifted. It was an almost physical sensation—the sensation of something moving, sliding, clicking into place. Tory would never be my lover. He could never be my lover. I didn't *want* him for a lover—not really. He was my brother. We were—we *are*—brothers.

In the living room, the stereo had gone quiet. The record—one of those lush Ravel ballet pieces, full of harps and flutes—had ended. Without Peanut's constant stream of chatter and prattle and fussy tears, the house was as hushed as a library. We sat looking out the window.

Tory said, "You know, it was my fault, too."

"Your—. What?"

"*Grieving Songs.* What happened to *Grieving Songs.* I should never have given up the only copy."

By then I'd apologized countless times and in various ways for the loss of the poems. Of course I'd simply told him I was sorry. But I'd also written him notes and letters. I'd found some poems about loss and remorse, and had copied them out and had given them to him. I'd even bought him flowers—purple hyacinths, because a florist told me that, in the language of flowers, purple hyacinths say, "please forgive me."

Eventually Tory *had* forgiven me. Now, I couldn't quite muster another apology.

"I was just so eager to hear them set to music," he said. "I just couldn't wait to see what you'd do with them. I thought if you had to wait for me to make a copy—. I mean, I would have had to take them to the office the next day, or type them up again. It would have been days before you got the copy, and I thought—."

"You thought I'd lose interest."

"Yes."

I made another apology after all, and then I said, "I can't explain what happened that night. I was—."

"Don't take me wrong," he said. "I'm over it. I was mad, sure, but I'm over it. I'm grateful, in a way, now that I've had some time to think about it. I needed to let all that go."

I set my hand on my knee and stroked the stiff linen of my napkin. I worried the hem with my thumbnail. "The new poems are certainly more—."

He held up his hand to stop me. "They're getting there. I still struggle with the long lines. Too much room to move around. But what I was saying is that—. I didn't mean to open up a rehash of this whole thing. I forgave you for losing the poems. It took me longer to realize that I needed to forgive Adam for dying, and let go of the grief." He looked out the window. It was still early, maybe nine o'clock. Across the street, in a neighbor's yard, the dewy, silver-green leaves of a young Russian olive tree shimmered like jewels. "And I needed to forgive myself, too. It was partly my fault, and I needed to forgive myself."

• • •

"I'd better get out there," I say to Michael and James. "It's cold. I need to get warmed up."

Michael nods gravely. "Call me or come by the clinic if—."

I hold up my hands. "Okay, okay."

He hugs me again. His sweatshirt is damp with sweat. His hair smells of apples and limes.

James hugs me. As we part, he says, "I almost forgot. Did you apply yet?"

Apply to the School of Music, he means, to the master's program. I shake my head, "Still studying for the GRE," I tell him. "Taking it next month. I'm taking some classes in the meantime. I'm weak in Form and Analysis, and I need to learn German." German, Italian, or French, actually, but since Tory speaks German, that's the language I've chosen.

"*German*," Michael says, as if I've just said I've taken up neurosurgery as a hobby. "How's *that* working out?"

"*Nicht so schlecht*," I say. "*Nicht so gut.*"

Michael crinkles his nose. "I don't know what that means."

James lays his hand on Michael's shoulder. "Not so bad, not so good." To me, he says, "What are you doing for Thanksgiving? We're having some people over."

I wince. "A lavish feast of tofurkey and vegan stuffing? I don't think so."

Michael winces. He looks at James. "He's talked me into having an actual turkey." He touches his belly. He cuts his eyes at James. "A living creature with a face and a brain, butchered and plucked in some factory."

James rolls his eyes. "It's one day out of the year. You can just deal with it, or eat your weight in green beans and yams." To me, he says, "So, what do you say? Join us?"

"I'm going to San Francisco again this year. Visiting my mother. I'm flying out tomorrow morning."

I'm looking forward to the trip. Barbara's taking a whole week off work. She's promised we won't set foot in a winery. There's been some intimation of a blind date with one of her neighbors, someone named Bryce Murray. "No relation," Barbara keeps saying with a hearty laugh, as if it's some great joke.

"Don't do anything I wouldn't do," Michael says. It's the kind of thing people usually say light-heartedly, but Michael says it in all gravity.

"Check," I say. "No fun whatsoever, I promise."

With a deep sigh, Michael says, "I need to change my image."

They lift their boats and trudge up the bank to the boathouse. As I slide *Ruby* into the water, I hear them talking, laughing, teasing each other.

I push off the dock. I look back and see the two of them drying their boats.

All around me the river prattles and blathers. I can no longer hear the men's voices, but I watch them come together in an embrace—a tight, full-body embrace. They kiss. It's a long, deep kiss, the kiss of two people much in love.

◆ ◆ ◆

I spoke too soon. I feel a headache coming on, a black flower blooming at the base of my neck, rising at the back of my head.

I stop pulling the oars. I float. The shell drifts westward, to starboard.

I close my eyes. I hold both oars in my left hand, knead my shaven scalp with my right.

Must it be? I think.

The pain dulls, subsides. I open my eyes. The sky is blue now, a pale shade of blue, thin as gruel. On the west bank, leafless trees sway in the cool breeze. Bare branches—the trees' nude limbs—clatter and creak.

It must be.

Plainly, manifestly, unequivocally, it's too late in the season to be on the water. But I woke early this morning—from the AZT, perhaps, or from a dream I've since forgotten, or from simple worry. As I lay in my bed I discovered that I needed one more morning on the water before the river freezes. That was my excuse. As for Michael and James—. They must be—plainly, manifestly, unequivocally—out of their freaking minds.

◆ ◆ ◆

I forgot—I am carrying the Walkman in the pocket of my sweatshirt. I feel it, now, the square bulk of it against my belly. Still holding the oars one-handed, in my left hand, I reach into my pocket and pull out the earphones. I stuff them into my ears. I feel around for the Walkman, for the play button. I find it, press it.

Beethoven. The Seventh Symphony. The first movement, the end of the slow introduction, the *Poco sostenuto*.

I've been listening to this symphony for weeks, immersing myself in it. I have a paper due next week in Form and Analysis. "The Use of Rhythm in Beethoven's Seventh," I'm calling it.

The Seventh is built on rhythm. Rhythm is everything, it seems, in the Seventh. Rhythm is the ore, and the symphony is the glinting rapier Beethoven forged from it.

The flutes break in with the main theme, their voices thin, tremulous. All at once the strings take up the melody. A dactylic rhythm thrums away in the horns and timpani.

My blood races. Everything in the world is contained in this music. The rhythms are as old as the world—the rhythm of galloping horses' hooves, the stroke of oars, the beat of tribal drums, the cadences of ancient poetry.

Everything in the world—work, play, dance. The thrust and recoil of tides, the rise and fall of sex and love, the cycle of death and renewal. The surge and subsidence of the earth itself, of the tectonic plates. The whole world is contained in this music.

I pull the oars. They pull easily.

There were other topics I might have considered—that I *did* consider—for the Form and Analysis paper. Tory suggested "Beethoven's Happy Endings," an idea he picked up from reading McNamara.

In Beethoven—according to McNamara—there is always a happy ending. But for Beethoven joy never comes without sorrow. Before the establishment of order, there is chaos. Before the safe haven, there is peril. Before the ascent to heaven, a descent into hell. Before resurrection, death. Before light, darkness.

Before the achievement of peace, of tranquility, in Beethoven, there is often a pause. It's as if you stand at a threshold, pausing, uncertain, before you pass through it—as if the entryway is also a barrier. A moment of stillness, of pondering, of uncertainty. To go forward may mean the attainment of paradise—or the loss of everything—or both.

The sun is up. The river is quite still, as if the water is on the cusp of freezing. The water is a plain of glitter and glare, a prismatic dazzle of light.

My face—my cheeks—feel colder, suddenly. My cheeks are wet. I am crying.

On my left, the upward-sloping strand slides by, a brown blur of tall oaks and steep sandy banks. I row harder. This part of the beach makes me think of Tom, of humid air and pounding sunlight, of lustrous summer afternoons we spent here, driving the men crazy with our aloofness, our conspicuous togetherness.

It takes less than this to remind me of Tom. I often think of him. I miss him. When we were happy, when things were good, he was the whole world. Maddening at times—*anyone* can be maddening at times—but loving and attentive and beautiful. The whole world. When we were happy—when things were good, when I knew that he loved me—nothing made me feel safer or luckier than the warmth of his body beside me.

If only I could see him one more time, even at a distance, even if his ghost emerged, shady and incorporeal, from the thicket of willow saplings on the shore—.

But no. He won't emerge from the willows. I won't see him again. He is gone, except in my memory.

Whatever it was that changed him—something I said or did, some feeling of guilt or shame that he discovered in himself, some random alteration of his brain chemistry—whatever it was that made him unhappy—.

Whatever it was—and I will never know what it was—I can do nothing more than forgive him for leaving, and go on missing him, and know that some part of me, at least, will never stop missing him, even if I think of him less and less each day.

Lately, we've all been going to Jonquil's church. I still can't get the name straight—Word of the Spirit? Spirit of the Word? It doesn't matter.

Last Sunday, Jonquil buttonholed me on my way out. She said, "Someday you'll have it again." She swung her hips, shaking out the folds of her pearly robes. She blinked. Kohl flecked her sleeves.

"Have what?" I asked her.

"Love. Marriage. Someone you love, someone who loves you, someone to share your life with. You'll have that again."

I felt my mouth curve into a big, open smile. My jaws ached from it. "I suppose I will."

"God loves you whether you're celibate or not," she told me. "He told me so himself."

I love Jonquil, but I've gradually come to conclude that she's slightly mad. This, more than anything, explains how it came to pass that, every Sunday at noon, Christa sets foot in an actual church.

The air is sharp and cold. Around me the river smells of mud and peat. I miss Tom.

The music is beautiful, jubilant, rapturous. The whole world is contained in this music. Work, play, dance. Rise, fall. Life, death. Departure, return.

Everything and everyone is forgiven. Whatever I've done—*everything* I've done—I am forgiven. I've learned to forgive myself. Every day, I forgive myself. Every day, I decide to forgive myself.

Must it be?

In chaos there is the promise of peace. In descent there is the promise of ascent. As Eve was hidden in Adam's rib, the spring is hidden in the gut of winter. In estrangement there is the promise of reconciliation. To be human is to be holy. It is all the same thing. In winter, the promise of summer's green is hidden under the white snow, under the blue ice.

Everything. Everyone. I decide to forgive.

My cheeks are wet. I am crying. Tears of joy, tears of sorrow—they are the same thing.

The strings play an obsessive figure. They climb the scale, tenaciously, as if slogging up a muddy hill. The horns pound away at their cretic rhythm, their horses' gallop. And then here is the melody again, in the strings. They have crested the muddy hill.

Everything in the world is contained in this music. Birth, life, death. Canticle, ballad, elegy. The ebb of the tide, the flood. Departure, return. The descent to hell, the ascent to heaven.

Everything stops. The entryway is the barrier.

The flutes, again—tremulous, tentative—take the melody. They play the brave tune that a frightened man might whistle as he wraps the palm of his hand around a candle flame, shielding it against the wind and dark.

It must be.

The wind is still. The river is still, as if on the brink of icing over, as if at any second it might congeal and freeze solid.

Feeling muscular, loose, strong, I pull the oars harder, rowing at full pressure.

The strings have the melody again, singing it loud, a full-throated cry of joy. The music is merry, ebullient, ravishing. The air is sharp and cold, smelling of mud and peat.

I pull the oars harder.

It must be.

I forgive.

The current draws me southward, downstream.

ACKNOWLEDGMENTS

I suspect that writing a novel is an act of such unsurpassed folly that anyone who attempts it is either quite mad or has a lot of help. I admit reluctantly to the former, and gladly to the latter.

For wholehearted encouragement and practical advice when I was hopelessly and haplessly stuck at the threshold of chapter three, I owe all praise and thanks to Carol Bly and David Leavitt. I learned much from each of them, and the book never could have been completed without their help.

For a clean, well-lighted place to write, and a fair amount of free coffee, I'm grateful to George and Michele and the staff of Muddy Waters Coffee on James Island, where I completed about ninety percent of my final draft.

For a deeply respectful reading of each chapter and countless percipient suggestions, I am grateful to Clif Mason, my good friend and compassionate reader. I'd always assumed that writing and revising were an entirely solitary pursuits, followed by the end product's release into the world. But Clif's comments inspired many new ideas and shaped the book-in-progress very much to the better. I'm particularly thankful, on Jonah's behalf, for the gift of the sporty yellow Walkman.

For their enthusiastic reception of the book and helpful feedback, I'm also grateful to other readers, including Linda Scott, Meg Scott-Copses, Kristeen Broussard, Vina McAllister, Ethel Frech, and Dee Miller.

For much-needed help with the intricacies of German case endings, *ein recht herzliches Dankeschön* to Doro Schwolgin.

Finally—last but not least, as they say—for listening with seemingly endless patience as I talked through one idea or another, for having faith in me even when I've had no faith in myself, for loving me even when I can't quite manage to like myself, for being my champion and my partner and my best friend, I thank my "immortal beloved," Todd Frech. Without him, I am entirely certain that this book would not exist.

COLOPHON

The text of this book is set in Whitman, a typeface designed by Kent Lew.

Whitman combines the qualities and character of classic American book types with a contemporary, digital aesthetic. The design was largely inspired by the work of W.A. Dwiggins, a book designer who also created a number of successful text typefaces in the first half of the 20th century.

Whitman received an award from the Type Directors Club in 2002.

www.ingramcontent.com/pod-product-compliance
Lightning Source LLC
Chambersburg PA
CBHW021425240626
47153CB00001B/34